Dear Readers,

Since we first started advertising *Scarlet* books we've had a lot of positive feedback about our covers, so I thought you might like to hear how we decide which cover best fits each *Scarlet* title. Well, when we've chosen a manuscript which will make an exciting addition to our publications, photo shoots are arranged and a selection of the best pictures are sent back to us by our designers.

The whole *Scarlet* team then gets together to decide which photograph will catch the reader's eyes and (most importantly!) sell the book. The comments made during our meetings are often intriguing: 'Why,' asked one of our team recently, 'can't the hero have even more buttons undone!' When we settle on the ideal cover, all the elements that make up the 'look' of a *Scarlet* book are added: the lips logo, the back cover blurb, the title lettering is picked out in foil . . . and yet another stunning cover is ready to wrap around a brand new and exciting *Scarlet* novel.

Till next month,
Best wishes,

Sally Cooper

SALLY COOPER,
Editor-in-Chief – *Scarlet*

PS I'm always delighted to hear from readers. Why not complete the questionnaire at the back of the book and let me know what *you* think of *Scarlet*!

About the Author

Jill Sheldon is a multi-published romantic/suspense author. *Summer of Fire*, her first novel for **Scarlet**, will be followed in 1997 by *Colour Me Loved*. In 1995, Jill's first novel was a finalist in the prestigious North West region's Romance Writers of America's 'Lone Star Writing Competition'.

Jill majored in journalism and has written many short stories.

She lives in Southern California, USA, with her husband and three young children and is an active member of the Romance Writers of America organization, particularly in her local area.

JILL SHELDON

SUMMER OF FIRE

SCARLET

Enquiries to:
Robinson Publishing Ltd
7 Kensington Church Court
London W8 4SP

First published in the UK by Scarlet, 1996

A copy of the British Library Cataloguing in
Publication data is available from the British Library

ISBN 1-85487-709-7

Printed and bound in the EC

10 9 8 7 6 5 4 3 2 1

To my family for always
believing in me.

PROLOGUE

'Yesss.' The hidden figure hissed in pleasure as he brought the camcorder up and hit the record button. 'That's it.'

Red balls of flame shot twenty-five feet into the night, making fiery streaks in the black sky. The explosion rang out, shaking the earth. Intense heat forced the hooded figure to move back, but he didn't want to. His eyes streamed, but went unnoticed. Smoke tortured his lungs and pulled his facial skin painfully tight. None of that mattered. Nothing, absolutely nothing compared to the unmitigated thrill of the fire itself.

Flames consumed the entire industrial building; in another few seconds there would be nothing to save. Huge roof chunks collapsed with loud crashes and a shower of sparks. The watching figure groaned with satisfaction, nearly overwhelmed by euphoria.

Another window blew outwards, shattering across the gravel car park. He giggled insanely at the deliciousness of it. He loved the intense, building anticipation while carefully planning the fire, and then the climax – watching it burn. The only thing that could possibly have improved it would have been to watch the firefighters perform their desperate dance to try to save the property, but they hadn't yet showed on the scene.

Suddenly, in the distant night, the sirens sounded. He sighed with contentment and lowered the camcorder. With any luck the rest of the roof wouldn't give until the firefighters clambered inside.

Grinning, the watcher pushed back the hood and reached into a pocket for a cigarette and a lighter, lost for a moment in the sheer beauty of the small flickering flame as he lit the cigarette.

The firefighters leapt off their trucks, rushing towards the building, shouting in alarm as another explosion sounded and shook the already weakened foundation. Breathing hitched and body tightened in excitement, the man drew the camcorder up again. Next came the best part – the finale, so to speak. Angry, harsh flames scorched and twisted high into the air, endangering each life struggling to fight the inferno.

Nothing beat this.

CHAPTER 1

The memories that assaulted her as she entered the house nearly brought Annie to her knees. Almost ten years, but little had changed. With a small sigh she forced herself over the threshold, but no amount of pressure could make her bring herself to go further. From the foyer she could see into the kitchen, the living room, up the long curved stairway that led to the bedroom she'd slept in throughout her childhood.

The smell was the same – the vague scent of lilacs that brought back her mother so vividly that she could see her standing in the kitchen, wooden spoon in hand, gently admonishing Annie to shut the door quickly before she let in the cold sea breeze.

Her mother and stepfather Ross had loved this house, had loved San Rayo's exclusive, California beach style, and the sort of life that had come with it. And so had Annie. With crime nearly non-existent, and the locals consisting mostly of devoted, hardworking white-collar types, Annie and her brother Jesse had known no boundaries, except the ocean itself and the mountain range behind it.

She'd had a childhood that had resembled a fairy-tale. Love, laughter and respect had been plentiful. She'd never doubted how important she was.

But she was alone now, both her mother and brother long gone.

And she had more important things to be doing than daydreaming. After all this time, Ross was going to sell the house. He'd written to her to say that he could no longer keep it – the pain it caused him was too great. He'd invited her to come and take whatever she wanted from it.

Purposefully she moved into the kitchen, ignoring the pang her heart sent up at the flowered wallpaper – faded now – that reminded her so sharply of her mother.

She dropped her bag on the table and glanced around. Ross was obviously at work, and she felt regret that she hadn't called ahead. But she'd wanted to make this first reacquaintance by herself. Ross understood all too well that the memories had kept her away, so *he'd* come to see *her* sporadically over the years. She'd never known her biological father – he'd died before she was even born. Ross had been her real father in all respects, and, as a real father, he had deserved more contact from her than he'd had.

She couldn't give more.

4

Her heels clicked on the tile floor as she walked past the refrigerator. She swallowed hard, remembering. It was hard to be in this room – Jesse's and her mother's favourite – without being overwhelmed by memories. Jesse had been notoriously in a constant state of hunger, and her mother always anxious to feed him. The kitchen had been the busiest room in the house.

Motivating herself to go up the oak staircase wasn't as difficult as seeing the kitchen, though she felt the fatigue in each muscle as she climbed. She wanted something of her mother's and Jesse's before the house was gone to her forever. Something to keep, to remember it by. As if she could forget anything about her home.

Home. Annie grimaced as she opened Jesse's bedroom door. She hadn't thought of this house as home since her mother and Jesse had been killed the night of her high-school graduation. She'd left immediately after the funeral and hadn't been back since. But now, she was risking her heart and soul for one last memory. She could be risking her job as well: her editor at *Time* hadn't been thrilled. As a travel writer she had a job to fulfil, and that didn't involve dropping a story to run home on a whim.

She dropped down on Jesse's bed, wondering why Ross had kept the house exactly the same for the past ten years. Surely it would have been easier on him if he'd made some changes? She opened the night-stand drawer and wasn't surprised to see Jesse's stuff scattered in it, just as it'd been when he was alive. A small pad of paper caught her attention. It had one name scribbled on it in her brother's bold scrawl. Noah Taylor.

The name alone made her smile. Jesse's best friend. And the first boy she'd ever had a crush on. Make that a crush of astronomical proportions.

Noah Taylor had been the local bad boy – the boy every mother dreaded. Withdrawn, moody and a loner, Noah was Jesse's opposite in every way. About the only thing they had in common was an insatiable love for computers, yet the two had remained fast friends until Jesse's death. In fact she and Jesse had been Noah's only friends – and she was only included because she was 'the little sister' – a term she'd grown to greatly resent. She hadn't seen Noah since he'd graduated with Jesse five years ahead of her, but she'd certainly heard of him; anyone even remotely interested in sports had. He'd become – unlikely as it seemed – a tennis pro. Annie had been as close to Noah as any outsider had been allowed and she'd never even known he could play tennis. How like him to go on and become not only a professional, but one of the best of all time.

She wondered if he was still troubled and sullen, then shook her head. His widely reported affairs with famous royalty, actresses, fellow tennis pros and even reporters told her that he wasn't. Women loved him.

6

She couldn't reconcile that with the taciturn and brusque Noah she remembered. Back then he was still physically undeveloped, his curly brown hair always too long, hanging continually over his eyes, so that even now she wasn't sure what colour they were.

Suddenly restless, she rose. Unready to deal with her task of going through her mother's things, Annie decided on a reprieve, and Noah Taylor was going to be it. She grabbed one of the few things she'd brought with her – her camera. Nothing soothed her nerves quicker than a jaunt of picture-taking, and there was no better place than the California coastline.

The walk to the beach was short – just across Noah's mother's property, which was adjacent to hers. With any luck, just maybe she'd run into Noah and they'd laugh at old times.

Noah returned the sharp serve with a backhand that would have stunned most of the tennis world. But not the small, undeveloped eleven-year-old Martin Hope. Martin made a valiant effort to reach the ball, but it was just physically impossible. So he did what any other overly streetwise punk who had been running wild too long would have done. He cheated.

'Out!' Martin shouted cheerfully. He pointed to the line. 'Definitely out, Noah.'

Noah snickered good-heartedly. 'Right.' But he gave it to the boy anyway. 'Your serve.'

He pretended to be dazzled by Martin's next serve and proceeded to lose the match. He struggled to look defeated when, in truth, he couldn't he been more pleased. Martin was coming along better than he'd ever hoped.

Since Noah had come back to his home town several years ago, he'd been teaching neglected and abused teenagers the joys of tennis. He'd beaten the best in the tennis world, bowed to royalty, travelled in nearly every country in the world. Yet nothing compared to this. It was the single most rewarding thing he'd ever done.

'Noah?' Martin asked tentatively as he gingerly placed the racket Noah had lent him in its case as if it were precious gold. 'How . . . how long can I stay here?'

Noah looked up in surprise as Martin chewed on his lip. The bruises his last foster father had given him were just fading, but the anger rose freshly in Noah. 'As long as you want to,' he told the boy, wishing he could pay back bruise for bruise to the man who'd inflicted them.

He watched as Martin looked across a great expanse of green lawn towards the huge house on a bluff high above the Pacific Ocean. It could have passed for a mansion. Instead, it was used as a safe haven for other boys like Martin. It was called the Taylor House, and Noah himself had grown up there. In those days, Rosemary Taylor had run the place. And when a bedraggled, sorry and pathetic little ten-year-old named simply Noah had shown up there one night, she hadn't thought twice. She'd taken him in. Later – in a move she hadn't made before, nor since repeated – she had officially adopted him, making him Noah Taylor.

'What if *they* make me go back?' Martin asked, fidgeting nervously on the bench at the edge of the court Noah had been playing at since he'd found Rosie's racquet twenty years ago.

They, of course, were Child Services. 'They won't,' Noah assured him. He didn't have the heart to tell the boy that no one else wanted him. No one wanted to bother with a kid who was nearly a teenager, and one who had been switched from foster home to foster home. It spelled trouble.

They stood and Noah winced as his left knee spasmed. It was bothering him more and more lately, and he knew it would only get worse. It was a harsh reminder that he was considered a has-been by most. The only thing it reminded him of now was that he wasn't as healthy as he'd once been. He had no regrets, certainly not even a single wish that he were still playing professionally. At thirty-two he was still young enough, but not even perfect health could convince him to go back and have his life dictated by ratings, championships, reporters, fans. He liked his life right now, playing tennis occasionally and only recreationally. Helping kids by running the Taylor House. Running his computer consulting business.

Nope, no regrets. And if he was vaguely uneasy that his life was indeed missing something, he continued to shrug it off. What more could he need?

Together they walked across the grass towards the house, Martin keeping a safe distance between the two of them that tore at Noah's heart. Martin had seen such vicious and repeated abuse that he found it impossible to trust completely, even here. No one understood that better than Noah. He'd come from that world once, too.

'Who's that?' Martin asked in an awed voice, pointing to the porch of the house where a young woman sat in the swing, sipping from a tall glass.

Noah recognized the glass filled with Rosemary's famous lemonade. When his eyes lifted to the woman's, he felt a sharp shock of recognition and a familiar dash of humility. Annie Laverty. The closest thing to a pesky younger sister he had. And the only woman alive who had the uncanny – and very provoking – ability to make a fool of him.

Annie glanced at them and raised her eyebrows in surprise as her gaze lingered over him, setting off that familiar jolt of irritation.

Growing up, the only females who gave Noah a second glance were Rosemary *and* Annie. Rosemary, because he belonged to her; Annie, because she'd followed him and her brother around relentlessly.

10

He had been nothing but skin and bone, even as a teenager. It wasn't until Rosemary had found him a good tennis coach and he'd made the tennis circuit that he had physically matured, years after he'd left San Rayo. From the moment he'd hit maturity, women had looked at him differently. He'd become – against his wishes – a hot commodity. Fans screamed for him, reporters tried to get into his dressing room, women wanted him. At first it had been amusing, and he had definitely spent time using it to his advantage. A lot of time.

Eventually, the thrill had faded when he'd realized that they only wanted a piece of his fame, his money, his reputation. And he quickly got the message. He was immensely physically appealing and that was all that mattered to the vast majority of the women he met. No one was interested in the real Noah Taylor. He knew it would be next to impossible to find a woman who could look past the exterior, the fortune and fame, to find the *real* him. He'd stopped looking long ago.

Now, Annie watched him in frank admiration, which not only made him very uncomfortable, but which was something she never would have done in the past. For one thing, she'd been a good many inches taller than him for most of their childhood. And for another . . . God, he hated to think about it. But he had always harboured secret feelings for her – his best friend's sister. A girl he should have thought of as his

11

own sister. It was as sick and pathetic to remember now as it had been to deal with then. Annie had never known how he'd felt, nor had Jesse; he'd always managed to hide it behind his mock boredom. And he'd choke before admitting it now.

Yet Annie sat, staring at him in a way he thought he'd never see, and it was surprisingly insulting. As was the quick flip his heart did at the sight of her dazzling smile. 'Hey, Laverty,' he said in a carefully neutral voice unintentionally cool and distant. He sighed, wishing he could just enjoy seeing an old friend without the painful and embarrassing memories.

She shook her head, her surprise obvious. 'I can't believe it's you.'

Noah ignored the pang of regret with a wry smile and introduced Martin to her. Annie smiled at the boy, whose tongue was practically dangling from his lips.

'Uh . . . hi,' Martin said, and Noah could have laughed if he hadn't so completely understood the boy's thoughts.

Annie had changed quite a bit herself since the last time he'd seen her. When he'd left town she'd been thirteen, a tall, gawky girl with straggly hair and braces who had tagged after Noah and Jesse wherever they went. Stubbornly she'd stuck with them, no matter how hard they'd tried to lose her, until eventually she'd become a natural part of the group.

12

She was gawky and straggling no more, Noah thought as Annie stood. Tall and willowy came to mind, as her startling eyes met his. They were the colour of a foggy morning sky, her golden hair cut in a graceful bob at her chin. The fact that she had turned out so coolly beautiful aggravated him all the more.

'It's been a long time, Bones,' Annie said, eyes narrowing as she studied his considerable height. She laughed softly when he winced at the old nickname. 'You've changed.'

'You haven't.' He bit back his caustic smile, enjoying her flash of annoyance.

Eventually she laughed again, a musical sound that took him back years. 'Heard you played some kind of game for a living, Bones. Croquet? Badminton? Wait . . . don't tell me – ' Her face lit up. 'I remember! Water ballet!'

'That's it, Annie.' He leaned a shoulder against the wooden banister, enjoying the banter. He'd forgotten how much fun they'd had, bickering constantly. Poor Jesse, he'd never known whether to referee or run for cover. 'Kind of you to remember me.'

'Hard to forget,' she said. Her eyes raked over him again and she shook her head. 'But I can't believe it's you. No wonder they've been falling at your feet. Look at you! You finally grew – you must be over six feet tall.'

He was six feet two inches, but who was counting?

'Yeah, well,' he said evenly, 'I got tired of bossy women pushing me around.'

She laughed in delight, but it embarrassed him, her frank approval of his body. He'd been eighteen when she'd seen him last, and in those days she wouldn't have thought of him that way – he was practically her brother, for chrissakes. 'Annie – '

'Who would have thought?' Her mouth quirked. 'I bet the women around here have been trying to atone, huh?'

He decided to give it right back. Maybe it would shut her up. 'Yeah. In the meantime you've been quite the busy one yourself, haven't you? Dressing up in style.' He paused to study her bright and sporty teal jacket, short skirt and heels. 'Though I have to say, the Annie I remember much preferred T-shirts and cut-offs. I hear you've been travelling around, flitting in and out of countries, having tea, going to parties, meeting celebrities and politicians. Shopping. Gossiping. It's amazing what people will pay you to do these days.'

Her easy smile faded, and her eyes frosted over. 'Why is it people assume that as a travel writer I'm on a perennial vacation?' Annoyance flashed over her face. 'I've been working, not "flitting".'

Noah stared at her in surprise, for he'd truly been joking. He knew and admired the reputation she'd earned for herself writing. She worked for one of the biggest magazines around, writing their travel

14

section from first-hand knowledge. 'I was just – '

'I'm sorry.' She set the glass down on the porch and stepped off to the grass. 'I've . . . got to go.'

Martin's awestruck face whirled to Noah, and Noah's eyes automatically shifted to Annie's heels, knowing they'd sink into the soft dirt.

'I'll see you around,' she said, trying to raise a stuck heel with casual nonchalance.

He wisely didn't offer her help and kept his amusement to himself. 'Wait – '

She turned from him, her veil of hair shimmering about her face, her short, full shirt whirling about her thighs. 'I can't.'

His good humour faded, sensing that something was bothering her deeply. 'No need to run off,' he said mildly, knowing from experience that Annie tended to use temper to ward off emotions. He was well familiar with the technique himself, and knew to tread lightly. He turned to Martin, wanting to spare him the exchange he knew was coming. 'Great game today. Could you – '

Martin shot him a look of such understanding and sympathy that Noah blinked in surprise. 'Yeah,' he said quietly. 'I'll catch you later.'

The kid was ahead of his time. Noah's attention returned to Annie. 'OK, I think we've established you're not here to socialize. So why don't you tell me why you are here?'

'Forget it. It's nothing. I was wrong to come.' Her

15

voice was calm and strangely subdued, her eyes filled with what could have been apology and sorrow. She turned and walked away.

Annie headed down the path, hoping to put the Taylor House behind her as quickly as possible. But the driveway was long and she could feel Noah's eyes imprinting her back. She slowed, knowing that she'd taken out her stress over being home again on someone who didn't deserve it. She felt like a fool and knew her tongue had got the better of her.

To make matters worse, her brain chose that moment to remind her why Noah had stopped playing professional tennis. A couple of years ago he'd disappeared from that whirlwind world after a tragic knee injury had ended his career at the age of thirty.

With a sigh, she stopped. Off to her right, the Pacific Ocean surf arched on to the shore with a soothing and hypnotic regularity. The California coast stretched out below in its lush beauty. For the first time since she'd been home, her sense of panic receded, and she felt relaxed. It suddenly felt good to be back.

She turned back towards the Taylor House where, even from her distance, she could see a tall figure sitting on the swing, watching her. From the wide, set shoulders there was no doubt who it was. His hair was still too long, and his face lean and tough, but he had grown, far surpassing the skinny kid he'd once been. Swallowing her pride, Annie made her way back to the house and stopped at the foot of the porch to meet his challenging expression.

'I'm sorry,' she said quietly.

Noah's expression was hooded, guarded. 'What are you so angry about?'

His voice had a deep, rough timbre to it that soothed her nerves. 'I'm not angry. Upset.' She sank down besides him, uninvited, on the swing. She didn't bother with casual banalities. 'When's the last time you thought about Jesse?'

His cool indifference vanished, and he looked off at the ocean for so long she wasn't sure he'd answer. 'This morning,' he said finally.

He said nothing else, even though she waited. He had always been miserly with words. 'Tell me,' she pushed.

He glanced at her, his expression distant. 'I couldn't start my car this morning. Jesse loved that damn car. It'd run for him every time, never hesitating. I have to beg it, cajole it, coax it – and it irritates the hell out of me.'

Annie smiled. Jesse used to have a way with cars, Noah's especially. He should. He'd rebuilt the '62 Mustang convertible for him and had loved every minute of it. That Noah still had the car unexpectedly touched her. She was sure he could have afforded ten new cars if he'd wanted to.

'How long have you been back here?' she asked him.

He shrugged. 'A couple of years.'

She thought of his injury and nodded. She still couldn't believe the change in him. His face was the same rugged from too many years in the sun, with heavy squint lines surrounding eyes holding a wealth of knowledge. His mouth was wide and firm. And still. Noah didn't smile often. But the years had given him a physical maturity she never could have guessed at. His body was well developed and toned in the way only a dedicated athlete's could be, lean and strong, but without excess bulk. He looked solid, sinewy, mysterious and dangerous. Entirely and completely masculine from head to toe –

'You're staring again,' he said, eyes narrowing. 'Did I grow a third eye?'

'No.' She grinned. She would absolutely *not* renew her silly, childhood crush – no matter how handsome he'd turned out to be. She didn't have the time, the energy, the . . . oh, who the hell was she fooling? For ten long years, she simply hadn't had the heart, the passion for something which could take so much from her. Lost love for her family had taken its toll, and she still wasn't ready to risk her heart. 'I'm sorry,' she said to Noah. 'Do you realize how many years it's been? I was thirteen when you left.'

'I saw you after that.'

'No.' She shook her head. 'I don't think so.'

'At the funerals.'

Her eyes met his for a heartbeat before they danced away to study the distant, almost indistinguishable line between ocean and sky. 'Oh.' She didn't remember much about that day. Unbelievable pain, shock and disbelief that both her beloved mother and brother were gone, and the vague memory of Ross, inconsolable in his own grief.

She looked at Noah again. He and Jesse had been so close. She wondered if he still hurt, still missed him, as she did. It was impossible to tell from his shuttered features.

'Heard you were in London working,' he said in a surprising move towards a friendly conversation.

'I was, until yesterday.'

'You live there?'

'No, my apartment's in New York, but I haven't been there in a while.'

'So, what brings you back after all this time?'

She shrugged, though it was disconcerting how he'd been able to bring her around to what was bothering her. 'You're full of questions today,' she said uneasily.

'Yeah,' he conceded with eyes that told her he was not going to give up until he got the answers he sought. 'Does Ross know you're back?'

He always was perceptive. 'No,' she answered, feeling the guilt sneak through her. Why hadn't she called? She knew he would have come to meet her, thrilled to have her back.

19

'He's away a lot.'

'Always was,' she said shortly, Noah-style. Ross was the head fire marshal for the entire county, investigating all counts of arson and any questionable fires. It was a rough job, one that frequently took him away for days at a time. In his letter to Annie, he'd written that he spent less and less time at the house and it deserved more.

She'd thought so too.

Annie wondered if Ross would come home tonight. The truth was, she hadn't told him she was coming because she hadn't meant to come. But in the end, she hadn't been able to resist taking one last peek at the house that had given her so much pleasure, joy and love.

'Ross wants to sell the house,' she admitted, looking away. Damn, her voice shook. She couldn't believe it. He'd probably just ignore it, giving her the same rude treatment she'd given him. Yet he said nothing and after a minute she turned back to him. His eyes searched hers. They were a deep, rich brown, and so fathomless that she couldn't imagine how she'd gone all those years without noticing them.

'That bothers you?'

'I don't know,' she answered truthfully, stretching her legs out in front of her and studying her feet. Her favourite heels were ruined because of her ridiculous stomp across the grass. Served her right. 'He never even packed their things, Noah.'

'Maybe he couldn't bring himself to.'

She shrugged.

'It's not so strange, Annie. You never came back.'

He had her there. The two things weren't so different after all. Still, she wondered how Ross could stand it, day after day. 'It was just so hard to walk through the house, much harder than I thought it would be.' She shrugged. 'So I came here instead.'

The side of his mouth quirked, almost but not quite in a smile. 'And now your pretty heels are ruined.'

Annie smiled. 'So they are.' She sighed. 'It was the stocked refrigerator that did it, I think.' That the refrigerator had been so full, as in the old days, had made her stomach clench painfully. The milk had expired two days ago; back then Jesse would have downed it from the carton the day it had been purchased.

Noah frowned. 'Stocked refrigerator?'

'Ross has it full now, but our food supply was always dangerously low when you and Jesse were about.'

'We always did spend most of our time swiping food; from school, from here, from your house. It was a wonder we ever graduated.'

Annie stiffened. She had a sudden vivid memory of getting ready for her own graduation. Dressed in a beautiful satin peach gown and primping in front of the mirror as if she hadn't a worry in the world,

21

gabbing on the telephone with her best friend, Tori. Ross had torn into her bedroom then, grabbed the phone and hung up – only to immediately start dialling.

It had taken her several seconds to realize why. Her mother and brother were out the front, trapped in the burning car, dying a hideously slow and painful death. Revenge, she'd later discovered. Revenge against the fire marshal. She couldn't bear to think about it, then or now. While she didn't exactly blame Ross, it was still hard to accept that it was his job that had killed her family.

She heard a soft sound and realized that it was her own sigh of distress.

'What is it?' Noah asked, leaning forward to study her.

She couldn't tell him, she couldn't tell anyone the thoughts that were beginning to haunt her all over again – just from entering a house. He opened his mouth to say something else when a soft, hesitant voice stopped him.

'Who's there?'

They both turned at the frail-sounding voice. An old woman stood in the doorway, staring at them. Annie stifled her gasp as she recognized Rosemary Taylor. Once a robust, formidable woman whom no one in the town would have messed with, fighting like a mother bear over her troubled teens as if they were her cubs, she was now a shell of that figure.

Pathetically thin, her features seemed to sink into her face, and her once glossy red curls were straight and grey.

'Rosemary,' Noah said in a gentle voice that Annie had never heard before. He rose, and so did Annie.

Noah reached for Rosemary's arm and helped her into the swing they'd just vacated. Annie watched as Noah crouched beside Rosemary, dwarfing her with his large frame. He smiled warmly, but Rosemary simply stared off into space.

'How are you today, Rosemary?' he asked, but the old woman just looked at him blankly, without recognition.

'It's me. Noah,' he said easily enough, but even from Annie's distance she could sense the strain in his body.

Annie saw the brief flare of light in Rosemary's eyes. It faded immediately and Annie could see Noah's bitter disappointment, though he managed to mask it quickly.

'Do you remember Annie Laverty, Jesse's sister?' he asked her in an achingly patient voice.

Rosemary frowned without glancing in Annie's direction. 'Noah?'

'Yes, I'm here.' His broad shoulders slumped in relief.

'The tomatoes are turning, and no one's picked them,' Rosemary said in a petulant voice. 'Now listen, young man. Go out there and take care of it

23

for me. If you need some help reaching the tall vines, get one of the older boys to help you. Tell them I said so. You hear me?'

Noah's gentle voice never faltered as he stood, though his eyes were troubled. 'No problem, Rosemary. I'll take care of it.'

Rosemary squeezed his hand and smiled up at the tall, lean man before her. 'Good boy. I want to make you some of my special spaghetti sauce for dinner. It's your favourite. How was school today?'

'Just fine. You go rest, and I'll take care of the vines for you. I promise.'

Annie stared, stunned, as Noah carefully led Rosemary back into the house. Never had she heard Noah speak so gently or kindly. Never had she known he could be so patient and understanding. Never had she witnessed such a touching, devastating exchange between mother and son.

'You're such a good boy, Noah.' Rosemary sighed, as a woman dressed in a white uniform came from nowhere and nodded pleasantly to Noah before leading Rosemary away.

Noah turned briefly back to Annie, his face impassive. 'Annie?' he said in his old Noah voice – as if the kind and loving man she'd just witnessed didn't exist. 'I'll be right back. Don't go.' His casual yet bossy tone was reminiscent of their childhood when she did everything that he and her brother had asked of her. How could she not have? She'd thought the

24

sun rose and set on her brother's shoulders and she'd been more than half in love with Noah since she was five years old. They'd run her around and she had never hesitated, knowing how they'd have protected her against anyone else daring to talk to her in such a way.

Annie watched them go, wondering how it was that things had changed so much, yet so little.

She shouldn't have come – there was nothing here in this town for her now. Trinkets of her mother's or Jesse's weren't going to bring them back. She had all the memories she needed in her own mind. And being near Noah was dangerous as well, though she wasn't quite ready to admit that. She jumped up and, with determined strides, headed across the green with the intention of getting out of town as soon as possible.

She never left San Rayo. Late that night, Annie finally settled down on the couch in the living room. Her stomach grumbled, reminding her that she'd skipped dinner rather than face the kitchen. And this time it wasn't nostalgia that did it – she was absolutely useless in the kitchen. Hotel living had made her dependent on room-service and pizza deliveries. She should have called out for Chinese.

Her own helplessness, especially on her home turf, brought back amusing memories. Noah, choking down some hard-as-rock brownies she'd slaved hours over – and swearing he loved them, even as he downed a gallon of milk to wash them down. Jesse, rather than face her home-cooked dinner, faking the flu, then really catching food poisoning – from her beef stew. Ross, so kindly offering to pay for a private tutor when she'd come home from school crying because she'd failed cooking class. Her mother, desperate to instil some sort of domestic skill, attempting to teach her to cook eggs. Everyone can cook an egg, she'd said, laughing. Annie smiled, remembering. Yes, everyone could cook an egg. And it was about all she could cook.

Those were the memories she could stand to remember, the happy and carefree ones. From the good old days.

It wasn't until she tried to settle in her own bedroom that she had problems. She simply couldn't sleep there without reliving haunting childhood memories, so she ended up on the downstairs couch. It wasn't that any one memory was bad – the opposite was true. That was what made it hurt so much. No less than five times she decided to go, but something stopped her. Whether it was the rows and rows of her mother's precious books or the garage still full of Jesse's prized tools, she didn't know. But she couldn't imagine letting strangers pack the place up, nor could she see Ross doing it by himself.

He must miss them as much as she did, she realized with a pang. She'd been selfish . . . and she hated that. She knew then that she'd see Ross through this, no matter what. It simply wasn't fair to make him face it alone.

She never should have let so much time go by without seeing him. Being back in this house reminded her that she did have family left and she'd sorely neglected him. Earlier, she'd called her editor and asked for a week off, then had regretted the move. But now she knew she'd done the right thing, and she settled herself down to wait for Ross. He'd probably work all night, as he tended to do. There wasn't a man more completely dedicated to his work than Ross Laverty, whether that work be finding arsonists or being a father. How many nights had the positions been reversed, with him waiting up for her to come home safely from a date? It seemed so ironic now.

She missed him, she thought. And sighed, slowly drifting off to sleep.

She slept fitfully and dreamed of fire. Dreamed of her mother's screams, dreamed of her trapped in the family car, unable to get out. Dreamed of a vague but haunting and disturbing thought that there was more to remember, but the more she reached for it, the more it eluded her.

The moon rose high over the restless sea as Noah watched. He sat in the dark on the porch, unable to sleep. Midnight, Martin's black cat, crunched his dry food in a bowl at his feet.

A chill crept through the air, making it seem more

like September rather than July. The cold ocean breeze blew over him, but still he sat. He loved the sea at night, loved the cool, salty air, loved hearing the crashing of the waves over the dark sand. Leaning back on the swing, arms outstretched, he felt relaxed. At peace.

Suddenly, Midnight stilled. As Noah watched, the cat stiffened, the black hair rising along its neck. A split-second later, the motion detector on the driveway came on.

Noah's head whipped towards it, but nothing came into the light and there wasn't a sound. He waited another minute, wondering what the cat sensed. After a few more seconds, the light flickered out and the cat resumed eating.

It couldn't be a coincidence. The cat had heard something and the light sensor had sensed something. Noah stood and walked up the drive, around to the back of the house. He passed several sheds that stored pool equipment, tennis equipment and various other sporting equipment.

At the edge of the large property were seven small cottages that housed the permanent staff of the Taylor House, allowing them to care for up to twenty children, though they rarely had more than ten at a time. Beyond that, a green belt. And beyond that, a housing development where the first house he could see was where Annie Laverty was at this very minute.

She'd bolted on him this afternoon. Respect for her

privacy and for her obvious wish to be alone had kept him from following her, though the urge to ignore that and go anyway had been strong. Strong enough to startle him.

He'd long ago buried his totally inappropriate feelings for his dead best friend's sister. A woman who thought of him as a brother figure.

To his disgust, her haunted grey eyes hounded his thoughts. A long time ago he would have known what she had on her mind, but that had changed. She'd grown up.

He'd thought about her often over the years, just as he still grieved over Jesse. It should have been painful to see her, a sharp reminder that his first and only best friend was dead. A vivid memory of humiliating feelings for a woman he could never have. Instead, it had felt right to see her. So right that he didn't want to admit it.

Now, at the edge of his property, he caught a shadowy movement in the trees ahead. Sure that he had caught one of the boys doing something he shouldn't, Noah moved forward.

What he saw nearly stopped his heart.

Annie struggled to clear her head, but couldn't. Her vision blurred, leaving everything in a haze around her and she coughed violently.

She sat straight up on the couch, then bent over immediately as her head swam.

29

Smoke! It wasn't a nightmare. Surrounded by smoke, the frightening licks of flame were too close. Heat overwhelmed her as she fought unconsciousness.

Oh, God, she thought, she couldn't die – not like this.

Not like her mother.

CHAPTER 2

There were flames all around her. The curtains were dancing with them, the smoke intoxicating. Annie jumped up and immediately collapsed to her knees as nausea overcame her. She managed by sheer force of will not to get sick and started to crawl towards the front door, concentrating on her one clear thought: getting a fresh breath of air before she passed out.

The smoke was so thick that she could see only a foot or so in front of her. Everywhere around her, ashes were falling like rain and wood was crackling. A few feet from the front door she cried out in pain as she crawled with bare knees over a hot spot in the carpet. Pausing to rock in pain, her body jerked when the living room window exploded, and a scream ripped from her parched throat.

The front door crashed open and Annie, her thoughts becoming muddled, dropped her head between her shoulders, panting for air.

'Oh, God.' Hurried hands scooped her up, shifting

31

her against a hard chest. 'Jesus. Annie, hang on.'

Her head lolled back against a solid shoulder and she caught a brief glimpse of Noah's tense face before a coughing fit seized her. He ran with her out of the door just as two fire engines came tearing around the corner, sirens blaring and lights flashing.

She was immediately covered in blankets and given oxygen, which was convenient as well as necessary. No one could ask her to talk with a mask over her face – which suited her. Shaken to the core, she sat and watched as the firefighters worked their magic and put out the fire, aware of Noah hovering protectively over her.

The fire wasn't as big as she had first thought. It was mostly contained on the first floor. But staring at the last of the flames before they succumbed to the steady streams of water took her back in time to a place that was even more terrifying.

To the day she watched in horror as her mother and brother died in front of her eyes.

Noah watched as Annie squeezed her eyes shut, a small cry escaping her lips. He'd been watching her, his heart in his throat, since he'd pulled her out of the house. He still couldn't believe it.

He dropped down besides her. 'Annie.'

She didn't open her eyes. He glanced back at the house, well aware of what bothered her. The same thing bothered him – Jesse and her mother – but for him the memories were different. She'd actually seen it happen.

'Annie,' he repeated more firmly. 'It's over now.'

She shook her head, looking so shaken, pale and sick that he wondered if the paramedics were wrong. They'd decided she didn't need to take the trip to the hospital; the burns on her knees had been treated and she was breathing fine. But she was trembling and he worried about delayed shock.

'Annie, look at me.'

She lifted her head and stared at him with misty eyes. Her hair fell back from her face; dark streaks of dirt covered her cheeks. Without warning she leaned forward, setting her full weight against him, then tucked herself into his arms. Either he wrapped his arms around her or they'd both fall to the floor. It was no choice, he thought as he held her. Her breath warmed his neck and suddenly his own breath halted.

He had held her this way countless times as children. Once she'd jumped on a bee, and when her foot had swollen to twice its size he'd carried her the half-mile home. Another time, she'd been about eleven and unceremoniously dumped for a prettier, more popular girl by a thoughtless, stupid boy. Her heart had been broken and he'd consoled her with an awkward brotherly hug, while wanting to smash in the face of the punk who had hurt her. He'd even given Annie her first kiss when she'd been twelve. Well, he corrected, she'd kissed him and he'd been shocked. And then a little mad because his body had reacted to her. He remembered pushing her away, feeling as if he'd just kissed his own kid sister. And wanting more despite that.

With her face snuggled under his chin he felt no disgust now, no casual solace either. Just an electric bolt of shock. And arousal. 'Annie,' he said in a low voice as he tried to push her away. 'The fire's gone now. It's going to be all right.'

She pulled herself closer to him. 'I know,' she whispered. 'It was just such a shock.'

He allowed himself one brief spontaneous, reassuring squeeze.

'I just kept seeing – ' She stopped abruptly.

'I know,' he said, seeing the same thing himself and wondering – as he had thousands of times – how much Jesse and his mother had suffered.

The blanket fell back from her arm as she reached up and snaked it around his neck, pulling herself even closer in the safe haven of his arms. 'I thought I was going to die the same way.'

He held on tight, having given up disentangling himself, and lightly brushed a kiss over her hair. 'You took ten years off my life tonight, Laverty. Nearly killed myself getting here after I saw the smoke from across the green. Then I heard you scream . . . Jesus.' He shook his head, then leaned down to kiss her head

34

again at the same exact moment she lifted her face to look at him.

His lips skimmed her cheek instead and his entire body reacted.

She stared at him, her own expression startled.

'Excuse me,' came a male voice besides them.

They each started and looked at the firefighter paramedic. 'We're wondering if you've thought about where you're going to stay for the rest of the night.'

Noah swallowed hard, then cleared his suddenly parched throat, unable to speak.

'I – ' Annie started.

'What the hell's going on?' a deep male voice called out.

'Ross!' Annie exclaimed, pushing shakily to her feet and pulling the blanket tight around her. 'Over here!' She stepped out from the dark shadow of the fire truck they'd been sitting near.

Ross Laverty had just got out of his car and was staring miserably at the house. The wind whipped noisily over them; everywhere people were shouting to one another and radios from the police cars crackled. Hazy, thick smoke made the dark night even darker. Through the gloom and over the din, Ross didn't hear nor see Annie.

Noah took a second to glance at the house, then wished he hadn't. It was hard to see the extent of the damage in the dark, but the bottom half of the house appeared charred. Water dripped everywhere. The smell of fire hung heavy in the air. There were still two fire trucks, an ambulance and a sheriff's car parked haphazardly in the street. And there were people with white, sleepy, concerned faces everywhere.

It was a disaster zone. One that Annie had nearly perished in.

When she stepped closer to Ross, Noah did too, knowing he should give them their privacy but still concerned over Annie's shakiness and her pallor.

'Ross,' she croaked in a smoke-strained voice. 'Ross.'

He whirled. 'Annie?' Ross turned to her and his eyes widened. 'Oh, my God. Annie.'

Annie's mouth turned up in a pale resemblance of a smile. 'Not exactly a great way to have a reunion, is it?'

Tall and generously shaped, Ross resembled a large koala bear. He had a tuft of grey hair that stuck up on his head and a rounded belly. But his shape and cuddly air were deceptive – he was smart, shrewd and the best in the business. Noah knew that in the world of firefighters he was a god.

But none of that mattered now as Ross enveloped Annie in his arms, closing his eyes. 'When I heard the call on the radio, I couldn't believe it. You – you were inside?'

She nodded.

Noah watched, feeling a strange sense of envy overcome him at the easy show of affection – even after being separated for ten years. Rosemary had been everything a foster mother could be, but she herself had come from an abused family. Kisses and hugs didn't come easy to her, and casual affection was unheard of. She'd cared for him enough to keep him, and that had to be enough. But never had he been shown the kind of natural physical contact that Annie and her father were sharing now.

'Are you all right? Did the paramedics check you out?' Ross held her at arm's length, running his gaze down Annie's dishevelled figure. 'Why aren't you in the hospital? Don't they know – '

'Ross,' she said, in a surprisingly firm voice. 'I'm fine. Believe me, Noah already gave them the third degree.'

'But you could have smoke inhalation, or – '

'I'm going to be all right, really. Don't worry.'

'Don't worry, she says,' he said on a harsh laugh, yanking her back in his arms. 'My God, how the hell am I supposed to do that? Why didn't you tell me you were coming, honey? I could have been here for you.'

For several moments they just stood there, holding each other, while Noah stood by fidgeting, uncomfortable.

The firefighters recognized Ross, the chief inspector, and after giving him a few private minutes came to fill him in on the details.

'Definitely arson, sir.' The firefighter shook his head grimly.

Ross's eyes wandered back to Annie in disbelief. 'What?' he said, looking shocked.

'We smelled gasoline immediately, sir, and you can see from the deep charring of the outside walls that it had been splashed liberally. Without an accelerant, the blaze would have given the walls a light scorching and skipped on in search of better, more combustible material, probably even burning itself out. Instead we have this mess.'

Noah's stomach flip-flopped at the thought of what could have happened. Some mindless savage had deliberately set the fire while Annie slept. If he hadn't come when he did . . . Jesus. He could hardly stomach the thought.

By the looks of Ross, he felt the same. Sickly white and sweaty, Ross looked ready to pass out.

'Inspector?' one of the firefighters asked. 'You OK?'

He waved them off irritatedly, then shook his head at Noah and Annie. 'My God,' he whispered. 'Arson. Here. In our house. My God.'

The fire chief pulled up then and Noah watched as he consulted privately with Ross and the others for a few minutes. He and Annie appeared forgotten, at least for the moment. Finally, Ross came back over, nodded to Noah as if seeing him for the first time, and looked at Annie, the concern and worry evident in his taut stance.

'Annie, Jesus. You could have been killed tonight.'

'I'm fine,' she said, trying to smile.

He took her hands, staring deep into her eyes as if gauging her answer for honesty. 'Why didn't you tell me you were coming?'

'I didn't think I was,' Annie told him. 'Ross, I'm so sorry.'

He grimaced. 'Don't – it's not your fault. They assured me you're OK. Are you really?'

She didn't look it with her large, haunted eyes, skin streaked with dirt and hair tangled about her face. 'Yes. Really, I . . . I'm OK.' She glanced at the house and took a deep breath.

Her knees poked out of the blanket she gripped so tightly around her. Ross looked at the bandages on her knees, then back at Annie's face. She still stared at the house.

'Burns,' Noah told Ross. 'She was crawling on her hands and knees out of there when I found her.'

Ross shook his head again, looking more and more upset as everything sank in. The noise around them increased, if that were possible, but Ross, probably used to such things, didn't seem to notice. Noah didn't know Ross well; over the years his unusual job had kept him away for much of the time. But Ross's reputation as a hardworking and tough investigator were well known.

Ross paused, staring at Noah. 'You pulled her out?'

Noah nodded, knowing he'd never in his entire life

39

forget how he'd felt in those awful first seconds, before he'd known Annie was all right.

Ross looked sick. 'God. If you hadn't been there . . . Thank – '

'Don't,' Noah said quickly. He didn't want to be thanked for something he'd done without a thought. He wanted to think anyone would have done what he did. He'd do it again in a heartbeat. 'I . . . don't need to be thanked,' he added gruffly.

Ross looked at him, then nodded. 'All right, then. But you have my eternal gratitude.' He put his arm around Annie.

Noah glanced at her. She stared directly back at him with those amazing grey eyes, just the look making him ache with something deeper than lust. He wondered what exactly what they'd shared a moment ago, before Ross had shown up. Jesus, she was practically his sister and he'd wanted to kiss her. He remembered the shock that had run through the both of them and he imagined now that hers had been from disgust.

Annie blinked, breaking the spell, and Noah could see the weariness and stress etched deeply in her face. 'You need a place to stay tonight, both of you,' he said them. 'We have plenty of room – '

'No, son,' Ross broke in, looking miserably at the house. 'You've done more than enough for us. Thanks for the offer, but we'll be fine.' He turned to Annie and without hesitating – in the way only a father could do to his own child – he took charge. 'We'll get a room for tonight. We'll be fine. Thanks, Noah.'

Annie remained suspiciously mute and Noah knew she was in bad shape if she let someone speak for her. He watched her carefully for signs of shock. She didn't appear to be shaking, just quiet. And after what she'd just been through, who could blame her? Besides, Ross was more than capable of deciding if his daughter needed further medical attention. Without a choice or a say in the matter, he watched as Ross led Annie towards his car, leaving Noah with nothing else to do but to head home.

As he always did, he checked on Rosemary first. She was safely and soundly asleep with the nurse posted at her bedside. It was a sad but necessary measure. Her Alzheimer's steadily worsened, with more bad days than good, and though it killed him to see her deteriorate so, he insisted on having her here instead of in a care unit. She deserved to be here, at the only home she'd known, and he felt lucky enough to be in a position to pay for it.

All was quiet from the boys' rooms, which wasn't so unusual. They played hard and slept just as hard.

He walked slowly to his cottage. He could have lived in the big house. He had, until he'd gone off on the tennis circuit. But when he'd come back two years ago he'd claimed the last cottage as his own. When he'd retired from professional tennis because of his knee, he'd planned to run a computer consulting business for his career. He'd always planned that, even as a child. He hadn't planned on running the Taylor House. But, with Rosemary sick, that job had fallen to him, and he didn't have the heart to shut it down, didn't have the heart to turn away kids that had come from their own private hell. A hell he personally understood. So he did both – equally well.

Too keyed up to sleep, he sat down in front of the computer. He had at least three programming jobs waiting for him, each one a rush.

Yet, as his fingers sped over the keyboard, his mind turned to Annie.

Sleep eluded him, the memory of the delicious fire too much for his over-stimulated brain. Flat on his back in bed, he watched the moonlight play over the ceiling and bit back a giggle.

Just the thought of how bright the flaring flames had been was enough to excite him all over again. God, he loved fire. He loved the pureness of it, the heat, the brilliant colour. He loved it all. And already he wanted more.

Then he remembered, and he sobered quickly. He loved fire, not necessarily death. Oh, he'd caused death before, but not by design. And each time he'd felt remorse, heavy remorse.

No, he never planned death with his fires; just the thought had a chilly trickle of sweat pooling at the base of his spine.

He shivered, despite the warmth of the room. Death.

It was exactly what had *almost* happened tonight.

By eleven the next morning, Annie couldn't stand the hotel one second longer. Ross had insisted on checking the house alone, saying it would upset her too much. Now she regretted letting him go, since he had looked more than a little upset himself. He had aged, she thought with regret for lost years.

After three showers she still smelled like smoke and hurt like hell, but she had to get out. Sitting was driving her crazy; she had far too much time to think. And she didn't like where her thoughts were leading her. Some time in the night it had occurred to her. Not sleeping in her bedroom the night before had saved her life. If it hadn't been for the fact she couldn't stand the memories her room brought, she'd have slept there – and died of smoke inhalation.

The fact that her nightmarish memories of a fire from ten years past had saved her life from a fire in her present was mightily unsettling.

She called a taxi, no easy feat in a town of three taxis total, but it was that or walk, and she had no shoes.

She supposed she should count herself lucky that San Rayo, being a beach town, had several decent hotels – and boutiques. Even luckier, she'd been able to have something sent up to wear, since she'd arrived in a T-shirt and blanket. The short sundress had been a find, but unfortunately there hadn't been a pair of shoes even remotely close to her size.

Shrugging off that concern, she directed the taxi driver to the house, preparing herself for what she'd see.

She couldn't contain her gasp of dismay as they drove up. The grass, once so green, now lay flattened and muddy, the flowers trampled beyond hope. Glass from two of the windows scattered the front lawn, yet the upper floor remained eerily untouched. The white paint was gone in spots, peeling and curling off in others. A steady flow of ashes covered the driveway and street.

It broke her heart.

Annie stepped out of the cab, once again seeing a flash of another time and place. If she closed her eyes it could be ten years ago and she was staring at her garden wondering how her mother and brother could be there one minute and gone the next.

A flickering memory nagged at her for a second, but before she could grasp it, it was gone. Firmly she put the thoughts of that fire out of her head. She'd go out of her mind if she didn't.

Ross was nowhere to be seen. She must have missed him. Gingerly and cautiously, she made her way to the front door, watching where she stepped. It was locked. She made her way around to the back where the fire might never have happened, except for the heavy scent of fire still in the air.

The same smell she hadn't been able to get rid of ten years ago, no matter what she did, how far she moved, how much she tried to forget. It had taken years finally to dispose of it, and now in a flash it overwhelmed her again. It wasn't fair.

Lost in time, she reached the back door of her house. She was a kid again, tagging after Jesse and Noah. She'd beg them to let her go along with them on their adventures. They could never refuse her, Noah especially. It seemed funny now. Though he'd never seemed to mind having her along, he had never opened up to her, never let her get too close. She'd never noticed it back then, but now she wondered. What made him so cynical, so withdrawn and distant? He could be kind and gentle; she'd witnessed it herself yesterday with Rosemary, though if she hadn't seen it with her own eyes she might not have believed it.

And then there was last night. He'd pulled her from that fire without a thought for his own safety. Yes, they were friends. Yet she knew he still held a part of himself back. In comparison, Jesse had been an open book.

In the old days, Jesse and Annie would come home after a hard day of play or school and the house would carry the unmistakable scent of freshly baked cookies. Then together they'd laughingly recount their adventures for their interested and loving mother. Ross would come home from work and the fun would begin all over again.

Her mother and Jesse had died, supposedly because some crazed arsonist had tried to get revenge on the investigator who had him put in jail. Ross had been that investigator. Silly, petty, useless revenge. Worse yet, the arsonist had never been caught, despite Ross's best efforts.

Annie knew how much that ate at Ross; they'd talked of little else those first few years after their family's death. He couldn't stand it that the fire, no matter how indirectly, had been his fault. He'd worked like a fiend, he and every other man on his team, for months, then years, on the case. No leads, no clues, nothing.

Sometimes it was hard to believe that ten years had actually gone by. In those ten years, she and Ross had slowly drifted apart. Painful memories kept them that way, despite the occasional visit by Ross, letters, and both of their phone calls. She was well aware that a small part of her blamed Ross for the car fire that had killed her mother and Jesse. It was wrong, but she couldn't help it. She knew also that he was well aware of how she felt, and that it hurt him.

She turned the knob of the back door, hearing Ross's voice in her head over and over again, his anguished words whispered so desperately to her at the funerals. *'I'm so sorry . . . so sorry, Annie. So sorry –'*

'Annie.'

Still lost in time, she nearly jumped out of her skin. Whirling around, she flattened herself against the door. And then sagged in relief at the sight of Noah. 'God, Noah. You scared me to death.' Her heart raced.

He gave her a long, cautious look. 'You all right?'

She found her humour. 'Great. I'm great.' She tried to look casual. 'And you?'

His eyes narrowed and his hands rode low on his hips. 'You know what I mean.'

With a lock of brown hair falling across his brow and his dark scowl he looked dangerous, almost mean. He'd become the grumpy, angry Noah of her childhood and it made her smile. 'It is you,' she said, finally recognizing the moody loner. Yesterday she had imagined he'd mellowed, gone gentle and compassionate. They must have been figments of her overly active imagination. 'I wasn't sure. Yesterday you were so . . . nice.'

'Annie,' he said warningly, taking a step towards her.

'Not that you weren't always nice,' she said hurriedly, flattening her palms back against the door. 'You just seemed . . . more tempered.'

He took another step towards her, glowering.

'That must explain the women thing,' she went on inanely. 'That and the fact that you turned out pretty decent-looking, Bones.' More than decent-looking,

47

but why swell that ego of his any further?

He stopped and tilted his head slightly, his eyes never leaving hers. 'The way you keep mentioning my so-called women, Annie, one would almost think you cared.'

'Oops,' she said, smiling wickedly. 'I gave you the wrong impression. It's just that when I knew you, you couldn't care less about such silly things as girls. The only thing that managed to capture your attention back then was your computer.'

'You're wrong there, Annie,' he said, matching her sardonic tone. 'It's just that the only girl who would even look at me back then was a long-legged, scrawny punk of a kid who wouldn't stop following me and her brother.'

She actually blushed. She couldn't believe it. But that was nothing compared to how she felt a second later when he took the final step between them and captured her chin in his firm hand, tilting her face up to his. He looked into her eyes, the depth of emotion swirling in his brown eyes taking her breath away.

Confused suddenly, she sought to fight back with words. 'Well, someone had to – '

'Shut up, Annie,' he said easily.

Her mouth clamped shut, though she couldn't keep the smile off her face.

'What?' he demanded.

'You do know just what to say to a girl.'

He raised an eyebrow. 'So they say.'

It was hard to think, especially with his hand holding her face so lightly, like a caress. If she was shocked at the strange and not entirely wanted yearnings flowing through her for someone she'd known all her life, she chose not to think about it.

One thing her life had taught her: live for the moment.

'Don't you have a bunch of kids to take care of?'

'I have a large staff. And we don't have very many kids right now.'

'Oh.' She ran out of small talk.

'So,' he said quietly, his eyes serious. 'Are you going to tell me how you really are?'

His fingers released her, taking with them the sweet feel of his touch. 'I'm really not so good,' she admitted. She lifted her hands between them. 'I smell like smoke. My knees hurt. My head aches from thinking. And my favourite T-shirt is ruined.'

He smiled then, his first since she'd seen him, and it was so infectious she could see why every red-blooded woman in the world had coveted it.

'One too many complaints,' he told her with a shake of his head. 'Now I know you're going to be all right.' He reached around her and opened the door. 'Are you ready for this?'

'Yes.' She hesitated. 'But I want to be alone.'

'Too bad,' he said, nudging her inside. 'Because I'm coming with you.' When she opened her mouth to protest, he placed a finger on her lips. 'Don't bother,

49

Annie. You shouldn't do this alone. You probably shouldn't do this, period. I'm coming with you.'

That superior tone again. If she weren't so damn tired, she'd fight him and win. Next time, she promised herself. Besides, she thought as her heart crumbled a little at the sight of the soggy carpet, it was nice to have the company after all.

She walked slightly ahead of him. It was a mess, much more than she could have thought possible. But despite the singed and blackened curtains, blown-out windows and ruined carpet, little besides the living room was affected.

'I thought Ross would have been here,' she said, taking care where she stepped, though it no longer mattered. Her bare feet were already muddy.

'He was here for nearly three hours,' Noah told her. 'Taking samples, making notes . . . mumbling to himself. He just left.'

The wallpaper in the kitchen was ruined. The beautiful faded wallpaper that her mother had loved. She ran her fingers along it, getting them sooty. 'Did he say what he found?'

'Found?'

She turned in the hallway to face Noah. He was studying her with that damned shuttered expression and she knew what that meant. 'Yes. Found. What started the fire?'

His eyes moved from her to study their surroundings. 'I'm sure that he'll tell you what he knows.'

'Noah!' she demanded, putting her grimy hands on her hips without a care for her new dress. 'Tell me.'

'No.' He eyed the smear on her hips. 'You're ruining your dress.'

'Damn it, Noah. I have a right to know.'

His deep eyes came back to hers and there was surprising flicker of something besides the normal standoffish and detached expression, reminiscent of how he'd hovered protectively over her last night.

'Annie,' he said solemnly as he came closer. 'I don't think – '

'Just tell me,' she said tersely, swiping her hair from her eyes and smearing dirt across her forehead.

'Arson,' he said tightly, watching her carefully.

She closed her eyes against the wave of disbelief, shock and betrayal that overcame her and clutched the doorway as if it were a lifeline. Belatedly she remembered overhearing what the firefighter had said about the smell of gasoline last night. She must have been in more shock than she thought to have forgotten that. 'No,' she whispered. 'Not again.'

'Annie.'

'And it was just a horrible coincidence that I happened to be here.' She laughed, a high, hysterical sound, then clamped her mouth shut, afraid that she'd never be able to stop. 'That kind of coincidence belongs in the book of records, don't you think?' she asked bitterly, opening her eyes to his.

He stepped closer. 'What are you saying?'

She shook her head, feeling weary. 'Nothing, forget it.'

'No. Tell me.'

She lifted her face, then at the intense look on his, closed her eyes. 'I'm afraid,' she whispered. 'I can't help but wonder . . . is it the same guy who killed my mother and Jesse?'

He made a soft sound, and she felt his fingers lightly brush her face, but she still didn't open her eyes. 'I know it sounds paranoid.'

'No.'

'I mean, it has been ten years. Why would someone want to kill me? It's really just that – '

'It's OK to be afraid,' he said quietly. 'Anyone would be.'

'I'm just tired.'

'I can imagine. Have you eaten?' His gaze ran down the length of her. 'Don't take this wrong, but you look like something the cat dragged in.'

She smiled then – she couldn't help it. 'There's your skill with tender words again. You've got to stop before I swoon over you.'

A small grin tugged at the corner of his mouth. 'Just so that you know – I'm not easy.'

'No,' she said, studying him. 'I don't imagine you are.'

His gaze narrowed on her bare feet. 'Annie, Jesus. You're going to cut yourself in here! And what are you all dressed up for?'

'I dressed like this because I thought maybe I'd have a tea party to go to today,' she snapped. 'What do you think? I came out of here last night wearing only a T-shirt. I – '

'Annie,' he interrupted with a soft gleam in his eyes. 'I was kidding. That dress . . .' he paused and she watched his eyes take in the short, snug yellow sundress that exposed her arms and long legs '. . . is . . . something, and so are you in it.' His eyes met hers. 'And no one knows better than I how little you were wearing last night.'

With those dark, mesmerizing eyes holding hers, she couldn't move. Her breath caught. His words were hypnotic and all her troubled thoughts flitted away. What he had said told her he was as aware of her as she was of him. What he didn't say spoke volumes. It shouldn't have been a turn-on, the memory of him carrying her out of a life-threatening situation. But she could see him, hear the rough concern in his voice as he had scooped her effortlessly in his arms and sprinted out of the door with her. Then he'd set her down outside, running his large hands the length of her, searching for injury. Last night there had been no room for modesty, no place for embarrassment.

Now she didn't know what to say. He was still looking at her and she realized in sudden horror that she hadn't thanked him. He'd saved her life, risked his own and she had done nothing but snap at him. She felt mean and churlish.

'What you did last night was amazing,' she said quietly, all signs of her earlier temper gone. 'To say thank you doesn't seem nearly appropriate enough.'

'Then don't say it,' he said, looking piqued.

'But – '

'I don't want your thanks, Annie,' he said brusquely, shoving his hands into his worn and faded jeans that emphasized his long, muscular legs and narrow hips. His loose polo shirt stretched across his broad shoulders and he looked so like the young, steadily removed Noah of her past that for a minute she could actually believe that they were teenagers again. And, as in the past, she couldn't resist teasing him.

She covered the remaining space between them and put her hands on his chest, tilting her head back to meet his eyes. 'But I feel I must thank you,' she said in an affected, throaty female voice – one he'd always hated. His eyes narrowed and he stepped backwards, away from her touch. Undeterred, she took another step forward in the mud and water, watching with amusement as he backed another step, coming up against the wall. 'What's the matter, Noah? I just want to thank you properly.'

He grunted in response and pushed past her into the living room.

She followed. 'I think I make you nervous.'

'Knock it off,' he said irritably. 'Get what you need out of here and let's go.'

She sighed with pleasure. He was still great fun to tease. 'Hard to understand how you got that womanizing reputation, Noah,' she said to his back as he stalked away from her. 'I can't even get you to stand still long enough to – '

'Do you ever give up?' he wondered aloud, tossing his hands up in frustration. 'Christ! You talk more than anyone I know.'

'What's that?' she asked, gesturing to a small video camcorder slung over his shoulder.

He turned back to her. 'I found it on the green between the Taylor House and yours. Do you recognize it?'

She shook her head. 'No.'

'Then hurry and get whatever it is you want. Let's go.'

'Go where?'

His hands were on his hips again. He sighed, the sound of a man heavily frustrated. 'You can't stay here. You know that.'

'I have a hotel room.' She hated that thought. Hated knowing she'd have to go back to the empty, lonely, stark room. Ross worked like a fiend. He was even more likely to do so now, and she couldn't handle the thought of being alone. Funny to feel that way when she'd been alone for years now, but it was so.

'We have two empty cottages,' he said, then looked as if he greatly regretted it.

She smiled. 'That's very kind of you, Noah.'

He didn't bother to respond.

Annie looking vulnerable was new for Noah. Maybe that was what had hit him when he'd offered her a place to stay, because God knew he hadn't been thinking clearly. She was wearing a sophisticated yellow dress that would have knocked his socks off if it hadn't been for her bandaged knee, with her pale face and shaking limbs. And he couldn't dismiss her haunted expression. Alluring, definitely, but bewildered too. And shaken.

Whoa, Noah, he told himself grimly. *Brotherly* feelings was what he would allow himself with Annie. *That was it.*

He was a sucker.

He took her to the furthest cabin from his – protection, he knew, but he wasn't sure from what. On the way they'd stopped for fast food because he suspected she hadn't eaten anything.

She smiled as they stepped over the threshold. 'This is pretty.'

He was pleased, ridiculously so. To cover it up, he slapped the key in her palm and glanced at the small room. The great room, as he called it, held the kitchen, dining room, living room and family room all in one. Bright colours, Indian rugs on the wooden floors and the huge brick fireplace gave the place a warm sense of home, even with the sparse furniture. The tiny bedroom held only a twin bed and small oak dresser, but it had character.

Annie went immediately to the dresser and dropped something in the top drawer.

'What was that?' he asked.

'I found one of my mother's earrings upstairs in the house. It reminded me of her. It was her favourite.' She shrugged as if it was no big deal.

'You should keep it locked somewhere.'

'I imagine a single earring should be safe enough here.'

He dropped the bag of food on the table and motioned her towards it.

She dropped in a chair and started in on the french fries. 'Noah, why did you come back here?'

'What do you mean?' He pulled a hamburger towards him and grimaced. He hated fast food, much preferred to cook, but he hadn't wanted Annie near him that long. He needed to leave. To go and check on the kids. To go and play tennis. To work on his computer. Anything, but sit in the company of the oddly beautiful and irresistible Annie Laverty for another minute. Ridiculous as it seemed, he didn't trust himself.

Yet he couldn't bring himself to leave. Not when she looked so unfamiliarly lonely and sad.

She swallowed, gulped down her iced tea and studied him with her bright eyes. 'You could have gone anywhere, done anything. Why did you come back here?'

He couldn't mistake the fact that she saw this as a step down for him. 'Maybe I wanted to,' he said evenly enough.

'I've upset you,' she ventured – correctly. 'I didn't mean to insult you, Noah. Did you come back for Rosemary?'

'Among other things.'

'How bad is it?'

He glanced at her, caught the compassion and sympathy in her eyes and it made him angry. He didn't want pity, for God's sake. He'd chosen to be here.

'Alzheimer's,' he said bluntly. 'She'll never get better. Only worse.'

Annie winced, her hair shimmering like gold. 'She was always so healthy. That must be hard to take, watching your mother fade away like that.'

'She's not my mother,' he corrected, then shut his eyes briefly. What was it about Annie that set his tongue and thoughts loose?

'She's not your mother?' Annie slowly set down her french fry.

He sighed and rubbed a hand across his face. 'Forget it.'

She looked at him from under long dark lashes, her eyes the colour of steel. It matched the strength of her determination. He recognized that look well – it would be far easier on him if he just told her. 'She adopted me when I was twelve. I came to her a couple of years before that, just one of thousands of kids who have passed through here. You couldn't have known, you were too young.'

'No, I didn't know.' She shook her head. 'All those years I just assumed you were her son, helping her with the others.' She started to say something, then changed her mind. Carefully she wiped her hands, pushed away her food. She leaned forward and planted two elbows on the table, staring at him with warm eyes that he didn't want to meet. He couldn't believe he'd just told her about Rosemary. He'd never voluntarily told anyone anything about himself and rarely – since Jesse – even allowed himself the luxury of a friend. It was so much simpler that way.

'So you run the place now?'

He nodded, then rose. Annie's curiosity had been like a healthy dose of vitamins. Colour now shone on her face, her eyes sparkled, and strength seemed to vibrate through her. She didn't need him any longer, and he felt the sudden need to get as far away from her as he could.

She stopped him with a hand on his arm. As he stared at it she said in a voice that tugged at him, 'That's the most noble thing I've ever heard of – apart from yanking me out of that fire last night.'

His reaction to her made him furious, only it died in his throat at the honest, sincere expression on her pale face. 'I'm not, and never have been, noble,' he bit out. He stormed towards the door, angry at himself for having offered her the cottage, mad at her for tempting him to lust after the one and only sister he'd ever had, and raging at the fates that had brought them together.

She followed him to the door and again restrained him with a hand on his arm. 'Noah,' she said softly. 'Why are you so angry?'

He looked down at her in confusion. He suddenly couldn't remember. Her elegant hand looked so small against his dark arm. She squeezed his arm gently and tried to move closer, her chest brushing against his elbow. Lust flowed freely through him. 'Noah – '

'Don't, Annie,' he ground out, moving back. 'You can stay as long as you want.' He brushed past her and slammed the door behind him, then jumped at the sight of Martin waiting for him.

Martin had taken to doing that; following him everywhere. Noah had not objected because he understood Martin's need to be near him. Together they walked, neither saying a word. He didn't take a deep breath until they were across the green and heading towards the courts. He should have been on the courts to meet four of the kids fifteen minutes ago. He blamed Annie because it seemed easier. These kids needed regularity, needed to know they could rely on him. They didn't need some heart-sick counsellor, pining away for what he couldn't have.

She had rubbed against him and his bones had nearly melted. It had been a struggle not to jump her right there, just toss her down on the hard floor and bury himself deep within her. Noah walked on to the court and forced a cheery smile for the kids sitting on the bench waiting for him.

They hadn't even started, and sweat trickled down his forehead.

He swiped at it and spotted Martin. The boy smiled sympathetically.

CHAPTER 3

Annie made her way to the big house, wanting to use the phone to call Ross. There was a pleasant hum of young voices, moderately loud music and the clanking of dishes, but Noah couldn't be found. Not surprising, just confusing.

Why did she need to catch a glimpse of the man anyway? Face it, Annie, she thought, Noah Taylor intrigued her every bit as much as he had as a kid.

Even when he didn't want anything to do with her. Noah had always been unpredictable and moody; she should be used to it by now. But she couldn't help feeling that somehow she'd caused Noah's current lousy mood.

The Taylor House interior was clean but in a constant state of comfortable disarray. Annie had only been inside a few times, but she remembered the kitchen well. It was a large, efficient one, run smoothly by the staff. As children, Jesse, Noah and herself had often sneaked food from the shelves. She smiled at the memory of them being secretive, when in truth if they had only asked, they could have had whatever they wanted.

Odd moments like that stuck out in her mind, tumbling through her head since she'd come back. Mostly of Noah. He'd been a tough kid, and it had been difficult to know his real thoughts. But there had always been an innate kindness in him that made him difficult to dismiss.

It had been what drew her to him when she was young and it was what was drawing her to him now. What would he think, she wondered, if he knew she'd always had a crush on him? It would swell that huge ego of his to unbearable proportions.

She could never tell him. It would be far too humiliating.

She sighed, smiled at several of the young staff as they passed her, and forced Noah from her mind. Using the phone mounted on a wall, she caught Ross in his office.

'Noah told me you suspect arson,' she said without preamble.

'That boy talks too much,' he muttered, and Annie could hear the strain, the weariness, the shock in his voice. It scared her.

'Ross, this has nothing to do with Noah. You should have been the one to tell me.'

'Oh, Annie.'

They listened to each other breathe for a minute, both thinking about the past. 'Ross,' she whispered finally. 'Tell me. Please. Is it the same one as last time? The same guy?'

'I don't know,' he admitted. He sighed. 'Where are you? I tried to call you at the hotel.'

'I'm at Noah's.'

Silence. Then, 'Annie, after an . . . accident, sometimes people get scared. And vulnerable. It would be easy for someone to take advantage – '

'Noah isn't taking advantage of me, Ross,' Annie said, trying to stay patient. 'I couldn't stand being in the hotel for one second longer. You just left, without a word.'

'I'm sorry, honey. I had a job to do.'

'Would you have told me?'

Again, silence.

'Ross.' She sucked in her breath. 'Tell me you would have told me about the suspected arson.'

'I would have told you, Annie. Eventually. When I was sure you were . . . all right.'

'I am fine,' she gritted out. God, fathers were unreal. She knew he was protecting her from unnecessary heartache, but it was more irritating then anything else. 'Do you have any clues? You must have something!'

'Annie,' he sighed. 'It's all still under investigation.'

'You're not going to tell me,' she said flatly, disappointed. 'Ross, you can't protect me from this. It involves me every bit as much as you.'

'Annie, please,' he pleaded, and she felt a twinge of

remorse for pushing him. 'Let the investigation run its course. Then I'll tell you everything I know.'

She twisted the phone cord and thought.

'Annie?'

'OK,' she said finally. 'Do you promise to tell me everything?'

'I promise.'

'But Ross,' she said quietly, unable to stop herself. 'It could be the same guy, couldn't it?'

He sighed again, heavily, and she could picture him leaning his bulk back in his chair with his feet on his desk. 'I've made a lot of enemies over the years,' he said with even greater sorrow. 'It truly could have been any number of people. I've brought hundreds of cases to trial, thousands of suspects in total. And it could be any one of them.'

Her breath whooshed out. *Thousands*.

'I just wish I could have spared you this – especially with what happened before.'

'Who's going to spare *you*, Ross?' she asked gently. 'It's hard for you too.'

'I'll be all right, honey.' He hesitated. 'I'll be working late tonight, but I can take a break for dinner.'

She heard the apology, felt his pain and regret. 'It's OK, Ross. Do what you have to do. I'm going to stay here. Do you mind?'

'With Noah?'

She almost smiled. He was such a dad. 'No, Ross. Noah gave me one of the cottages. I'll be there alone.'

65

He chuckled. 'Just checking. I'm glad you'll have better company than me.'

'You're fine company,' she insisted faithfully. 'I'm . . . staying another week. I thought I could help you decide what to save in the house, help pack or whatever you need.'

'I don't want you to have to do that.'

'I want to,' she assured him, knowing he couldn't face it alone. She wasn't sure she could face it at all, but she'd try. She'd deserted him once – for ten long years – and she wasn't going to do it again. 'I have a week. Please let me help.'

'On one condition,' he said firmly. 'You don't go to the house alone. *Ever*. Wait for me.'

'I won't go there alone,' she promised, knowing that was one promise that would be easy to keep.

She called her editor next. Sue, a bossy, competent woman who ran the New York department with the efficiency of a drill sergeant, had a deep soft spot for Annie, and Annie knew it.

'How are you, sweetie?' Sue asked, her voice heavily accented with Bronx.

'Fine now,' Annie told her.

Sue listened in horrified silence as Annie told her what had happened the night before. 'And you're all right? Really?'

'I'm fine.'

'Good.' Without mincing words she added, 'Then hurry up and get back here.'

Annie laughed. One had to love good, sweet, dedicated Sue. 'Your concern is touching.'

'Annie,' Sue said sternly. 'You've been with me for years. You know how I feel about you living alone, never finding Mr Right, no family. Last week you spring your stepfather on me, give me some pathetic story about him selling your family home and you without a keepsake of your mother or brother. Of course I fell for it and gave you your time off.'

'It was the truth,' Annie said with a smile. Sue loved dramatics.

'Sure it was,' Sue answered. 'Now – and I can hear this coming, mind you – you're giving me this fire story and I know what's next. You want more time. And no one deserves it more than you, I know. You haven't had a vacation in years. I appreciate the dedication, I really do. But I have an edition coming out without a travel article, the one, might I remind you, that was supposed to come from London. The story you reneged on without warning.'

'I remember.'

'So hurry up and get back. You owe me.'

She did. 'Next week.' She hung up and smiled. Which faded abruptly when she spotted Noah, leaning against the refrigerator with a quiet watchfulness that had her heart leaping strangely. She had a new picture of him now in her head, and it was so much more than the angry, withdrawn Noah she'd thought she'd known. He'd given up a lot to care for Rosemary, to care for the kids he surrounded himself with, and he'd saved her from the fire without hesitation or thought to his own safety. OK, he would hate it if he knew she had elevated him to hero status, but for a minute she couldn't help it.

She thought of him as a hero – her hero.

'Noah,' she said, annoyingly breathless. 'I didn't see you there.'

He held up the soda can in his hand, saluting her. 'Just getting a drink.' He took a long sip and Annie watched with fascination while his throat contracted as he drank. 'It's hot out there,' he said, licking his lips.

Annie just looked at him. It wasn't a hardship. The man had a body that amazed her, and it didn't hurt that he'd just been working it out on the court. His shirt clung to him in an interesting way and those shorts showed his long, powerful legs to their advantage.

'Why are you looking at me like that?' he asked, frowning and straightening. 'Stop it.'

She lifted her gaze to his and forced herself not to blush. She'd been gawking at him and he'd noticed it. What was the matter with her? 'You've been playing tennis,' she said stupidly.

His mouth curved slightly. 'You're quick, Laverty. Real quick. Always knew you'd turn into something.'

Oddly speechless, she turned her back to him, still sitting at the table. But she knew when he came up behind her.

'So, you're doing better?'

That couldn't be concern she heard, no matter how much she wanted to hear it. 'Better than what?'

He cursed under his breath. 'Better than when I found you white as paste about to walk through your house alone. Better than when I left you back at the cottage looking as if you'd misplaced your favourite doll again.'

She smiled. He'd just reminded her of a time she'd long forgotten. Once when she'd been about five, she'd left her favourite doll – Susie – on the beach. High tide had claimed it by the time Noah and Jesse had gone back to look and she'd cried at night for a week. Out of desperation the boys had even pooled their resources and bought her a new one, but Annie wanted her old Susie back. She'd been inconsolable. Then, miraculously, one week later, Susie washed up on shore – minus an eye and a foot. It didn't matter, Annie loved her all the more for it.

She risked a look now at Noah over her shoulder. His scowl was back, and it looked particularly fierce. She refused to be fooled. He cared. 'I'm fine.'

He didn't believe her, she could tell by his expression. 'Really, I'm just fine.' But for just a second, she wished for something completely out of her reach – like a hug.

Before Annie could guess Noah's intentions, he slid her chair out from the large table and turned it to face him. He squatted before her and pulled her calves from beneath the chair.

'What – ?'

'Be quiet,' he said, his voice gruff but kind. 'I want to look at your burns.'

She opened her mouth to retort, but with his rough, warm hands on her bare legs she couldn't speak. 'They're fine. I told you before, they're just fine,' she managed, but he paid no attention to her. Tongue between his teeth, he meticulously lifted her bandages, glancing up sharply when she squealed and winced.

'That hurts?'

'Yes!' She gritted her teeth and gripped her chair with white knuckles. 'That bandage was attached to hair!'

'Toughen up, Laverty,' he said mildly, though he did flash her a quick grin. 'But a tip – next time shave before you apply this type of bandage.'

Her legs were smooth, damn smooth. And she could tell by the high gleam in his eyes as he ran a hand up and down her leg that he knew it too.

'I didn't know I was going to be inspected.' She tried to jerk her legs from his grasp, embarrassed, but he held firm. Their gazes met and Annie's breath stopped. They were close, too close. It shouldn't feel so good to have his hands touching her burns, should it? It shouldn't feel so right to have him look at her like that, should it? Heat flooded her face, her body. His fingers continued to touch her legs and suddenly, it

70

felt far too warm in that kitchen. She needed air. Fresh air. 'Move.'

He cleared his throat and dropped his head to peer at her legs intensely, but she couldn't help but feel that he was as shaken as she.

'Please move,' she said again, softly.

'Not yet.' He carefully reapplied the adhesive, his brows furrowed in complete concentration. 'They look pretty good.' He glanced up at her, for the first time letting her see his concern. 'Do they hurt much?'

'No,' she lied. Just a minute ago, she'd felt a powerful surge of lust. Now, looking at his face close up, seeing the compassion in his eyes, she felt a lump stick in her throat. How nice it felt to have someone worry about her. How unusually nice. 'It's sweet of you, Noah.'

His frown came back and she just barely suppressed the urge to smooth the furrow between his brows. 'What's sweet?'

'For you to care.'

He leaned back on his haunches. 'Well, the way you've been moaning and groaning about the smoke in your hair and your ruined clothes . . . someone has to feel sorry for you.'

She found she could laugh at herself. 'I still smell the smoke.' She leaned close and offered him the top of her head. 'Smell.'

He stood abruptly, backed away and slipped his hands into his pockets. His gaze became distant.

'Yeah, you stink all right. Try peanut butter. I heard that works.'

'I have *not* been complaining about my lost clothes.'

His gaze ran over her, leaving her hot and cold at the same time, if that were possible. Then he purposely took another step back.

Annie tilted her head. So he couldn't handle the closeness. Very interesting. She dragged her lower lip over her teeth as she rose, feeling uncertain of her next move. When had things changed between them, so that she didn't feel natural? A minute ago she'd needed to escape. Now she didn't want that at all. 'I know you don't want to hear this, but I want to thank you for letting me stay here – '

'Don't thank me. I would have done it for anyone who looked as bedraggled as you did the other night.'

'Gee, thanks. I think.' To test him, and herself, she stepped closer. What was it about him that had her wanting to throw herself against him and cling? She never did that. 'Noah – '

'I said I don't want to be thanked.' And he backed away another step. Why did she scare him – a man who reportedly was scared of nothing and no one? She should let it go, Annie thought, but she couldn't. Right now, he was her only friend, and all she wanted was a hug and some comforting words. That couldn't be asking too much. Just a hug.

'Noah.' He took another step towards the door, backwards. 'Noah?'

He looked at her. 'I'm pretty busy right now, Annie. I've got to – '

A loud humph escaped him as he backed into the door.

Annie swallowed her laugh, her need to weep gone as quickly as it'd come. But a hug would still be nice. 'I just wanted – ' She stopped, feeling silly.

'What?' he demanded, glancing blackly at the door.

'Nothing,' she whispered. He wanted out – and as quickly as possible. It deflated her. 'Just . . . Nothing.'

Two days later Annie decided that cleaning up after a fire was dirty, depressing work. Very dirty and very depressing.

Ross was buried in work. They'd hardly had more than ten minutes together, and though they both regretted the lost time, Annie encouraged him to work. She knew neither of them would relax until he'd solved the case.

No one wanted the arsonist caught more than she. Except maybe Ross.

But she was lonely.

And Noah . . . well, Noah was being Noah.

Parked at the large block table in the Taylor House kitchen, she was waiting to catch a glimpse of him. They hadn't spoken more than a handful of words since he'd stormed from the kitchen days ago. She knew he was avoiding her, but couldn't figure out why. What had she said or done to scare him off?

Tired of guessing and unwilling to play the game any more, Annie intended to force the issue.

The thought brought her up short. *Force the issue?* Who was she kidding? She had no idea how to do that, or why she even wanted to.

For ten long years she'd been busy travelling the world, trying to make a name for herself. Living as she had, she'd got to see worlds she'd only read about, meet people who graced the covers of newspapers and magazines across the globe, and come and go as she pleased.

But it was a lonely existence. One that allowed for few, if any, personal relationships. Her closest friend was her editor, and that was because they had to speak frequently by the very nature of her job.

The truth was, for ten years she'd managed to avoid any kind of permanent relationship because it was safer that way. To care, to need, to love someone – it all brought the possibility of great pain. She'd learned that the hard way with the loss of her mother and brother.

If her heart wasn't involved, she couldn't get hurt.

Now she wasn't sure that was the right way to go about things. Maybe love, true love of any kind, was worth the risk.

A noise brought her head around, and her gaze met Rosemary's, though a very different-looking Rosemary from the woman seen the other day. She was dressed nicely in a trouser-suit, the old robe of yesterday nowhere in sight. Her hair, although grey, curled softly about her face in a way that complemented her age. She even had make-up on, making her look more like the Rosemary of old. 'Hello,' Annie said softly, not wanting to startle the woman she'd known all her life, yet hardly recognized.

'Annie?' Rosemary asked with obvious delight and surprise. 'Little Annie?' She reached out with a hand that was surprisingly steady. Her eyes sparkled with happiness.

Annie took the offered hand and nodded, struck by the difference between today's sure and confident Rosemary and yesterday's sad and bewildered one. 'Rosemary. How nice to see you.' She knew a little about Rosemary's disease, knew that in the early stages of Alzheimer's one could be completely normal one day and gone the next day, without a single memory to fall back on. 'How are you today?'

A cloud passed over her features. 'I've been better.' She turned her head away. 'You've already seen me, then.'

Annie nodded.

'I . . . don't remember.'

The words, spoken so quietly and with such dignity, tore at Annie. She'd never known a disease so cruel. 'It's OK, Rosemary. I understand. You're feeling fine today?'

'For now.' Rosemary shrugged and moved to the counter, pouring herself a cup of coffee. 'Coffee?'

Annie shook her head, wishing she could somehow ease the awful pain she could see etched in Rosemary's face.

'It's just as well,' she said mildly. 'I could forget to bring the coffee to you. Or, even worse, halfway through pouring it I might forget what I'm doing, and spill it all over the place.' The words were spoken with mild self-disgust, making it difficult to know how to respond.

With any other woman, Annie would have hugged her tight and told her not to feel self-conscious, that she did truly understand. But Rosemary was different – she always had been. Though she opened her home and resources to children in need, she never seemed to allow anyone into her heart. Including Noah. In all the years that Annie had known them both, she had never seen any real mother-son affection between the two. She had wondered about it in the past, especially when she compared her own mother and Jesse's extraordinarily close relationship. Now that she knew Noah wasn't Rosemary's true son, it made more sense, but it was still hard to get close to the woman.

That didn't change the fact that Rosemary suffered now, and Annie never could stand seeing anything or anyone suffer.

'I'm so sorry, Rosemary,' Annie said, feeling overwhelmingly helpless. Rosemary had always been the most independent, strong woman she knew. To know that was all being ripped away from her was beyond comprehension. 'Tell me what I can do.'

Rosemary sighed and looked around the kitchen. 'I love this house.'

Annie smiled. 'You know, I do too. You should be so proud, you help so many kids here.'

'Noah does it all now, not me. He's . . . been wonderful.' She walked slowly to the table and sat next to Annie. 'But I'm becoming more and more of a burden to him – '

'No,' Annie said quickly, shaking her head. 'He would never see it that way.'

'And that's the problem,' Rosemary said stubbornly, sighing. 'He worries about me, I know that, and . . . I don't want him to.'

Despite knowing Rosemary didn't weather physical touch well, Annie reached out for the woman's hand. 'You could never stop your son from worrying about you. He cares too much.'

Rosemary looked down at their joined hands. 'What would you say if I told you I don't deserve him?' she asked very quietly.

'Oh, Rosemary,' Annie said, her throat suddenly clogged. She knew very little about Rosemary's background, other than that she had supposedly had it as rough as any one of the kids she took in. 'Everyone deserves love, don't you think?' She gently squeezed the older woman's hand. 'Besides, your son is so set in his ways and so stubborn, I doubt that even you could command him to stop caring about you.'

77

A short laugh escaped Rosemary. 'He is stubborn, isn't he?' Her gaze, suddenly curious, settled on Annie. 'And very handsome. Don't you think?'

Recognizing the eagle eye of a mother honing in on a prey, Annie shifted uneasily. 'Uh, yeah. He's . . . all right.'

Rosemary laughed. 'Oh, Annie. You're good for me. And I'm so very glad you're here. Whatever took you so long to come back?'

Annie thought of the years on the road, the hundreds of stories she'd written, the things she'd seen. And then thought of her family and what she'd lost. 'It just seemed easier to stay away.'

'And now that you're back – '

'For a short time only,' Annie corrected.

'For a short time,' Rosemary repeated with a little smile, 'you and Noah have renewed your . . . friendship?'

Annie shrugged non-committally, and Rosemary's smile increased.

'You'll be good for him too, Annie. He could use a friend.'

Annie sincerely doubted that, but didn't want to spoil Rosemary's mood. 'While I'm here, surely there's something I can do to help?'

'Well, now that you mention it, maybe there is something you can do.' Rosemary shot her a wry grin that reminded Annie of Noah. He might not be her biological son, but that didn't matter when it came to shared mannerisms. 'Can you can wield a shovel as well as you can a typewriter? I just got in from looking at my garden. It's a disaster. Weeds everywhere. The tomato vines have taken over the squash – as if they should have ever been given a chance to get that close!' She shook her head ruefully. 'I really shouldn't complain, Noah is doing the best he can. Our place has never been run so smoothly or with as much joy among the kids. But a gardener he's not.'

Annie smiled, her thoughts spinning. Noah spreading joy and affection among the kids here was a picture she couldn't get.

A din out in the hallway caught their attention, and both women rose, startled, only to stop short in the doorway.

A young boy of about thirteen was standing on the second stair from the top, having just tossed a basket of apples down the entire flight. Some had split open, some had just bruised – but it was a sticky mess. Each stair had apples or apple parts scattered on it and the tile landing was covered.

The boy was standing there trying not to shake and struggling to contain his tears, but he still managed to send a defiant look to his right. Annie looked over and saw Noah standing there, studying the mess. Slowly his eyes rose to the boy, whose eyes were heavy with unshed tears.

'I did it on purpose,' the boy called down in a wavering voice. 'And I'm not going to clean it up.'

'Yes, you are,' Noah said quietly, but without rancour or anger. 'Start now and I'll help you.'

The boy took a step down and stopped. 'Why?' he asked bitterly. 'Why should I help you clean it up? You're going to send me away anyway. But it doesn't matter, cuz I won't go back. I'll never go back there.'

'No,' Noah agreed solemnly. 'You'll never go back.'

The boy swallowed and continued as if he hadn't heard. 'I won't let him touch me again, I swear,' he said with false bravado. 'I'll kill him first.'

Noah's eyes never left the distraught boy's and what he said next endeared him to Annie forever. 'No, Gerry. If he touches you again, *I'll* kill him for you.'

The boy absorbed that and tried to control his emotions, but couldn't. The tears fell freely and he launched himself down the flight of stairs and into Noah's waiting arms. He sobbed openly and Noah let him, softly stroking the trembling back, whispering soft words that Annie couldn't hear.

The emotions the interaction had caused in her were stunning. If she'd been alone she would have released the tears that were threatening. Though her childhood had been cut short by tragedy, what she had experienced was loving, joyful and carefree. Never had she feared a serious reprimand, worried about physical or mental abuse, or suffered through unwanted sexual advances.

The children and teenagers here all had, and she realized with a jolt that most likely Noah had also. The implications of that hit her hard. Now that she knew he hadn't come here until he was ten, she worried about what his life had been like before that. Watching his strained face now as he tried to comfort the weeping boy, a dread filled her heart and iced her limbs. He had indeed suffered, and she suffered now knowing it.

If true, it would explain a lot about his nature. By turns taciturn and surly, angry and withdrawn, he held much bitterness and a latent, unleashed violence. It had always been that way. But now she knew it was because of deep scars – scars that would take a lot of healing.

Noah squeezed Gerry close, letting him know he wasn't alone. The gesture tore at Annie. Never had she seen Noah give casual affection, nor had he ever given it to her unless she'd taken it. Yet now he showed it freely and without reserve.

Her eyes ached and her throat tightened at the beautiful sight of Noah bestowing love on the boy. When a man loved like that, gave of himself like that, he became absolutely, stunningly gorgeous. What made it even more so was how natural and uncalculating it was, how it came from deep within his heart.

Being at the Taylor House wasn't a step down for him. It couldn't be a sense of charity – he had none. He was here because he *wanted* to be – and because he was damn good at it.

Annie turned to Rosemary with a whimsical smile,

81

but it faded immediately at the frosted, vague look on her face. Rosemary had disappeared back into her shell.

At the soft sound of dismay behind him, Noah glanced over his shoulder. Rosemary was looking around her, obviously confused. Annie was standing next to her, looking concerned.

He sighed, wondering why everything always happened all at the same time instead of one crisis at a time. Gerry hiccuped in his arms. Noah stood, holding the boy firmly against his side. 'Rosemary?'

She didn't respond.

'Rosemary.'

She looked down at her hands, her eyes limpid and lifeless. 'I have to get out here and get the vegetables under control,' she said in a quiet, shaky voice. 'They're a mess.'

He looked around for Rosemary's nurse, but she was nowhere in sight. Gerry hiccuped again. Noah wanted to howl at the injustice of what the boy had been through. At the very least, he wanted to smash something, but he forced himself to remain calm. First things first.

The spilt and spoiling apples gave off a sweet scent that made him feel sick. Rosemary was looking at him with the fiery expression a mother gives a wayward child.

'The vegetables, Noah.'

'I'll take care of it,' he told her.

'No, you won't,' she said sternly, wagging a finger at him. 'You said you would take care of it before and you didn't. I should ground you for disobeying me, but I'm too tired.' She sighed. 'I just want to get my garden under control and no one will help me.'

What Annie did next cast her in his eternal gratitude. She stepped towards Rosemary and smiled gently. 'Let me help you, Rosemary. I'm excellent in the garden and I'd love to do it.'

Rosemary looked at Annie sternly. 'Who are you?'

'Annie Laverty,' she said with the same gentle smile. It warmed Noah's stressed, tired heart. 'I live on the other side of the green and I'm Noah's friend. Can I take care of your garden for you?'

Rosemary considered Annie's height, slender body and her lack of shoes with distaste and Noah almost smiled. For as long as he could remember, Annie had hated wearing shoes. 'You look pretty scrawny to me, Annie Laverty. Don't know that you'll be much help.'

'But I will,' Annie said calmly. 'I promise you, I know what I'm doing. Let me help.'

Rosemary took one last look at the bright sundress that Annie wore and shrugged resignedly. 'I don't have much choice. Come on, I'll show you where it is.' She took Annie's arm and started towards the slippery stairs.

Gently but firmly Annie turned her around and led her towards the back where the garden lay. Noah watched with amazement as Rosemary allowed Annie to lead her. Normally when Rosemary was 'in a mood' as the kids called it, she refused to listen to rhyme or reason from anyone, – including him. It was hard to take when she reverted back in time, hard to allow her to talk to him as if he were a boy again. But she couldn't help it and he just wanted her to be comfortable. And in her own home. She would hate being confined in a nursing home – just as he would hate it for her.

Gerry pulled away from Noah and sniffled. Nervously he looked up at Noah and hiccuped again. 'Are you gonna make me go now?'

'Nope.' Noah smiled a little. 'But I am going to make you clean up the mess.'

Gerry flinched. 'You don't have to make me – '

'Not that way, Gerry,' Noah said with gentle calm, though the icy rage was flowing through him again. Gerry stood there shaking as if he were waiting for Noah to beat him. 'I'll never lay a hand on you in anger. I swear it.'

Gerry absorbed that quietly, testing the words for honesty. 'I'm sorry about the apples,' he said finally.

'I know you are,' Noah told him. 'So help me clean them up.'

Together they bent to their task, Gerry bouncing with the energy of the resilient youth and Noah dragging from the drained emotions of the day. He watched Annie's slender back as she walked with Rosemary. The way she'd stepped in to help touched

84

him. Defusing Rosemary was a tricky business at best, and never yet she'd handled it with grace and aplomb.

At the sliding glass doors, Annie paused with Rosemary and glanced back at Noah. Even from that distance, he could see her warm, appraising eyes on him and it turned his insides upside down. He was crazy, insane, a fool to be contemplating the things he was contemplating about her. He dropped an apple back into the basket and returned her long look. Neither smiled.

'Laverty,' he called.

Her eyes brightened. 'Yeah.'

'Stay out of trouble.'

She smiled then, and left without a word.

It was hours before Noah was free again. He'd had to break up two fights, organize a softball tournament, supervise dinner and make preparations for the annual charity ball in three weeks.

He considered the ball a necessary evil and would have loved to skip it altogether, but he couldn't. The Taylor House made thousands of dollars from it every year and the locals loved it. It gave them a reason to dress to the hilt, hobnob with some local famous celebrities – including him – and drink too much.

By the time he had finished and given his computer business some desperately needed attention, he felt starved. But he had to check on Rosemary, as he did every night.

Her bedroom was empty. Not yet worried, he checked the kitchen. Often on bad days like today her nurse would take her to the kitchen before bed for a snack so that Rosemary wouldn't rise hungry in the middle of the night.

The kitchen was also empty, and he began to get anxious. He roamed the house, relieved that the staff had the boys under control. But still no Rosemary. He checked the doors, fretting. God, he thought, he couldn't take this. Every week seemed to get worse for her, and soon, he knew, she'd be gone from him entirely.

Just like everyone else in his life.

He shook his head sharply as he checked the back door. That wasn't right. Rosemary wasn't leaving him on purpose. She certainly hadn't chosen this vicious illness. He sighed and leaned against a wall. It just wasn't fair; she'd already had such a tough life. Her own parents had severely neglected her, her husband had abused her and still she'd dedicated her life to others. So what if she was sometimes distant and undemonstrative? She'd cared for him when no one else had wanted him. That alone was reason enough to make sure she lived out the rest of her days as comfortably as possible. And at the only place she'd ever considered her home.

Think, Noah, think. Where could she have wandered off to? And where the hell was her nurse?

When he heard the telltale squeak of the swing on

86

the front porch, he sagged with relief. Then he tore through the living room and yanked open the front door.

He stopped short.

Rosemary sat on the swing, the nurse kneeling at her feet. 'I don't recognize any of this,' Rosemary cried, dropping her face into her hands. 'I . . . don't even know . . . my name.' She sobbed quietly, a sound that wrenched at Noah's heart.

'It's Rosemary,' the nurse said quietly. 'And you're in your favourite place in the house, your swing.'

Rosemary's sobs broke the night silence. 'I hate this place!'

'No,' the nurse murmured, patient and understanding. 'No, you don't.'

'This isn't my home and I don't know you,' Rosemary cried, lifting her tear-streaked face. It was ugly in its fierce, unrelenting anger. 'Get away from me.'

Noah took a deep breath and stepped forward. 'It's OK, Jeannine,' he told the nurse. 'I'll get her to bed.'

The nurse nodded reluctantly, looking with sympathy at Noah. 'I'll wait in her room for her.'

Noah nodded his thanks and sat next to the woman who had been his only mother. 'Rosemary, it's me. Your son, Noah.'

Rosemary narrowed her eyes on him. 'No.'

'Yes,' he assured her quietly. 'You raised me, don't you remember? You used to make ice-cream sundaes for me every Sunday night because I loved them so.

And I'd sit with you in the garden for hours and hours, just because I wanted to be near you. One time, I pulled off all the blooms from the roses because I thought they were weeds. Remember how furious you were?'

Rosemary shook her head, unsmiling. 'No. Did I hit you?'

'You never laid a hand on me,' Noah said, reaching into his pocket for a tissue. He handed it to her, but when she didn't take it, he wiped at her tears himself. 'But you could terrify me with just a look.'

Her lips curved slightly. 'You're a big man, whoever you are. I doubt anyone could terrorize you.'

'Oh, but you did,' he assured her. 'Believe me, Rosemary Taylor, your temper is not something anyone – no matter how big – takes lightly.'

She actually laughed then, and in a very rare show of public affection Noah took her hand. 'You *are* home, Rosemary. Can you trust me enough to believe that? To believe that we care about you very much?'

'It's hard,' she whispered, her eyes filling again. 'I feel so lost . . . so alone. And . . . I'm scared.'

His own throat tight, he nodded. 'And it makes you angry, I can understand that. It's hard to be confused.'

'And humiliating. I hate that,' she said in a low voice. 'I really hate that.'

For a minute, they each leaned back in the swing, lost in their thoughts. The night closed around them comfortably. The distant sound of the pounding surf that was so much a part of San Rayo, and the salty night air soothed and relaxed.

'I'm so tired,' Rosemary said suddenly. 'So very, very tired. I want to be in my bed.'

Even her voice sounded weary, he thought, as he rose. 'Let me take you to your room.' He watched the flare of panic in the confused eyes, and tried to put himself into her position. Terrified, because nothing – not one thing – around her was familiar, she had to trust a perfect stranger. Anyone would be scared. 'It's going to be all right,' he promised her, helping her to her feet.

If only he could believe that. He hated seeing Rosemary so frail, so vulnerable. It took him ten minutes to get her into the house and up the stairs – she absolutely refused to let him touch her, much less carry her. And while he forced himself to understand, it hurt.

Especially when he knew that the good days were going to get fewer and farther between the bad days. He paused outside of Rosemary's door, waiting to hear the latch of the lock that would tell him the nurse had secured them both into the room. A sad, but necessary measure. If Rosemary wandered off into the night, she could get badly hurt.

He didn't know if he could take it. God, he needed a friend.

An unbidden image of Annie in her sunflower-yellow dress – the one that hugged her lithe body and drove him to distraction – came to mind. His body demanded food and bed, but for some strange reason he wanted to see her first.

Brotherly concern.

Bullshit. But he wanted to see her. Badly.

Her dark cottage could only mean one thing – that the woman couldn't follow directions worth a damn.

He walked furiously across the green and around the back of her house. No one answered, but he knew he'd find her there.

He entered quietly, not caring if he scared her to death. She had no business being back in this house alone – though he couldn't quite put his finger on the reason. Maybe because he knew it would upset her. Maybe because she could get hurt. Maybe he simply worried about her.

The last thought bugged him most of all. He had enough people in his life to worry about.

He found her upstairs in her mother's room, sitting cross-legged on the floor with a jewellery box opened in front of her. Gone was the elegant sundress; in its place she wore cut-offs and a white T-shirt that only emphasized her vulnerability. Her golden hair spilled from its precarious position on top of her head. Her face looked too pale, her mouth too tight, and he could tell she'd been crying. Instead of softening him, it made him all the more irritable.

'What the hell are you doing up here?' he asked roughly.

She jumped. 'God, Noah.' She swiped at any lingering tears and shakily stood to her feet, anger giving her two matching splotches of red on her cheeks. 'Don't do that.'

'You shouldn't be here.'

'Why not?'

Her eyes were like sparking flint, hard and defiant. She knew she shouldn't be here alone, too, he thought. He watched as she placed her fists on her hips, hypnotized by the gap between the hem of her shirt and her shorts where he could see a smooth, flat expanse of stomach. He shoved his hands in his pockets to keep them off her.

Brotherly concern, he reminded himself.

'This is my house, Noah,' Annie snapped. 'And I'll come here whenever I want to. Just because I'm staying on your property, it doesn't give you the right to – '

He reached for the light switch on the wall because the light was fading. A bright flare of blue light flashed and a loud pop smacked throughout the room as the light bulb blew.

A small cry came from Annie's lips and she dropped to the floor with her hands over her head.

It was just a blown light bulb, but the terrified huddle that was Annie wrenched at him. He kept his hands in his pockets, afraid to touch her.

'Annie.'

She didn't move but he heard her whimper.

91

With a creative and long oath he went to her, lifting her up and against him. It was a mistake, he thought as his hands came in contact with bare skin. And it would cost him. 'Annie, it's all right.'

She clung to him, her eyes squeezed tightly shut.

He knew what was happening to her, could feel the tremor that shook her body, the fierce pounding of her heart. 'The light bulb burned out, that's all. There's no fire.'

Another tremor shook her and he ran a hand down her back and closed his own eyes as a wave of what could only be described as powerful lust raced through him. He told himself that she didn't smell soft and flowery to drive him crazy, that her skin wasn't smooth as silk just to torture him.

'Annie,' he said in a strangled voice. He tried to push her away but she burrowed herself tighter against him. 'Annie, please.'

She sighed and straightened, pushing a stray tendril of hair from her face. Her eyes were weary and shadowed. 'I don't bite, you know.'

He ignored the hurt in her voice and said nothing. He didn't trust himself to.

'I sort of lost it, didn't I?'

'You're entitled,' he said quietly. 'What you went through was enough to spook anyone.'

She lifted her eyes to his and he was startled to see stark terror there. 'It's not that,' she said, her voice quivering slightly. 'It's not the fire. It's what happened ten years ago that I can't get out of my mind. I keep reliving it over and over in my mind and . . .' She trailed off with a shrug.

'And what?'

She lifted enigmatic grey eyes to his. 'And there's something I'm missing, something I'm forgetting. It's like this little, nagging memory that my brain lost and it's driving me crazy.'

His eyes narrowed thoughtfully as he weighed what she wasn't saying along with what he already thought. 'You think there's a connection between this fire and that one?'

'Yes,' she whispered. 'I do.'

Though he hadn't wanted to believe it, had spent days silently disputing it, he did too. Rage filled him just at the thought of someone out there, silently stalking Annie. Looking at her now, staring into her deep and troubled eyes, he promised himself he'd let nothing happen to her.

Because he couldn't live with himself if something did. He couldn't even stand to think about the possibility – because to lose Annie the way he'd lost Jesse would kill him.

'Come on,' he said. 'I'll walk you back.' Together they walked down the stairs and through the back door.

Annie stopped at the edge of the yard and glanced back, her eyes shadowed and full of sorrow. Without thinking, he took her hand and squeezed gently, then tugged her away from her house and across the green. 'Hungry?' he asked.

She shook her head.

'Tired?'

Again, she shook her head and he forced himself to give up the hovering mother routine, but it was difficult. Yes, Annie was a grown woman, but he could see her pain, and suddenly – he wasn't sure exactly when – it had become *his* pain. He wanted to pull her into his arms.

The night had darkened and a few long streaks of pewter cloud shifted over the stars. In the distance, the surf hammered the shoreline and the night noises engulfed them. Still, Noah could feel Annie's tumbling emotions. But she looked so absolutely lovely standing there, it became difficult to keep his mind on merely comforting her.

But he had to try.

'Remember the night Jesse and I decided to camp out on the green?'

Annie's head lifted, but she mutely shook her head.

'Come on, Annie,' he chided, swinging their joined hands, striving to make her smile. 'How could you forget? You teased us for months afterwards. Jesse and I thought we were hot stuff then. We must have been about twelve. At midnight on the dot, you and Ross – '

She laughed suddenly, a beautiful, musical sound that made him smile. 'I remember!' She laughed again and tossed him a look of his Annie of old – defiant and saucy. 'We knew you'd been reading ghost stories and that Jesse would read his favourite – the one about the headless turkey terrorizing the farm boys. Ross and I snuck up on you guys, gobbling and hollering – ' She snorted with laughter and stopped walking. She turned to him, smiling broadly. 'We scared you guys to death that night.'

'We weren't *that* scared,' he said, feeling as though he needed to put up a token defence for those two terrified twelve-year-olds. 'Not really.'

She shook her head, a fresh peal of laughter escaping her. 'Jesse almost wet his pants that night and you know it, Noah Taylor. He went running cross-legged as fast as he could for home.'

And he'd done the same, Noah remembered. But he felt momentarily sidetracked by how her smile lit her face. 'You told all your friends, too. What a brat you were.'

They laughed. When she stopped, she swiped at her eyes. 'I wasn't always a brat.'

'Yes, you were.'

'But you guys always let me hang out with you.'

'Did we have a choice?'

'No,' she smiled. 'You didn't.'

'Besides, Jesse made me. He felt sorry for you.' Noah laughed at the lock she gave him. 'OK, we *both* felt sorry for you.'

She tilted her head up and stared at the stars. Noah

95

stared at her smooth neck and gave serious thought to lowering his lips to the spot where her pulse beat.

'Every time you both ditched me,' she said, her voice dreamy as she remembered, 'I'd tell on Jesse, and both of you would get in trouble.' Her smiled faded a little and she started walking again. When he caught up with her, she said quietly, 'I guess I *was* a brat. Why did you always put up with me?'

'Did you ever think maybe we had to?'

Her gaze shot to his and he suddenly didn't feel like teasing her. He wanted her to feel better. He wanted to see her smile again. He wanted to kiss her. 'We liked you,' he said simply, reaching for her hand again.

She smiled and he struggled to keep her hand lightly in his, a difficult task when every muscle of his clenched body demanded more.

'I liked you guys too,' she said lightly. 'All my friends thought I was so cool. It was the two of you that made me so popular.'

'No,' he said with certainty. 'It was Jesse. I wasn't well liked then, remember?'

'The girls loved you.'

'They did not.' They walked some more, Noah wrestling with the memory of those unhappy days. 'Well, maybe a little they did.'

She laughed and they fell silent. Satisfied that some of the sorrow had faded from her eyes, Noah let the silence hang. It was a pleasant and easy one, something

Noah would have to think about. It'd been a long time since he felt so at ease with a woman, maybe even since all those years ago with Annie.

'I miss Jesse,' she said eventually, quietly. 'This is nice, but he should be here.'

Well, if that didn't put things into a sharp, painful perspective for him. He was a fool, a complete fool, to be even contemplating the strangely erotic things he'd been thinking about her. She thought of him as nothing but the 'friend' and he should remember that. 'I miss him too.' He would never forget Jesse.

'I miss Mom, too. Everything here in San Rayo reminds me of them.' She sighed. 'They say it's supposed to get better with time. It's not supposed to hurt so much for so long.' Annie shook her head slowly. 'It's a lie. It never gets easier, does it?'

Not for me, he almost said. But he didn't want her to be sad tonight. 'You don't have to forget them, Annie. What I think people mean is, it's supposed to get easier to remember them.'

'Well, it's been ten years and it still feels like yesterday. Especially since – '

He knew what she'd almost said, and he let the silence hang. *Especially since she'd come back*. It was hard to be completely sorry, since her coming back had given him the opportunity to know her again. But she would leave, he reminded himself, and probably soon.

Whether she stayed another week or the rest of the

summer, he couldn't imagine what his life would be like when she left.

This time, the silence deepened and he could tell she wanted to be alone. He felt a strange reluctance to leave her, but he didn't know if it was because he was worried about the bleak and lonely expression in her lovely eyes he'd seen at her house before, or because he wanted to be with her. In case of the latter, he intended to leave immediately.

He had to.

He opened the front door of her cottage for her, frowning as the knob turned easily in his hand. 'Why didn't you lock this?'

She shrugged, walking past him, her sexy, light scent taunting his nostrils. 'I didn't think it was necessary.'

'Well, it is,' he said gruffly, shutting the door behind him. 'Just because this isn't the big city, it doesn't mean – '

He stopped at her harsh intake of breath. She had flipped on the light and stared in shock at the large room.

It was in shambles.

CHAPTER 4

'Shit,' muttered Noah, coming forward to grab Annie's arm as she started towards the bedroom. 'Go to the big house and call the police.'

He pushed her back behind him and headed towards the bedroom himself, wanting to make sure they were alone. They were, but the place looked like a disaster zone. Annie's clothes had been dumped out of the small dresser, the mattress turned, the cupboard emptied.

'Shit,' he said again. What would have happened if Annie had been here alone? His blood ran cold at the thought. Anything could have happened to her.

'What do you suppose he was looking for?' she asked in a small voice behind him.

He cursed again. 'I asked you to call the police.'

'You didn't ask, you told.'

Noah slammed his eyes shut and pinched the bridge of his nose with two fingers, mentally counting to ten. When he was calm he looked at her. 'Could you go call the police?' He paused. '*Please.*'

'No.'

God, she was irritating. 'Why the hell not?'

She lifted her chin and her golden hair swung against her cheeks. 'I don't want to leave you alone.'

A short bark of laughter escaped him. 'What are you going to do – protect me?' Her eyes glinted dangerously. 'Never mind,' he said, still amused. 'We're alone. Good thing too, Laverty. Jesus.'

'I could have hit him over the head or something,' she mumbled, looking around at the mess. 'Pretty thorough guy, huh?'

'Did you have anything valuable in here?'

She started to shake her head, then stopped abruptly. Looking stricken, she raced for the bedroom. The top dresser drawer was ajar but she yanked on it anyway.

She reached in and ran her hand around the interior with a moan. 'Oh, no, not the earring.' She raised devastated eyes to his. 'My mother's earring is gone.'

He didn't think this would be a good time to remind her that he'd warned her to lock it up. 'Why was there only one?'

'It's all I had. I brought it here so I could look at it – ' She dropped her face into her hands and he couldn't stand it any longer.

He went to her and wrapped his arms around her trembling form. Fury filled him so that it was hard to speak calmly, but she needed him to, so he managed it. 'We'll find your mother's earring, Annie,' he promised, resting his chin on her head and looking over her head at the forced chaos. 'We'll find it, and we'll find whoever did this.'

And he wondered, as she was most likely doing, how exactly this break-in, the fire and the car bomb that had killed Jesse and her mother were all connected.

As quickly as it'd come, the fury dissolved, leaving in its place a deep-rooted fear. Fear for Annie's life.

Ross was stunned. Standing in the middle of Annie's torn-apart cottage, he divided an uneasy look between Noah and Annie.

'The police just left,' Noah offered, waiting for the man to say the police weren't needed because he'd solved the case, waiting for him to say the arsonist was at this very moment being charged, waiting for him to say anything, anything at all that would ease his mind about Annie's safety.

'This is . . . insane,' Ross said finally. 'What could he have possibly been looking for?' He looked at Annie, and from where Noah stood he could have sworn Annie was squirming. If the situation hadn't been so desperately out of control, he might have enjoyed it.

'Annie?' Ross asked, stepping close to his daughter.

'I took Mom's earring,' she said softly, staring at her feet. 'I found it in the house when I was looking through her things, and it reminded me of her, of how she looked that last night . . . before my gradua-

101

tion. She looked so beautiful that night, so excited, so happy . . . she was so proud of me.' She swallowed hard, still not looking at either man. 'I just slipped it in my pocket, Ross, then brought it here, even though Noah told me it wasn't a good place for it, I just wanted it close . . . and now it's gone.' She covered her face with her hands and Noah clenched his fists, shoving them in his pockets, wishing he could have just one minute with whoever was doing this to them. It killed him to see Annie like this.

'I just wanted a part of her,' Annie said, lifting her face in mute misery to look at Ross, 'and now it's gone forever. I'm so sorry, Ross. I – '

Unable to stand her despair, Noah moved closer to Annie, reaching for her, but Ross beat him to it, pulling Annie against him. 'Shhh,' he said, his voice hoarse. 'Don't blame yourself.'

'It just doesn't make any sense,' she murmured. 'The police said they have nothing to go on.'

'They'll be contacting you,' Noah told Ross, studying the older man's tortured expression, unable to shake his sudden feeling that Ross was holding out on them. 'Wondering if you have anything to tell them.'

'I don't, unfortunately.' The two men's eyes met over Annie's head, and Noah knew, in that moment, that whatever information Ross was keeping to himself was solely for his daughter's benefit. The thought was chilling.

Ross shook his head grimly. 'But before this goes

any further, I will. I can promise you that.' He squeezed Annie. 'I won't see you hurt. I won't let anything happen to you, honey, I swear.' He pulled back, holding Annie's shoulders. 'You can't stay here. It's not safe.'

'They took what they wanted,' Annie told him wearily. 'I'm perfectly safe now.'

Ross glanced at Noah, and Noah felt the full weight of his disapproval. Frowning in surprise, Noah said, 'She's as safe here as she is back at your house.'

Ross glanced in the small bedroom door, his eyes resting on the tiny bed. 'It's not right.'

Annie pulled back and shoved her hair from her face. 'Ross,' she said warningly. 'I'm fine here. We discussed this.' A long look passed between the two of them that spoke legions.

Noah didn't know whether to laugh or be insulted that Ross thought he and Annie were sleeping together. That the older man didn't approve irked Noah, but even more irksome – Noah himself had thought of little else *but* sleeping with Annie.

'Well, I don't have to like it,' Ross said, looking peeved. 'You're never home any more.'

'And neither are you,' Annie told him gently, giving him a hug.

'I would be,' Ross growled, 'if I could solve the goddamn case.'

'It's not your fault, Ross,' she said, looking suddenly exhausted.

'But it is my job to get it stopped.' He glanced down at the girl in his arms. 'And to keep you safe. I will do that, Annie, I will.'

Noah watched the embrace, and hoped to God Ross could. Because, unlike Ross, Noah was convinced Annie was in danger – and until the arsonist was caught, she'd continue to be, no matter what they did to protect her.

Two days later Annie was kneeling in Rosemary's garden, her hands deep in the dark, earthy-smelling dirt. She loved the cool feel of it between her fingers so much that she'd forgone gloves. Each day she'd spent some time watering, tending to the ripening fruit and vegetables and fighting the weeds. Rosemary was right, the garden was sorely neglected, but she was pleased to see the changes that just a few days of careful tending had wrought. She truly did love to garden. Once it had been a true passion but living as she had for the past ten years had made it a difficult one to keep.

Living as she had made anything difficult to keep; plants, animals . . . friends and lovers. She sighed.

Ten years ago she had run away from San Rayo, convinced she'd never love nor care about anyone again. Yet it would be all too easy to settle back into this life, living in the town she'd grown up in with people she knew and cared about. She could have a garden, be with friends and family. But could she really allow herself to do it?

Could she allow herself to let go enough to love again, and then possibly lose that love?

She shoved her fingers into the dirt and ruthlessly tore out a stray weed. Gardening was one way to forget the haunting memories of her mother and brother's death that continued to plague her, to forget the nightmares of her recent escape from the house fire, to forget the fact that someone had methodically searched her cottage for God knew what.

The police had found nothing – as she knew they would. No fingerprints, no motive, no clue. They had suggested it was one of Noah's kids, but she knew better. She'd met all of them by now and knew it wasn't possible.

If only she could sleep, she might feel better. But she'd been robbed of even that. Her thoughts wouldn't allow her to relax enough to get into that so badly needed, deep sleep. Everything was connected, she was sure of it.

Al, one of the staff, walked by with two kids in tow. They each held a tennis racket and the boys wore enthusiastic grins of their faces.

'We beat him,' they proudly told her as they passed.

Al, who couldn't have been more than twenty-five, rolled his eyes and rubbed his shoulder. 'Yeah, well,' he called after them, 'that's only because you took advantage of my age.'

She laughed dutifully, though she felt a funny little pang inside. The kids were getting to know her and she them. She liked them. The longer she stayed, the harder it would be to leave. She should get in a plane and go now, but she couldn't. She told herself she couldn't leave Ross with that mess of a house to pack up, couldn't leave Rosemary's garden unfinished, but they were all excuses. She had to be honest with herself. She couldn't leave until she knew what was going on, and not just regarding the fire.

It was about Noah, too.

So she stayed and ruined her fingernails in the dirt. Each day, little by little, she cleaned and packed the Laverty house for Ross, who didn't have the time – or the heart – to do it. And each day, little by little, she lost a piece of her heart to the Taylor House, the bright and miraculous kids in it, and their enigmatic leader, Noah Taylor.

She smeared some dirt on her shorts. Looking down at the stain, she sighed. Damn. Being about as skilled at laundry as she was at cooking, she knew she'd never manage to get the spot out. She'd have to go shopping.

She looked up at a sound on the path behind her. Rosemary was smiling, looking more excited and animated than Annie had ever seen her. Noah looked cool and distant – his usual charming self. Except that for the briefest second his eyes warmed, were no longer aloof, and she wanted desperately to think that was because of her.

'It looks beautiful,' Rosemary breathed, clasping her hands together. She turned to Noah and slapped a hand to his chest. 'You see? That's what it's supposed to look like.'

'Rosemary,' Noah sighed. 'I don't know why you can't just buy the damn vegetables.'

'Because,' she said gleefully, 'now I don't have to. I have Annie.'

Annie stirred uncomfortably from her position on her knees. Rosemary and Noah had stepped closer so that her eye level was at their waist. She was face to face with Noah's hips. Feeling the distinct disadvantage of that subservient yet unmistakably erotic position, she stood.

It was no use denying to herself that she had renewed her childhood crush. She definitely had, and it felt as strong and as painful as the first time – especially since the grown-up Noah had no more intention of doing anything about it than the younger one had.

She tried to remember the last time she'd been so undeniably attracted to a man, but couldn't. Her relationships had been pathetically few and far between, countable on half the fingers of one hand. In fact in the past few years she'd given up altogether, unable to find a satisfying combination between her job and a relationship.

It didn't help to know Noah felt the attraction too. She couldn't imagine what held him back, what made him fight it so, but it was strong enough that he'd managed to avoid her entirely the past few days.

Pride alone had kept her from seeking him out.

Ignoring Noah's inscrutable eyes, she smiled at Rosemary. 'I'm glad you're pleased, but you'll be on your own soon.'

She could feel Noah's dark, curious eyes on her, stabbing little pinholes of speculation, but he said nothing.

'Are you leaving soon, then?' Rosemary asked, the disappointment heavy in her voice.

'As soon as I finish boxing up the house,' she said. 'It should take me another week at the most.'

'Oh, you have to stay for the ball,' Rosemary said firmly. 'You remember the annual charity event?' She spared Noah a quick glance of disapproval before spearing Annie with determined eyes. 'I suppose he forgot to tell you about it?'

Noah shifted, with, Annie imagined, great discomfort. Annie's eyes rested on him with amusement, thinking how lovely it was to see the unflinchable Noah squirm. 'Wouldn't you know it, he did. When is it?'

'Two weeks from Saturday.' Rosemary's face was bright. 'Try to attend . . . please? As you know, it's the highlight of the year around here.' She glanced down at Annie's shorts. 'It's formal.'

Noah stirred then and there was no mistaking the humour in his tone. 'Rosemary, you have the subtlety of a bull in a china shop. Trust me – Annie knows how to dress.'

108

His mocking, challenging eyes met Annie's and she had to laugh, knowing they both were thinking about the yellow sundress. 'That I can do,' she agreed.

'It's settled, then,' Rosemary said with relief. 'I wanted Noah to have a date. He hasn't brought one since that silly woman he called a fiancée several years ago, and people are starting to wonder if he's . . .' She lowered her voice to a conspirator's whistle. 'Well . . . *you know*.'

Annie managed to contain her grin, but was difficult, especially with Noah scowling at her so. 'I see.'

'Rosemary,' Noah said warningly in a voice that would have made most men quiver. Rosemary paid no attention.

'You'll come, then? With Noah?' Rosemary asked hopefully, gripping Annie's dirty hand.

Something stirred deep within Annie; a need to be frivolous, an urge to do something other than work for a change; a craving to let go. She didn't dare look at Noah. 'I wouldn't miss it.' Fiancée, she thought, avoiding Noah's eyes. *What had happened to her? And how much did she have to do with Noah's reluctance to trust?* She risked a glance at him.

He was positively glowering at Rosemary, who looked completely unconcerned about her son's wrath. Annie couldn't help it; she smiled right into his rebellious eyes. Things were looking up after all. He didn't want her as a date, and it wasn't concern for her feelings that kept him silent – he couldn't care less about appearing surly and rude. It was his concern for Rosemary that did it; he couldn't possibly back out without disturbing her and her mood.

Annie wasn't concerned. Noah didn't want a date with her, and it wasn't because he couldn't stand being in close confines with her. In fact she was betting it was the opposite. She could feel his hungry eyes devour her whenever he thought she wasn't paying attention. It excited her in a way that she hadn't thought possible. But something was holding him back and she wanted to know what. She could only imagine the dark things that lurked in his past that made him so unwilling to give any part of himself, so unwilling to trust. It made her ache for him and want to ease the pain. If only he'd let her.

In that moment, she knew. For Noah, she'd risk all the heartache in the world, if only to be with him. Through tragedy, she'd learned: the future couldn't be depended on, it was the here and now that counted. She'd love for the present, and hope the future would follow.

She looked at Rosemary's happy face and at Noah's glowering one and felt a contentment she hadn't felt in years. This was where she wanted to be.

Yep, things were looking up.

After another sleepless night that had been filled with burning images and horrifying memories, Annie felt groggy and out of sorts. Not at all the sort of mood that was good breakfast company, but she'd promised Ross.

They sat across from each other in a small café in town, and laughed over fond memories until Annie had left her rotten disposition far behind.

'Remember that time you and Jesse came to the station to visit me at work and you climbed into one of the rigs while I was on the phone?' Ross asked her. 'You were about five.'

She smiled, remembering perfectly. 'I fell asleep waiting for you.'

'Then they took the rig out on a call and we had no idea where you'd gone to.'

'You had every police car in the city searching for me,' Annie laughed. 'And I woke up as the rig pulled back into the station, yawning and wondering what the fuss was all about.'

Ross shook his head. 'You slept like the dead.'

She wished she still did, she thought, hiding a yawn. Sleep didn't seem to come so easy any more.

As if he read her mind, Ross said, 'You're worried.'

She opened her mouth to tell him she was fine, but he waved her words aside brusquely. 'I hate this, Annie. I see you losing sleep over this, I see you struggling with what happened all those years ago and I just want to tear the guy apart.'

'I know you do,' she said softly.

He rested his fists on the table, grimacing. 'And I can't. Because I can't find him. It's killing me.'

111

'It's going to be all right, Ross,' she said, trying to lighten the mood. 'We're going to be all right.'

'Yes,' he agreed. 'We will. I have every man in my command making sure of that.' He took her hand. 'Thanks for coming, Annie. We don't spend too much time together any more, but the little time we get is good. You'll be gone again soon.'

She nodded. 'But we won't lose touch again. Not like . . . before.' She refused to let that happen. He was all she had left.

When she arrived back at the Taylor House, she felt a little better, and far less grumpy. Hearing a shout of laughter as she walked by the main house, she changed direction, following the sounds of kids whooping and clapping all the way to the tennis court. There she found herself watching a game between Noah and Adam, one of the permanent staff. Several boys were cheering wildly – for both men.

It was a pleasure to watch the absolute joy and thrill on the young faces – until her own eyes got hooked by the game. She'd never thought of tennis as particularly exciting.

Until now.

Noah was closest, his back to her. As she watched, he ran gracefully, his long, powerful legs bending and stretching for each return. The muscles in his arms and shoulders bunched as his racquet collided with the ball, his face tight with concentration.

Her gaze spellbound, she suddenly felt ridiculously

112

breathless. The two men volleyed back and forth for long moments, their awed crowd completely silent with amazed respect. The pop of the racquet hitting the ball came quicker and quicker as each man tried to best the other.

Noah slammed the ball into Adam's court and took the point. And the next. And the next. Then Adam foiled Noah with a sweet, clean slice down the side of the court and gained a point. The kids yelled good-naturedly. Sweat trickled down Noah's forehead and he swiped at it with his wristband before diving for a net shot that left him on his hands and knees, gasping for breath.

Adam laughed triumphantly and the kids booed cheerfully. 'Beat that, buddy!' Adam shouted, laughing again. 'And I thought you were the pro.'

Noah smiled evilly and slowly stood, pulling another ball from his pocket. Adam sighed and backed up, his face resigned. Noah gestured with his hand that Adam should back up even more, which he did with a look of mock fright on his face.

Noah served twice in a row. The ball soared so quickly it was a blur. Annie couldn't follow it with her eyes. Neither could Adam.

The kids went wild and Annie let out a breath she hadn't even realized she'd been holding. Her heart pounding strangely, she backed out of the court before Noah could see her.

In all the time that he had played professionally, she

had never caught a game on television, and she was sorry now. He moved on the court with the grace and sureness of a gifted dancer, with the power and prowess of a panther. His body was perfectly in tune, beautifully made – except for the five-inch-long jagged scar she'd seen on his knee. She wondered if it gave him half as much pain as just seeing it gave her.

She must be more tired than she thought. The last thing Noah wanted from her was concern.

The phone was ringing. Annie could hear it as she walked through the Taylor House. It rang again. And again. She glanced around, but there was no one in sight. With a shrug, she answered it and got Bess, the secretary for the City Planner. She was desperate to speak to Noah.

'I'm sorry,' Annie said quite honestly, though she disliked the soft, breathy voice on principle. 'He's not in at the moment.' The memory of where he was, what he was doing and how he looked doing it had her heart tripping again.

'Oh,' Bess breathed in a sexy Marilyn Monroe voice that grated on Annie's nerves. 'He has some information for the work he's doing for us and I gave him my only copy. I have to speak to him.'

Annie rolled her eyes. Sure she did. 'All right,' she said casually. 'I'll go to his office and see if I can locate what you need. How's that?'

The woman, put in the corner by her own trap, had

to agree. Annie put the reluctant Bess on hold and went to Noah's office. It was closed, not locked, but still she hesitated. Noah was a bear about this room, he hated to be bothered when he was in it and he hated trespassers even more. His privacy was sacred and Annie had respected that. But it was the alternative – letting Bess come to the house – that decided her. She really wasn't in the mood to watch a simpering female fawn all over Noah.

The room was large and masculine. One dark oak desk had a computer, the other was completely covered with papers and files. The deep forest-green carpeting was nearly invisible beneath the stacks of papers and books. Two walls were all shelves and they too were filled to capacity. Another wall was dominated by large windows overlooking the cliffs and ocean. It was obviously a worked-in office. There wasn't empty space anywhere. Annie had to step over stacks of papers and books on the floor just to get in.

She glanced at the expensive computer set-up on one desk, fully aware that Noah had an entire and separate career right here in this room. His vast and widely reputable computer knowledge probably earned him more than he had playing tennis – and that had not been peanuts. Sitting in the chair – the only spare space in the room – she picked up the extension.

Bess was eager to talk. 'Are you Noah's sister?'

'No,' she said wryly, smiling at the youth in the voice. 'Just a . . .' What the hell was she? 'A friend.'

'Me too,' Bess said conspiratorially. 'Though not for lack of trying. He's so soft-spoken and shy. So gentle, too, you know? And sexy.' She sighed in the dreamy way that only a teenager could come up with.

Annie stifled her laugh as she glanced at the papers on Noah's desk for the one that Bess needed. Noah, soft-spoken? Sexy, most definitely – but never gentle or shy.

'Find anything interesting?'

Annie jumped nervously and glanced over. Noah's shoulder was holding up the door-jamb, his arms crossed, his hard gaze leveled right at her. His voice was ice-cold – in complete contrast to the heat in his eyes.

'Shy and gentle like hell,' she muttered under her breath as she rose from his chair. 'Bess is on the phone and she needs – '

'Fine,' he said curtly, pushing away from the door. 'I'll take it.'

'OK,' she said awkwardly, knowing she'd trespassed into forbidden territory. She was at the door when he called her. Slowly she turned back, hating the flush she felt on her face.

'If I needed a secretary, I'd damn well hire one.'

'Fine. Then get an answering machine!' Softly she shut the door behind her, though the urge to slam it was strong. She was only interested in getting out of that embarrassing situation as quickly as possible, but when she heard Noah's voice talking sweetly, kindly and yes, even shyly, to Bess through the door she exploded.

She yanked it open again just in time to see him hang up the phone with a small smile playing about his lips. It set her off even more. 'I'm not going,' she said defiantly.

'I can see that.' With a sigh, he pushed away from the desk and looked at her. He was still in his tennis clothes and the stark whiteness of his shirt and shorts set off his tan and dark eyes. His hair clung damply to his forehead.

He looked far better than any obnoxious male had a right to look.

'Tell me, Noah Taylor, what gives you the right to be so damned rude and moody? I can't keep up with you. One minute you snap my head off, acting like you can't stand the sight of me. Then the next you seem kind of . . . well . . . attracted to me. I want to know – need to know – which it is.'

'Which it is?'

He was carefully expressionless and she was beginning to sorely regret her outburst. She put her hands on her hips and sighed. 'Which is it,' she repeated. 'Can't stand the sight of me – or attracted.'

His gaze met hers and she noticed with fascination his eyes were no longer cool, but filled with warmth, humour and something else. 'Attracted,' he said simply.

117

Thank God. 'OK,' she said, ignoring her fluttering heart. 'So you're attracted.'

His lips twitched once. 'That's right.'

Damn him, he was enjoying this. She thought of how long they'd known each other, how he'd pulled her from the fire and she knew she had to ask. 'Are you attracted to me because you think I need you?' She gestured to her remaining bandage on her burned knee.

'Annie,' Noah said with a short, frustrated laugh, ploughing a hand through his hair. 'You don't need anyone. You know that as well as I do.'

Maybe not, she thought, as she made her escape from him. But it would sure be a luxury to give in and try it some time. Just for a little while. Surround herself in his capable arms and cry, really cry, as she hadn't allowed herself to do since she was a child. She could almost try it now, except that would prove her point: that he was only attracted to her because she needed him.

The thought that maybe it was true wasn't comforting.

Annie spent another sleepless night. Long, haunting dreams kept her tossing and turning. Visions of her mother and brother, then of Noah floated in her mind and she couldn't shake them.

At dawn she gave up the effort and made her way to the big house. She'd promised Ed the cook that she would have fresh tomatoes for him from the garden so he could make his county-famous omelettes.

Wearing her favourites cut-offs and a loose T-shirt, she threaded through the pre-sun garden, enjoying the fresh, cool air. She'd treat herself to a run on the beach, she thought. As soon as she delivered those tomatoes. Gathering them in the hem of her large shirt, she hummed lightly to herself and walked in the back door.

Ed sent her a grin. 'You remembered!' He was a short, large man with black hair and deep set eyes that gave him an imposing look that was at complete odds with his soft, gentle manner. He'd been at the Taylor House forever and he remembered Annie from the days when she, Noah and Jesse would steal his freshly made cookies.

She set the tomatoes carefully on the table. 'Look how big they are. Rosemary should be pleased.'

Ed's smile faded. 'It's a bad day, Annie.'

'Oh.' She knew what that meant. Rosemary didn't know who she was or where she was. It made it very difficult for everyone around her because sometimes she got angry and mean in her frustration. Especially to Noah, who seemed to take it all in stride, but Annie imagined that deep down it hurt horribly. 'Is there anything I can do?' They both knew that there had been far more bad days than good lately.

'Well, actually, yes,' Ed told her gratefully. 'You

could run to the store for me. We'll need all the hands around here we can get and I hate to leave. But I have to have pepper, hamburger buns, milk – '

'Wait,' Annie laughed. 'I've a rotten memory. Let me get a pen.' She grabbed the pen and pad by the telephone and tried to write. 'Oh, this pen is out of ink.'

'Here, let me show you a trick,' Ed said, whipping a lighter out of his pocket. 'This always works.'

He flicked the lighter and Annie promptly dropped the pad with a small cry. Her eyes were riveted on the small flame, her mind lost in time.

She could see the family wagon, swallowed by flames and smoke. Screams were everywhere, though she knew they were her own, not her mother or brother. It was too late for them.

'Annie?' Noah came into the kitchen. He glanced questioningly at Ed.

She was dressed in her beautiful graduation dress, screaming, being held back by Ross. She clawed and scratched at him, desperate to get to the car, but he was strong. 'It's too late, honey,' he sobbed. 'I'm so sorry, it's too late.'

'*No,' she cried. 'It can't be!'*

'Annie,' Noah said again, in real concern. Ed was still holding the flickering lighter in front of Annie and Noah pushed it aside. 'The flame's gone now. See?' He grabbed her arms and gave her a little shake, waiting until she looked at him.

120

'Noah?' she gasped, gripping his forearms like a lifeline. God, it had seemed so real. As if it were happening all over again. What was wrong with her?

'It's me,' he murmured, leaning down to study her face. 'It's just me.'

She flung herself against his chest, taking comfort in the fact that though he hesitated, his arms eventually surrounded her. 'Oh, God, Noah. I'm so afraid, I'm losing it.'

'No,' he said against her hair. 'You're going to be all right, I promise.'

Suddenly she pulled back, staring up at him in stunned shock. 'The earring, Noah. I just remembered. Oh, my God.'

'OK,' he said calmly, shoving his hands into his jeans pockets. 'What do you remember?'

She drew a ragged breath. 'The earring I found in my house – they were my mother's favourite pair. When she was pulled from the car fire she had been wearing only one, though it was melted beyond repair.' She swallowed hard on the ball of bile blocking her throat.

'Why was she wearing only one?'

'Exactly,' she murmured. 'My question exactly. I never thought about it before. But now the other one has been stolen.'

He studied a point beyond her, deep in thought. 'Why?' he asked finally.

She shook her head. 'I don't know,' she said,

backing away. And when he would have pulled her back to him she stepped back further. His hands dropped to his sides. This is how it needs to be, she reminded herself. She didn't need him any more than he needed her. If only she didn't still crave his arms around her, she'd be all right.

'You're white as a sheet.'

And she was still shaking, but Noah looked less than thrilled to be the one stuck offering her comfort. It hurt more than she wanted to admit. 'I'm fine. Thanks.'

He didn't believe her. 'Annie – '

'I think I should find out about that earring.' And she walked out of the kitchen and out of the Taylor House.

As she crossed the immense garden towards her cottage she could hear the wonderful, noisy sea from the cliff below and abruptly changed direction. On the far edge of Noah's property was a steep set of steps that led down to the beach. She ran down them and looked longingly at the small pier where as a kid she used to fish.

She kicked off her tennis shoes and the instant her toes hit the sand she started running. The nightmare surrounding her seemed oppressive, overwhelming. And her strange desire for a man she'd known all her life left her uncertain and wary. She ran without a thought for the beautiful sunrise coming up over the mountains to the east. She ran and ran, not realizing how far she'd gone until suddenly she knew she wasn't alone.

Whirling in fright, then sagging in relief, she dropped to the sand. She gulped in big breaths of air as her lungs screamed at her.

She felt raw. For years she had managed to deal with her grief and sorrow by burying herself in work. Now she was being forced to face it all and it was so difficult. She wanted to lose herself, forget just for a little while.

She glanced at the man besides her, standing so rigid. Noah sank to his knees, his own breath ragged. Head dropped between his shoulders, hands on his thighs, his chest heaving, he said nothing.

Beneath them, the sand vibrated with the force of the powerful waves. The sky lightened with the new day. Their ears filled with the glorious music of the surf.

Her annoyance at how he'd talked to her the day before in his office vanished. After all, she had been the one invading his privacy, and she somehow knew that his anger hadn't been at what she was doing, but because of how she affected him. She should know; he affected her in the same disturbing manner.

It was time to do something about it.

Sliding closer, she manoeuvred in front of him, their bodies nearly touching. He lifted his head and she saw he was scowling, causing a deep groove between his dark eyebrows. On their own her fingers reached out to smooth it over.

He caught her hand. 'Don't,' he said harshly.

'Why?' she whispered, brushing her body against his. 'What will it hurt?' She raised her face and delicately grazed her lips against his, feeling the tautness seize his body. 'Please, Noah. I . . . need this.'

'Annie,' he warned in a deep voice that was in direct contrast to the tremble she felt in his hands as he tried to push her away. 'Stop it.'

'I can't,' she admitted, refusing to be shoved aside. Her hands grasped his face, holding it prisoner as she trailed soft, moist kisses along his tight jaw. 'You won't touch me . . . kiss me . . . and I can feel that you want to. Why, Noah?'

'It's wrong,' he ground out, his hands on her shoulders, neither pulling her close nor pushing her away. 'You're Jesse's sister. Christ. You're practically *my* sister.'

'No,' she murmured. 'I'm not your sister. You'd never feel this way about your own flesh and blood.' She took a nip out of his ear and his breath hissed out. 'Kiss me, Noah. Please.' She flicked at the sensitive spot beneath his ear with the tip of her tongue.

He groaned, then tumbled her down on the sand, following with his own body over hers. She tensed, prepared for a violent, angry, hot kiss, but he surprised her.

It was devastatingly gentle, unbearably tender. And

so slow and thorough that her bones went limp, making her thankful she was already lying down. His arms surrounded her, turning them so they lay on their sides facing each other. His hands slid beneath the cotton of her shirt and caressed the bare skin of her back as his mouth slowly, exquisitely made love to hers. Her heart was pounding out of control and she felt flushed, moist and unbelievably ready for the lean, hard and aroused body pressed against her.

Noah pulled back and stared at her, for once his expression clear. He was as completely stunned and overwhelmed as she.

'God,' she whispered, her eyes on his unsmiling, sexy mouth. 'My God.' She was imprisoned by his arms, his legs were entwined with hers and suddenly she yearned for more with such intensity that it scared her.

In response, he rolled her back, plunged his hands into her hair, tilted her head up and took her mouth again in a long, wet, deep kiss that was so erotically charged she could do nothing but helplessly respond. His sure, strong hands on her overheated skin caused her to shiver in delight, and in response he pulled her closer against his sheltered warmth. She wanted him, wanted him more than she'd wanted anything in her entire life.

In the distance, the waves pummelled the shore, matching the ferocity of their heartbeats, but there was something else too. And gradually they realized it was voices, laughing voices that were getting louder and louder as they came over the high rift of sand that hid them.

Noah released her and she sat up, licking her swollen wet lips, smoothing down her rumpled T-shirt. He stood and reached down a hand to pull her up. His breathing was uneven, his heavy-lidded eyes dark with passion and regret.

She, so brave and sure only a moment before, was suddenly and inexplicably terrified of the feelings coursing uncontrollably through her veins. There was only one thing to do.

She turned tail and ran.

CHAPTER 5

Noah watched her go, still reeling from the kiss. Heart pounding, breath uneven, he had just enough time to swipe the frown from his face before Martin and two other boys trudged over the sand, smiling and waving at him.

With a sharp eye, Gerry watched Annie's quickly disappearing figure. 'Whatcha doing?' he asked slyly.

'Just . . .' Oh, hell. 'Talking.'

Gerry grinned. 'Uh huh. How come you're out of breath if you're just . . . talking?'

Smartass. 'I'm old.'

Gerry's grin widened and Noah felt a burst of pride. Making Gerry smile, no matter that the kid was laughing at *him*, was a feat.

'How old are you?' Martin wanted to know, curiously running his gaze down the length of Noah.

It wasn't ego that told Noah he had the body of a man ten years his junior, and that people frequently noticed. It was fact. He was a trained athlete. 'Too old to admit.'

'Rosemary once told me she beat you wrestling.'

Noah felt himself smile. 'I was eight, Martin.'

'I'm older than that.'

His eyes shone with challenge that was a thrill to Noah and he nodded with mock seriousness. That Martin was, in a roundabout way, asking him to wrestle, was a milestone. 'You are, aren't you?' He touched Martin's bicep, whistled slowly. 'You been working out?'

Martin shrugged modestly. 'A little.'

'Me too.' Gerry casually crossed his arms across his chest. Then flexed his muscles.

Noah raised his eyebrows and nodded. 'Winner gets loser's dessert.'

'Deal,' both boys said, and Noah let them tackle him down.

Twenty minutes later they were all sweating, huffing and laughing. Noah let them talk him into a game of volleyball after that. Then they wheedled and cajoled until he finally agreed to take them fishing by the pier.

It was the dream stuff that for young, healthy boys summers were made of, and he didn't even slightly begrudge the time he spent with them. Martin and Gerry were both coming out of their shells and twice Gerry had even let Noah touch him as he'd helped bait the fishing pole.

But Noah couldn't be blamed if a large part of his mind remained on the sand rift with Annie's hot, delicious body spread beneath him, her low moans ringing in his ears.

By the time he got to his office and sat at his computer desk he was beyond frustration and ready to snap the first person's head off that he saw. He forced himself to concentrate on work, which happened to be a large computer job he was doing for the city of San Rayo. He was reconstructing their central computer program to integrate the police, fire and paramedic departments. Everything had to be reprogrammed, from their personnel schedules to the 911 emergency service. It was a complicated job, but one that would certainly take his mind off a certain blonde.

It didn't.

After an hour of trying to get into the work, he shoved away from the desk with a long and lurid curse. He stormed to the window and stared out over the Pacific Ocean.

He'd kissed Annie. Jesse's little sister. Despite all his good intentions to stay out of reach, he'd kissed her. And liked it far too much.

He was allowing himself to think about her constantly. So much for brotherly feelings. He should be strung up for thinking about her the way he was, but no one knew but himself. In caring as much as he was starting to, he was giving her the power to hurt him, and he couldn't allow it to continue. Hadn't he learned his lesson the hard way? He couldn't give his heart away and expect it not to be stomped on. His mother had taught him that, and his fiancée had drummed the lesson home.

Only another week or so, he told himself. Annie would be gone, back to her whirlwind life of travel and writing – and out of his life.

It was for the best.

So why then was he afraid – an emotion he hated with a passion? He knew first-hand what fear was and he had hoped to never feel it again.

Only this time, his fear was nameless. Part of it was genuine fear for Annie's safety. He couldn't dismiss the feeling, even though Ross had assured him Annie wasn't in any real danger. But a much larger part came from his fear of Annie leaving.

'Noah.'

He tensed at her soft, musical voice.

'Do you have a minute?' she asked.

God, no. If he gave her a minute, he'd give her another kiss that neither of them would ever forget. 'I'm busy.'

Annie glanced through the window that he'd been daydreaming out of and sent him a sad, whimsical smile. 'I can see that.'

He sighed. 'What is it, Annie?'

She stepped over some files with a soft-hearted smile on her lips and came to stand next to him. They stood side by side looking out of the window, not quite touching. He caught her pretty flowery scent, watched the fading sunlight shimmer in her hair like spun gold. Her expression was distant, almost forlorn, and he knew a stab of real regret.

He had put that look there. Because he had lost control on the beach, things would never be the same between them again. Hell, even now all he could think about was kissing her again, how absolutely perfect she'd felt in his arms. His hands slammed into his pockets and fisted with the struggle not to grab her and lose himself in that warmth again.

The violence of his need shook him, but even so he wanted nothing more than to shove his work off his desk and toss her upon it, to feel her body strain beneath his, her legs wrapped around him . . .

'Why don't you trust me?'

He shot her a startled glance. 'What?'

She looked at him evenly and with infinite patience. 'Trust, Noah. Why can't you give me some?'

He stared at her, unable to answer.

'It's just a question, Noah,' she smiled gently. 'You're looking at me as if you're facing the inquisition.'

He might as well be. Trust. Why didn't he trust her? That was the question of the century, one that he knew the answer to all too well. It still didn't make it any easier.

He could still remember the first time he'd trusted and what it had got him. *'Don't you dare cry, kid. If you do, you're outta here. Don't forget it.'* That

131

from the woman who had given him life. Apparently he had forgotten it, because his mother had dumped him.

He turned from her and looked out the window sightlessly. 'I don't trust anyone.'

'Not even Rosemary?'

'Rosemary isn't Rosemary more than half the time. I *can't* trust her.'

Her incredible eyes were on him but he kept his own on the window. The ocean was rough, as it usually was at sunset. It was his favourite time of day. He longed to be on the beach now. With Annie.

'You could trust me,' Annie said softly.

'Can I?' he asked, hearing the doubt weighing down his words.

She heard it too. 'You trusted me once.'

'We were kids then.'

'We're not all that different now. Can't you tell me about it, Noah?'

'No,' he said curtly.

'Is it about your real mother?'

'I don't remember her.' But he did.

'She gave you up when you were ten. You must remember something.' She moved closer to him so that her shoulder brushed against his bicep and in the reflection of the window their eyes met. Curious, warm grey met hostile, tense dark brown.

'Why did she give you up?'

'She sold me. For drugs.' Jesus, why had he told her

that? He could feel her stiffen, feel her horrified eyes on him and he hated it, hated knowing she felt sorry for him.

'Noah.' She tried to turn him towards her but he was far too strong for that.

He smiled coldly into the window. 'Luckily she screwed up and an undercover cop bought me.' It had left him so insecure that he couldn't make friends in school and for years he suffered their tauntings in silence. Until Jesse had come along, befriending him, making them leave him alone. His last real friend – and now he was dead. Years later, as a hot tennis pro, people had suddenly wanted to be his friend, be seen in his company. He'd accepted that at face value only, knowing it wasn't him that they wanted, but his fortune, fame and glory.

Indignation, fury and something else he didn't want to see flashed through her magnificent eyes. 'How could a mother do that – ?'

'It's done,' he said flatly, refusing to discuss it.

'But – '

'I don't want to talk about it.'

'OK,' she said unevenly, and he could tell she was shaken. 'What about your fiancée?'

He should have known this was coming. He leaned a hand on the sill, watching the beach. 'You're full of questions tonight, Annie.'

She shrugged apologetically, looking not at all sorry, and he had to bite back a reluctant smile.

133

'Occupational hazard, I suppose. Tell me about your fiancée.'

'What about her?'

She sent him a long look in the window. 'You can be as surly, rude and cynical as you want, Noah Taylor – I'm not budging. So tell me, could she cook or do laundry?'

His lips twitched. God, she was a treasure. 'No.'

'Good,' she said with relief. 'Neither can I. Why did you ditch her?'

'She asked too many questions.'

She had the good grace to smile, then laugh. 'Yeah, well. It's a bad habit.'

'What makes you so sure I ditched her?' he asked suddenly, looking at her.

She turned to face him, her eyes soft and warm. 'Don't tell me she got tired of your incredible mind-blowing, bone-melting kisses. That I'd never believe.'

His breath caught and he went very still. If she continued to look at him like that, he was not going to be responsible for his actions. He plastered a bored smile on his face. 'Actually, it was something like that.'

'There's no way, Noah.'

She sounded so sure. But she was wrong. How could he possibly explain that he'd been engaged to a woman he thought he loved at the time, but later realized that had been impossible? Why else had he never been able to tell his fiancée that he loved her?

Her name was Tracey Popewell, the same gorgeous, sensuous young actress who was currently in any number of popular films. She was wild and beautiful and an orphan, as alone in the world as he'd felt at the time. He'd fallen in deep lust with her on sight. She had just gone through a rough time, having been sexually abused by her director and lead co-star. She'd been in need of someone who wasn't aggressive or demanding – and he'd been lonely on the circuit, surrounded by people he couldn't get close to or trust. She'd convinced him that they'd belonged together, and for nearly a year he'd believed it. She was clingy and needy but he had been at a point where it was nice to be wanted. She was a professional socialite, loved by everyone around her and knew it, but underneath it all she had a heart. Or so he'd believed.

'She decided she didn't want to be associated with a cripple,' he said calmly. 'She left the day after I was injured.'

Annie's eyes trailed down to his knee, her eyes resting on the scar he knew was a vivid white against his tanned skin. She looked neither repulsed or full of pity, just curious. Her disbelieving eyes slowly met his. 'She left you while you were suffering in agony in the hospital?'

One corner of his mouth tilted up. 'How do you know I was suffering in agony?'

'Weren't you?'

Just the memory of those days and the pain he'd

gone through brought a fine sheen of cold sweat to his skin. 'Maybe.' He shrugged as if it didn't matter.

She sighed and put a hand on her hip. 'I guess,' she said slowly, 'you've had no one to trust but yourself. Until now, that is.' Her knowing gaze met his and held them prisoner. 'You've surrounded yourself with people who need you, Noah. Who trust *you*. The kids, Rosemary, your employees. You don't need them back. You've convinced yourself that's the best way. And God knows, after what you've been through it's no wonder – but there's more. There's so much more to life than this.'

'My life is fine,' he said tersely. 'And I don't need you to psychoanalyse it.'

She smiled sadly, reaching up to softly stroke his cheek. 'Trust is a hard-earned gift, Noah. If you gave yours to me, I'd treasure it for always.' He struggled not to give in, not to turn his face into her hand and kiss her palm.

He knew she was right. Trust didn't come easy for him – not when he was young and certainly not now. That was what frightened him, more so than at any other time in his life. More than when his mother had beaten him and sold him, more than when he'd been surrounded by bullies in the school yard, more than when he'd lost his competitive edge by blowing out his knee.

Brotherly feelings to hell, Annie Laverty was seeping into his blood, claiming his soul, and he didn't have a defence left against her. He moved away from her and turned his back, leaning with arms that trembled against the window ledge. He was afraid to give in to his feelings for her, afraid of what it would do to him when she walked away. Because eventually she would go back to her job, back to her life.

God, he was lonely. He couldn't believe it was possible to still miss Jesse so much – even after so much time had gone by. But he did. He wondered what his best friend would have thought about his lecherous thoughts of his sister. He couldn't imagine he'd be pleased. 'What about you?' he asked her reflection in the window. 'You make it sound so easy, this trust thing, but I don't see you giving it away.'

'Me?' she asked, obviously startled. 'What – what do you mean?'

He looked at her. 'Why did you never marry?'

She lifted her chin. 'I'm young yet. Plenty of time.'

He shook his head sadly and touched her cheek, watching as she closed her eyes and turned her face into his palm. A hot, hard ball of desire curled within him. 'It's not your age, Annie, and I think you know it. Don't you?'

She stepped back, biting her lip softly. 'I don't know what you're talking about.'

'Yes, you do. It's about Jesse and your mother.' His

heart twisted a little at the slash of pain he saw cross her face. 'I think you're afraid.'

'I'm not.' But she took another step backwards.

'It's OK, Annie. Believe me, I understand completely. Once you've loved and lost, it's hard to trust enough to do it again. It's hard to trust, period.'

'I trust you,' she said softly, stirring his soul.

'Do you?' he whispered, turning back to the window. God, the look in her eyes terrified him. He couldn't, simply couldn't, handle it. Why had he started this?

'You can trust me, Noah,' Annie said softly behind him, but he couldn't answer her. 'Think about it,' she said.

Wave after wave smashed on to the sand as he watched, thinking. He heard his office door shut quietly.

Then he was alone.

He sighed with pleasure as he lit the match, his heart-rate beginning to race in anticipation. He smelled of oil, which had irritated him so that he almost couldn't enjoy what was coming. Almost.

He hadn't want to use oily newspapers to start this fire, but it was important that he alter his methods so they couldn't catch him. He knew the consequences well enough.

All thoughts left him then as he bent down to touch the match to the soaked papers. It caught immediately, flaring hot and bright and racing away from him, following the fuelled path.

'Ahhh,' he sighed, feeling the usual adrenalin-rush, the excitement surge through him. The deserted house caught quickly, its timber old and dry. There was no one in it, which suited him. There was no use hurting innocent people unless there was an excellent reason. The last time had been too close a call for comfort.

The roof was ablaze now and in the far distance he could hear sirens. Rage flowed through him; it was time to leave – but he didn't want to go yet. They always came too soon, far too soon. And this time he didn't have his camcorder so he could play the tape over and over again. He'd been foolish enough to lose it at the last fire.

Sometimes he stayed up all night watching his tapes. They were his greatest thrill and he was proud of them. He had one for each fire he'd made – except this one. It bothered him that the camera was missing because that meant that someone had it, someone had watched the tape he made.

It didn't matter now. What mattered was getting off the scene before the danger-loving and thrill-seeking firefighters arrived. He sighed again, a sad sound. The firefighters loved only the glory, not the fire, not like him. They'd have to be punished.

Annie talked to Ross nearly every day. They ran into each other at the house, they had an occasional meal together or they talked on the phone. Their one-time easy relationship had been restored and for that Annie was thankful.

Or she would be if she still weren't so distinctly uneasy about the circumstances of the fire and the plaguing memories of her mother and Jesse's death.

She had asked Ross again about her mother's earring. The more she thought about it, the more the whole situation hadn't made sense. Why had Jesse and her mother got into the car to go to graduation without her? And why had she only been wearing one earring?

Even more puzzling, why had the other earring been stolen? The police had shrugged off the incident. After all, no one had been hurt and next to nothing had been taken. To Annie's way of thinking, that made it even more disturbing. In her mind, it somehow connected everything that was happening – only she couldn't figure out how.

Ross had no answers for her, and the more she brought it up the more distraught he became. She finally, out of reverence for his feelings, dropped it.

But she couldn't forget it. There was something else she couldn't forget.

It had been a week since Noah had kissed her on the beach. Kissed her like she'd never been kissed before. The memory alone gave her weak knees and a pounding heart.

She hadn't been alone with him since she'd talked to

him in his office, though she'd seen him often. If her feelings had been as frivolous as infatuation, they would have faded by now, but they hadn't. Something which left her sure that she'd long since passed that stage. If only she could say the same of Noah's feelings.

She could feel his eyes on her whenever they were together in a room, his serious deep brown eyes, and she wondered if his thoughts were similar to hers. She'd meet his solemn eyes and see a flicker of heat and she would know that they were.

She wanted him to kiss her again, but she wouldn't rush him. Not after the things she'd learned about his past. Bad childhoods like his weren't easy to recover from, but it wasn't impossible. He just needed the right person in his life to help him, someone he could care about and trust. Someone to be his friend.

She wanted badly to be that person, but time was against her. She was planning to leave San Rayo in one week – just after the ball.

She lay in her bed staring at the ceiling. Sleep was eluding her, just as it had for too many nights now. Longing for rest but afraid of the dreams she knew would plague her, she lay in that impossible state between wakefulness and peaceful bliss. A glance at the clock by her bed told her that it was only eleven-thirty. Since sleep was not even a distinct possibility, she gave it up and tossed her light covers off.

She pulled on her clothes in the dark, thankful for

the warm summer night. The lights were all off at the big house and she wondered if Noah was sleeping. Just the image of his long, sinewy body lying amid tossed sheets had her hot and bothered and she had to stop to laugh at herself. She was acting like the lovesick teenager she'd never been. Pining away for what she couldn't have was a waste of time.

She jolted at the voice as she passed the big house.

'Annie.' Rosemary stood from her perch on the swing. 'Come join an old woman for a glass of iced tea.'

Annie breathed a sigh of relief. She'd panicked at the sight of Rosemary, unsupervised on the porch. On a bad day, and there hadn't been many good, she could wander as far as the driveway and then get lost, but thankfully she was lucid tonight. 'I can't. I'm going to do some more packing at my house.'

'Well, then,' Rosemary said, putting down her glass. 'Let's go.'

'Let's?'

'You helped me – my garden is gorgeous, never better.'

'Rosemary,' Annie said slowly, 'I don't think you should be packing heavy boxes.'

Rosemary gave her an ironic gaze. 'Honey, I've raised boys all my life – hundreds of them. I think I can handle a few boxes.'

Annie smiled. 'It's awfully late.'

'I know,' Rosemary said, 'but it's so rare that I feel

good.' Annie's smile faded when Rosemary added, 'I mark my days on a calendar in my room, Annie. The days I know myself. There aren't so many any more.'

'Come,' Annie said gently. 'The company would be lovely.' The night was seasonably warm as they crossed the green with her flashlight towards her childhood home.

Ross was out. Typical. She let them in, knowing that she could be staying here again if she wanted to. The ground floor had been cleared, the carpet pulled, the walls stripped. Ross had a contractor working on restoring it. The upstairs was eerily untouched and available to her.

She hadn't wanted to sleep there.

She flipped on lights as they went, still not entirely comfortable.

Rosemary tutted at the damage. 'What do you want me to do?'

'I'm working on the kitchen.' She showed Rosemary the empty boxes and stack of newspapers to wrap the glass. To Annie, who had seen the kitchen in times much better than these, the half-packed room looked empty and forlorn, void of life. Unexpectedly, she felt overwhelmed by emotion and she knew she needed a minute alone. 'I just want to finish the shelves in the upstairs hallway and I'll be right back down.'

'Annie,' Rosemary said with a restraining hand on Annie's arm. 'I may be losing my mind, but – '

'You're not losing your mind,' Annie insisted fiercely.

Rosemary sent her a sad little smile. 'Yes, honey, I am. And I know I sound like a meddling mother when I say this, but I'd like to know: is something going on between you and Noah?'

It was the last thing she had expected to hear. 'Going on?' she asked weakly.

Rosemary patted her arm and smiled. 'Come on, Annie. Do you have any idea how many boys I've raised? You can't fool me.'

'I'm – I'm not trying to fool you,' she said carefully.

'So then tell me what's between you and Noah.'

'Very little.'

Rosemary looked unconvinced. 'I've seen the way you both look at each other when you think no one's looking. Those are some . . . pretty complicated looks. The kind of look that says more than nothing is going on.'

Annie's laugh sounded nervous, even to her ears. And why was it exactly that she was having so much trouble admitting she was attracted to the man? 'Looks can be deceiving,' she said carefully.

Rosemary nodded thoughtfully. In a voice completely absent of malice, she said, 'I don't want Noah hurt.'

Annie laughed again, this time for real. 'What makes you think I have that sort of power over him?' *She only wished.*

Rosemary wouldn't let it go. 'I've seen you two, the way you avoid each other,' she insisted. 'And Noah isn't really very good at this sort of thing.'

Annie's already aching heart lurched. 'I would never hurt him.'

'Not intentionally, maybe,' she conceded. 'But despite his tough exterior, Noah's vulnerable, open to heartache.'

'You couldn't be more wrong there, Rosemary,' Annie disagreed quietly. 'He isn't open to heartache at all. He doesn't *allow* himself to be.'

Rosemary's protective expression gentled. 'He doesn't *want* to trust you, Annie. He doesn't want to *need* you. *But he does.* And that's what he's fighting. Not you, but himself.'

'It's the same outcome.'

'All he needs is the right person.' She looked at Annie with a kind, soft smile. 'I like you, Annie, so I'm going to tell you something.' She fiddled with a box, her smile suddenly gone. 'Noah's not an easy man to know,' she grimaced, looking chagrined. 'And maybe that's my fault. I haven't been a great mother to him all these years.'

'Wait a minute,' Annie said, stopping Rosemary's nervous hands with her own. 'You took him in, didn't you? Made him yours when no one else wanted to?' Annie asked. 'You even gave him your name. I'm sure you did the best you could.'

'No,' Rosemary denied vehemently. 'Honestly. I

didn't. I – I know that now. When he was young, I was still so hurt over things in my past. I gave him shelter, some comfort and food. And yes, even my name. And maybe I thought I gave him everything I had inside me, but I didn't. I know that. Because I never did give him my unconditional love – and that's what he needed most of all.' Rosemary turned away. 'It shows now.'

'A person isn't just a product of his environment,' Annie told her, even as she wondered how she would feel if she'd gone all her life without the love her parents and brother showered over her. 'Whatever you think your shortfallings were, Noah is old enough to develop his own life and lead it the way he wants to.'

'It's not always that easy.' Rosemary sighed, pacing the room. 'You had it good, Annie, you and Jesse both. But it was different for Noah. He was shown over and over again, told in so many different ways if not words, that he was worthless. Useless. A burden. Not worth loving. That kind of a thing sticks with you.' Rosemary's eyes filled with regret, concern. 'I love him, Annie. I do. I couldn't love him any more if he really were my own. But I never once told him that or showed him properly. His real mother – '

'You are his real mother,' she said fiercely, grabbing Rosemary's hand. That other woman who had given him birth didn't deserve the title. 'No one else exists.'

'I'd like to think so,' Rosemary said sadly. 'He told me about her once. She didn't feed him, she kicked him out at night so she could come and go with whomever she pleased. If he so much as whimpered, she'd beat him senseless. Then, years later, that awful, clingy fiancée used him and then left him when she thought his career was over. You have no idea how all that can damage a person.'

Annie looked into Rosemary's anxious face and tried to smile reassuringly, but she felt sick. 'And despite all that, Noah's OK. Look what he's done for the Taylor House.'

'And what he hasn't done for himself,' Rosemary countered. 'He needs someone he can trust.'

'I know,' she whispered, wanting so desperately to be that person.

Rosemary smiled. 'Just be good to him. And patient.'

'I will.'

She left Rosemary there happily boxing dishes that her mother had treasured and wearily climbed the stairs, thinking about Noah.

He'd given his life to children who had been seriously abused and neglected. He opened his heart and home to them, without a concern for himself. It must be difficult to relive his pain through theirs. How badly could a man as sensitive and caring as Noah be hurt by the dreadful, sickening things in his own past? Pretty badly, she admitted. But was he willing to give her a chance?

* * *

Noah leaned back in his chair in his office and stared off into space.

It had been an unusually good few days for Rosemary. Noah knew he had Annie to thank for that. She had spent hours with Rosemary in her garden and then on the ball preparations and Rosemary was so happy, so excited that her thoughts just somehow seemed to stay with her.

The darkness out his window was complete. The line between cliff, ocean and sky was indistinguishable, though he could hear the unique sounds. Water smashing on to hard sand, crickets playing their music, the wind rustling through the loose rafters above.

He had avoided being alone with Annie. But he couldn't stop thinking about her. About their kiss on the beach. About Annie asking for his trust with her clear, thoughtful eyes.

Trust – that was out of the question. But another kiss . . . one taste of her hadn't been enough. He knew he could never get enough, but she was going to leave after the ball and he had to remember that. She'd leave and his life would go on, but now he would know exactly what was missing in it.

He'd spent the past week pretending it didn't matter, that everything would be just the same without her. The fact that he was fooling himself had him in the foulest temper in recent history.

And Annie was doing her damnedest to make it worse.

She had joined an impromptu tennis match, playing doubles against him with two of the kids. She'd looked so damn irresistible in her short skirt and matching top that he'd wanted to toss his racquet aside and drag her down on the floor of the court. He couldn't focus on the game because every time she served, reaching high in the air, her shirt lifted tantalizingly. Every time she bent to retrieve a ball his eyes soaked up long legs and luscious thighs. And despite himself he had grinned uncontrollably every time she laughed in delight at her own shot, thankful that the persistent, haunted look in her eyes had started to fade.

He hadn't been able to concentrate worth a damn. That was the only explanation he had for Martin when they lost.

It wasn't until the boys were in bed that Noah remembered the camcorder he'd found the night Annie's fire. It was the evening news that reminded him, with its report of the thoughtless burning of a vacation home by some sick pyromaniac.

He got out of his chair and inserted the tape into his VCR, hoping that he would see some clue as to the owner of the small, expensive camcorder. The fact that he'd found it on the green between his property and Annie's had to limit the owner to someone he knew, but he'd heard nothing about it.

And then the tape came on and he stiffened.

The fire at Annie's house filled the screen with flames so bright, so real he could almost feel the heat. A low, grisly voice whispered and moaned how the fire turned him on.

Noah skin crawled. He couldn't have felt more spooked – or full of uncontrollable rage.

Then came the scream. He heard it clearly on the tape and remembered it first-hand. It was Annie's scream, the scream he'd heard seconds before he'd crashed open her door to find her nearly unconscious, crawling on her hands and knees, inches from the blaze.

On the tape the voice wobbled and haltered. 'Oh, God,' he heard, followed by a tortured moan. 'Oh, God, no.'

The tape went blank.

Noah sat staring at the white, fuzzy screen. His limbs were icy thinking of the implications of that tape. He knew Ross and their department suspected arson, but hadn't been – as yet – able to come up with a suspect or concrete proof. He was looking at that proof now.

Then he remembered something else. The night of the fire he'd been sitting on his porch when the motion detector light had gone on – for apparently no reason what-so-ever. He had thought it was strange enough to walk about his property to check things out; and thank God he had, because that was when he had seen the fire. He'd raced down the hill in just enough time to haul Annie out of the house.

But someone else had been on the green that night,

and that someone had set off his motion detector. That someone had been the arsonist – someone he probably knew.

He rewound the tape, his mind on the events of the past two weeks. Someone had methodically searched Annie's cottage. It seemed far-fetched, but couldn't that someone have been looking for the camcorder?

He ejected the tape and stared down at it. If so, why had the earring been taken? A random theft? He didn't think so, but the alternative was worse. It meant that their suspicions were right. Not only was the fire and the break-in connected, but the death of Annie's mother and Jesse as well.

It didn't help that deep down he'd known it all along.

Whoever had set that fire was a cold-blooded psycho case. And if that person thought Annie knew who he was or that she knew about this tape, she was in the gravest danger.

He had to see Ross, give him the tape. But there was something he had to do first.

Suddenly he wanted more than anything to see Annie, his reasons for avoiding her seeming silly and petty now. He wanted to know that she was all right, that she wasn't still tormented by terrifying flashbacks. He wanted to see her, to have the simple pleasure of her company.

He stopped off at his cottage and hid the camcorder and the tape. It would have to go to Ross, of course, as soon as possible, but for now he could think of only one thing.

Annie's cottage was dark. He knocked for a few minutes then stepped on to the green, straining his eyes down to the tract of homes below.

Damn her, the lights to the Laverty house were on. If she was alone in that house he would kill her.

No, scratch that. He'd kiss her again; then he'd kill her.

Annie dropped a load of books off the hallway shelf into a box and sighed. The ball was coming up and her packing was half done. There was no getting around the fact that she'd be entirely finished by next Saturday's big bash and she'd have no further reason to stay.

She ignored the protest her heart sent up. Noah would be relieved and, in a way, so would Ross. They'd be free to get on with their lives.

And she'd get on with hers. Travelling, writing, meeting new people, seeing new things. She'd always loved it so much in the past. So why then did it sound like a death sentence? Because she lived on planet reality and she knew very well it meant meals alone in strange cities, quiet hotel rooms without personality, boring plane trips and long, lonely nights.

It meant being a lifetime away from her family, her house . . . and Noah Taylor.

She pulled another armload of books off the shelf.

Suddenly the hair on her neck rose. She was being watched. She went completely still except for her heart ricocheting off her ribs – then remembered. Rosemary was downstairs and she would have alerted her if someone had come. She started to twist down to dump her load of books when she was grabbed from behind and swung around.

CHAPTER 6

Books flew everywhere. The scream died in her throat when she caught a brief glance of Noah's strained face a split second before he yanked her against him, slamming his mouth down on hers. Her hands gripped his shoulders as she sought her balance, letting her body take the impact of his as it rocked against her.

Annie could taste his desperation, his confusion laced with fear, and she pulled him tighter, letting him know she would never let go if he didn't want her to. He gentled the kiss immediately, softened his hold on her, his relief evident as some of the tension left his tight body. Then his lips left hers and he put his open, wet mouth against her neck.

The sensations that sky-rocketed through her left her weak and trembly. Joy, sweet and overwhelming, swept through her as his lips nibbled on her skin. She slid her hands under his loose shirt to feel the smooth, sleek muscles taut in his back. 'Noah,' she whispered. 'Downstairs is – '

'Shh.' His hungry lips came back to hers, his hands possessively running along her body.

'But, Noah.' He backed her up against the hallway wall and his hands slid under the hem of her shirt. She closed her eyes on a moan as his thumbs grazed slow, lazy circles over her nipples. 'Oh, my God.'

She felt him smile against her jaw. 'Do you have any idea what you're doing to me?' he asked, nuzzling her.

She actually lost her vision to the flurry of heat and lights dancing through her head. 'To . . . you?' she murmured as his wandering mouth left a hot, scorching trail down her neck. 'I – I can't stand, Noah.'

He took her weight against him and his lips came back to hers; questing, searching, until she opened her mouth for him, savouring his tongue, the roughness of his teeth. She thrilled to his low sound of approval and pressed closer to his long, lean length. Somewhere, in the nagging recesses of her mind, she remembered Rosemary. 'Noah, I think – '

'Don't think,' he ordered in a husky voice that provoked images of wild and passionate love making. It had been so long, so very long since she'd craved a man's touch, and never had she felt such spearing sensations vibrating through her. It was foreign, exotic and she didn't want it to stop.

Except she didn't want to be just another one of Noah Taylor's women. She wanted so very much more than that. The thought was like a dousing of iced water. She pushed at him until he released her

155

and he stared down at her with fever-glazed eyes.

'I – I don't want to have a quickie affair with you,' she said in a tremulous voice she didn't recognize as her own.

He took a deep breath and pulled his arms back from around her, though their bodies were still close enough to touch. 'OK.'

She regretted the loss of his warm arms. 'And I don't want things to get out of control here in the hallway. We're moving too fast.'

'Annie,' he said quietly. 'We've already known each other a lifetime – it can't be *fast* enough. And you're not just a quickie affair – you could never be that. You're different and I think you know it.'

'You've ignored me.'

'I didn't want to want you, not like this – but I can't help myself. God, Annie. I can't stop thinking of you, seeing you, wanting you.'

His sweet words and intense eyes melted all resolve. 'Rosemary's downstairs in the kitchen,' she said inanely, feeling ridiculously flustered.

He looked at her, his eyes suddenly lit with a touch of amusement. He reached out and touched her cheek with long, sensual fingers. 'Annie,' he said on a ragged sigh. He leaned closer, brushing his thumb across her lower lip, causing a tugging sensation in her lower body. 'This thing between us has a life all its own. I've tried to control it and can't. I want you, I dream of you, I crave you. When we make love – '

'When?' she whispered, her body tingling with delicious anticipation.

'Yes. When – and we will, Annie, I promise you that – ' He paused and her stomach muscles quivered as he brushed his lips across her forehead. 'It won't be rushed . . . it won't be on the spur of the moment . . . and it sure as hell won't be in a dark hallway with my mother downstairs.'

He tilted her head back so that her eyes drowned in his. 'It will be some place warm and soft, some place that I can touch you how I want to touch you, and kiss every inch of your incredible, slender body. I want to hold you as you tremble and feel your long legs wrapped around me. I want to watch you come, hear your soft cries and gasping breath, and know that it was all for me.'

His lips brushed against hers once, twice and then he straightened and backed away. She was left to stare at him, using the wall behind her as support – having been effectively seduced, melted into a little pool of longing by nothing other than his words.

'And,' he said, his eyes narrowing, his eyebrows coming together in one stern line, 'don't ever come here at night again.'

She went from limp with lust to rigid with anger in less than a heartbeat. 'Excuse me?'

'It's not safe, Annie.'

'Don't,' she said, coming away from the wall and pointing a shaking finger at his chest. 'Don't tell me what to do.'

157

'I have my reasons.'

She laughed shortly as she looked at him in wonder. 'Do you have any idea how . . . conceited you sound?'

'Do you have any idea how bull-headed you are? No,' he said, shaking his head at her peeved expression. 'I can see that you don't. Come on, then.' He grabbed her arm and started to pull her to the top of the stairs.

She dug in her heels, refusing to be manipulated, but he ruthlessly tugged her along, ignoring her struggle. 'Stop it,' she cried at the top step. 'Where are we going?'

'To show you how stubborn and – '

'Noah!'

He sighed and relaxed his hold on her wrist. 'Let's get Rosemary.' When he saw that she was going to protest again, he stopped. 'I have to talk to you, Annie. And I have something to show you – something that you need to see.' He looked at her with a solemn expression. 'Do you trust me?'

She wanted to laugh. It wasn't a question of her trust – it never had been. He'd had it all along. She wanted *his* trust, craved it and wouldn't be happy without it. 'Yes,' she whispered. 'I trust you.'

'Then come.' He let go of her then, giving the choice entirely over to her. He backed down a step, watching her.

She didn't hesitate, but walked to the top of the staircase and took his outstretched hand. He stood two steps below her and she was actually taller than him. She liked it and it made her smile. But then she caught his expression. For a brief second, his lips curved and his eyes burned bright. But then the flash of heat was gone, leaving Annie to wonder exactly what emotion she'd seen. Her smile faded as she stared at him.

Had anyone ever infuriated and aroused her at the same time the way he had done?

'Annie,' he murmured, squeezing her fingers gently. 'I want to kiss you again.'

She couldn't speak.

'Tell me to go away, Annie. Tell me you don't want me to kiss you. Tell me again we're moving too fast.'

She could only shake her head.

He curled an arm around her waist and brought her down the two steps to fit in his arms, his wonderfully warm, strong arms. 'You didn't tell me.'

'No,' she managed, clinging to his neck and pressing closer.

He groaned and buried his face in her hair. 'It isn't right,' he said, then gasped when her teeth nipped his ear. 'Tell me it isn't right. I shouldn't want to kiss you so badly.'

Annie knew Rosemary could walk to the staircase and look up at any second, but she couldn't rouse herself enough to move. 'I want you to kiss me.' There. She'd said it.

He pulled back to look into her eyes. Holding the

stare, he gave her a quick, hard kiss, then pulled back with obvious reluctance. 'What is it about you?' he wondered aloud, reaching for her hand. 'You're driving me crazy.'

She didn't know, but she was thankful he felt that way. Because he was doing the same to her. He led her down the stairs, where they found Rosemary, happily packing boxes and whistling softly to herself.

'Noah!' Rosemary smiled brightly. 'I didn't hear you come in.' She paused, then divided a speculative glance between both Annie and Noah.

Annie shifted uncomfortably. Were her lips still wet from Noah's kiss? Or was it her blush that gave her away? Whatever, she knew they hadn't managed to keep anything from the sharp-eyed older woman.

'I found something,' Noah said, apparently unconcerned about his mother's curious gaze. 'It's important.'

'What is it?' Rosemary asked, wiping her hands.

'A camcorder.'

Annie didn't like the tightness to Noah's mouth, or the strange gleam in his eyes when he said that. 'The one you already told me about?'

He nodded. And was that regret she saw in his eyes, competing with anger?

'It had a tape in it,' he told them, shutting the kitchen window Rosemary had opened. When he'd locked it, he ushered them both to the back door, carefully locking that as well. They stood on the patio,

160

looking at him, and Annie's unease grew. He was stalling, but why, she couldn't imagine.

'What's the matter, Noah?' she asked quietly, knowing she wouldn't like the answer. 'What's the deal with the camcorder?'

He looked at her, then chose his words with obvious care. 'I think I'd rather show you. Come on.'

He started across the green, but Annie's stomach had started tossing and turning, and she couldn't let it go. 'Does it have anything to do with the fire?'

Noah didn't spare her a glance, or bother with an answer.

'Noah!' Rosemary admonished, struggling to keep up. 'What's the mystery?'

Noah slowed, and guided Rosemary across the damp lawn. 'Let me take you back to the house before I walk Annie back. You're tired.'

'Oh, no, you don't, Noah Taylor,' Rosemary said. 'I want to know what's going on.'

Noah stopped. 'Rosemary, please, do this for me. I have some things to work out. I'll talk to you about them in the morning. OK?'

She stared at him, and Annie was sure she was going to refuse. But then, Rosemary's expression softened with understanding. 'If that's the way you want it.'

He gave her a brief smile. 'Thanks.' They started walking again.

And as they did, idly discussing the fire and the camcorder that Noah had found, nobody noticed the dark figure that watched them go. Or the stark, desperate rage that poured from his eyes.

Noah and Annie saw Rosemary safely in the big house before they turned towards his cottage. Curiosity made her steps quick – he had not yet told her what was on the tape. 'Are you going to tell me?' she asked.

'I'd rather show you.'

His words brought delicious thoughts to mind, but she knew they'd been spoken innocently. Yet she hesitated on his threshold, then tried to hide it with a bright smile. She wasn't ready for this, she thought frantically. She'd thought she was, especially when he'd kissed her senseless, but she felt so nervous. This thing between them had become far too important to rush. She'd been right when she'd said they had moved too fast. She needed to slow things down, didn't she? She glanced up to find him studying her, his expression soft.

'I'm not going to ravish you,' he promised. 'At least, not tonight.'

'That makes me feel much better,' she murmured, feeling oddly disappointed – which was ridiculous considering she was the one holding things up. 'Where's the tape?'

'It's – ' He broke off at the loud shot that rang out in the night. 'What the – ' He peered out the front window.

162

'That sounded like a gun,' Annie said with apprehension. 'Didn't it?'

'Yes,' he said tersely, yanking open the front door. 'It did.'

'Where are you going?' she asked, panic flaring in her voice.

'Stay here.'

'Like hell,' she muttered, peeking out the window as he started to disappear across the green. She followed him out soundlessly.

Noah could have sworn that the shot came from near Annie's house. But the house was deserted and there was no one in sight. The street was dark, not a single light in any of the surrounding houses.

A prickle ran along his spine and he went utterly still, knowing he was being watched. Casually he traced his steps back past Annie's house, making his movements slow and precise. At the last second he made his move and leaped out on the shadow on his left, flying through the air to land on whoever had been following him.

He heard her muffled squeak of surprise and twisted in mid-air so that Annie landed on him. Rage rumbled through his every vein so much so that he was able to ignore the sharp shaft of pain in his knee as he roughly rolled her off him and sat up.

'What the hell do you think you're doing?' he whispered furiously.

She looked up at him, the laughter quickly dying out of her eyes as she saw his angry expression. 'Who did you think I was?'

He reached down and yanked her to her feet, giving her shoulders a hard shake. 'I thought,' he hissed through his teeth as he tried to ignore the agony shooting up his knee, 'that you might be the one with the gun. I thought that just maybe you might be the arsonist who almost made ashes out of your home. I thought maybe you were the dangerous psycho who rifled through your cottage.'

She paled at his words and he was just mad enough, scared enough to shake her again. 'I told you to stay in the goddamn cottage – '

'I'm sorry,' she whispered, her arms limp at her side.

'You could have . . .' He yanked her back into his arms and squeezed.

Her hands went about his waist. 'I could have what?'

For a minute he didn't trust himself to speak. Could have been killed like Jesse, he wanted to say. 'You could have listened,' he said instead. He let her go and stepped back, his face carefully expressionless.

'I said I was sorry.' Her eyes were huge and stormy.

'Forget it,' he said succinctly. He turned from her then and gasped in pain as his knee gave out. One more step and he dropped to the ground.

'Noah!'

From the foggy depths of near-unconsciousness he glared up at Annie, a hot retort on his lips. And he gasped again.

Behind her, over the green and beyond the Taylor House where the seven cottages stood, was a thick cloud of smoke, and hovering in and around it was a wall of flame.

Annie sneaked into the big house and then into the room Noah was sleeping in. The sun wasn't quite up, but sleep had been impossible after the cottage fire last night. She was armed with the best breakfast she could cook. Coffee and toast.

Gingerly Noah sat up at the sound of the door, unsuccessfully hiding a wince as he straightened his knee. Annie tried to hide her response to how magnificent he looked, rumpled and rough from sleep. Tousled brown hair and a day's shadow should have made him look sloppy and unkempt, but it only made him look more appealing. Younger. As did his bare torso. It was the most magnificent chest she'd ever seen, and she had to force her eyes up to meet his.

Lack of sleep made her own eyelids heavy and she had a headache that wouldn't quit. Awkwardly she placed the tray on the low table by the bed. 'How do you feel?'

'I'm not on my death bed. Yet,' he grumbled, grabbing greedily for the coffee.

She stood there staring nervously at him, twisting her hands and not knowing what to say.

That alone was so uncharacteristic of her, he levelled his sleepy gaze on her. 'What?'

She nearly crumbled right then into a mass of stupid tears. He was in immense pain, she could see it in the dull glaze in his eyes, the careful way he held his leg. And the guilt was overpowering. Gently she sat on the edge of his bed, meeting his eyes. 'I'm so sorry,' she whispered, grabbing his hand. 'Please believe me.'

His brows shot up and the hard edge disappeared from his face. 'You're *sorry*?'

She nodded, desperate for him to forgive her, sick with worry and weighted with reproach. 'If I hadn't followed you last night, if I'd listened when you told me to stay – '

'Christ, Annie. If you hadn't followed me last night – ' He stopped short when his voice cracked. He held her hand, the low timbre of his voice and the urgency of his whispered words soothing away her own pain and suffering. 'If you'd listened to me you'd have been caught in that fire. And I'd be the one racked with useless guilt.'

'But your knee – '

'My knee was injured on the court, not last night. I just aggravated it, that's all. In a few days I'll be as good as I was yesterday, for what that's worth.'

She watched him shrug lightly, in complete opposition to his heavy words. What he didn't say told her far more than his words. 'You miss it,' she guessed. 'Competing.'

'Yeah,' he admitted. 'I miss playing competitively – more than I ever thought I would.' He smiled at her, one of those glorious rare smiles that warmed her insides. 'But I don't miss the travelling, the bullshit sucking-up to reporters, the back-stabbing, the thoughtless invasion of my private life.' He tugged her hair teasingly. 'So don't feel sorry for me – I don't.'

'OK,' she said, squeezing his hand. Happy for a brief moment. 'Last night – '

'Was a set-up.'

A set-up. She stared at him, assembling thoughts. 'What started it?' she asked. She'd spent a sleepless night trying to figure it out. They'd only been gone a few minutes. Afterwards Ross had come and spoken to Noah for a long time, though neither of them had seen fit to tell her what they'd talked about.

He took a long, grateful sip of the coffee and gave the overcooked toast a sceptical look. 'This is breakfast?'

'Noah,' she said with determination, recognizing the delaying tactic.

'I'm a growing boy,' he complained, rubbing his very flat stomach. 'This won't sustain me.'

'Tell me,' she grated.

He sighed, took a wary bite and said, 'You remember the shot we heard?'

'Yes.'

'It was a lure. Staged to get us away from my cottage so he could torch the place. It worked, all too well.'

'But . . . why?'

He tossed the toast down. 'I was afraid you'd ask that.' He brushed the burnt crumbs from hands. 'All right, but remember I'm an injured man, you wouldn't want to hurt – '

'Noah!'

'Somehow our arsonist found out I was holding proof of the fire at your house.'

It took less than three seconds for Annie to grasp what he was saying. 'Proof! You had proof!'

'So I did, though I didn't even realize it until yesterday. The camcorder I found held a tape of the fire at your house. It had a recording of some sicko describing how beautifully sexy the fire was and how all he wanted to do was stand there and watch it burn forever. If we could have identified the voice, it would have been enough to put him away for a long time.'

'Would have?' Annie asked weakly. 'The tape burned in the fire?'

'Yes,' he said darkly. 'As did just about everything else.'

'I'm so sorry,' she said softly. 'I know how hard it is to lose your things to fire.'

'I lost nothing I can't replace,' he said with an offhand shrug that brought her eyes back to his bare, tanned shoulders.

168

The fire had gutted the cottage. He had to have lost plenty. 'What about clothes, pictures . . . stuff?'

'Annie,' he said eloquently, 'none of it means anything.' He brought her hand to his lips, his eyes glowing in a way she couldn't begin to interpret. Kissing her fingers softly in a touching gesture that unaccountably brought tears to her eyes, he sent her a look that made her feel more special, more treasured than she'd ever felt before. 'God, Annie, I don't know what I would have done if you'd been caught in that fire, so help me I don't.'

He brought her hand to his cheek and rubbed against it softly, his rough whiskers tickling her. 'I couldn't have stood it if you'd . . .'

'If I'd what?' she pushed when he didn't finish.

His beautiful eyes were haunted, lonely, empty. 'My last true friend was Jesse. I couldn't have stood it if you'd left me too, and in the same agonizing way.'

She could only look at him, stunned by the admission, unbelievably touched. Then, in typical Noah fashion, he ruined the mood in an instant.

'You look like hell, Laverty.' His eyes touched her dull hair, tired eyes and haggard expression. 'Take a nap.'

She gritted her teeth as she stood, then headed for the door.

'I've got room here,' he called out to her, patting the spot besides him in the large bed.

'Bite me, Bones.'

'I'd like to.'

The man was infuriating, though she did indeed go back to her cottage. For the first time in her adult memory, she lay down during daylight hours and took a nap.

Only to awaken an hour later, sweating and gasping and horrified, the lingering nightmare of slowly burning to death sticking with her for the remainder of the day.

It was days before things settled down. Annie shoved the hair from her eyes with soapy hands, blew at the bubbles that drifted near her nose and shoved her hands back into the water.

Of course the dishwasher at the Taylor House had chosen this perfect time to break down. It wasn't enough that Noah was forced to stay off his knee and Rosemary was sick and that they were horribly short-staffed. Nope, the worst of it was she hated washing dishes.

'Here's the last of them, Annie,' Martin said, lugging a large tray stacked with the rest of the lunch dishes. 'Great time for Ed to go on vacation, huh?'

She sighed. Ed had left the day before the fire and they were at a loss without him and Noah. Rosemary was back in her fantasy land and Annie had somehow found herself taking over the kitchen.

It wouldn't be a problem – except for one teeny, tiny little thing. She still didn't know how to cook. Breakfast cereals and sandwiches had allowed the last two mornings and lunches to be faked. But they'd had take-away pizza the night before and she couldn't imagine that they'd fall for that trick twice in a row.

Racked with guilt, she thrust another dirty dish into the water and punished it for her sins. Haunting her was the memory of helping Noah across the green, calling for the firefighters, watching Noah's cottage burn. But the worst part of it was Noah's knee, watching him fight the pain.

And she'd caused it.

OK, he'd told her not to worry. And she believed that he didn't blame her. But she couldn't help but know that the arsonist's grudge wasn't against Noah or the Taylor House, couldn't help but believe that, without that tape of her fire the arsonist never would have bothered with Noah's cottage. She had brought this trouble on him. And despite the fact that he wasn't concerned with the money it would take to reconstruct and to replace his material things – she was. No one knew better than she that money didn't grow on trees. Regardless of how much money Noah had, it wasn't fair that he was going to have to shell it out because of her.

She had only seen him once since she'd brought in that pathetic breakfast and watched him choke down the burnt toast. It had been on the green at the cliffs and she'd been taking pictures of the beach, something that never failed to cheer her up. Shouts and laughter had drawn her to the sidelines of a volleyball game between some of the boys, with Noah – his injured knee still wrapped – as their coach.

Rosemary had come up beside her as Annie had started clicking pictures of the game, mesmerized by the euphoria on the kids' faces. They were so into their game that they didn't even notice the two women watching.

'Look at them,' Rosemary said with mock disgust. 'Every last one of them needs a haircut. Including their fearless leader.' Then she looked at Noah's hair – which was long enough to be pulled back when he wanted – and sighed. 'They all want to be like him, you know.'

Annie studied Noah's concentrated expression through the lens of her camera as she adjusted for the bright sunlight. 'They could do a lot worse.'

Rosemary smiled a proud, very mother-like smile. 'I know.'

Just then Noah had turned from where he was standing in mid-court with a whistle hanging around his neck and his eyes met Annie's. She snapped several shots as his expression changed from loose and easy to surprise, then a brief flare of gladness before hardening to annoyance at the sight of the camera. Annie had sighed as she'd pulled it from her face. Nothing tightened a person up quicker than a camera.

The minute the camera was lowered, his expression changed again and their eyes locked. For Annie, everything around her receded except for Noah and his hot, hungry eyes. Martin shouted something to Noah that she missed and his mouth turned up slightly in a self-mocking smile. He'd turned back to the game without a word.

Now she was slaving away in his kitchen and was going to have to cook dinner for no less than twenty-five people. 'Oh God,' she mumbled, feeling panicked. Maybe the local Chinese food place would deliver . . .

'Annie,' Martin said with a worried look on his face. He was standing in front of the open refrigerator. 'Ed took this roast out of the freezer before he left. If it's not cooked soon, it will go bad.'

Annie studied Martin's nervous face. She'd noticed over the past few days that he couldn't stand it when food went to waste. Knowing what kind of world he came from, it was no wonder. He used to be forced to live from meal to meal, never knowing when the next one would come around, getting lucky if he got one a day.

'Don't worry,' she said with false courage. 'I'll cook it for dinner tonight.'

He brightened immediately. 'Well, you'd better start now because it's huge. It will take hours – don't ya think?'

'Uh . . . yeah.' She flipped off the hot water and dried her hands. 'Sure, no problem.' She walked with confidence to the pot and pans, stalling as she pretended to search for what she needed.

173

'Want some help?' Martin asked.

Annie whirled back towards him. 'Do you know how?' she asked hopefully.

'Um . . . no,' he admitted with a small frown. 'But I think you just stick it in a pan and that's it.'

'Sounds easy enough, doesn't it?' she said cheerfully into the cabinet, hiding her dread. A cook she definitely wasn't. She didn't know how she had managed to live on her own for so long without learning that basic skill, but the truth was, she could barely scramble an egg. Wondering if it was the right one, she pulled out a pot.

'I don't think that's big enough,' Martin said with a sharp shake of his head. 'Is there anything bigger?'

'How about this?' It was a huge frying pan.

'I think a casserole dish would work better in the oven than a frying pan.'

Annie spun around at the sound of that achingly familiar deep voice. Noah was standing in the doorway, wearing a crooked grin that had her immediately on guard and wary. Noah was not easily amused.

'Since you're up,' she said slowly, trying to ignore the fluttering in her stomach at the gorgeousness of his smile, 'why don't you take over here?'

'Noah,' Martin said with obvious relief. 'You know – '

'Hey, guys,' he said easily, interrupting Martin with a long look, 'you're doing a fine job.' He smiled at

Annie. 'You were just about to show Martin how to cook the roast.'

'Right,' she said. Hell, she thought. No help there. He probably didn't know any better than she did. 'You suggested a casserole dish, Bones?'

'Yes,' he said, his lips twitching suspiciously.

'All right, then.' She pulled out a shallow baking sheet, twirling back to Noah when he started to choke, then cough.

Martin ran over to him, slapped him on the back and looked at him with deep apprehension. 'Noah?'

'I'm fine,' he insisted in an odd voice. 'Really.' He looked at Annie then and she could have sworn his eyes were alight with laughter.

Her eyebrows furrowed tightly together as she stared at him with mistrust. 'Bring me the roast, Martin.'

Together they centred it on the pan, eyeing the plastic wrapped around it.

'Are you going to take it off?' Martin asked her.

She didn't know. Obviously Martin didn't either. Martin opened the flour bin and peered in. 'Don't you need flour?'

This was getting worse and worse. 'I don't think so.' She looked over at Noah who was bent over at the waist, shaking.

'Noah!' she cried, and then he straightened.

He was laughing so hard that tears were running

175

down his face. Her first thought was that she'd never seen him so carefree and happy, but it was her second thought that proved deadly. *He was laughing at her.*

'You son-of-a – '

'Careful,' he managed, swiping at his tears and holding up a hand in protest. 'There's an impressionable kid present.' And then he cracked up uncontrollably, sliding against the wall and holding his flat belly as it shook. 'Oh, God, Annie. A cookie sheet . . . the plastic . . . flour – ' He broke off, snorting hysterically.

She stood there feeling the anger and humiliation sweep over her. 'You knew how to cook it all along, didn't you?'

'Yeah.' He sniffed and sighed, still wearing that stupid grin on his face that made Annie want to smack him.

'He's a great cook,' Martin added, coming to Noah's defence. 'You should taste his awesome breakfasts.'

'Really.' Annie's eyes narrowed dangerously on Noah. 'He can cook pretty good, huh? Especially breakfast?'

'He's better than Ed,' Martin said faithfully. 'But we can't tell Ed that, cuz he'll quit.'

'Hmmm,' Annie said thoughtfully, picturing the pathetic breakfast she'd brought him and wanting to die of mortification.

'Annie,' Noah said in a warning voice, straightening

in alarm. 'I remember that hmmm. That's the same noise you used to make before you sought revenge on Jesse and me for some imagined crime. I – '

'Don't worry, Noah,' she said sweetly. 'I've grown up.' She came around the huge block counter in the centre of the kitchen, fixing her bright smile on him. 'Besides, I don't hold grudges any more – I just get even!' She dipped her hand in the opened flour container and flung it at Noah, hitting him full in the face and across his chest.

His reaction was comical. His eyes widened and he slowly looked down at his black shirt, smeared with very white flour. His fingers touched his face and came away white.

Martin gasped and started to laugh but, at the look he got from Noah, choked it off. 'I, uh . . . gotta go now.' He dashed from the room.

Noah's smile turned wicked as he advanced slowly on Annie and she instantly realized her mistake in not planning her exit.

She backed up, feeling the block table against her hip. 'Noah,' she gasped, struggling not to giggle at the destruction she'd wrought on his clothes and face. 'Your knee. Be careful.'

'My knee,' he said calmly, taking another step, 'is much better today, thank you very much.'

Annie dashed around, putting the table between them, but she definitely underestimated her opponent. With one fluid motion he scooped up a handful of flour and reached over with his long arm, snagging the front of her shirt.

Now she was left with the very sorry choice of pulling back and ripping the shirt right off her back or standing still and praying for mercy. She did neither.

Grabbing her tall mug of lemonade that stood on the table between them, she flung the contents at him – ice cubes and all – and then stood in rooted horror as he slid an evil gaze on her. He didn't move, didn't flinch for a full ten seconds as he absorbed the very cold fluid down his chest and trousers. Then he tugged – hard – on her shirt and she had no choice but to go with it. When he had moved her around the table and in front of him he dumped his handful of flour down the gap between her chest and the shirt he was holding away from her. Picking up Martin's deserted lemonade, he gave her a slow, thoroughly nasty smile. Slowly he poured it down her shirt, watching intently as the thin cotton and then her skin became soaked.

Annie gasped, sucking in her breath sharply as the cold liquid spread across her skin. She raised her eyes to Noah's as he gripped her arms tight to prevent retribution. All the amusement had fled from his, leaving his eyes dark and fierce as he studied her thin shirt clinging to her damp skin. Recognizing the look, Annie panicked. He was going to kiss her. If he did, she'd melt into a bowl of jelly right there on the kitchen floor. Her heart was drumming and everywhere his eyes landed, her skin heated. Her insides were starting to quiver and she was going to beg him in a minute if she didn't put a stop to it right now.

'Don't,' she whispered, pulling her head back a fraction.

His hands tightened on her arms and his lips remained with close range. 'The first time you begged me to kiss you,' he reminded her softly. 'And the second time you couldn't get enough.'

'My actions are coming back to haunt me, then?' she murmured, dropping her gaze. His mouth quirked and she stared at it, then back at his eyes, feeling a strange sort of lethargy come over her.

'So to speak.' His hold on her softened to a caress as he tried to pull her wet body closer to his. 'Come on, Annie. It feels right.'

Annie took a deep breath – not easy when she was as cold as she was – and said, 'On the beach I could only guess how it would feel to kiss you.'

'And now that you know?'

His voice was soft, husky. She wanted to give in to that, could so easily give in to that – but she held back. He still didn't trust her – or didn't want to – and, hot as she knew their affair would be, she wanted more. It was already going to be hard, so hard to leave when the time came. It would kill her to settle for less than one hundred per cent of his love.

Love.

The thought had her reeling.

When she didn't answer his question on how his kiss had felt, he smiled self-deprecating. 'And it was so awful that – '

'No.' She managed to laugh, shaking her head. She sobered. 'It wasn't awful at all . . . but then again, you know that.'

'Yes,' he said quietly, pulling her close when she shivered.

'And,' she continued, resting her head against his damp chest, 'that day on the beach, you didn't want to kiss me. We can't forget that.'

'Ah,' he said, pulling her head back so she stared up into his amazing eyes. The gold flecks in them danced brightly. 'But that was before.'

'Before?'

'Before I knew what it would be like.'

He lowered his lips to hers.

'Ahem.'

Noah lifted his head, eyes slitted in provocation. At his soft oath, Annie turned her head, still chest to chest with Noah, her mind turned to mush by a simple kiss.

Standing in the doorway were Martin, Gerry and three other boys, crowding and shoving to catch a glimpse of their treasured leader, Noah, in the clutches of a – dread – female.

Feeling the reluctance in Noah's arms to release her, she stepped back and grinned broadly at the boys. 'You missed the food-fight guys, but believe this.' She laughed and leaned close. 'I won.'

'She did not,' Noah said evenly, stooping to retrieve the plastic beaker that had held Martin's drink. 'But a gentleman never argues with a lady.'

The boys snickered and sent Noah appreciative looks so that Annie rolled her eyes. 'Oh, please, you can't expect us to believe that you're a gentleman.'

His eyebrows rose as he eyed the length of her, taking in her long flour-stained legs, soaked blouse, flushed face and leaving her with her breath caught in her throat.

Good God, she thought, when he looked at her like that she simply couldn't function. So she did what was beginning to become a habit for her when her thoughts and heart fought valiantly over her mixed feelings for him. She escaped – as fast as she could.

CHAPTER 7

Quickly and efficiently Noah dealt with the roast as Martin and Gerry watched.

'You know how to cook?' Gerry asked, his eyes watching doubtfully as Noah skilfully handled the meal.

'Yep.' Noah pulled off the plastic.

'How come? Only sissies cook.'

'You're wrong!' Martin declared indignantly, giving Gerry a horrified side-glance. 'No way is Noah a sissy.'

No, he wasn't a sissy. Noah had been cooking for himself since he was five, not out of any great love of it, but for mere survival. His biological mother had tended to forget that there was an extra mouth to feed. How many times had he watched her spend an entire week's supply of food stamps on two large, juicy steaks – one for her and one for her current lover – and then toss Noah a cracker or two before locking him in his room for the night? He had been lucky to get a meal every few days.

'Cooking isn't for just sissies, Gerry,' he said with a grim smile. It had been many years before he'd grown to enjoy it. 'Nor is it just for girls.'

Gerry still looked uncertain. 'Then how come aprons are made like dresses?'

Well, the kid had him there. 'Want to learn how to cook?'

'Nah,' he said, eyeing the roast hungrily. 'Some day I'm gonna get me a wife to do that. Maybe even a cook. I'm gonna be rich.'

'Noah's rich,' Martin said. 'He's so rich he doesn't need to get a wife. Huh, Noah?'

'Uh, no, not exactly,' Noah said, tucking his tongue against his cheek. 'Money has nothing to do with it, guys. You get a wife just because you want one.'

They looked at him as if he'd grown antlers.

'Well, I don't ever want one,' Martin said emphatically. He shivered. 'Yuck.'

'I want one. That way you can have sex whenever you want it. Women like that.'

Noah set the roast in the oven and lifted a brow as he studied Gerry. He knew that Gerry had come from a situation worse than his own had been. His mother was a prostitute and had no idea who had fathered Gerry. Her current boyfriend had tried on several occasions to molest Gerry. 'How do you know what women want, Gerry?'

Gerry shrugged, his eyes clouding over. 'The jerk that stayed with my mother used to kick me outside at night to sleep on the grass. He said they wanted to have sex in peace. I only went so that he couldn't – ' He turned away. 'Never mind,' he mumbled.

Noah's gut wrenched at the thought of Gerry, all of four feet seven and eighty pounds, fighting off his mother's boyfriend. 'You're safe here, Gerry. No one will do anything to you, no one will force you to do things against your will. Remember that.'

'My mother . . . liked the things he did.'

Noah wiped his hands on a towel and looked at both of them. 'Not all women want sex. In fact, most don't. They want love.'

Now where the hell had that piece of infinite wisdom come from? He didn't know the first thing about love. And he didn't want to, he thought, watching as the boys left. So why, then, did Annie come to mind just then?

As he forced his mind to something new, it was no wonder that the fire was his next thought. Someone had purposely deterred him the night of the cottage fire, sending him and Annie on a wild-goose chase with the noise of the shotgun. It had been done with calculated timing. Once they'd left his cottage, the fire had been set.

Ross claimed not to be able to share information on the open investigation.

But it didn't take a genius to figure out why the fire had been set in his bedroom, specifically the mattress.

He'd hidden the camcorder – with the tape of evidence – directly beneath it.

Ross knew the details because Noah had told him – what Noah didn't know was what Ross thought about it. That night Ross had been too busy studying the fire and the evidence and hadn't been willing to discuss what he thought. But it had been days, and Noah needed to know.

It was after dinner before Noah managed to break free, and by then his knee was throbbing with the not-so-dull reminder that he was supposed to be taking it easy. Glancing at the full bottle of Demerol in his medicine cabinet, he gritted his teeth and slammed the door shut, leaning against the bathroom sink. He had avoided taking drugs to overcome the pain because he hated the way they made him feel, but the pain was beginning to overwhelm him. He sighed and reached again for the bottle. Just this one time, he told himself as he took the prescribed two pills, just this one time he'd give in.

As if to prove to himself that he could, he ignored the pain and walked to the Laverty house, hoping to catch Ross. He got lucky.

Ross opened the door wearing filthy jeans and a torn T-shirt, holding a hammer. His grey hair was spattered with black specks that looked and smelled like ash.

'Noah!' Ross said in an unusually boisterous voice. 'C'mon in, son. I'm . . . doing demo work. Hoping to please the contractor so he'll lower 'is price.' He laughed.

The sound was so unlike Ross that Noah blinked in surprise. He took in Ross's bloodshot eyes and red, blotchy cheeks. If he didn't know better, he'd guess Ross was well on his way to blissful drunkenness. But Ross didn't drink, never had, and loathed that weakness in others.

'Everything all right?' Noah asked, following gently weaving Ross into the living room.

'Couldn't be better,' Ross insisted, smiling glibly and waving the hammer wildly. 'Wanna help?'

The casual friendliness made Noah wonder. In all the years they'd known each other, they'd had less than a dozen short conversations – and most of them since Annie had come back. But Noah needed information, and he was just stubborn enough to get it, no matter what Ross was up to. 'Sure, I'll help,' Noah offered, gingerly taking the hammer Ross thrust at him. 'I wanted to talk to you about the fire at the cottage.'

'Terrible thing,' Ross muttered under his breath, teetering his way to the far wall in the living room. He picked up another hammer and took a swing at the wall, throwing his entire and considerable weight into the punch. Noah flinched at the incredible destruction it wrought and spent a quick moment being relieved that they were on the same side of the law.

'What did you want to know?' Ross asked, taking another swing.

Noah's eyes narrowed as Ross tripped on his own feet and slammed into the wall with a noisy grunt. 'What have you been able to do about the evidence I told you about? The destroyed tape, the stolen earring? The fact that both fires were set on purpose and so close to each other?'

'Now, Noah,' Ross said, resting next to the hollowed-out wall he'd been sending his hammer into. 'It was your property and you've a right to demand answers.' He rubbed his face, then hiccuped loudly. 'Believe me, I know first-hand what kind of rage overtakes you when you've been violated in that way.' He glanced around him at the destruction from his own fire. '*I know exactly how you feel*, Noah.' He paused, letting that sink in, and Noah had a quick vision of Jesse and his mother's coffin being lowered in the ground. He shuddered.

Ross took a deep breath, and shook his head as if to clear it. 'But it's nearly impossible to pin this on someone without specific evidence. And we have none, not even a suspect.'

'Are you telling me you don't believe those fires are all connected?'

'I'm telling you I haven't finished the investigation yet. That's all.'

Noah bit back his frustration at the lack of a satisfying answer. 'You *have* to believe that these fires are all connected. The circumstances are just too damn strange!' Noah stressed. 'The tape, the earring – '

Already Ross was shaking his head. 'The tape was destroyed and the earring means nothing, Noah. Not without a suspect. I'm sorry.' He tossed the hammer down and walked to the stairs, dropping down on the first one. Grabbing the half-empty bottle of Jack Daniels that sat there, he took a quick swig with Noah staring on in stunned shock.

He *was* drunk, Noah thought with disbelief.

'What are you staring at?' Ross demanded. 'Haven't you ever seen a man have a well-deserved drink at the end of the day?'

'Just not you.'

'Christ,' Ross moaned softly, dropping his head into his hands. 'I'm sorry. I just can't believe it's happening all over again. Can't stop it now any more than I could then.' He tipped the bottle to his lips again, then wiped the back of his hand across his mouth.

Noah ached at what the man had suffered, but he wanted to shake him for losing it now when things were getting a little hairy. 'You're only a man, Ross. Maybe you just need more help.'

Ross closed his eyes. 'I have every man available already on it. My men are doing the best they can. It's just . . . not good enough. Not when it's this close to home.' His words came quickly and were slurred together, making it difficult to hear him.

Then Ross went so still that Noah's heart leapt. He came forward. 'Ross?'

Ross lifted his head and Noah shifted with unease at

the suspicious wet streaks on Ross's face. 'Can't stop it, Noah.'

Concern swirled within Noah as well as a sharp pain over what they'd already suffered. Ten years and still it hurt to think of Jesse. 'It's not your fault, Ross, you know that.'

'I miss 'em, miss 'em to this day.' He offered Noah another chance at the bottle, but Noah shook his head.

'I miss them too,' he said. 'I think about Jesse every day.' The ache in his chest grew. Slowly he lowered himself to the step below Ross, thinking he'd never seen a man look so tortured, so lost. He remembered how much he'd always envied Jesse's and Annie's happy, close-knit family, then tried to imagine how he'd feel if it were suddenly yanked away.

'You and Annie,' Ross said suddenly, raising his head and settling his red eyes on Noah, 'are a thing.'

'No, we're not.'

'You . . . like her.'

The topic threw him.

'Don't you?' Ross pushed.

It felt more than a little unnerving having Annie's tipsy father interrogate him about Annie, especially after having known her his entire life.

'You like her,' Ross repeated, again offering the bottle to Noah. Noah shook his head and Ross shrugged, chugging down another shot. He winced. 'Yeah, you like her. I can tell.'

Noah leaned back and stared at the ceiling. How the hell had this come about?

'I remember what s'like, ya know,' Ross said, then laughed softly. 'Her mother was . . . the same way. Independent, beautiful, stubborn . . . a modern enchantress that you can't do with or without.' He dropped his head back into his hands. 'Shit.'

Noah was beginning to regret turning down that drink.

'Saw you kiss her on the beach,' Ross mumbled, rubbing his head. 'I's standing on the cliff above.'

Ross was looking at him expectantly and he didn't know what to say. 'We're . . . just friends. Practically brother and sister.'

Ross flicked him a knowing smirk, then tipped the bottle again. 'Right.'

They *were* just friends, Noah thought. Weren't they?

'That kiss looked pretty friendly.' Ross nodded seriously and Noah winced. 'Very friendly.'

Noah decided he could use a shot after all, though he choked as the fiery fluid scorched its way down his throat. The memory of that spine-tingling kiss was a sharp reminder that there was definitely something more than just friendly feelings between him and Annie. His feet tingled funnily and he thought that was strange, so he looked down and gasped. They were gone.

'My feet,' he mumbled, feeling with his fingers. 'Oh,' he said slowly. 'They're there.'

Ross laughed at him, which rankled. 'You're a lightweight.'

'Am not,' he insisted, thought it was suddenly difficult to talk. 'Don't mix pain killers with booze.' He squinted. 'Makes it hard to see.'

'Well, I see just . . . fine,' Ross said stubbornly. 'And I saw you kiss my girl.'

Noah's thoughts fuzzily jumbled together in his mind until he could almost feel Annie's soft, giving body pressed against him, the sound of the waves crashing in his head, the grit of the sand beneath them. He blinked as the sound of Ross's voice snapped him out of it.

'"Just friends."' Ross snorted and his head dropped back as he studied the blackened ceiling. 'Annie'll leave again, break our hearts, ya know.'

The next shot didn't burn nearly so much as the first and Noah grinned broadly at Ross. He felt vastly amused. 'That's a'right . . . cuz I don't have a heart,' he confided, making Ross snicker. Knowing Annie was leaving next week made it easy for him to repeat, ' 'Sides, we're just friends. Really.'

'Whatever you say, chief,' Ross told him.

'No,' Noah said, shaking his head, then reeling from sudden dizziness. 'You're the chief.'

They both laughed uproariously at the joke. Then Ross sobered. 'If you hurt her, I'll have to . . . get rough.'

Noah eyed the bigger man. Even drunk, he believed the threat. 'Wouldn't dream of it.'

'Good. I'd hate to mess up that pretty face of yours.'
They both snickered and snorted at that.

'Annie'd mess up both of our pretty faces if she could see us now,' Noah said, slurring his words crazily. 'She doesn't like it when people talk about her.'

'She also doesn't like drunks.' For some reason they found that hysterically funny and it was several minutes before they managed to stop laughing. Noah wasn't too far gone to realize he was going to have a hell of a time getting home.

Tongue inexplicably three times too thick for his head and hands absolutely refusing his brain's signals, he had to work simply to stand up.

'I . . . really don't want her hurt,' Ross said suddenly. 'I mean it.'

'Me neither,' Noah said solemnly, weaving slightly. 'But she . . . attracts danger.' Including me, he thought. 'I gotta go – ' Shit, what did he have to go and do? 'Uh, check on the kids.' That was it – wasn't it?

'Maybe it will be better when she's gone.' Ross dropped the now empty bottle of whisky at his feet, watching it roll away. 'Won't have to worry so much. It'll be safer for her.'

For the first time, Noah realized they weren't discussing him being the danger factor, but the arsonist. To know that Ross, despite his denials to Annie, was worried about her safety wasn't reassuring. 'I don't like knowing she could get hurt.'

'She'll leave soon,' Ross said, frowning as though he couldn't decide whether he wanted her to stay or go.

'Yeah,' agreed Noah. It would be better for everyone. The ground tilted crazily towards him and he braced his arms out to steady himself. He held his head still with two hands and muttered something about his own stupidity.

'Gonna miss her,' Ross mumbled, leaning against the banister and closing his eyes. 'Gonna miss her.'

Not him. When Annie left, he wouldn't have to think about her, dream about her, want her until it was a physical ache. He wouldn't have to feel guilty about wanting her so much either.

She'd leave and his life would go on.

Pushing the swing idly with one foot and watching the moon cross the dreamy night sky, Annie thought about her life. And decided that maybe it was a bit lonely. There hadn't been a real home for the past ten years and for the first time she began to regret it.

At the Taylor House, despite the turmoil and the terror of the fires, she'd been happy. She knew Noah was a big part of that. Though he wouldn't admit it, Noah felt the same.

In another day or two she would have finished packing up the house. Ross had helped a bit, but it had been difficult for him and Annie didn't mind. During the hours she had spent putting away bits and pieces of her childhood, her mother and Jesse had

193

been brought back to her. The memories had been so vivid that she wouldn't have been surprised actually to see her mother or Jesse standing next to her as she filled box after box.

A noise across the green made her straighten. It sounded like singing. Cocking her head, Annie listened. It sounded as if someone had left a radio on. A loud radio with a very off-key voice. When she stood to catch a better glimpse, Annie's mouth dropped open. Then she laughed.

Noah was crossing the green with a funny gait, singing at the top of his lungs, throwing his hands about him in conjunction with the ridiculous – and dirty – limerick. One gasp escaped Annie as she heard the next raunchy line of the song and she realized he was most definitely drunk. He did a little jig and she clamped a hand over her mouth, muffling her laugh.

Then she frowned. Despite Noah's flaws, which she was beginning to suspect were many, over-indulgence was not one of them. Noah might have been the local bad boy for years, but he never drank and never did drugs.

But, God, did he sing terribly.

Then she realized he wasn't dancing or strolling along as she'd first thought. He was limping – and badly.

She waited at the top of the driveway, watching with wide eyes as Noah flung his arms wide, then did a lopsided cartwheel. He straightened with a chuckle and a proud little impromptu dance, only to collapse seconds later in an undignified heap on the grass.

She ran to him and dropped down beside him, staring into glassy, limpid eyes that were distant and unfocusing. 'Noah? Oh, God, what's the matter? Where are you hurt?'

He didn't answer, but closed his eyes and shifted into a more comfortable position on the grass, as if he planned on staying there for a long time.

'Noah?'

He settled, then was still.

'Noah!' she said sharply, worried now.

'Yep,' he mumbled, his eyes still closed. 'That's my name – don't wear it out.' He snorted indelicately, amusing himself, and Annie nearly choked at the alcohol on his breath.

She'd never seen him like this, so out of control. 'What's the matter with you?'

One eye slitted open, settled on her, then slammed shut. He grinned foolishly then, a total and complete mocking grin. 'Hey, babe. I can see right up that dress. Nice . . . view. *Very* nice.'

With an exasperated sound Annie yanked at her loose but short sundress, then gave up to shake him. 'Noah!' she cried in frustration when he couldn't be budged. 'Are you sick?'

'Nah . . . just a little toasted. Polluted. Soaked. Juiced. Tanked. Shitfaced – '

'I get the picture,' she said tightly, sitting back on her heels. 'But why? You don't drink.'

'Demerol and whisky . . . don't go together.' He raised a weary hand to his eyes. 'Don't . . . feel so good.'

'No kidding. Why on earth did you drink on top of a pain-killer?' she demanded, her eyes shooting to the knee he was so obviously favouring. And why was he out walking when he was hurting still?

'Ross said you and me weren't just friends and I said we were.'

'So you had to drink him under the table to prove it?'

'Only two shots, swear.' He brought a well-intentioned hand towards the region of his chest to prove his oath, then missed, slapping himself in the face. 'He doesn't think I'm good enough for you.'

Annie rolled her eyes. 'Men!' she said in disgust. 'Why were you talking about me?' she demanded.

'I told him you'd be mad.'

She was not, *was absolutely not*, going to lose her temper with a man too drunk to hold a decent conversation.

'Said you'd leave me, break my heart. Told him – ' His voice faded to a whisper. 'Couldn't break what I didn't have.'

Her own heart constricted, remembering how he'd escaped from a mother who didn't care, dealt with a system that didn't always have a child's best interests at heart and had ultimately landed in a house with another mother who hadn't been able to give him what he'd needed. Yet, despite that, he'd grown up to be a man who was undoubtedly tough-minded, but tender-hearted as well. He took care of kids in need, alternately giving them the tough love and sweetness they needed. There was a heart inside Noah Taylor all right, whether he wanted to admit it or not. Just watching him care tenderly for Rosemary through her difficult illness when he could have put her in a home was yet another example. And she knew she'd never forget how he'd helped her through the first fire with calm compassion when he could have handed her over to Ross or the firefighters and gone back to bed.

'You have a heart, Noah.'

He denied that with a shake of his head. 'Ross's worried about ya. Told him you're . . . stubborn, independent – don't need anyone.'

In just shorts and a T-shirt, lying on the dew-damp grass, Noah shivered. Concern filled Annie and she knew she had to get him inside and warmed, well aware of how dangerous the combination of pain-killers and alcohol could be. 'C'mon, Noah.' She put her hands under his shoulders and tugged, getting nowhere. 'Help me help you up.'

'And you certainly don't need me,' he continued, staring thoughtfully at the star-riddled sky.

Nothing but a dead weight, she thought helplessly,

watching as he shivered again and closed his eyes. 'Noah,' she cajoled. 'Open your eyes, Noah.'

Nothing.

'Noah, please.' He didn't budge. 'C'mon, don't you want another glimpse up my dress?'

His eyes flashed open and he leered at her. 'Knew you'd beg me some day.'

She still couldn't move him. 'Get up, Noah Taylor. You're a foot taller than me and at least seventy pounds heavier – I can't do it by myself.'

Her sharp tone evidently broke through his stupor. Dilated brown eyes opened slowly and fixed on her. 'When you look at me like that,' he said slowly, enunciating each syllable carefully, 'makes me want to do things for you.'

'Do things?'

'Yeah. Conquer the world. Tame the beast. Shit like that.'

A quick laugh escaped her, then she caught the graveness of him. She sobered. 'I don't want you to do things for me,' she said carefully. Something seized her heart as she wondered again if he was attracted to her because he thought she needed him? All around him were people who needed him; he made a business of making sure he didn't need any of them back. She didn't want him to collect her as one of those people. 'I can do for myself.'

'I know. I tell myself that.' A sad smile escaped him. 'Can't help myself, Annie.' Awkwardly he

198

pushed to his feet, weaving and teetering wildly. Annie threw her arms around his waist to hold him steady and he plopped his chin down – hard – on top of her head.

'Ouch,' she complained. 'Now, walk. One foot in front of the other – that's it,' she encouraged him as he shuffled forward, leaning on her.

'We grew up together, didn't we?'

'Yes, Noah.' God, he weighed a ton.

'Like siblings.'

'Uh – ' She hesitated, thinking of how unsiblinglike her feelings were. 'Not really like that. Different.'

'Don't leave me, Annie.'

'I won't. I'm taking you home.'

'You're gonna leave me . . . they all do.'

Her heart stopped. God, Noah, she thought, will you constantly put a knife in my heart? Women left him. Even Rosemary had left him in her own way. That he cared warmed her heart. That she had the power to hurt him terrified her.

'I'm not going to leave you, Noah.'

'Yes, you will,' he insisted. The dew seeped into her sandals as they crossed the green. Halfway there he sagged heavily against her. 'Tired.'

'I know.' What was she going to do with him? She certainly couldn't get him up the stairs of the big house and he would make such a ruckus anyway. She headed towards her cottage.

Halfway there he stumbled, nearly tumbling them

both down on the wet grass, but Annie somehow managed to straighten them. 'Does your knee hurt?'

'Nah,' he denied. 'Can't feel a thing.' After another minute he said, 'Hard to walk when you can't feel your legs.' And he chuckled, blowing a draught of Jack Daniels in her face.

'You're a funny guy, Noah,' she said drily.

'Too far,' he muttered when they were almost there. 'My head's falling off.'

'Well, you shouldn't have been walking at all,' Annie shot back, full of concern that had turned into anger and irritation. 'Serve you right if your head did fall off.'

'Annie,' he sighed. 'Where's your heart?'

Somehow she managed to unlock the cottage without losing her grip on Noah. In the bedroom she pushed him down on the bed. He lay where he fell, silent. Already asleep, she thought with disgust. Sighing, she looked at him.

And knew she loved him.

Trying not to panic at the knowledge that she was set to leave in less than a week, she picked at one of his high-top tennis shoes and pulled it off his foot.

He stirred. 'Annie,' he whispered, turning to hug her pillow to his chest. 'Kiss me again.'

She yanked off the other shoe, then his socks. She tried to turn him over so she could get a look at his knee, but he was a dead weight. 'Noah, I need you to help me here.'

'You don't need me,' he muttered, turning over for her. 'Wish you did – like I need you.'

Her hands stilled.

'Can't stop thinking of you, Annie.' His head tossed restlessly on the pillow.

Did he know what he was saying? Wanting desperately to believe so, Annie sat besides him and reached for his hand. His face was tight with pain and his body tense. Smoothing his hair back from his face, she let her eyes wander down the length of him, catching sight of his knee, which was swollen and puffy.

Hurrying to her freezer, she pulled out an ice-pack and returned to the spot besides him on the bed, debating whether or not to call his doctor. 'Noah,' she said, shaking him gently. 'How many pain-killers did you take?'

'Two,' he mumbled, then swore. 'I couldn't move to save your life. Hope there's no dragons lurking.'

'And only two shots of whiskey?' she pushed, wanting to smile at his frustration. He hated being out of control as much as she hated seeing it.

'Yeah. Don't worry . . . not going to die yet.'

'Good,' she said with more than a little relief. He'd be all right, she thought, as long as she watched him. It meant another sleepless night, but she doubted she would have slept much anyway. She lifted the ice-pack.

'I want you, Annie.'

Her hands fumbled. He couldn't know, couldn't

imagine what those words did to her insides. He yelped in shock as she settled the pack around his knee.

'Cold!'

'You deserve it,' she said calmly, covering him with a sheet. The chair near the bed looked mighty uncomfortable. Shrugging, she stripped off her dress and slid under the sheet next to him. The twin bed was small indeed, with his large frame in it. He immediately pulled her close and she sighed against his deliciously warm body.

'You're naked,' he accused in a small voice. 'I can't feel my limbs or open my eyes and you're naked. Shit.'

She smiled as she soaked up his body heat and slid even closer, chest to chest, hip to hip.

'God, you're a witch,' he said with a moan, his mouth nuzzling her ear.

'You definitely deserve it, Noah Taylor.'

'I know,' he mumbled, snuggling tight against her. 'I know.' He was asleep in two seconds.

It had been a close call, the cloaked man thought. He walked the beach as the moon rose, as he always did. If the tape had been seen, it would have been all over for him.

He couldn't get so careless again.

What he needed was another fire to cheer him up. A bright, hot, glowing fire. And maybe . . . just maybe an explosion. Nothing did the job like a loud bang.

202

Death, gloom, destruction . . . it all would boost his spirits.

It had to; he had nothing else.

The hoarse scream stirred him; the ugly, heavy panting had him crawling his way from the drunken stupor he'd seeped himself in. His head felt as if a tractor were ploughing through it. Noah blinked in the dark, trying to place himself.

The muffled, tortured sob did it.

'Annie?' He tugged at the huddled form, tangled in the sheets next to him.

Her breathing terrified him. Gasping as if she were suffocating, she twisted herself further in the covers. Noah squinted in the dark room, then nearly groaned as the slight movement sent pain bouncing off his set teeth.

'Annie, what's the matter?' He dragged her to him, ignoring his own agony, concern for her causing his heart to pump. *What the hell was he doing in her bed?* She fought him, but he managed to uncover her head and tuck her still wrapped body against his.

She cried out, the sound twisting at him.

'God, Annie, talk to me. What hurts? What's wrong?' Had he hurt her? Had they –?

'Mom!' she moaned, her arms flailing, her legs kicking.

'Oh, Annie, it's just a dream,' he said softly, realizing that she still slept. He shook her gently, then smoothed her hair back from her damp brow. 'Come on, Annie, wake up.' He cursed when her head turned quickly and bumped his chin, sending shockwaves of pain through his aching, pounding head. She tossed restlessly and he ducked, just barely missing a right hook that would have knocked him out.

'Annie, wake up.' Did she dream like this every night? Was this why she looked so tired lately? His stomach hurt to think about her suffering this way. Why hadn't she said something? She moaned again. He ripped away the sheet and pinned her body with his – then cursed again.

She wore nothing but soft, warm skin.

He slammed his eyes shut and his hands stilled on her slender back. With her plastered against him, he could feel her every, perfect curve.

Her next sob wrenched at him. 'Annie,' he whispered, struggling for control in a world that had slipped from its axis. 'It's OK, I'm here. It was just a bad dream, OK?'

He could tell by her stillness that she had awakened, but her breathing still rasped, sounding especially loud in the suddenly quiet night. 'Noah?'

'Just me,' he said, much more lightly than he felt. She trembled in his arms and he struggled with the urge to yank her close and never let go. His head throbbed with the effort – and the lingering effects of his earlier stupidity. What the hell had happened, that he'd ended up in her bed? *And where were her clothes?*

'Noah,' she breathed, gulping in air. 'It was a horrible dream.'

Her arms snaked around his neck and she pushed close. So close he could feel her . . . Oh, God, he thought desperately. How was a man supposed to handle this? His body was reacting, and violently. His head hurt so badly he thought he might die.

'Annie,' he whispered, 'you're killing me here.'

She didn't seem to hear him as she burrowed into him deeper. Muffling his moan, he smoothed his hands over her back and closed his eyes. Her hardened nipples bored holes into his chest, the heat at the apex of her legs had him nudging a thigh between hers before he could think. She adjusted her hips close to his, rubbing—

He had to open his mouth to breathe. Slowly, he shifted to his back, but she clung to him so tightly that she came with him. Now she lay sprawled across the top of him, her breasts crushed against his chest, her legs over his, the juncture between them snuggled firmly against his very hard erection. When she shifted slightly, sliding over him, he cursed and forcibly slid her off to his side.

He wanted her – badly. But there were rules to such things, weren't there? How could he take advantage of a terrified woman? And how the hell was he supposed to make certain parts of his anatomy work properly when his head was in serious danger of falling off from the mountain of a hangover he was starting?

Well, OK, that wasn't going to be a problem. Every part of his anatomy was working *more* than fine. It was in overdrive.

'Annie,' he said, practically begging her. 'Let me up.'

'Mmmm. No.' She plastered her face into the crook of his shoulder, slid a bent leg up and over his thigh and placed a hand on his chest.

'Please. You've got to let go of me. We're moving too fast, remember? Your words, Annie. Not mine. I'm sorry, so sorry, you had a bad dream. We can talk about it, OK? We should talk about it, that way maybe you won't have them anymore, but *you've got to let me up*.' He was rambling, but he couldn't help it.

She became a dead weight.

'Annie?'

No response.

'Annie?'

She exhaled softly, deeply. Well, shit. She'd fallen back to sleep, if she'd ever even awakened. The small, delicate hand on his chest slid lower, down to his belly button. Through his shirt he could feel her heat. He felt as though he held an entire bundle of cotton in his mouth and yet he was still hard for her, desperately.

Noah took a deep breath and willed his body to relax.

It didn't happen for a long, long time.

Pain, excruciating and sharp, sheared through Noah's head when the bright light bounced into the room. He

206

groaned and pressed his hands against his head to hold his eyes in. 'Who the hell turned on the lights?'

'No lights, Noah,' a disgustingly cheerful voice sang, 'just sunlight.' And then that voice – the one he was going to strangle when he could see again – laughed. 'Come on, Noah, it's getting late. The kids are going to start looking for you and— '

'Shit.' It wouldn't do for them to find him in Annie's cottage. It was all coming back to him, the ridiculous over-indulgence with the scotch at Ross's house, Annie putting him to bed. Her dream. He managed to open one eye and saw Annie place a cup of coffee on the bed stand. Reaching for it gratefully, he pushed himself up, flexing his sore knee. It was surprisingly better.

Too bad his head was killing him.

Annie folded her hands in front of her and leaned against the bed. She had showered and was dressed in a bright red shorts outfit, looking more lovely and alert than anyone had a right to look on a morning such as this.

'You dream like that often?' he asked.

'Dream?' She frowned. 'I didn't dream.'

'The hell you didn't. You practically crawled all over me afterwards.'

Her frown deepened. Her next words rankled.

'I don't remember that. You look awful.' Then she smiled wickedly. 'Still feeling sorry for yourself?'

Annie's sparkling observation, tinged with amusement over his discomfort, grated on his nerves. The fact that he remembered next to nothing of the night before didn't help. 'I never feel sorry for myself.'

She raised her brows with a saucy look that would have cracked Noah up at any other time. 'You were definitely feeling self-pity last night.'

'Oh, yeah?' His dizziness forced him to grab for the wall as he headed for the bathroom. He paused at the door. 'For your information, Laverty, I remember everything that happened last night.'

'Oh, well, then.' She sent him a smug sort of look that made him want to growl.

He shrugged and started to shut the bathroom door, then paused. She looked smug, but there was something else too. A nervousness that was very unlike her. Oh, please God, if he had had that delectable body of hers, wouldn't he have remembered? 'We didn't – ' He vaguely remembered her putting him to bed, but then nothing until she'd woken him up screaming. Surely he would have remembered if they'd –

'No.' She gave him an indecipherable look so that he couldn't tell if she was pleased or not. 'We didn't.' Her confidence was back. 'But since you remember everything, I don't need to tell you that, do I?'

He was definitely missing something. He sighed and glanced out of the window at the perfect summer morning. 'Just give it to me, Annie. What did I say?'

She shot him a little smile. 'You really don't remember?'

208

His sigh was much louder this time. 'Look, my head is going to fall off, my body feels as if I used it as a punching bag and the kids are probably at this very minute raiding my bedroom. I'm not in the mood for games – and no, I don't remember every little, tiny detail. OK?'

'OK,' she said softly with a secret smile that made him hesitate. 'If I told you that you declared your undying love for me, would you believe it?'

'No,' he said flatly, ignoring her sudden flicker of emotion. He definitely hadn't said that, he'd never in his life said that and he most definitely would have remembered it.

'All right,' she admitted quietly, her good humour gone, her eyes flat. 'You didn't say that. How ridiculous that would have been.'

He frowned. 'Annie, if I did or said anything that hurt you or your feelings last night, I'm very sorry. I didn't meant to do that. But having you laugh at something I can only imagine is more than a little infuriating, so just tell me.'

'Are you sure –?'

'Tell me,' he said curtly, losing patience.

'You said you needed me.'

His knuckles turned white as they gripped the wall even tighter and he closed his eyes briefly. He did say it, he remembered. In fact, the entire evening was coming back to him. Annie's concern, Annie dragging him to the cottage. Annie slipping into the bed naked to torture him.

After a lengthy silence, during which time Annie just stared at him, he shrugged, setting off fireworks in his protesting head. 'Well, no wonder you're so amused. I must have been a barrel of laughs last night.'

'You also said . . .' She trailed off.

'What? I said what?'

Her stormy eyes met his. 'You said you wanted me.'

I want you, he remembered telling her in a tortured voice. She'd looked so irresistible last night in that summer dress, struggling to help him across the green, then later stripping it off and keeping him warm with her body heat. Yes, he'd definitely wanted her. Still did. 'I do want you, Annie.' He took some pleasure in her hitched breath. 'And if you had awoken after your nightmare, you'd know that. Believe me.'

It had felt so good last night to give in to the mixed effects of the alcohol and painkiller, knowing Annie would take care of him. But now, in the harsh reality of day, the same thing that had comforted him last night struck terror in his heart. He did want her, he did need her and it had to stop. Forget that he *should* have had only brotherly feelings – he had always had more than that.

But to need her, to want her and care for her only, gave her an immense power over him that couldn't continue. Allowing his pride to speak for him, he shrugged nonchalantly. 'But want and need are two different things.'

Her twisting hands defied her calmness. 'I see,' she said quietly.

'I don't need anyone,' he reiterated.

'I heard you.'

He eyed the bed they'd shared during the night, his mind on the warm, soft body that had snuggled against his aching one. He turned and entered the small bathroom. Leaning on the sink, he stared at his bedraggled self in the mirror then dropped his head down between his shoulders.

And nearly flinched out of his skin when Annie's arms circled him from behind, her head resting against his back. 'Is it so hard to admit, Noah? Is it so bad to need someone, care for someone?'

He stiffened. 'I care for you, I told you that.'

With a gentle squeeze, she peeked around his side to meet his eyes in the mirror. 'But you don't need me, right?'

He nodded. He didn't want to need her. Needing someone had never worked out well for him, never given him anything but pain. And trusting someone went along the same lines. He was done in both departments.

Annie shook her head slowly. 'I'm leaving in a few days, Noah, after the ball. Can't we just enjoy what's left? Be honest with each other?'

Pulling away from her arms, he moved as far away from her that the tiny bathroom allowed. 'Damn it, I am being honest with you.'

'You think so?' she asked softly, tilting her head and studying him with a dignified air that only tormented him all the more.

He didn't want to hurt her, didn't want her to care for him because that gave him an obligation to her, an obligation he didn't want. Deciding retreat was the best move, Noah moved around her and out of the door. Ignoring his socks, he painfully yanked on his shoes and looked at her. 'I'm not sure what you want me to say here, but you can't manipulate me into it.'

'Do you really think I would?' Sad eyes tore at him.

As he watched the change in her mood, his heart constricted, knowing it was his fault. He ignored that too, using his uncertainty and concern to fuel an anger that was never far below the surface. 'Look, I've got to go. You're looking for something that isn't there, Annie.'

'Are you trying to fool me or yourself?' she asked quietly. 'Or are you that scared you can't help yourself?'

He *couldn't* help himself. That she hit it so directly on the nail was frightening enough. It infuriated him. 'And are you so conceited that you can't believe someone may be invincible to your charms?' The minute the words were out, he wished them back. Never before in his adult life had he used words so purposely to hurt someone. That he did so now to hurt Annie was like ripping his heart out.

'No, it's easy enough to believe that someone could

resist me,' Annie said, walking around him towards the bedroom door. 'What I refuse to believe is that *you* can resist me.' She gave him one last knowing look as she left.

He heard her front door shut a minute later and he sank to her bed, momentarily giving in to the urge to lie back and close his eyes. But he found he couldn't lie there without dwelling on last night, couldn't stop wondering whether Annie was right about him needing her. Slipping into her shower, he scrubbed with soap that reminded him of Annie's soft, smooth skin and washed his hair with shampoo that smelled deliciously like Annie's own golden hair.

Feeling marginally better after the long, hot shower, Noah walked through Annie's kitchen as he prepared to leave. The pictures on her table stopped him short. They should; they were of him.

There were pictures of the stunning cliffs, the sandy beach and the wide green. There were some of the kids playing volleyball. All were great shots. Each kid's personality leapt out on to the page: Gerry with his eyes full of neediness, wanting to belong. Martin and his big, cheeky grin as he threw the ball high.

Then there was the picture of himself as he prepared to serve, body extended and eyes squinted in concentration. The next picture had him looking directly into the camera lens and his expression stole his breath like a fist to the gut. Standing at the net with a whistle around his neck, he looked poised to call a shot, only his body was twisted to catch a look at Annie; mouth unsmiling, jaw tight and his eyes full of hunger, need . . . love.

A sound escaped him as he tossed down the picture and walked towards the door. Heart pounding, emotions high, he left, not looking back – and missing the shadow standing besides the house watching him go.

Annie stormed to the kitchen in the big house, sure that a large, fattening breakfast would cure her sudden blues.

But the kitchen was empty, which meant if she wanted breakfast she'd have to cook it herself. She frowned, knowing exactly how unappetizing that would be.

'What do you think you're doing here, girl?'

Annie jumped at the sharp crack of Rosemary's voice. The older woman stood in the doorway, wearing a ratty-looking robe, her grey, limpid hair sticking out in messy clumps. There wasn't a spot of make-up on the pale, angry face. 'I asked you a question.'

Annie stepped towards her hesitantly. 'Rosemary? Is everything all right?'

'No, of course not.' Rosemary stormed into the room, obviously oblivious to the fact she wasn't dressed. 'I called for you an hour ago, and I expected you to be on time. Let's go.'

'Go?' Annie repeated in confusion. She glanced quickly in the hall, looking for Jeannine. She was almost sure Rosemary was having a bad day, but sometimes it was hard to tell . . . she seemed so lucid. And very angry. 'Where do you need to go, Rosemary?' she asked gently.

Rosemary whirled, the confusion and scared eyes in complete contrast with the rage on the face. 'I told you the address on the phone. You cab drivers are supposed to keep track of such things, I can't possibly be responsible for not knowing – ' She ended on a quick sob, stuffing her fist in her mouth.

'It's OK, Rosemary,' Annie said quietly, going quickly to her.

'I can't remember where I'm supposed to go,' she whispered. 'I don't remember where I belong.'

Jeannine ran into the room, looking wild with worry. Her shoulders slumped with relief when she caught sight of Rosemary. With ease, she led the woman out, cooing softly to her.

Annie's breath whistled out and she leaned back against the counter, feeling drained. God, she thought, how could Noah keep his cool and deal with this every day? It must be killing him.

She heaped a plate full of cinnamon buns and then loaded on the butter, ignoring the sound of the back door behind her. She wasn't ready to face an angry Noah.

But a second later, she whirled in fright as the unmistakable stench of burning wood and paint hit her nostrils. The back door to the kitchen was ablaze.

Instead of running out of the hall door to safety, instead of grabbing the phone and dialing the emergency services, instead of trying to extinguish the flames with the fire extinguisher she could see so plainly on the wall, she did the only thing she could.

She screamed.

CHAPTER 8

Noah was halfway between Annie's cottage and the big house when he heard her scream. He started running, the sound of her cry shaving years off his life, but the smoke rising from the back of the house spoke for itself.

'Call 911,' he shouted to one of the older kids who was standing in alarm on the porch.

The petrified boy nodded and ran.

Skidding to a stop, Noah stared in shock at the back door to the kitchen. It was the only thing on fire, yellow, hot flames licking at the frame. Noah yanked the garden hose off the grass, turned it on and held it to the fire, realizing that it was a relatively small blaze and easily extinguishable.

The door was still smoking when he jerked it open, hose in hand. Annie was frozen in place against the table, eyes wide, hands behind her to brace her. Sirens wailed in the distance as he dropped the hose and crossed the kitchen to her.

She flew into his arms, trembling violently.

'It's all right, babe,' he said, the endearment slipping off his tongue with such ease he didn't even realize he'd said it. Stroking soothing hands up her back, he tried to dispel her racking tremors. 'It's out. The fire's out.'

'He's at it again,' she gulped against his chest, gripping handfuls of his shirt in her fisted hands. 'I can't stand it, Noah.'

An overwhelming anger at whoever was doing this to them took hold of him. That the fire had been set to terrorize, not damage, spoke for itself. They were dealing with a desperately sick pyromaniac.

And despite his best intentions, Annie had nearly been hurt. Again.

When Ross arrived, looking wan and shaky himself, the first thing he did was hug a pale Annie. The man had downed more than twice the alcohol Noah had and yet he managed to put it behind him to give his daughter comfort. Noah felt as if a train were charging through his head, so he knew exactly how bad Ross must feel, and he felt his respect for the man grow. Even if Ross didn't think he was good enough for his daughter . . .

Ross took one look at the metal-sheathed door that was scorched black and the carpet rug in front that was singed to the floor timbers and shook his head. To one side of the door, still soaked by the water from the hose, were crisps of cardboard, a mangled umbrella, and a woman's molten wellingtons. Ross lifted the rug, smelled it, then looked around for a long, silent moment.

'What?' Noah demanded.

Ross sighed. 'It's under investigation. I'm sorry, Noah, that's all I can tell you.'

Noah's frustration exploded. 'Damn it, Ross, screw your investigation! This is my house and I want to know what you found.'

Ross raised his head and looked sadly around the room. 'OK. But you're not going to like it. Judging from the severity of the burn marks in the floor underneath here, I figure someone poured gasoline into this box of rain gear and then set it alight. It's a good thing you were so close and could contain it so promptly. It could have brought the rest of the room down in a few more seconds, the entire house in minutes.'

Jesus. 'I thought we were safe. Isn't that what you told us, Ross? That we were safe?'

'Noah – ' Annie started in a defensive voice. 'It's not Ross's fault.'

'It's all right, Annie,' Ross said quietly. 'This investigation has gone on too long; we're all on edge.'

'So is it the same pyro who gets his thrills from haunting you for some petty revenge?' Noah asked furiously, reaching for Annie's cold hand.

The sadness fled Ross's eyes, to be replaced by a cool, simmering anger. 'If it is, we'll catch him. But I think that we'd do better to look closer to home this time. You have any troublemakers here?'

'No,' Noah said quickly, forcefully. '*Absolutely not. And you're way off base.*'

'Now, Noah,' Ross said quietly, his eyes showing his sympathy at having to ask. 'I know that you take in kids who have had a rough time. These kids can hold their problems in pretty deep. A fire like this isn't necessarily anger against you, it's a release of their frustration.'

'None of my kids would do this,' Noah said adamantly. And he believed it with his whole heart. He wished for a bottle of aspirin.

'Have you had any kids lately cause any damage around here? Any kind of damage at all?'

Noah's eyes rolled to Annie and he knew she was thinking of Gerry and how he'd tossed the apples down the stairs. But that had been different. Way different. Gerry would *not* set fire to his back door. 'Nothing like this.'

Ross sighed, slid his eyes to the kitchen door briefly, and slipped his hands into his pockets. Noah knew he was well aware, as he himself was, that most of the boys were eavesdropping from the other side of the door.

'Well,' Ross said slowly and clearly, 'that's all the questions I have for now. The fire was a relatively small one and there were no injuries.' He paused meaningfully. 'But if that fire had been able to spread, everyone in this house could have been gone before the firefighters had even shown. I would hope that if anyone knew anything about this fire – anything at all – he or she would be able to come forward and be honest about it.'

No one said a word.

But Noah had never been more sure of anything in his life. This wasn't the work of anyone in this house – and, judging by the panic in Annie's eyes, she knew it too.

Everyone seemed on edge. Noah felt it even more than the others. Fear motivated him, fear for Annie's life. He caught her walking along the bluffs in the late afternoon, looking alone and frightened.

'Ross is wrong,' she said flatly without looking at him as he caught up with her and matched her slow stride.

'I know.'

'None of those kids started that fire.'

He wanted to smile at her vehement protection of his kids, but the topic was far too serious. Every last one of them had been shaken by the fire. Noah had tried to explain to each of them that he didn't blame anyone in his house, but he wasn't sure the message had been clear.

'I don't think so either,' he told her, startled when she grabbed his hand. But she made no other move towards him and they just kept walking.

The sun made its lazy descent over the deep blue ocean to their left, casting a yellow glow over the water. The sound of the surf soothed, the warm salt air invigorated. Noah felt some of his tension drain away.

'Sometimes,' she said so quietly that he had to lean closer, 'I think it would have been better if I'd stayed away.'

'Better?'

'Safer.'

She was scared. He hated that. 'I won't let anything happen to you.'

She glanced at him, smiled wistfully. 'My hero?' He scowled and she laughed. 'I'm kidding,' she assured him. 'You aren't hero material.'

Well, he knew that, but he didn't especially like her pointing it out. 'I've saved your hide several times, if I remember correctly.'

She ignored that and took the concrete steps down that would lead them to the beach. At the bottom, she slipped out of her sandals, gave him an impish look and headed for the water.

For a minute he watched her walk away, his gaze caught by how nicely her cut-offs showed off her legs and hips. The shirt she wore didn't quite meet the waistline of her shorts, showing him smooth skin he knew would feel warm and soft to his touch.

Noah rolled his eyes at himself and followed her. 'What are you up to, Laverty?'

'Absolutely nothing, Bones.'

He knew that tone all too well, or at least he remembered it from his past. She *was* up to something, and it was no good.

She stepped into the wet sand, played her toes in it. The next wave splashed to her ankles. 'Feels good.'

'I'm *not* getting into a water fight with you.'

She glanced up innocently, flashing him a sweet smile as he stood on the edge of the wet sand, his hands on his hips. He couldn't possibly stay way out here on the beach with her looking like that and not kiss her. And he *absolutely* wouldn't kiss her. 'I've got work. I've got to get back.'

'So go.'

She turned her back on him and her shoulders sagged slightly as if he'd rejected her. Damn it. He sighed. She shouldn't be alone. Not when she felt down like this. 'Come on, Annie, come back with me.'

'I'll be back later.'

She didn't look at him. He stepped closer, cursed, then slipped out of his shoes. 'I can't just leave you out here.'

'Sure you can. Just go.'

'Damn it, Annie.' He came up behind her and the next wave hit at his calves. 'I – '

The air whooshed out of his as she bent, scooped a double handful of icy ocean water and tossed it into his face. She straightened and turned, giggling.

He stared at her, water dripping off his nose. 'I can't believe you did that.'

'I'm . . . sorry.'

'No, you're not.'

She slapped her hands against her mouth, but the laugh still escaped. 'Really, I am sorry.'

'You looked sad – '

'Because you wanted to go back to work?' She laughed again. 'And you didn't want me to feel bad? It's OK, Bones. I'm used to being alone. Go to work.'

She didn't need him, didn't want to weep on his shoulder. He should be greatly relieved; he *wanted* to be greatly relieved.

Instead he was the opposite. 'You weren't sad,' he said, knowing he was repeating himself. He couldn't help it, he was shocked. Cold water seeped into his T-shirt and he narrowed his eyes. 'You fooled me.'

'Yeah.' Her eyes shone, her cheeks flushed. She looked adorable.

He was going to get her back. And he was going to enjoy it. Slowly he stalked her. She held up her hands, laughing, and backed away, further into the ocean. 'Now, Noah.' She laughed again. 'It was just a little splash. Just a teeny, tiny little splash to lighten the mood, you know? I mean, the water isn't even that cold and I didn't get you all that wet.'

'Mm-hm,' he agreed, taking another step. 'You would have thought you'd learned your lesson in my kitchen with the flour and lemon-aid.'

'What lesson?' she asked, her eyes widening as a wave hit her at high thigh.

'I *never* lose,' he said softly.

'Oh.' She gasped.

He smiled, albeit a wicked one. He knew exactly what had happened. That last, very cold wave had hit her a little high. The crotch of her shorts was wet. 'What's the matter, Annie? The water isn't all that cold, remember?'

'You – you said you had work,' she said quickly, obviously deciding further retreat wasn't smart. She held her ground as he came to a stop in front of her. 'I'll walk you back,' she offered generously.

'I don't think so. Not yet.' This time she jumped up with the wave, but her shirt got wet. And her body reacted in interesting ways.

'Cold, Annie?' he asked innocently, enjoying her blush.

Her next smile came as quick as the water she splashed against his chest, but he was ready. He scooped her in his arms.

She squealed and wrapped her arms around his neck. 'Noah! Put me down.'

'Nope. Not until you're as wet as me.' He tossed her in the air, easily catching her. She grabbed at his shirt, screaming with laughter.

'Stop!' she demanded. 'Put me down right this minute!'

225

'If you say so,' he said innocently. And he dropped her in the water.

He had to admit later, he made his second mistake by turning his back on her. But the next thing he knew, he was flat on his back in the water next to her. He'd just swiped the water from his face and narrowed his eyes on her laughing one when a huge wave crashed down over both of them.

Noah's fingers flew quickly over the keyboard as he stared at the computer screen in his office. A quick glance out of the window told him the night was a dark one. And seeing as it was the night before the big ball, he should have been tucked into bed getting sleep – but he couldn't.

He'd got a late start at work, thanks to Annie and her antics at the beach. He still couldn't believe she'd bested him and he'd take great joy in planning his revenge. He wouldn't be allowed to forget what had happened for a long while, because Annie had told everyone in the house she'd beat him at his own game.

The boys had eaten it up.

His smile faded quickly. Every boy but Gerry had got a kick out of Noah getting drenched by a girl because he was missing. Martin said it was because of the kitchen fire. The thought that he was running because of that disturbed Noah, because he knew Gerry couldn't have set it. Martin swore that the two of them had been together in their room – and Noah believed him.

So why would Gerry run? The answer tore at Noah's heart. He had run because he thought he would be blamed. The kid had so little confidence in his own ability to prove his innocence and so little faith in the people around him that he felt running was his only alternative. Noah had been forced to call the police and notify them that the boy was missing because of the regulations of foster care, but he hadn't wanted to. The police would only terrify him and what Noah wanted was to bring Gerry back himself, convince him that he wasn't a suspect and help him to understand that Noah was on his side. Hope had bloomed earlier when Ed discovered food missing from the kitchen. Noah was positive that Gerry was hiding somewhere close by and that Martin was squirrelling him food – which was more than fine. As long as Gerry was close by, he was relatively safe and that was Noah's main concern. Purposely he and his other staff had spread the word that the arsonist was a pyromaniac who had nothing to do with the Taylor House and that none of the kids was suspected.

He hoped that would be enough for Gerry and that he would come back soon. If not, Noah would find him. He'd grown up here once too, and he knew every hiding spot for miles around.

There was something else keeping Noah awake – and it had nothing to do with the Taylor House. It was his golden-haired, stormy-eyed house guest. He was unable to stop thinking about her. Images of her were haunting him. How small and vulnerable she was. How terrified she'd looked after the kitchen door fire, the way she'd looked in her cabin when she had told him he had said he wanted her.

They agreed on that one point – they wanted each other. But to take that step with Annie would be different from the way it had been with other women. It would mean other things, things he wasn't capable of.

It didn't matter – she was leaving.

Firmly ignoring the ache in his chest over that depressing thought, he forced himself to remember – it wasn't safe to let his heart loose. Pain always came with it. He wasn't up to the heartbreak.

He thought work would ease his mind. He was staring at the city's computer program. To his surprise he found he had been cleared for access to complete employee records, including the fire department. An idea struck him and for the next few minutes his fingers worked fast and furious, his mind absorbing the interesting information. Work succeeded in taking his mind off things, specifically Annie – until she showed up.

'Could you stand some company?'

He jumped and whirled in his chair at her soft voice. She stood in his doorway, wearing a soft-looking sweater, faded jeans and a spooked expression that explained her presence.

'Bad dream, huh?'

She nodded.

He kicked another chair towards her and she sat down with a grateful look that eased her taut and strained features. 'Another fire?' he asked her, wishing he could ease her mind enough that she wouldn't have those nightmares. The only way that was going to happen was for the arsonist to be caught.

'It was a bad one.' She sighed, looking down at her hands, which she spread wide. 'I tried to yank Jesse and my mother out of the car, but all I did was burn myself. And the pain was so real . . .' She turned her hands over as if she expected to see horrific burns spread there.

He understood all too well. 'For years after it happened,' he told her, 'I'd dream about it every night. Different kinds. One night I was with them, trapped in that burning inferno. Another I'd be on the outside, trying to get at them – but I never could. It went on like that . . . over and over again.'

'Me too,' she told him. 'But after a while they faded away. Now that I'm back here they've started again. And it doesn't help now that the arsonist is at it again.'

He wanted to tell her that between what he was beginning to suspect and what the fire department and its team of investigators knew, the arsonist would soon be caught, but he couldn't. To tell her would be to put her in even more danger. But he hated the worry and pain he saw swirling in her eyes and knew that if something happened to her before they solved the crime he would never forgive himself.

Scooting his chair forward, he reached for her hands. 'It will soon be all over.'

'You think so?'

He nodded, his senses reeling from being in such close confines with her.

'Any word of Gerry?' she asked, those stormy eyes anxious and tormented.

'No, not yet. I'm still sure that Martin knows more than he's telling but I'm not going to force the issue. I'd much rather Gerry come back on his own.'

'You think he'll resent you if you force him to come back?'

'I would have,' he said wryly.

'Noah,' she said with a small smile, 'at Gerry's age, you resented everything and everyone.'

'True,' he admitted with a shrug. 'It leaves me in a perfect position to understand, doesn't it? But if he's not back in another day or two I'll bring the country-side down looking for him. We'll find him.'

Her smile lingered as she studied his face.

'What?'

'Whatever happened to that earring you used to wear? The one that Rosemary always threatened to yank out?'

'You remember that?'

'Yeah' Her smile softened as their eyes connected,

holding until he actually felt a physical jolt. 'I remember a lot of things.'

He did too. He remembered how he'd always worried about her following them, worried about her getting hurt or in trouble. Jesse had always laughed at his concerns, saying that his sister was very capable and could handle herself. Noah couldn't help it, he worried anyway.

'You were a handful back then, Annie.' He ran a finger across one cheek. 'Still are.'

'I know. Stubborn and persistent, too. So what happened to that earring, Bones?'

'Persistent isn't the right word,' he said mildly, sitting back. 'People in the tennis world were calling me the Bad Boy of Tennis. And – '

'And you couldn't stand being labelled so you took it out.' She grinned. 'Oh, Noah, you always took such pleasure from being totally unpredictable. It's nice that some things never change.' Her warm and steady gaze never left him. 'Thanks for sending some of the kids to help me pack. They were a great help.'

'They're good kids.'

'I know. I think so too,' she said with the soft smile that never failed to warm him.

'They like you. You made it seem so effortless.'

'It breaks my heart to know what they've been through and how they've suffered.'

Her expressive eyes told him that she hadn't forgotten he'd started his own life in the same way.

231

'Kids are amazing that way; they bounce back well. They're getting better here.' Of their own accord, his fingers reached out to massage hers gently.

'Thanks to you. They worship you, you know.'

'I don't want that.'

'I know. But they see what you've done with your life and it gives them hope. It encourages them.' She hesitated. 'I think what you do here is pretty terrific. You didn't have to come back here and continue the Taylor House after your tour. You could have let Rosemary close it down.'

He frowned and pulled his hands back. 'Anyone would have done it, Annie. Don't make me out to be some kind of saint.'

'No,' she said with a quick shake of her head that had her hair flying, teasingly tickling his face. 'A saint you're not, and I'm in a position to know. But you are a compassionate, sensitive man who knows first-hand what those children have experienced – and one I respect with all my heart. I think you're wrong, Noah. Not just anyone would have continued the Taylor House, supporting it with his own earnings. Most people would have shut it down because of how difficult it is to run or let someone run it for them.'

'That would have killed Rosemary,' he said. 'This place is her life.'

Annie smiled, a beautiful smile that did something to Noah's insides. 'I know that. I just wanted you to know that I think what you're doing is special.' She leaned forward and grabbed his hands again. 'And I think you're pretty special too.'

He brought her hands to his lips and kissed her fingers while he slid her chair closer. She was between his legs now and he ceased to think, just acted with the emotions that were humming within him. Leaning forward slightly gave him all the access he needed and he settled his mouth against her neck, closing his eyes to savour the softness of her skin.

He was still holding her hands, and the sense of power he garnered from her wildly scrambling pulse was pure ego, but he couldn't help it. When she pulled her hands from his and put them on his shoulders, gripping tight, he brought his own to her waist to pull her to his lap. Her sweater was soft and giving and her jeans snug enough that he could feel her every curve.

'The last time we were alone,' she reminded him breathlessly as his arms curved around her waist, holding her close, 'we argued.'

'No,' he murmured against her neck, pressing soft kisses along her jawbone. 'You were looking for trouble – and got it.'

'I . . .' She paused with a gasp as his teeth raked at her earlobe. 'I . . . never laughed at you, Noah. I just wanted you to need me the way I need you.'

He went still, remembering how shaken he'd been to see those pictures of himself, how fierce his own expression had been as he stared at her, how much emotion he'd shown her without even knowing it.

Annie's hands slid from his shoulders to around his neck, pulling him close. 'Don't,' she whispered. 'Don't you dare pull back now, Noah Taylor. I didn't mean to bring it up again.' She bent her head and nuzzled his ear with her lips. 'Please.'

His eyes slammed shut with a groan as she pressed herself tight against him, her lips drawing shivers down his spine. 'Annie,' he said hoarsely, needing to tell her before he lost all capability of thinking. 'It's OK to tell me what you're thinking – I don't want you to hide it.'

'No matter how it makes you feel?'

'Yes,' he said intensely. 'And if I'm a jerk, just kiss me.'

He felt her smile against his neck. 'All right, then,' she murmured, raising her head, and with her eyes wide open on his, she kissed him.

And as always, he was lost.

When she lifted her head a minute later, he was dazed.

'I think,' she said with a dreamy little smile, pushing herself off his lap. 'I can definitely sleep now.'

'But – ' He watched her, making a disparaging sound as she pushed the other chair aside, stepped over a pile of papers and headed for the door. 'Where are you going?' Damn it, she couldn't just kiss him like that – with her mind, body and soul – and then leave.

'To bed.' She sent him a special, knowing look that was filled with such tenderness and passion that he was momentarily struck dumb. 'Goodnight, Noah.'

'Annie,' he said, standing and moving towards her. One hand reached for hers, his other curled around her waist, drawing her close. 'I want you.'

'I know. You've told me.' Softly she ran a finger over his lips, her eyes sparkling with desire. 'And I want you. But you've already promised me that when we make love it will be some place warm and soft, some place where we can be alone.'

He cursed his own words.

'You wanted to kiss me all over, "every inch of my body" you said, and I want to be able to do the same.' Her light fingers brushed over his cheek as excitement stirred his blood and his body tightened with an ache only she could ease. Gently she disentangled herself from him and stepped over the threshold of the door, looking back at him with eyes that smouldered like ashes.

'It will happen, Annie.' He wanted it so badly, it had to be true.

She smiled, a wicked, hot smile. And then she was gone, leaving him far too keyed up to even think about sleeping. He was uncomfortably warm . . . and un-believably aroused.

The annual ball was something every local looked forward to. Held at the historical City Hall, which was an old brick building dating back to the beginning of the century, it was the event of the year. Anyone who was anyone attended, and the local stations covered it on the news. Annie remembered its reputation from when she was a child and her parents had gone. So it seemed strange – and nostalgic – to be making her own preparations to go.

There wasn't a mirror, other than the small one covering the medicine chest, to be found in the entire cottage. For weeks she'd got along fine without one; she wasn't working and it was summer. There'd been no need for much make-up and she'd dressed mostly in her favourites – shorts and T-shirts. But now she was on the date of her life – she hoped – and she wanted to make sure everything looked perfect.

She could see the top half of the slinky black sheath that was posing as a formal dress. Held up by thin spaghetti straps, it showed off her lightly tanned shoulders. Jumping up once, she was able to catch a glimpse of the bottom half of undeniably the sexiest thing she owned. Deciding against stockings at the last minute – mostly because she hated them, but also because she laddered the only pair she owned trying them on – she silently thanked her mother for handing her down a decent pair of legs.

She artfully piled her hair on top of her head, secured it with a handful of pins and left the bathroom. A quick glance around the small cottage verified what she'd been trying to deny in her heart for weeks.

She was leaving tomorrow.

Knowing it was for the best didn't help. Knowing

she had a job to do, one that she wanted to hold on to, didn't help either.

She didn't want to leave Noah. Unfortunately, she didn't have a reason to stay.

A knock at the door came simultaneously with the ring of the telephone and both startled her out of her thoughts. Noah had installed the telephone after the intruder had been there and she hadn't yet got used to it. Jittery, she reached for the door first.

Noah was standing there looking too magnificent for words in his black dinner-jacket. His dark hair was still damp from his recent shower and he smelled heavenly. Heart aching, Annie watched Noah's moody eyes roam over her, her skin tingling everywhere they touched.

'Wow,' was all he managed to say, his eyes finally meeting hers.

The phone rang again and she laughed nervously as she reached for it, her eyes glued to his. 'Hello?'

'Well, you've outdone yourself this time, Annie.'

'Sue.' There was no mistaking that New York-accented voice.

'None other.' She laughed in delight. 'Simply outstanding, darling.'

'What are you talking about?' Annie asked her, still staring at Noah. He came in and shut the door from the cool night air, watching her with a matching gravity.

'The photos you sent me. How could you have

forgotten? The coastline, the cliffs, the green – they're absolutely stunning.'

'Thanks. I thought you might like them, since you've complained about never having been to the west coast.'

'Like them?' Sue asked incredulously. 'I love them. And it's your new assignment. I need more. We're going to do an entire issue on California.'

'An entire issue?'

'Yep. And I need hundreds more shots. Can you handle it?'

Annie dropped into the chair by the telephone. Sue was offering her a chance to stay around for a little while, giving her an excuse. She glanced at Noah, only to find his intense eyes on her. 'I don't know,' she said weakly. Could she handle staying here, loving a man who wasn't willing to return that love?

'Think about it, honey. It's the chance of a lifetime. I'll call you Monday.' And the line went dead.

Annie stared at the receiver in her hand, then slowly hung it up.

'Everything all right?' Noah asked her when she didn't move.

'Yeah.'

He took her arm as she stood and suddenly he smiled.

'What's so funny?' she asked, a reluctant grin tugging at her mouth. He was so irresistible when he smiled.

'You're wearing heels. Tall ones.'

'You're observant.'

'And you're a smart ass.'

'Is there a point here?'

'The point is,' he said huskily as he drew her close and kissed the top of her nose, 'that you're nearly as tall as I am. I like it.'

She snickered. With her high-heeled sandals she neared six feet. He topped her by only a few inches. 'Most men would feel threatened.'

'Is that what you were hoping for?' he asked in an amused voice, his eyes lit up.

'Nah. But a little intimidation never hurts.'

'Baby, with those legs, intimidate me all you want.'

She rolled her eyes. 'You're sick.'

'I know, but you like it.'

Outside, they walked back towards the main house where Noah kept his car.

'Where's Rosemary?'

He levelled his dark gaze on her and smiled sardonically, looking so devastatingly handsome that Annie wanted to cry. How was she going to leave?

'I was informed that this was a date – between only you and me,' he said.

Whatever amount of joy she'd managed to retain about the evening faded into a growing sense of sorrow and gloom. He was doing nothing more than fulfilling a promise. A promise that had been extracted against his will. 'I'm sorry if you feel you had to do this,

Noah,' she told him quietly, willing her voice to remain strong. 'But it's not too late to back out – '

'I've no intention of backing out,' Noah said with equal solemnity, startling her by touching a loose strand of her hair that had already escaped its hold. 'Have you?'

His eyes were alight with challenge – and mischief. Relieved to see it, and some of her old Noah, she smiled. 'Not a chance.'

'Well, then,' he said, holding out his elbow for her to take. 'Shall we go?'

He held the car door while she slid into the seat of his Mustang. When she straightened her legs he slowly shook his head, his expression one of stunned marvel. When he folded himself in next to her, his eyes once again travelled over her. 'I mean it, Annie. You look . . . ravishing.'

His choice of words, warm smile and sparkling eyes had her heart-rate accelerating. She wished things could have turned out differently . . . but she wasn't going to waste tonight on regrets. 'You look pretty OK yourself, Bones. It's amazing how well you clean up.'

He chuckled, then laughed. 'You always had a smart mouth on you, Laverty.' He glanced at her and shook his head. 'But that body . . . now that's new. You were a skinny runt last time I saw you.'

'I was thirteen,' she said indignantly. 'And you liked me well enough.'

'I tolerated you,' he corrected, turning on the engine and pulling away from the house.

He and Jesse had more than tolerated her. In spite of their five-year age-difference, they had treated her as an equal and had looked out for her with a care and patience not usually found in kids – especially teen-agers. But she was feeling enchanted enough with the forthcoming evening to let his comment slide.

Nothing was going to ruin this evening for her. Not Sue's offer, which threw her off balance giving her an option she hadn't considered, not Noah's hesitation to give her what she knew he was capable of giving, not the as-yet-unfound arsonist who couldn't seem to get enough of the Lavertys.

And certainly not the fact that she was desperately in love with the man sitting next to her.

They arrived before any of the other guests did, by design. As host, Noah was expected to be there to greet the guests and offer small talk. A task he hated, but tolerated because of the cause.

The Taylor House.

And he'd do anything for it, including giving up one night a year to pretend to be social.

He sighed, knowing he'd deliberately misled Annie into thinking Rosemary would be here tonight. She wouldn't. When he'd left her in the care of her devoted nurse, she couldn't even find the door to her room without forgetting where she wanted to go.

Pain shot through him, but he wouldn't give in to it, not tonight. Tonight he'd get through the dreaded ball by himself, and he'd do it for Rosemary. She would want it that way.

He craned his neck past the new arrivals, wondering where Annie had disappeared to. She was nowhere in sight. For the next hour he shook hands and smiled more times than he cared to count, but the entire time his eyes were searching through the DJs and formal gowns for Annie.

His popularity gave him no sense of satisfaction. In fact, it bothered him greatly. There were hundreds of people here, all wanting a moment with him. Yet every last one of them ignored the fact that when he was growing up here he was an absolute nobody. Worse than a nobody, he had been the butt of their jokes, their punching bag.

Funny to be in a room, surrounded by people who were familiar, yet feel totally and completely alone.

He wanted Annie.

He walked and smiled some more, nodding at Ross and some others he recognized as the fire chief and city commissioner – all of whom he now knew personally, thanks to his computer job and the arsonist. Soon, he silently promised Annie, soon it would all be over.

But where was she?

It was then that he saw her. His hungry eyes ran over her and his blood started pumping. She was wearing that dress that should have been outlawed,

surrounded by a group of locals that he recognized –
most of them men. Probably begging her for a dance,
he thought with some disgust, and she was holding
court with more dignity than the Queen of England.

It didn't matter; he wanted to be with her and no
one else.

Her dress was glimmering under the colourful
lights, her hair shining like fire. And he wanted her.
He came up besides her in time to hear her light
laughter.

Grabbing her hand, he brought it up to his lips,
meeting her startled eyes. Slowly, softly, he kissed her
knuckles while his ravenous eyes roamed over her.
'Hi,' he said quietly, completely ignoring the others
standing around them.

'Er . . . hi,' she stuttered, as he squeezed her hand
gently. She looked at the others, obviously flustered.
'Noah, you remember . . .' At her horrified blank
expression he smiled knowingly, rescuing her with
ease.

'If you'll excuse us, gentlemen,' he said, his eyes
directly on Annie's, 'I need to steal Ms Laverty away
for a few minutes.'

He pulled her from the elegant ballroom so that they
stood in the hallway before the kitchen. She smiled up
at him uncertainly and he pulled her to him and kissed
her.

The din around them waned so that the roaring in
his head was all he could hear. Annie made a soft

sound and pushed closer, returning his hard kiss without question, stealing what little breath he had left. Another little sound escaped her and he kissed her again, loving the sweet taste of her, loving the feel of her bare arms wrapped tight around his neck, loving the desperate feel of her caged passion and wondering what she would do if he dragged her home right then. Christ, his knees went weak just thinking about it.

The kitchen door opened behind them and a waiter carrying a loaded tray of drinks passed through, pausing to send them a sympathetic smile while they shifted out of his way.

Annie looked up at Noah with limpid eyes and a wet, swollen mouth.

'Your lipstick is gone,' he observed with a small smile.

She grinned. 'That's because you're wearing it.'

'Funny.' He wiped his mouth with his handkerchief and it came away peach-coloured. She smirked. 'Very funny,' he said again, shoving the handkerchief back into his pocket.

Knowing he should go back out and smile some more, but wanting only to be with Annie, he decided a compromise was in order. 'Dance?'

She glanced out on the dance floor where hundreds of people were swaying to the music, then to his knee. 'Should you?'

He thought about his host duties. 'Definitely not. But let's anyway.' It was easier said than done. The floor was crowded with couples, all dressed to the nines in glittering evening gowns and black jackets, but it didn't matter to Noah. Together they threaded their way towards the dance floor, hands entwined, souls colliding.

For Noah, dancing with Annie was like nothing he'd done before. She walked into his arms in the small space they found and they eased up against each other with the natural grace of two people who'd known each other forever. Holding each other tight, they swayed, dipped and glided together, their bodies clinging with a mind of their own.

Only this wasn't just two old friends having a dance together. It was much, much more. Her arms around him felt like heaven, the soft scent of lilacs and rosemary wafted up from her hair, and her glowing eyes were filled with yearning and desire – all for him. It ignited his own heat, his own need, and as they flowed together with a subtle movement he could feel her hitched breath, her tight nipples pressed against his chest, her hips moving against his. Squeezing her even closer, he knew she could feel his own arousal, his own frantic heart, and when she sighed, the sound filled with longing, he nearly groaned aloud with pleasure.

One song drifted into another as Noah tried to deny what he was feeling. When he closed his eyes against the onslaught of the unaccustomed emotions, his sense of touch was heightened and Annie's long, lithe body against his was almost too much to bear. The music faded and still they swayed together, his heart bouncing off his chest in response to what had been the most erotic, sensuous experience of his life. The hundreds of people swirling around them might never have existed, for he could hear and see nothing but Annie. Grateful for the dim light, Noah released her hand, but Annie stayed pressed against him. Sure that the desperate need for her was plastered across his face for the world to see, he averted it, but Annie touched his jaw with long, elegant fingers and their eyes met.

'I love you,' she said quietly, and as he looked at her – stunned beyond words – she reached up and kissed him softly once, pulled away, and disappeared into the crowd.

CHAPTER 9

The rest of the evening was a blur to Noah. He made his expected speech, toasted when there were toasts, smiled as required – but he remembered none of it.

Because Annie was gone. She was nowhere to be found and, because of the deep, empty feeling deep within him, he knew she'd left the ball. How could she just say what she'd said and leave? As much as he didn't want to talk about those three words, he knew they had to – or it would never be the same between them again.

Hell, who was he fooling? It wouldn't be the same regardless.

She'd said she loved him. Thirty-two years old and he'd never said those words, never thought he could. But Annie had said them to him, and he knew she meant it, could see it overflowing from her lovely eyes, could feel it in her body as she'd gently rubbed against him when they'd danced.

'Where's Annie?' Ross asked, coming up to him

near the flowing fountain of champagne. 'I want to dance with her.'

'She's – '

'She looks beautiful tonight,' Ross said proudly. 'I fool myself sometimes thinking she's still a kid, but when I look at her tonight, all I see is a stunning woman.'

'I – I think so too,' Noah stuttered, feeling like a stupid kid. He hated that. 'But I'm afraid you're too late for that dance.'

Ross's eyes sharpened. 'She's left?'

'I think so.'

'What's going on, son? I thought you had this thing handled between the two of you.'

Noah glanced at Ross's amused face with confusion. 'Not that whatever's happening between us is any of your business, but I thought you didn't approve.'

'Maybe not, at first. You'll have to forgive an old man, judging you for being the boy you were. But I realized, like Annie, you too had grown up. I like the man you've become, Noah. You make Rosemary proud.'

Noah blinked, uncomfortable and unused to such compliments. 'Thank you. As far as Annie – '

'You know,' Ross said, smiling broadly, 'the way you two deny there's anything going on is a dead giveaway.'

Noah closed his mouth, feeling the colour creep up his face.

Ross must have taken pity. He leaned forward and tapped Noah's arm. 'Don't worry, son. I'll cover for you. Go find her and fix whatever stupid thing you've done. Unfortunately it's the man's job to be the fool.'

Not knowing what the hell he was going to say to Annie, not even understanding what he felt for her, Noah took Ross's advice and left the ball to find her.

She wasn't in her cottage, nor in the big house. It wasn't until after he'd checked the Laverty house that he started to worry. Where could she have gone?

Sinking into the large swing on the porch of the Taylor House, refusing to give in to despair, Noah thought hard. Over and over again he heard her soft declaration of love and he had to admit – it thrilled him.

The sound of crashing waves carried over from the cliffs, enticing him, offering him comfort. Without a care for his dinner-jacket or leather shoes, he climbed down the steep steps, inhaling deeply the salty, wet air. It was a dark night, the sky full of deep grey clouds that churned angrily. A summer storm was brewing, he thought. Fitting.

If he hadn't been so in tune with her, so desperate to find her, he might have walked right past her as she sat on the beach, for she wore black against the black cliffs, the black sky, the dark sand.

Annie sat near the water's edge, staring out at the seething, foaming ocean. Tendrils of hair had come loose from their bonds and they whipped wildly about

249

her face in the wind. Her heels were off and lay in the sand next to her. One strap of her dress had dropped off her shoulder and, as he watched, she shivered, hugging her knees close. His heart clenched at the absolute misery on her face.

'Annie.'

She lifted her face. The cloudy sky was a perfect match for her glorious eyes – moody as hell. He heard her soft sound of distress when she saw him. Pushing to her feet, she picked up her heels and swung them in her hand as she stood staring mutely at him.

'I was worried sick,' he said. 'I couldn't find you anywhere.'

'I'm sorry,' she whispered, dropping her eyes. She sighed, then stared at him, her eyes shimmering. 'But I can't bring myself to be sorry about what I said. I didn't mean to say it, but it just built up until I couldn't keep it inside any more. I don't expect you to say it back.'

He opened his mouth to say something, he wasn't sure what. Before he could, she whispered, 'Have to go.'

And she turned and walked off into the dark.

Annie wanted to run down the beach as fast as she could, but managed to curb the impulse, since she knew Noah was watching her. Her vision was blurred with unshed tears, tears she refused to let go. All right, so she'd jumped the gun, spoken those three little words that she knew had struck terror into his heart. But she couldn't have stopped them and she refused to regret it.

She'd leave tomorrow, assignment or not. There was no way she could handle being this close to Noah, with him knowing how she felt about him.

The surf tumbled and roared on to the sand, making the earth tremble beneath her bare feet. The cliffs to her left were tall and imposing in the dark, disappearing into the black sky. And she had never felt so alone in her entire life.

A firm but gentle hand stopped her and turned her around. Noah's face was dark, intense. She waited for him to speak, but he didn't – a silent testament to why he had stopped her – and in response her heart started a heavy pulse and her insides tightened.

He stepped closer and cupped her cheek. Drinking in the hunger and longing in his eyes, her heart beat even faster as she raised a hand to cover his.

He kissed her then, using his tongue, his heart, his soul, until she was clinging helplessly to him, knees weak. By the time he lifted his head she was in a trance.

'I want you,' his low-timbred, husky voice said. 'I want you more than anything. But I won't lie to you.'

'I know,' she whispered, her heart cracking.

He seemed desperate to make her understand. Eyes as black as coal bored right through her. 'I don't know about love,' he admitted quietly, his thumb tracing her jaw. 'But you mean more to me than anyone I know, more than anyone ever has.' He watched her carefully. 'Is that enough?'

His eyes held passion, honest affection, a touch of fear and much, much more. He just didn't know it yet, she thought. 'Yes,' she whispered. 'It's enough.'

'I don't want to hurt you. God, that's the last thing I want to do.' He cupped her face, tilting it up, trying to see her expression in the dark night.

Annie knew it was inevitable, knew also that she wanted Noah Taylor, had wanted him from the first moment she'd come back into town, and she couldn't – wouldn't – deny herself. 'Kiss me again,' she whispered.

He did, almost before the words were out of her mouth. He sank to his knees in the sand, pulling her down with him. Deft fingers scattered the few remaining pins holding up her hair, then ran through it. Warm hands ran down her arms, her back, up her bare legs.

'All night I've been wondering . . .' he whispered hoarsely, 'what you're wearing beneath this dress.'

'Not much,' she whispered back, listening to his sharp intake of breath as his fingers discovered that fact for himself. He slowly, tantalizingly pushed the remaining strap off her shoulder, pulled the slinky material down as his fingers explored every inch of exposed skin. With similar care he looked at her body, eyes filled with such heat that she couldn't breathe.

Without a word he lowered his head and opened his

hungry mouth on a bare breast, one hand splayed wide against her back to hold her close. His lips, tongue and teeth suckled her, teased her, tormented her until she cried out with pleasure.

Shrugging out of his jacket, he spread it down on the sand, then pushed away her fumbling fingers and undid his shirt. They tossed aside the rest of their clothes, ignoring the distant thunder and rumbling surf. He pulled her down so they lay facing each other, rough sinew against soft, giving warmth. His arms held her close and her eyes fluttered closed as he kissed her, reducing her to nothing but a shaking, needing mass of nerve-endings.

She could feel him, heavy and hard against her, and thrilled to his groan as she encircled him with her hands. It gave her a courage she usually lacked and a sense of power that was heady indeed. When his fingers smoothed down over her breasts then her belly to the spot that was hot, wet and throbbing between her legs, her breath halted. And as those fingers started a rhythm that made her quiver, her breath started again, coming in quick pants. She felt as if she was going to burst . . . and then she did. Completely. A million stars shot across her vision, streaking the night sky until she could see nothing but brilliant colour.

And before she could catch her breath, before the last tremor shook her, Noah rose over her, spread her thighs and entered her with one quick, powerful thrust. She stared mindlessly up into his dark, intent features as her vision blurred. All senses deserted her on his first stroke and her eyes fluttered closed. And on the next she exploded again, her body lost in the rocking, endless, blinding sensations. Vaguely she was aware of Noah gathering her closer to him, burying his face against her neck and murmuring low words of endearment, then his own pulsing release.

Then he lay over her, his muscles still trembling, his breath as harsh as hers. She held him close, loving the sound of the waves, the glittering stars above. She didn't want ever to move, didn't want him to pull away from her. And maybe the most lovely thing he did was to be just as content as she to prolong their union, for he didn't move from her for a long time.

Eventually he did stir and pushed up to his elbows to cradle her face in his palms. He said nothing, just stared at her with an expression of dazed surprise. His thumbs softly caressed her lips. And, unbelievably, her body responded again, just from him towering over her, his eyes shining down on her as if she were the most special person on earth.

'I'm crushing you,' he murmured, moving to his side and pulling her with him. The sand crunched pleasantly beneath his crushed jacket. 'Do you want to get up?'

She shook her head, desperately wanting him to remain close. He did. Smoothing her hair back from her face, he softly kissed her damp brow. His fingers continued to run over her in tune to her still humming body, leaving thought nearly impossible. It had never been like this for her, she thought. She wanted more.

The oncoming storm had warmed the air and, though a low wind swept over them, it wasn't cold. The waves sounded gently, lulling them.

'I have sand . . . where there shouldn't be sand,' he said after a minute.

She smiled. 'Wimp.'

He ran a fingertip down her neck, across one breast, watching the nipple pucker. 'I love your body,' he said simply. As his mouth lowered, her thoughts scattered as carelessly as the wind around them.

'I want you again,' he murmured against her skin, his voice awed. His fingers brushed over her where she wanted them the most and she couldn't contain her moan. 'Let me make love to you again, Annie,' he whispered softly as his mouth ran over her. 'Please.'

'Yes,' she gasped, her fingers digging into the sand at her sides. 'God, yes.'

It wasn't hurried this time, it wasn't frenzied – not like before. It was soft, tender, and slow – torturously so. He used nothing but fingertips and then his tongue, driving her to the edge of sanity, watching her as she writhed and arched beneath him, making her soar over and over again. When it was her turn to pleasure him, she gave herself up to it until he was rasping her name helplessly as she trailed kisses along every inch of his body. Finally, he tumbled her over and slid so gloriously into her, loving her so magnifi-cently, so thoroughly, that she was robbed of thought, incapable of speech and sure she'd never move again.

The first thing Annie became aware of was the thundering of the waves. Then a large, cold drop landed on her. And another. A streak of lightning lit the night as the rain hit the beach, drenching them within seconds.

'Shit.' Noah leapt to his feet, pulling her up beside him. She swayed, still deliciously off balance, and he steadied her with a soft, knowing smile. He hurriedly helped her dress, then pulled on his very wrinkled, wet trousers and bunched up the rest of his clothes carelessly. 'Come on,' he said taking her hand.

They ran along the beach, shoes in hand. In be-tween the main house and her cottage they hesitated, then silently decided on her cottage. They went straight into the bathroom and shared a hot shower.

Annie ran her soapy hands over Noah's broad shoulders, his smooth chest and sleek back. She couldn't keep her fascinated eyes off his splendid frame and it seemed it was the same for him. He soaped her slowly, his eyes glowing as he watched his hands on her body.

When the hot water ran out he cursed, then pulled her dripping wet from the shower into the tiny space between the tub and sink. Amidst bumped elbows and tangled legs Noah laughingly decided they didn't have enough room for what he wanted to do to her, so he whispered naughty promises in her ear and pulled her gently towards her bedroom.

More than willing, Annie followed him down the hall, laughing at the water still dripping freely off him. At the bedroom door she turned to him, intending to tease him about the amount of water they'd lost in the hallway. It died at the sight of him standing with his back to her, his shoulders stiff, his splendidly nude body absolutely still. He was staring at where she had her things packed up and on the bed, ready to go tomorrow as planned.

She'd completely forgotten. She was leaving.

She had already told him how she felt and she couldn't, wouldn't pretend otherwise. If he didn't feel the same she had no intention of dragging this thing out, using her job as an excuse to stay. It would kill her. Heart in her throat, she approached him.

'You're leaving,' he said flatly.

'You knew I would eventually.' *Ask me to stay*, her heart begged. She could see the fear, the familiar sense of abandonment in his eyes and her heart bled a little for him, for her. 'Will you miss me?'

'No.' He turned from her towards the door.

She followed. 'Liar.'

He came back towards her so abruptly she blinked in surprise. 'All right,' he said tightly, gripping her shoulders and staring miserably into her eyes. 'I'll miss you. You know I will. But you said something

257

tonight, Laverty, that threw me for a loop and had you running tail. It's beyond me to understand how you could say what you did and still leave.'

She tried to shrug off his hands but he wouldn't let her. Never in her adult life had she felt love such as she did for Noah. Maybe she was a little slow in that department, but she understood one thing. Life was difficult enough as it was – and no one should know that better than Noah. Happiness should be taken where it could be found. She stopped fighting him and relaxed under his hands, aching at the tortured, confused look haunting his eyes. 'I said I love you, Noah. And I meant it.'

'But how do you know?' he whispered, convulsedly squeezing his hands on her. 'How can you be so sure?'

'It's just what I feel. I'm not asking you to say it back. Of course I want you to return that love, I can't help it. But my love is a gift, Noah, not a chore. You can't make yourself feel it, you can't force it and you sure as hell can't fake it.' Reaching up, she smoothed away the deep crease between his brows that always appeared when he was troubled. 'It's an offering. From me to you – one that you didn't ask for, but I can't deny. For tonight,' she shrugged helplessly, 'just enjoy it.'

He shook his head in denial of what she was saying. 'After all you just said – how can you just leave?'

How could she not? 'So ask me to stay,' she whispered simply.

Panic flared in his deep, brown eyes. 'I can't.'

Anger surged through her, giving her words a razor sharpness to them she couldn't hold back. 'Why? Because I don't need you the way everyone else around here does?'

Without a word he turned and left the room, going down the hall to the bathroom. He threw a towel to her, then while she wrapped it around herself, he took another and started to dry his body in long, jerky motions. 'That was a low blow,' he said between his teeth.

'Well, it's the truth, isn't it? You've surrounded yourself with people who need you – making sure that you never need anyone more badly than they need you.'

'Goddamn it.' He threw down his towel and turned to her, totally unaware – or uncaring – that he was completely naked. 'I told you – there on the beach – that I wanted you. I care about you. I don't want to hurt you. You said – '

'I know what I said,' Annie told him, her anger draining away. The pain in his eyes was killing her and the love in her heart was overflowing. Love had never been good for him, it had always been thrown in his face, and she had no right to do the same. Her love for him was stronger then that, better than that, and maybe, just maybe she could prove it to him enough so that he too could believe in it. 'I said it was enough.' She stepped towards him then, dropping her towel. 'And it is.'

For now, she thought as his desperate mouth closed hungrily over hers and he yanked her hard against him. It was enough for now.

The sun came up only a couple of short hours later. Annie was sleeping blissfully – with more than three-quarters of the bed and all the covers. Noah gave up the attempt to get even a corner of the blanket and stretched.

She was going to leave – probably today. It made him ache to think about it, but he didn't have any right to ask her to stay. He had nothing to offer her. Nothing at all. Money and material items didn't matter to her – she'd liked him enough long before he'd had any of those things. No, she wanted the one thing he was sure he wasn't capable of. His love.

How could he make her understand that he wasn't good at love? He used to believe he wasn't worthy of love; his sorry excuse for a mother had taught him that. The pathetic system that was supposed to rescue children only reinforced it. It had taken years to learn – everyone deserved love. But somehow, some time or another he'd decided that he didn't need it. Especially since pain always seemed to follow closely behind.

He slid out of bed, his stomach demanding sustenance. Slipping into his soggy, wrinkled trousers, he grimaced. His body was sore in that wonderful, vague way that it could only be after a night of wild sex. No, he frowned, it had been much, much more than just sex. And, with that thought, all his turbulent, confused feelings slammed back into him. It had been the most incredible, awe-inspiring lovemaking he'd ever experienced.

His stomach hurt thinking about it.

She's going to leave, his pathetic heart protested – don't let her leave. But, his mind argued, Annie had a life away from here – a good one. What right did he have to ask her to give that up for him? He had nothing to offer her.

All he had to do, she'd said last night, was ask her to stay, and she would. But he couldn't do that, it wasn't right. He would hurt her.

His stomach cramped again.

Food was what he needed. Annie would too. He wanted to grin foolishly, thinking how much energy they'd burned last night. But the day's reality took the pleasure away. Instead he would cook them a large breakfast and serve it to her in bed. He couldn't help it then, he did grin. Serving breakfast in bed posed some interesting possibilities.

As he stood in front of the stove frying an omelette, the phone rang. He picked it up quickly because he wanted the pleasure of waking Annie up.

'Hello?'

'Hello. This is Sue, Annie's New York editor. Is she in?'

Work was calling her already. Wasn't it enough that Annie was leaving to go back to them? Did they have

261

to call and occupy her mind for the few remaining hours she had? 'She's sleeping,' he said rather curtly.

'Never was a morning person.' Sue laughed. 'Don't wake her, then, she'll be of no use to me if you do. Just tell her I'm waiting on her decision on the assignment in that beautiful country you call California.'

'Decision?'

'Yes,' Sue told him in a New York drawl that grated on his nerves. 'I told her she had until Monday, but I need to know today so that I can prepare someone else for the job if she doesn't take it.'

'Prepare someone else?' He knew he sounded like a complete idiot, but he couldn't help himself.

'I figure that she should take at least a month – do it right. After all, you have more gorgeous scenery out there than I can imagine.' She sighed wistfully. 'Well, anyway. Have her call me with a yes, she's staying, or a no, she's coming back here. And it wouldn't hurt to sweeten the pot, since she's the only photographer who could really do it justice and then have the skill to write about it as well. Tell her I'm offering her more money than she earned on the Scotland piece. OK?'

'OK,' Noah said, dropping the phone back on its cradle. He stared at it, his heart pounding fiercely.

Annie had been offered a chance to stay. Stepping back from the phone as if it had bitten him, he shoved his hands in his pockets, feeling pain and betrayal wash over him. She could have stayed, but she had chosen to leave. Her packed suitcases attested to that.

She'd said she loved him and yet she was choosing – willingly – to walk away. Why? Why would she do that?

Angrily he flipped off the stove and left the cottage, appetite gone.

At the big house he discovered Rosemary was still sick. It was not going to be a good day.

In his office, he stepped over the mess and plopped down into his chair to stare moodily at his computer, booting it up for comfort rather than the need to accomplish work.

Had she lied when she'd said she loved him? Maybe she was no different from his legions of fans, wanting a piece of him and his fame, not caring a whit about the real Noah Taylor.

No, he denied vehemently, Annie wasn't like that – she had never been after who the public thought he was. She liked the Noah that she'd always known.

But, damn it, what the hell was he supposed to think?

He opened some files on the computer, wanting to distract himself. Entering into a classified file was no problem for him now that he'd been given free access. He read the fire department's arson file, nagged at by the suspicion that the answer to that problem was right in front of him, that he'd missed something of vital importance.

He flipped through the yet unsolved arson crimes, impressed with Ross's record. There weren't many open cases. In fact, the fires that had happened in the Laverty House and on the Taylor property was the majority of the county's arson problem.

It didn't bode well. And suddenly Noah couldn't shake the feeling that Annie was in grave danger.

'So this is what you prefer to do in the mornings rather than ravish fair maidens,' a sleepy, sexy voice said behind him. 'I can't say it's flattering.'

Noah turned from his computer and faced Annie. She looked incredible; rosy-cheeked with a saucy sparkle to her eyes that made him want to knock everything to the floor and ravish her right there on the desk. Until her curious eyes travelled to his computer screen.

Quickly he reached back and flipped it off, but some of his urgency must have transformed itself because her eyes narrowed thoughtfully as they levelled on him. 'What's up?'

CHAPTER 10

Noah's eyes and thoughts shuttered right before Annie's eyes, closing himself off to her so completely that his face looked blank. He had done that to her before, but she had thought they'd got past that. What on earth had happened between last night and this morning?

'Nothing's up.' Turning away from her, he busied himself with papers on his desk. 'I'm busy.'

'Well,' she said quietly, moving between him and his desk to get his attention, 'when you slink out of a woman's bed in the deep of the night without a word, it leaves her feeling a little . . . self-conscious.'

'I left after the sun was up.'

'Oh, well,' she said with a casual shrug. 'That's all right, then.'

Despite her light tone, she couldn't keep the hurt out of her voice. But damn it, it had hurt to wake up and find him gone, without a word of goodbye. She had accepted the fact that she wasn't going to get declarations of undying love, but a goodbye she expected. After all, she knew he thought she was leaving, though she had made the difficult decision in the middle of the night not to.

She couldn't go, not feeling how she did about him. After all, every woman he'd ever felt anything for had deserted him in some way. She couldn't possibly do the same to him and reinforce his assumption that love always ended badly. This time it wouldn't, she promised herself. And she could start by taking that job and staying as long as possible.

'I never pegged you for a coward,' she said lightly, gambling – correctly – on sparking his anger.

'And I never pegged you for a finagling game-player,' he said evenly, putting his hands on her hips. He attempted to move her to the side so he could get at his computer.

Annie slammed her hands down on his, refusing to be budged. 'What does that mean?'

When it became obvious he couldn't move her without physically shoving her aside, he sighed and removed his hands from her. Scraping his chair back so they were no longer touching, he looked at her with brown eyes devoid of emotion. 'I took a message for you this morning. Sue seems to think you'd be a fool not to stay – they're offering big bucks.'

Now she understood his mood. 'I see,' she said carefully. So was he pouting because she was leaving or staying? 'Noah,' she made a disparaging sound and spread her hands, 'I'm staying.'

He studied her silently a moment. 'Why did you let me think you were leaving?'

'I thought I was. Please believe me.'

'You thought you were leaving,' he said. 'But now you're not?'

She'd sensed his unleashed violence simmering at the surface before, but she'd never felt it directed at her. The mistrust it implied made her sick. 'No,' she said quietly, braving a little smile. 'I'm not.'

'Why? Because of the phone call this morning?'

She stared at him, wishing for some sign of encouragement, any sign at all. But there was none. 'No,' she whispered, leaning forward and grabbing his hands. There was more than just a little warmth and compassion inside this man, no one knew that better than her – especially after what had transpired on the beach.

But even that had been just a harbinger for what had happened later, in her bedroom. They had made love again; with Noah whispering soft, sexy words that she couldn't quite hear over the roaring in her head and the low sobs escaping her chest. Together they had experienced such a mind-shattering climax that she knew their souls had collided. Noah knew it too. He couldn't possibly have forgotten.

'I'm staying,' she said, 'because I've been offered a great job opportunity here, one that will last at least a month. I'm going to take it and just see where it leads. But most of all I'm staying because I decided in the middle of the night, while lying against you, that I couldn't possibly leave. I know,' she said quickly when he would have spoken, 'that you don't know how you feel. I know also how difficult this all is for you.' She shrugged helplessly. 'I love you, Noah. But I won't force that love on you, nor beg you to return it.' Still holding his hands, she leaned towards him and lightly grazed her lips against his cheek, his neck.

He groaned and pulled her down on his lap, squeezing her against him. 'Damn you,' he breathed in her ear. 'I can't get you out of my head. You demoralize me.'

The feel of his strong, sheltering arms around her, after she'd seen the frightening emptiness in his eyes, was like a warm balm over her heart. 'I'm sorry, Noah.'

'I thought the worst of you, you know. I thought you were trying to manipulate me and for a minute I wanted to believe that you were no different from – ' He stopped abruptly, his face hard again.

And the heart he had warmed only a minute before ached for him. 'I am different, Noah. I would never purposely hurt you.' She waited, content to stay exactly as she was as he absorbed her words.

'I wouldn't hurt you either,' he said against her hair, then took a deep breath. 'I don't know about relationships, I don't have very good experiences to base this on. I tend to have very bad luck at this sort of thing.'

'We're doing fine, Noah,' she said gently. 'Things are good. Look at what happened last night.'

'That was more than fine,' he agreed, a wicked light gleaming in his eyes.

She smiled dreamily.

'So,' he said, lightly grinding his forehead against hers. 'You're going to hang around for a while.'

'Yeah,' she smiled. 'Know a place I can stay?'

He shot her a quick, crooked grin, tinged with male satisfaction. 'Maybe.'

She brought her palms up to his cheeks, feeling the light stubble there. His hair was tousled, as it always was, and he was wearing only a pair of shorts, showing off his very well-made chest and arms. She sighed happily and rested her head on his shoulder. 'Admit it, Noah. Aren't you a little relieved I'm staying?'

'No,' he said adamantly, then ruined it by pulling her closer and nibbling on her ear.

'Just a little?'

'Maybe just a little,' he said with a another one of his rare, glorious smiles. 'But you're a pain in the ass. Always having to save you.' His eyes turned solemn.

'What is it?'

'There's no one more relieved then me that you aren't leaving, Annie. But you should consider something else. The fires.'

'What about them?'

'I think you're in danger.'

Not wanting to hear it, she stood up and nodded

269

towards the computer screen. 'What were you working on when I came in? You couldn't shut your computer off fast enough.'

'You're changing the subject, Annie.' But he clicked on the screen and his fingers deftly brought up some files.

She leaned over his shoulder, squinting. 'That's the City Fire Department's investigation files. What are you doing looking in those?'

'Annie, listen. Remember what Ross told us about the arsonist? That his department had a list of suspects a mile long they were currently investigating?

'Yes. And that they were certain that it wasn't just one guy. Or that if it was, it was someone new. Like Gerry, as ridiculous as that is.'

'And that it wasn't possibly related to the car bomb that killed your mother and Jesse.'

'I remember.' She swallowed with difficultly, instinctively knowing she wasn't going to like what was coming.

Noah gestured to the screen. 'So why then does this file indicate that they've exhausted their list of suspects, including Gerry? They're at a complete loss, Annie. Yet the guy keeps making fires.'

Annie tried to put herself in Ross's position. 'Maybe he didn't want to worry me. I was terrified enough.'

'Was?' Noah asked, with a slow shake of his head. 'Laverty, we should still be terrified. The guy's on the

loose and no one is even close to catching him. And
. . . he seems to have a thing against you.'

'You mean against Ross.'

Noah said nothing but she could see the uneasiness
in his eyes. 'Look, I'm supposed to go see Ross today.
He wants to talk about what to do with the house when
the construction is finished. I'll ask him about the
investigation. He's obviously just protecting me from
worry.'

'So the house is going on the market, then?'

'Actually, no. Ross told me last night at the ball that
he had just come from the house. He'd walked through
it and nostalgia caught up with him. He can't bear to
part with it. He feels that, since the house was my
mother's before they were married, he needs to buy
me out.'

'So he's moving back in?'

'I don't know what he'll do now. He mentioned
something about needing a vacation and wanting to
take off to some deserted island for several months.'
She stopped when she realized Noah wasn't listening
but staring off, deep in thought. 'And I thought,' she
continued in the same casual voice, 'that we could take
off all our clothes and have wild, passionate sex here
on this floor under your computer desk – which
happens to be the only space available in this entire
room.'

His sharp eyes flew back to hers. 'Annie, let *me* go
meet Ross today. You've got that photo job to work on

and I need to talk to his staff about this computer program anyway.'

'You didn't hear a word I just said.' She laughed in amazement, a hand on her hip. 'Did you?'

'Hmm? Oh, yeah. Right.' He grabbed at her again, yanking her down on his lap. The smile tugging at the corner of his mouth turned into a fully fledged grin. She struggled, just for the fun of it, gasping when he snaked a hand up her shirt and warm, rough fingers stroked a breast. 'And as soon as I get back, I'll let you seduce me – right here under this desk.'

Then he kissed her, long and hard until she was delirious and hot. With disgusting ease he lifted his head, retrieved his hand and set her aside. He got up and walked from the room whistling softly, leaving her to stare after him feeling ridiculously weak-kneed. She had to laugh at herself, getting so worked up over a kiss.

It wasn't until she was leaving his office a minute later that she realized it was Sunday. How could Noah meet with Ross's staff when none of them worked at weekends?

Annie occupied herself for the next few hours with her camera. Martin tagged along after her as she took pictures on the cliffs. With summer more than half over, the sun was no longer directly overhead and the lighting was perfect. The sun was warm, but not hot as most of California could be at this same time of year. It was the wonderful, cool ocean breeze that made this place so absolutely perfect, Annie decided. And she was very glad she wasn't leaving – yet.

Martin watched the ocean in the distance with a relaxed expression and Annie knew there was no better time. 'Martin,' she said offhandedly, her face against the lens. 'Where's Gerry?'

Martin said nothing and after a minute Annie lowered the camera. 'We're worried sick, Martin. Noah, Ed, Rosemary . . . all of us. He's just a boy – like you. He's done nothing wrong and he deserves to be home with us.'

Martin looked down at his feet. 'I don't know where he is.'

Experience had taught Annie to detect a lie and she knew she was getting one now. Gently she said, 'I don't think that's the truth, Martin. But I don't want to force you to break a confidence. After all, a promise between friends is the most important vow there is.' Martin looked at her, gratitude heavy in his eyes, and Annie knew she'd hit on the problem. 'I'm worried about him, Martin. Could you, if you happen to see him, let Gerry know that my house is empty and that would be a safe place to go when he needed one?'

'If I see him,' Martin said, his eyes back on the ocean.

'OK.' She knew the message would get to Gerry. And she'd make sure there was a sleeping bag and pillow at the house.

When they went in for lunch a few minutes later, Ed was in a whirlwind of panic.

'What's the matter?' Annie asked him, watching as he raced dramatically around the huge kitchen, noisily banging pots and pans, slamming the cabinet doors.

He stopped and threw up his hands at Annie's question. 'You'd do better to ask me what isn't the matter.'

'Let's start with what is,' she suggested with a hint of a nostalgic smile. Ed's temper tantrums were as much a part of her past as his apple pies.

His hands fisted on his thick waist, he scowled. 'The boys have a volleyball tournament all week and the uniforms haven't been cleaned, I've got a turkey dinner to prepare and I haven't got to the breakfast dishes yet. No one's bothered to do their chores and I don't have the time to yell at them.' He chewed on a nail as he paused to look at Annie. 'Sorry you asked yet?'

'Where's Rosemary?'

'She's in bed, Noah's working and I need help.' He eyed her with sudden interest. 'And I think you're it.' He thrust a basket of clothes into Annie's unsuspecting hands.

To say she was even less talented at laundry than she was at cooking a roast was being kind. She dry-cleaned nearly every item of clothing she owned. It was not only convenient, but cost-efficient as well. She couldn't ruin what she didn't wash. 'But Ed, I don't know how to – '

'Martin can help you,' he said hurriedly. 'Now leave me in peace, I'm swamped.'

'Ed, really, I don't know – '

'Please, Annie? Try. For me.' He rushed to the oven. She glanced over at Martin who shrugged. Together they dumped the entire basket into the washer and stared in confusion at the knobs. 'Hot?' she asked no one in particular.

'They're pretty dirty,' Martin said slowly. 'Hot sounds good.'

'What if one colour runs,' she asked warily as she eyed the bright white and blue colours. 'Doesn't hot make it do that?' She bit her lip as she worried. She wanted to laugh at herself. She spent less time contemplating the lighting for a photograph – but then again, she knew how seriously the kids took their uniforms.

'They've been washed before so they won't run. Right?' Martin looked as concerned over the uniforms as he had the roast, so Annie decided to take charge. Clicking on the hot and dumping in lots of soap, she did the only thing left to do – valiantly hoped for the best.

By early evening Noah was back at the Taylor House. All he wanted was to be alone to think. Ross had met him in his city office and the things they'd discussed had given him a headache. To add to his discourage-

275

ment, Rosemary was still ill enough to need round-the-clock supervision and Gerry was still missing. Noah had searched every square inch of the property without luck.

Walking into his office with the weight of the world on his shoulders, he stopped short.

Annie was sitting in his chair waiting for him, her eyes warm and full of emotion. For him.

A moment ago he had thought he wanted to be alone – now he couldn't imagine why. He smiled – an unknowingly weary smile – and came towards her, stepping over his own mess scattered across the floor. 'Hi,' he said softly.

'Hi yourself,' she said, standing.

He knew he should be annoyed at her invasion into his private space, but instead his insides melted at the sight of her.

He turned back to lock the door.

'What are you doing?' she asked breathlessly as he grabbed her and pulled her tight against him.

'I'm thanking myself for my wonderful insight in purchasing the best, softest carpeting on the market, and thanking God for my very large desk.'

She giggled against his neck, relaxing her wonderfully soft body against him. 'What does your carpet and desk have to do with anything?'

'Well,' he said, nipping her ear, drawing goose bumps which he promptly soothed with warm hands up and down her arms. 'All day I was distracted by your proposition this morning – something about wild, passionate love under my desk.'

He kneeled on the floor and pulled her down with him, loving the curious way she eyed the opening under the computer desk, as if checking it for size. Then she looked out the window at the early evening light still streaming through. She turned back to him, her eyes gleaming softly. She leaned a hand on his chest. 'Now, Noah?'

In answer he moved her hand lower, curling it around the bulge in the V of his jeans.

'Oh,' she whispered softly, as her fingers held him.

Her name was on his next breath, longing searing through him.

'What if someone comes looking for you . . .?' Her voice trailed off as his open mouth settled against her throat, nuzzling it, and his hands worked up the back of her short, full sundress. 'Uh . . . I suppose it's worth a try.'

He hummed his agreement, his hands gripping her hips and rubbing them hard against his. She made a soft purr of approval and arousal.

'Love that sound,' he murmured, lips against her neck. He slipped his fingers into her panties, wringing a helpless sigh of pleasure from her, watching as her incredible grey eyes turned dark.

'Noah?' She pressed herself urgently against him, her hands frantic against the buttons of his jeans. 'Now.'

He held her off, touching her intimately and watching the myriad expressions cross her face as his fingers played in her slippery heat.

'Please,' she gasped, clinging to him. 'Now.'

He shoved the piles of files and papers scattered around them out of their way as she worked open his jeans, dragging them desperately off his hips. He tugged on her panties and to his surprise the delicate lace fell apart in his hands.

'Hurry,' she whispered, then laughed breathlessly as he pulled her hard against him, tumbling them both over to the floor, only half under his desk.

With her hands on his tightened body, her tongue in his mouth, Noah was gone. No longer capable of rational thought, he felt a surging of heat through his body that refused to be denied. But Annie had no intention of denying him anything. She rolled them over and straddled him, taking in every inch of the largest erection he'd ever had, bringing them both to a wrenching orgasm within minutes.

Which, when Noah could breathe again, had him shaken to the core. When he was with Annie this way, he was shattered, torn apart as never before; just as when he was with her he was whole. Balanced. At peace.

It was as easy and as terrifying as that.

At dark Annie and Noah prepared to check the Laverty house for Gerry.

'I hope Martin got the message to Gerry,' Noah said as he checked his flashlight to make sure it was working. He glanced out the window of the kitchen where nothing but a dense grey fog was visible. 'Hell of a night to be out alone.'

'We know he's eating,' Ed said wryly as he came into the kitchen carrying a basket of dirty clothes.

'Food still being taken, then?' Noah asked hopefully, his worry wearing a deep groove between those dark eyes that Annie longed to soothe. The sweetness of his concern caused an ache deep inside her and she wanted to wrap her arms around him and never let go.

'Yes, thank God,' Ed said. 'The little guy is skinny enough as it is. When I see Martin hanging around after a meal, I make myself scarce for a few minutes so he can grab what he wants.'

'Good,' Noah said with relief. Ed turned to the laundry area and Noah looked at Annie with his hands on his hips. 'We've got to find him tonight. It's been too long.'

'At least he's eating.' Annie thought it was a good sign that Gerry had stayed close. She was certain he wanted to come back, but he probably just didn't know how to do it and keep his pride intact.

Noah shook his head and sighed, his jaw tight. He looked out of the window at the fog rolling in from the ocean, eyes narrowed in thought.

'What?' she asked softly. He looked so . . . sad.

'I know what it's like, Annie. I know what it's like to feel so completely alone. To feel utterly worthless . . . a burden.' He looked at her, his eyes bleak. He rubbed a hand across his chest as if it hurt. 'And I wanted so badly for all that to be behind him.'

Annie stepped closer, her heart in her throat. With gentle, delicate hands she reached up and touched Noah's face. 'Noah, you are the most compassionate, sensitive man I know. If anyone can help Gerry put his past behind him, you can.'

'I just want him to be all right.'

'He will be. He's older than you were when you were forced to fend for yourself.'

His eyes slid to hers and warmed. Reaching up, he covered her hands with his larger, rougher ones. 'Thanks for thinking about the empty house and telling Martin.'

'I want him to be safe and back here with his family as badly as you do.'

A small smile touched his beautiful mouth as he gave her a quick, impulsive hug. 'What would I do without you, Laverty?' he whispered against her hair.

'Well,' she said brightly, her heart racing at his words and loving tone, 'you won't have to find out for quite a while yet.'

'Er . . . Annie?' came Ed's choked voice behind them.

They both turned quickly at the strangeness of Ed's voice and stared.

Ed was holding up two uniforms for the coming tournament, formerly bright, stark white with a blue stripe. They were now a very definite, solid pink. 'I take it you were not a housewife in a former life.'

Annie was still staring in horror at the boys' prized shirts. Every one of the kids absolutely loved their uniforms. It gave them a sense of confidence, a sense of family and belonging. It gave them pride. She stepped closer and peered into the washing machine. And groaned. She had single-handedly wiped out the entire team. 'Oh, no,' she cried. 'What did I do?'

'Well,' Ed said, pulling out a red sweatshirt from the washer, 'I would wager that this had something to do with it.'

A strangled gasp behind her made her cut her eyes to Noah. His hand fell away from his mouth and the rare laugh escaped him. 'I'm sorry,' he managed, shaking his head. 'You weren't kidding when you said you couldn't cook or do laundry – '

The last word came out in one quick swoosh as Annie's elbow connected with his stomach.

'Ouch,' he complained, rubbing his belly. Ed snickered and Noah's eyes caught his. They both burst out laughing.

Annie felt humiliated to the core, wishing she could fall into a hole. 'Stop laughing at me.' Noah held up a hand and muffled his next laugh. Ed didn't even try.

'We're . . . not laughing at you,' Noah said, seconds

281

before he laughed again. Ed wiped his eyes, both managing to fall silent – until they glanced at each other. Both snorted hysterically.

'You are so laughing at me,' she told them, feeling the heat rise up her face as she marched for the back door – which had been replaced since the kitchen fire. She felt stupid and inefficient. She should have paid more attention in high school to home economics class, but she'd been too busy with her writing and camera.

She whirled at the door, eyes narrowed at their amused faces. 'I can't cook and I can't do laundry. I told you both up front and now you have no one but yourselves to blame if you have to wear pink clothes.' For dramatic effect she shut the door behind her.

The night immediately swallowed her up. The fog was so thick and so dark she could hardly make out the light on the driveway, only a few feet from her. It was eerie and she suddenly decided that laughing male chauvinists were better than being alone in the dark. Whirling towards the back door, she bounced directly against a solid wall – Noah's chest.

'Let's go, Laverty,' he said lightly, grabbing her hand.

She searched his face but it was entirely too dark to see his expression clearly. 'Are you done laughing at me?'

He squeezed her hand. 'I love pink shirts,' he said solemnly, though she was sure his eyes were twinkling.

It was a peace offering, she decided, no mockery or jest intended. She took it and his hand. 'All right, then. Let's go find Gerry.'

As they walked across the green, finding their way from years of practice rather than by sight, Noah still held her hand. The night was still and silent and dark in the hollow way that only a deep fog can provide.

'You OK?' he asked after a minute. She looked at him questioningly and he squeezed her hand. 'I didn't hurt you before . . . in the office – did I?'

Thankful for the dark fog that hid her telltale blush, she shook her head. 'No, Noah. I'm . . . fine.' Their lovemaking had been quick, hard and . . . raw. But it had also been staggeringly masterful and the most intense experience of her life. They had clung desperately to each other right there on the floor under his desk and she would never, ever forget the rush of pure power she got from knowing she could cause him to lose his tightly held control. She stepped forward.

He stopped her and turned her face to his. 'It got a little rough.'

'And,' she reminded him with a wry smile, 'I'm the one that started it, remember?'

He slowly smiled back. 'So you did.'

'I'm not all that fragile, Noah.'

'No,' he said softly, his thumb caressing her face. 'You're not. And you're not afraid to show how you feel; emotionally, physically, sexually . . . that's one of the things that attracts me to you.'

His eyes burned through her and she felt that invisible tug that she always felt when he looked at her like that.

'And . . . I owe you a pair of blue lace panties.'

She laughed and pushed him. The fog surrounding them was so thick he nearly disappeared standing three feet from her. She grabbed him back and snaked her hand into his.

'Scared?' he asked with a mocking grin that shimmered in the night.

'No way,' she assured him with false bravado, glancing surreptitiously around her. The waves crashed eerily in the deep black night, but there was no other sound. Not even the crickets were out tonight. She decided she didn't like the fog and pulled him with her towards her house.

'It must have been difficult to pack away your mother's and Jesse's things,' Noah said quietly a minute later.

She shrugged. 'What was difficult was the loss of my mother's earring.'

'It doesn't make any sense,' he said. 'Your mother was always impeccably dressed. Under what kind of circumstance would she wear only one earring?'

'She would have had to be rushed.'

'So the question is – what was the hurry and why does the arsonist need that earring?'

'What did Ross say about what you found on the computer?' she asked. 'Why did he tell us that they still had suspects when they don't?'

'I didn't ask him.'

She looked at him. 'Why not?'

'I couldn't very well tell him that I had been looking his department's private and confidential files. When I asked him about the investigation, he insisted that they were still checking out several suspects. I just couldn't call him a liar to his face.'

'He's protecting me,' Annie murmured, wishing Ross hadn't felt the need to do so.

'So it would appear.'

She didn't like his tone of disbelief but suddenly her house loomed up out of the fog. It was dark, as they knew it would be. The electricity had been shut off for the contractor. They turned on their flashlights, calling Gerry's name.

In the hallway, they heard a distinct clatter from upstairs. Together they took the stairs. At the top Noah turned to Annie and grasped her arm in a grip of steel. He said in a low voice laced with determination, 'Stay here while I check that far bedroom. That's where the noise came from.'

At her mutinous glare his fingers tightened. 'Please,' he whispered. His eyes spoke volumes.

She agreed with a short nod and watched him go. But a second later she forgot that promise when she heard a sound from the bedroom closest to her. Silently opening the door, she stepped into another world. The bedroom window had been left open and the thick, swirling fog had entered, leaving Annie unable to even see the far wall.

'Gerry?' she called softly. 'Are you in here?'

She caught a glimpse of movement to her right – a figure staring directly at her – and she swung up her flashlight to see.

It flickered once . . . then went out.

CHAPTER 11

Annie's breath caught as she was surrounded by thick, oppressive fog and darkness. It was hard to believe this nightmare was happening in the house she'd grown up in. 'Hello?' she called to the vague dark form she could see a mere five feet in front of her. Desperately she shook her flashlight, to no avail.

'Gerry?' she said again, her voice shaking nervously. She took one step backwards.

Whoever was standing there didn't answer, but took a matching step backwards. Her blood froze and she stopped. So did her company.

With a gulp of air, Annie again stepped forward and raised her heavy flashlight, prepared to scare away whoever it was standing there. A scream welled up as he raised a weapon over his head also, but she swallowed it, slamming down her flashlight with as much force as she could. A deafening shattering of glass accompanied her scream of panic.

In the distance, as glass rained down over her, she

could hear Noah shouting from the hallway as he searched for her. 'Annie! Annie, is that you? Goddamn it, where the hell are you?' He crashed into the room and splayed his flashlight into the room as her legs gave out and she sank to the glass-riddled floor.

'Noah, I smashed him,' she said shakily. 'Shine your light, I got him.'

Noah first illuminated Annie, his face in sharp relief behind the light, reflecting horror, concern. Then the light flickered to the source of the broken glass. A closet door hung open, its full-length mirror smashed to pieces.

'Oh, my God, Noah,' she said flabbergasted. 'I smashed my own reflection.' The hilarity of the situation struck her then and she laughed weakly, her hands over her thundering heart.

Noah divided a stunned look between the destroyed mirror and Annie, but eventually his mouth quirked. Then he joined her, laughing until they were both roaring and Noah slid helplessly to the floor, unable to contain himself.

Eventually they got it together. Nervous from the incident, Annie didn't leave Noah's side as they methodically searched the rest of house. There was no sign of Gerry. Downstairs in one corner of the living room was a rolled sleeping bag, a soft pad and pillow – the equipment she herself had put there earlier in the day.

'Look,' Noah said, crouching beside it, his face

lighting up with a hope that tore at her. 'Maybe this is where he's sleeping.'

'Um – ' she hesitated ' – I just put that here for him this afternoon.'

Noah looked at her.

'I wanted him to be warm,' she said with a helpless shrug. 'And since there isn't any carpet I left the mat too.'

Noah stood and reached for her, pulling her close. 'Annie,' he said with a small laugh and a shake of his head. 'You're amazing.'

The words warmed her chilled and worried heart.

'Let's go.'

At the back door, Noah paused. 'Are you sure the front door is locked?'

'No,' she said. 'But I want Gerry to be able to get in.'

'Not that way,' Noah insisted. 'It's too risky. You still have things here. I'll go lock it. Hang on.'

Two seconds later, the back door handle jangled as someone tried to open it. Annie had no more than a second to panic before she recognized Ross in the deep gloom of the night.

'Ross, what are you doing here?' she started to ask with a smile, only to have it freeze on her face at his thunderous expression.

'What the hell are *you* doing here alone at this time of night?' he demanded, brushing past her and looking around. He turned back to her with his face hard and took her shoulders in his large, firm hands. 'You have no business here.'

Cold surprise lashed at her. 'I still have a few things here, Ross,' she said coolly, unable to keep the stunned hurt from her voice.

'Jesus, Annie,' he said harshly, his own expression twisting from rage to pain. 'The electricity is off and it's late. What on earth made you come here? Don't you realize that this place – empty as it is – is a prime target for the arsonist?'

Noah came up besides her and put a hand on Ross's arm that still gripped Annie. 'Relax, Ross. She's not alone.'

'It doesn't matter,' he insisted, though he released Annie. He drew a ragged breath and dragged a hand through his mop of grey hair. 'I'm sorry.'

Annie let out a shaky breath. 'It's OK.' Never could she remember her stepfather speaking harshly to her. Not when she'd ditched class to go skiing at Mammoth Mountain with friends, not when she foolishly went ocean-swimming during a harsh riptide and had to be rescued by three lifeguards. Not even when she'd smashed his prized '74 Camero into a telephone pole. Something was very wrong.

'It's not OK,' Ross said, his face filled with disgust. 'It's not.'

'Ross?' She touched her stepfather's shoulder when he turned his back to her, watching his flashlight play idly over the kitchen floor. 'What it is?'

He settled his flashlight on the bare kitchen for a long minute. 'I saw you standing there, Annie, looking so like your mother. Gave me a start, you did. Standing alone, looking frightened and vulnerable, and I flipped.' He turned back to them, his eyes on Annie. 'There are things going on, Annie, things that I can't explain. But I have to believe that you're going to be all right. I have to know you're safe.'

She gave him an impulsive hug. 'I'm fine, Ross.'

'You don't understand,' Ross said with a quick shake of his head, looking shaken and upset. 'What's happening is – '

'All related?' Annie pushed softly. 'Ross, just tell us the truth. No more protecting me. Things are bad, aren't they?'

'Yes.' He looked at her and Noah miserably. 'And it's far from over. You need to be careful, Annie.'

All three thought about her close brushes with fire: the first fire here in this house, later at Noah's cottage and then the most recent in the Taylor House's kitchen.

'Why, Ross? Why is she attracting this guy?' Noah asked, his face tense.

Ross bit his lip and looked away. Finally he said, 'I can only come up with revenge.'

'So you do believe these things are all connected,' Annie breathed. 'I knew it.' Her stomach lurched at the sickness of it all. 'Well, then. He should be easy to catch. Just go over the cases that you were able to bring about convictions on, starting back before Jesse's and Mother's death.'

A harsh laugh rumbled from Ross's chest. 'Oh, Annie. If only it were that simple.'

'Why isn't it?' Noah pressed.

'I must have put away hundreds of sickos, all before the car bombing ten years ago. If it's someone new – since that time – make that number thousands.'

Noah and Annie looked at each other. Annie knew he was remembering what he'd found in the computer. *All suspects exhausted.*

'Do you remember last time, Annie?' Ross asked. 'I put every man within a hundred miles on that. We knew it was arson, knew it was revenge, and still we couldn't solve it. I drove my men crazy, worked them night and day and still . . . we came up with nothing.'

'You did the best you could,' she said softly.

'And nearly killed myself in the process. And my men. They hated working for me during that time and I don't blame them.'

'It's their job,' Noah said.

'It's not their job to work for a man possessed. And it's happening again. They're grumbling over the hours, grumbling over my . . . attitude. But I'm afraid, so afraid that if I don't press them, someone will get hurt next time. Like . . . before.'

'No one can blame you for wanting this case solved,' Annie said. 'And if they do, they don't belong there.'

'Aren't the police any help?' asked Noah.

Ross laughed, a cold, harsh sound. 'I'm sure you've heard of the intense competitive air between the detectives and our investigators. Often, as in this case, no one is sure whose case it really is, the police or ours.'

'It should be both,' Annie said indignantly. 'Competing for a case is sick. It just needs to be solved.'

'It doesn't work that way, Annie,' Noah pointed out. 'The fire investigators often do all the work, the detectives take over the case to make the arrest and they get all the glory, in and out of court.'

'And my men get disgusted, but there's nothing they can do. It's happened a hundred times,' Ross admitted. 'It makes it difficult, if not impossible, for everyone to work happily together now.'

'Well, it's wrong,' she insisted.

'Maybe this time there's enough suspects to go around,' Ross said.

'But Ross – ' she started.

'Ross is right,' Noah said with a slight shake of his head to Annie. She knew he didn't want her to press Ross. 'You need to be careful, more so than usual.'

'Yes,' Ross agreed with some relief. 'Please, Annie. It will make me feel better. Especially since you're staying longer than you planned.'

'I'll be careful,' she promised him duly with a fond smile. 'Don't worry about me.'

But as Ross gripped her shoulders and then hugged her tight, the relief and love pouring from him,

Annie's gaze met Noah's serious eyes. Why was Ross lying? his brown eyes silently asked her.

She didn't know.

But something was very, very wrong.

Over the next few days, the incident at the house haunted Annie. The only explanation for Ross's lying to them was that he was covering up his investigation. And the only reason he would do that, she was sure, was to protect her. That left her with the disturbing conclusion that whatever it was, it was bad.

Noah must have come to the same conclusion because he became reluctant to leave her side. He spent his nights in the cottage with her – which was heaven.

They had a way together, the two of them, and she knew that she wasn't the only one to feel it. They made love every night and they were the most passionate, incredibly mind-shattering experiences of her life. There was no halfway with them. Every time they came together it was a sharing of souls. And it would have been absolutely perfect – except for one thing.

Noah didn't love her. He had frozen that part of his heart, kept it successfully hidden for so long that he seemed unable – or unwilling – to do anything about it. They were close, but still Noah managed to keep some part of himself from her.

She began to think that because of his horrifying childhood and subsequent experiences he was incapable of taking that last step, of giving her his love. And it killed her. Because every day, as she shot her photos and sent film back east, she edged closer to the final confrontation – what would happen when the job was finished?

She wished desperately for Rosemary to talk to, but the poor woman was lost in her own world. Her doctor had told Noah there was little he could do except make her comfortable – and also suggested Noah put her in a special home. Noah, of course, refused.

It made Annie love him all the more.

But without Noah's love in return, she knew she couldn't stay. She just couldn't expose herself to that kind of hurt, not feeling the way she did about him. So she took her pictures, prayed for Gerry and wished the arsonist caught, all while loving Noah and wondering how everything would work out.

She sat in Rosemary's porch swing staring out at the late summer night sky. Out of the dark green ahead, Noah appeared.

He smiled softly as he sat next to her and pulled her close. She loved the warm, male scent of him, the way his arms surrounded her possessively. The moon was bright and in the distance clouds rolled, swayed, danced as they watched.

It was beautiful, Annie thought. 'You know, sitting watching the night like this, I can't remember why I ever wanted to live anywhere else.'

Noah's eyes were eloquent, dark. 'So don't leave.'

'Are you asking me to stay?'

'That would have to be your decision,' he said evasively.

She could feel him pulling away from her. 'It's not that easy.'

'Yes, it is,' he said, his eyes hooded. 'Either you want to stay or you leave. It's that simple.'

Straightening, she leaned back against the arm of the swing to get a better look at him. 'So I stay. Or I don't. It's no big deal?'

He made a sound that was half grunt, half exasperated sigh. 'I said nothing of the sort, Laverty. Don't put words in my mouth.'

'All right,' she said evenly, though her heart was pitter-pattering out of control, 'then just tell me what you feel.'

'About what?'

A frustrated sound rolled off her throat. 'About us.' She looked at him, looked through his tough exterior to the gentle sweetness she knew lay beneath. 'Will your life be the same whether I stay or go?'

He closed his eyes, leaned back against his side of the swing and fell silent. She waited, her heart cracking more with every second that passed.

Finally, he looked at her, his expression giving nothing of his thoughts away. 'I enjoy being with you, Annie,' he said cautiously. 'It makes me feel good, makes me as happy as I've ever been. But more than that, I don't know. As far as a long-term commitment – '

'I didn't ask you for a long-term commitment,' she interrupted quickly. Even she wasn't sure she was ready for that. 'I just want to know – will your life be the same whether I stay or go?'

He nodded slowly, his face still as stone. 'I would miss you, more than you'll know. But yes, basically my life would be the same.' He looked at her. 'If you can't live with that, you'd better let me know now.' At the devastation written so plainly across her face, he winced. 'I guess that means you can't.'

Annie's heart had lurched at his words, at the realization that nothing was going to change. No matter how much time she gave Noah Taylor, he still would not allow himself to need her, to love her. She owed herself more.

'I'm sorry,' she said softly, standing. Struggling against the tears stuck like cotton wool in her throat, she backed off the porch. 'I thought having you want me was enough. But it also means that what's between us is nothing more than a mutual physical attraction we satisfy with sex. And I don't like the way that makes me feel.'

'So that's it, then, Annie?' he asked wearily, his body leaning heavily back against the swing, his knuckles white from their grip on the wood, telling her he was not as indifferent as he wanted her to believe.

I want you to need me, to crave me, to love me, she wanted to cry. 'I don't know. I need to think,' she whispered.

'Well, you'll have to let me know what you come up with,' he drawled. 'Since I'm not a mind-reader.'

And as quick as that, he withdrew from her. He was still sitting in the swing but he was the quiet, moody, invincible Noah of the past. The one that hid his every thought and emotion.

'Well, then,' she said, swallowing a sob. 'I guess I'd better go.' And she turned and walked away, summoning every ounce of dignity she had not to tear across the green to her cottage. She could feel his eyes on her the entire walk.

Noah let Annie go; he didn't have much choice. He couldn't say what he knew she was waiting for. He simply wasn't ready. Hell, he thought, staring at the night sky riddled with sparkling stars as he remained on the swing. He didn't know if he'd ever be ready.

Did he love her?

He truly didn't know. He knew less than nothing about the kind of love she was looking for. All he did know was that a large part of him was dying watching her walk away. A dull ache in his chest was spreading slowly, wiping out any warmth that her presence had brought him, leaving in its place a chilling cold he couldn't shake.

For as long as he could remember, he had had only himself to rely on. And that had been more than fine. He'd got his satisfaction, his confidence from what he had been able to do for others.

Helping kids like Gerry and Martin was his life. He

298

gave to them what he had never had, hoping to give them a short-cut through the trials and tribulations of life. And taking care of Rosemary – after what she had done for him – was easy enough.

It was much easier to give love to only those who desperately needed it. And Annie was not in desperate need – he'd never met a more self-reliant woman. No matter what she said or thought, she didn't need him. Her very survival did not depend on him.

It had been a long time since he had allowed himself to care for someone who didn't need him, and he wasn't sure he was ready. He shook his head at himself, knowing it was far too late for that sentiment. He already cared. Much more than he wanted to.

Annie was right. He surrounded himself with only those who were dependent on him. Everything she had accused him of was correct.

But knowing that changed nothing. So as she disappeared into the night he was left staring, wondering if he'd just destroyed the best thing that had ever happened to him.

The next morning, Noah got up and went through the motions of living, but something didn't feel right. His heart ached.

Out of sorts, and definitely not in the best of moods, he decided a run was just the thing he needed to clear his head. He stepped off the back porch and froze.

Annie sat in a chair, head bent. She looked miserable and his heart slowly sank to the floor.

'Annie?'

Her head flew up and he saw that she hadn't been lost in personal misery as he'd figured, but that she'd been bent over something she worked on in her lap.

He felt like an idiot, especially when her eyes remained cool and distant.

'Good morning,' she said quietly.

'I'm just . . . going for a run.'

She nodded and bent back to her task.

'What are you doing?'

'I'm sewing Martin's favourite shirt. He ripped it in a game.' She didn't look up as she answered, but stuck her tongue between her teeth in concentration as she pulled a needle carefully through the material.

'You're . . . acting funny, Annie.'

'No, I'm not.' She stabbed with the needle again, and still didn't look at him.

'You are,' he insisted. Well, what the hell did he expect after the way he'd treated her last night? But he still didn't understand enough about his feelings for her to try to fix it. 'You've been thinking,' he said, and he hoped she wouldn't turn away from him just because he didn't know how to deal with their relationship.

'How do you know?' she asked in a deceptively mild voice, taking another stitch. 'You're not a mind-reader, remember?'

OK, he deserved that.

'Go away, Noah.'

Fear gnawed at him, but he couldn't understand that either. For lack of something to say or do, he stared at her sewing – and wanted to laugh. Her stitches were large, uneven and not in the right place.

'Do you, er . . . sew often?' he ventured.

She glanced at him then. 'Maybe.'

'Want some help?'

She jumped and cursed when she stabbed herself with the needle. 'Damn it.' She brought the injured finger to her mouth and sucked. Against his will his gaze was drawn to that mouth and even more amazing, his body tightened.

He blinked when he realized she'd said something. 'What?'

She made a noise of disgust and thrust the shirt in his hands. 'Who am I trying to fool?' She closed her eyes and rested her head in her hands. 'I can't sew. I can't do anything domestic. It's pathetic.'

He'd never in his life had such jumbled, confused emotions. 'You're good at lots of things, Annie. Who cares that you can't sew? Or cook without burning water? Or do laundry without turning the whites pink? You probably can't clean either, but you could always hire a maid.'

She shot him a wry smile. 'Thanks. I think.'

She might have smiled, but the sadness lingered. And he'd caused it. He tossed aside the shirt and sighed before kneeling down and taking her hand in his. She tried to pull it away, but he held firm. He kissed the sore skin where she'd pricked it with the needle and she jumped again.

'Don't.'

'Annie – '

'Please go away, Noah. I'm not done thinking.'

'About us?'

She nodded, and this time her misery was evident. 'I want to be alone. Go run.'

'But – '

She stood abruptly. 'Look, Noah. Last night you told me honestly how you felt. The honesty part is the best thing between us. Now I'm being honest with you. I can't handle this right now, I really can't. To see you and just be casual friends . . . it's really – ' Her voice broke and so did his heart. 'It's hard,' she managed. 'I just need some time to think. Please, please do that for me. OK?'

When faced with those gorgeous, drenched eyes, what choice did he have?

Two days later, Noah was losing his mind. His staff had set up their small annual carnival for the kids and everyone had got into it. In spite of himself, he had too – he'd always had a soft spot for carnivals. As a young child, he remembered stealing money from his mother's boyfriend and sneaking off to the local carnival. He'd loved everything about it: the

302

noise, the happy faces, the games, the sickening, sweet food. That his mother had been waiting for him with the beating of his life was a distant memory. What stuck with him was the thrill of the carnival itself.

When Rosemary had found out how much he loved the carnival she'd started the annual Taylor Carnival, earning his undying devotion. Even now, twenty years later, it still excited him.

Rosemary, blessedly, miraculously aware of herself, was directing with her usual flair. Just having her up and about put the entire house on celebration-alert. Ed had set up the booths on the large patio in the back of the house, complete with various games and loud music, and Annie . . . Annie was the source of his insanity.

She was laughing with the kids, helping with the games and throwing such life and joy into the place that he couldn't remember what it had been like without her. It didn't help that she consumed his mind night and day. He was terrified for her safety, worried about the torment he saw in her eyes and missing her friendship, all the while lusting uncontrollably after her lithe, trim body.

She hadn't ignored him; in fact she'd been very polite, making a point of speaking to him whenever they ran into each other – which was often. But it was obvious that things were different. No longer did she seek him out, no longer did she steal kisses when they passed in the hallway, no longer did she send him her special smile that warmed him from the inside out.

He missed that smile, the way she had of making him take himself less seriously, the way her sweet laughter lit a room.

Sitting on the edge of the patio with her camera slung around her neck, sandwiched between two of the kids, she seemed to be having the time of her life, completely unaware of how miserable he felt.

'OK, everyone. It's time!' Ed shouted. 'Let's go.'

Noah watched as Annie hopped off the patio with a graceful leap, then moved to help. She whispered something in Martin's ear which turned his fretting face into a wreath of smiles.

Making his way through his staff and excited kids, Noah edged close to Annie. For a long minute, he stood behind her, watching her buoy the kids' spirits. She laughed again, sending a wave of nostalgia through him that made his legs weak.

Suddenly she whirled and took a step, right into him. Her camera slammed into his stomach and took his breath, but still he steadied her with two hands on her shoulders. Through the blaze of pain in his gut he saw one brief flare of joy in her eyes at the sight of him. Then it faded, replaced by a dull sheen he had never seen before.

'Oh,' she said quietly, taking a step backwards until his hands fell from her. 'Excuse me.'

She looked beautiful, wearing one of the loose summer dresses that suited her so, her soft skin glimmering with the glow of a light tan and her grey eyes so deep he could drown in them. God, he wanted her. 'Annie – '

'I'm sorry, Noah,' she said turning, 'I'm running a booth. Gotta go.'

'But – '

She simply kept walking as if she hadn't heard him. 'Well, shit,' he said to no one in particular.

'Hey, Noah.' Martin came up besides him and together they watched Annie walk away. 'Why is she mad at you?'

Normally Martin's worried face tore at him. For weeks Noah had been trying to ease Martin's stress. But he was momentarily rendered unable to help anyone – especially himself. 'She's not,' he said lamely, eyes glued to the soft, gentle sway of Annie's hips.

Martin gave him a doubtful look. 'If you say so.'

Annie turned back then and beckoned to Martin. 'Gotta go,' he said, charging after Annie without a backward glance.

Ignoring the urge to follow like a silly puppy, Noah made his way to the booth he was due at. The dunking booth was easily the most popular booth at the carnival, and the reason was simple. For a penny, the kids got a shot at dunking each and every one of the staff, who took turns sitting in the hot spot.

Noah stood off the to side for a few minutes, watching as Tony, their youngest kid at the moment, hit the spot on the head and dunked Al.

Al made a big splash and thrashed around in the water like a fish, much to the amusement of the kids.

When he climbed from the tall, decorated tank, he smiled at Noah. 'You're up, boss. And let me tell you, that water is *cold*, my friend. Very *cold*.'

'Great.' The brightly painted tank had a huge sign hanging over it that read 'DUNK-A-HUNK'. He'd seen it earlier and had been informed by a laughing Ed that Rosemary and Annie had taken great pride – and amusement – out of the name they'd given the booth. He stepped up and the small gathering cheered. Then he glanced at the very full tank and wondered why he hadn't thought of using warm water.

'Come on, Noah. Get in. Give us a shot!' Ed grinned evilly.

'Kids only.' But Noah stepped up to the ladder that would take him to the top of the booth where he'd sit, suspended above the tank. Was it him, or did the sun suddenly duck behind a cloud? He looked out at the eager, smiling faces and sighed.

'Strip, strip, strip!' they chanted.

He kicked off his shoes and Martin shoved his way to the front of the line. 'Me first!'

Noah laughed, the euphoria contagious. 'All right, all right, I'm coming.' He reached for the hem of his

T-shirt and out of the corner of his eye caught sight of Annie. She came forward, slowly, her gaze on him.

The strangest thing happened. The sounds of the others faded away, and for a minute it was as they were alone on the green. Her eyes held regret, affection and a hint of a promise he didn't try to understand. He blinked, breaking the spell, and pulled his shirt over his head, tossing it aside.

Annie's gaze slowly lowered to his chest and he held his breath, feeling the caress as if it were her long fingers touching him.

'Hurry, Noah!' Martin called out, tossing a ball in his hands. 'I'm ready to dunk you.'

Noah glanced back at Annie as he climbed the ladder, but she'd turned her back. When he looked again, she looked at him, but with only vague interest. Had he imagined the rest?

As Noah settled himself on the seat, cheers rose up and he had to laugh. As a kid, he remembered, there was nothing more satisfying than dunking an authority figure in water. Some things never changed.

How the hell did he grow up to be an authority figure?

He couldn't even get his own life in order.

Martin wound up and threw the ball . . . and missed. Thank God. A cool breeze blew over Noah and he suppressed a shiver. No use egging the crowd on by showing them he was chilly. They'd love that.

He grinned. His kids had a collective sense of humour that was slightly twisted. He liked that. But damn, he was cold. Could he get so lucky as to not have to fall into the water? He glanced down at the ten-foot fall he'd have to take.

It didn't look nearly so much fun from his angle.

Two more kids tossed and missed. Everyone wandered over, and everyone yelled and screamed for Noah to get dunked. Al especially. Noah began to relax after two more unsuccessful attempts.

He was going to do it. He'd be the first one to not get dunked. Things were good.

Then Annie stepped up to the line and lifted the ball. She raised her head and their gazes met. This time he saw no sympathy, no longing, and certainly no affection. Her eyes were lit with pure challenge.

'No fair!' he called, ignoring the way his heart turned over just from looking at her. 'You're not a kid.'

That set off a loud, verbal debate from every which angle, the end result being that he was far, far outvoted. Annie wasn't official staff, therefore she could dunk Noah.

Shit.

She wound up, her tongue between her teeth, her jaw set in concentration. If he hadn't been hanging ten feet above ground waiting to fall into a tub of icy water, he might have smiled at how terrific she looked.

Then she dunked him. And his last thought before he hit the water: Annie, 2; Noah, 0.

An hour later, Noah was dry and once again feeling relaxed. Carnivals did that for him. It had nothing to do with the screaming, happy kids. Or the loud music. Or the games and action. No, it was the simple freedom. It reminded him of the youth he hadn't had.

The youth he was going to give as many kids as he could.

Funny, he thought, raising his eyebrows. Annie had made herself quite scarce since the dunking incident.

He couldn't blame her.

She thought he'd retaliate – and in the past he would have. Now, he didn't feel like it. He just wanted to see one of her smiles again. Maybe he could charm one out of her.

He found her behind a makeshift booth, surrounded by balloons. She smiled politely – and warily – when she saw him. The music blared and the kids seemed rowdy and noisy around him – not exactly the ideal setting to charm someone.

'Hi again,' he said stupidly.

'Hello. You're dry.'

'You have a good arm, Laverty. A real good one.'

She chewed her lower lip, but her eyes sparkled with suppressed humour. 'Are you mad?'

'Nah. I signed you up for the next hour.'

'Signed me up?' she asked, narrowing her eyes.

'Yeah. For the dunking booth. The kids thought it was a great idea. You don't mind, do you?' He looked at her innocently, and he got his wish. She smiled.

'You're a cheat. A penny, please,' she said sweetly, holding out an empty palm.

Her other hand held three darts. Fishing a penny from his pocket, he eyed the strategically placed balloons behind her. 'What's my prize?' he asked, sorting through all sorts of wicked thoughts.

Apparently some of those thoughts were written across his face, for a half-smile tugged at the corner of her mouth. 'The Kiwanis Club from town donated ice-cream sundaes. If you pop a balloon with a dart, I'll give you a ticket for one.'

An erotic picture of Annie wearing nothing more than the makings of a sundae left him temporarily mute. He weighed a dart carefully in his hand, studying his target. 'Would you share it with me?'

'Share what?'

'The sundae.'

She was eyeing him with more interest now. And leaning against the booth towards him, as if her body knew where it belonged, even if her mind didn't.

'That might prove interesting,' she answered as he threw his first dart.

It missed. He could slam a goddamn tennis ball anywhere he chose with pinpoint accuracy and he couldn't hit a balloon seven feet away.

She eyed the fallen dart with sparkling eyes as she bit her lip. Silently she propped herself on her elbows, allowing her dress to gape slightly, just as he threw his second dart.

The brief tantalizing view proved too much for his hungry eyes and the second dart also missed the target, but managed to stick pathetically to the board. The three kids behind him snickered lightly, then choked on it when he turned to them with an eyebrow raised.

'One dart left,' Annie said brightly over the loud music, straightening with a secret smile that tugged at his gut. 'I think you should be less interested in the prize and more on working on that aim.'

Being in such close proximity to her, after two long days of being unable to touch her or talk to her, was agonizing. He wanted nothing more than to wrap his arms around her and take her somewhere quiet. Just to talk, to look at her, to be near her . . . without a curious audience.

'I'll make you a deal,' he said smoothly, pulling out a pocket full of change.

'You're in no position to deal,' she said, shaking her head and looking around him at the next in line.

'Yeah, Noah,' Rosemary called out over the din. 'Now either get behind that booth and help out or move on!'

'Yeah, Noah. Hurry,' Martin shouted. His face was wide with happiness. Nothing suited a kid more than a carnival, Noah thought. He felt Annie's expectant gaze on him and he knew she was wondering what he'd do.

'What will it be?' he asked softly. 'Want some help?'

She shrugged indifferently. 'I'm fine. I don't need any help.'

He wanted her to want him there, but then again, he wanted a lot of things. And suddenly he could think of no place he'd rather be – forget that she didn't want him. As he bent under the wooden booth, she scooted over to give him plenty of space and refused to meet his eyes.

'I said I was fine,' she ground out under her breath as she handed out three darts. She took the penny, gathered some fallen darts, tried to pin up more balloons all while keeping up the pace with the kids. And there were more balloons to blow up, change to give and more darts to collect. She couldn't possibly do it properly by herself and they both knew she needed his help.

'I'm fine,' she repeated as he scooped up some fallen darts.

'But,' he answered as he ducked darts flying over his head, 'I wanted to help.'

He laid his hands on her waist to set her aside, but then she leaned towards him and he found he couldn't let go. Intently she studied his face, his eyes, and then her gaze dropped to his lips. He wondered if she was going to ask him to kiss her – he desperately wanted to. Abruptly she backed away. 'St Taylor,' she whispered beneath a charming smile for Martin who managed to pop a balloon. 'Always there when someone's in need.'

'Don't judge me, Annie,' he said quietly as he took the bucket of darts from her. She stared at him, her eyes showing her regret and sorrow. He nudged her gently aside and proceeded to handle the front line, leaving the balloons to her.

Without another word, they proceeded to work together in perfect harmony. Annie blew up balloons and kept the board full; he took the pennies and handed out darts. Both of them stooped often to pick up the fallen darts, and when they did, their bodies occasionally brushed together. Noah could feel the tremor go through her body at each contact and it set his own pulse racing that he could have that effect on her.

Children were cheering each other on and the music still blared, but within the booth Noah was only aware of Annie. Purposely he let his hand skim across her back as she bent for a fallen balloon and her startled gaze shot up to his. Bowed at his feet, her lips parted slightly in surprise and her golden hair flowing about her face, she looked like the most beautiful creature he'd ever seen. He drew her to her feet and their gaze locked.

And for just a minute the curtain of indifference fell from her eyes, allowing him to see the longing, the sadness, the love swimming there for him. He opened his mouth to speak, wishing for the first time in his life that things could have been different, that he could trust her enough to give her what they were both looking for.

But nothing came out. He didn't have the words.

CHAPTER 12

'Hey, isn't a penny good here?' Ed grinned at Noah and Annie, breaking the spell. The sounds of the carnival, which had faded when she'd got lost in Noah's eyes, drifted back.

And they got back to work, Noah more painfully conscious of her than he'd ever been. The few feet in which they had to work got smaller and smaller as the minutes passed. Their bodies brushed against each other often as he manoeuvred back and forth with the darts. Slowly the tension in that little booth built to a fevered pitch, until it was almost unbearable. Yet, through it all, Annie's face remained poised and serene.

When she moved just as one of the kids was about to toss a dart, Noah grabbed her wrist to pull her out of danger. Slowly, he smiled. In absolute opposite of her calm, cool façade, her pulse was frantically leaping beneath his fingers.

She glanced at his knowing smile and with a soft oath yanked her hand from his grasp. 'You're in my way,' she muttered, pushing past him.

He let her go, unable to contain his smug grin.

He had just bent down to pick up some darts when he heard Annie's squeal of delight. He glanced up in time to see her duck under the booth and gather someone tight against her.

'Oh, Gerry!' she cried, rocking him back and forth. 'You came back.'

Gerry winced in obvious embarrassment as everyone gathered around and started talking at once, yet he made no move to pull away from Annie's embrace.

Noah straightened and vaulted over the booth, gently drawing Gerry from Annie. 'Hey, it's about time,' he said, the smile breaking out on his face as he pulled Gerry close in a quick hug, pleased that the boy allowed it. 'What took you so long?'

Gerry looked down at his feet. 'Wanted to play,' he mumbled. 'And I got hungry. The kitchen's empty.'

Noah laughed. 'You mean all this time all I had to do was stop supplying food and have a carnival?'

Gerry gave him a nervous glance, then looked at Annie. 'Aren't you mad?'

'No, he's not,' Annie said quickly. 'No one's mad, we're just glad you're back.'

'You see?' Martin said, coming up from behind and punching Gerry on the arm. 'I told you he wouldn't be. Should have come back last week – you missed Ed's turkey dinner – '

'Wait a minute. Don't misunderstand – I am mad,'

Noah interrupted quietly, ignoring Annie's sharp look. 'But I'm very happy you're OK. I'm also relieved that you're back.'

Gerry's face had frozen at his first words and continued to look more and more uneasy. Noah sighed. Ignoring Annie's warning look, he pulled Gerry aside so they could talk in private.

'You're going to send me back now.' Gerry tried to look uncaring and defiant but failed miserably, looking like a young, scared little boy.

Compassion filled Noah as he remembered that it wasn't all that many years ago that he had felt as wary and untrusting of a friendly adult as Gerry. 'I told you before, I'm not going to send you away and I'm not going to hurt you. In return, I expect you to respect me and the rules here, and that means you don't just take off because your feelings are hurt. You talk to me about it.'

'I didn't set that fire,' he said quickly, biting his lip. 'I swear.'

'I know that. No one thought you did.'

Gerry's eyes slid to the booths of games in longing and Noah relented. 'Go play, Gerry.' He pulled out a pocket of change and handed it to the boy. 'We'll talk more later.'

For the first time Gerry's smile held more warmth and honesty than wariness, and it was all the thanks that Noah needed.

★ ★ ★

From the shadows on the green, he watched.

Something twisted in his gut watching the make-shift carnival, something that might have been envy. The happy shouts of the carefree kids brought a thickness to his throat he would have denied.

In his own childhood there had been no laughter, no smiling adults, and certainly never a carnival. There'd been nothing but anger, reproach and disgust for him.

The urge to be with fire was strong at any time, stronger now when he felt like this. Flame, red, hot and very real, was the only thing that could cheer him up.

Fire never rebuked, never snubbed, and absolutely never criticized. Fire was all he had.

Soon, he thought. Soon the next fire would come. He'd waited a long time, more time than he would have liked, but they were getting closer and he had to be careful now.

The next scorcher would have to be a large, hot one, sort of a reward for being so patient. He chuckled to himself. He couldn't wait. Already he was anticipating the thrill, the excitement.

Just for the pure pleasure of it he pulled a lighter from his pocket and flicked it, staring at the wavering flame. Ahh, he thought. Fire. It's the most beautiful, pure thing there is.

And all he had left.

It was midnight before Annie got back to her cottage. Wearily she slipped out of her clothes and slid into a hot shower, slowly washing away her sense of sorrow and regret.

She'd been part of a world tonight that she never wanted to leave. Letting the water flow through her hair, she closed her eyes. The pictures she'd taken during the carnival were among the best she'd ever taken – and she didn't even need to see them to know it. The kids had been in absolute heaven and Rosemary had never looked better. Even Noah had been relaxed and carefree in a way she'd never seen before.

Noah.

Just the image of him brought an ache to her chest. She wanted him. So many times she'd been on the verge of whispering that to him, wanting to tell him that it didn't matter that he didn't love her, but something held her back. Her pride, she supposed.

She soaped her body, ignoring the tingling in every nerve-ending, ignoring the throbbing tender warmth between her legs clamouring for release, ignoring the fact that she was trembling in desperate need for a man she could never really have.

Yet she knew with a disturbing certainty that if he appeared in the foggy mist of her shower she would beg him to make love with her.

With a small cry of frustration she reached mercilessly for the hot water and shut it off. Unable to stand the icy shower for more than a few seconds, she turned that off too and leaned her head against the shower wall.

God, she wanted him.

Eventually she shoved the curtain aside and wrapped a towel around herself. Shivering, she stood in front of the sink and wiped at the fog on the small mirror, staring at her reflection.

What was the matter with her, that he didn't want her as badly as she wanted him?

The soft knock at the bathroom door froze her limbs. When it came again, accompanied by the achingly familiar voice quietly calling her name, her body turned from steel to jelly in a heartbeat. She couldn't speak.

The knob slowly turned, then Noah was filling the doorway, his expression carefully masked.

She didn't turn; their eyes met in the mirror and she found she could talk after all. 'How did you get in?' She was surprised at how normal her voice sounded, though her fingers tightly gripped the towel around her shaking, cold body.

He lounged negligently in the opening, one long arm raised and braced against the jamb. His eyes were dark, intent and his gaze captivated hers so that she was incapable of moving. His stance suggested strength, an unleashed power and a hint of the desperation she felt. 'You didn't lock the front door,' he said, his voice low, almost rough. 'You should have.'

'Oh,' she said, releasing the breath she'd been holding since he'd appeared. She shrugged as if it didn't matter. 'Well, it's too late now.'

'Yes.' He pushed away from the door and still holding her eyes in the mirror, he came to stand directly behind her. Every inch of her body was aware of him, every nerve screamed for his attention. But, though he stood close enough for her to feel the coarseness of his jeans against the back of her legs, he didn't touch her. 'You made the carnival happen for those kids tonight, Annie. I wanted to thank you.'

'I didn't do it for you. Is that what you came to tell me?'

In the mirror, his eyes fell from hers to rest on her neck, then to her bare shoulders and to where she was gripping the towel against her breasts. 'No,' he said in a gruff voice. His hands lifted her wet hair aside and he lowered his lips to her neck. His arms came around her, his hands resting on hers where they held the towel precariously around her. Softly his strong fingers stroked hers, his knuckles brushing lightly the swell of her breasts that spilled over the towel.

Her eyelids fluttered closed as every fibre of her body responded to his touch. 'Go away, Noah.'

He trailed tender love-bites down one side of her neck and up the other, his hair falling over his brow, his features set and tight, his brown eyes feverishly bright. 'Don't send me away, Annie. Please. I . . . need this. I need you.'

His fingers moved over hers, taking her hands and placing them on the sides of the porcelain sink before her. With that barrier gone, he loosened the towel. His eyes pinned hers in the mirror as he held the towel against her. 'Please, Annie.'

'No,' she whispered. She could feel his hard arousal pulsing against her bottom through his jeans and the towel, and it was the most erotic thing she'd ever felt. With a subtle motion she couldn't control, she rubbed against it and he groaned.

'Annie.' His lips dropped to one shoulder, kissing it softly before moving to her nape.

Dropping her head in compliance, Annie gripped the sink as if it were a lifeline. Her knees had gone weak. Damn him, she couldn't resist him, never could. 'Noah,' she whispered, unsure whether she was begging him to go or stay. 'Please.'

'I can't leave,' his tortured voice came quietly in her ear. 'I want you so much.' He let go of the towel and it dropped to the floor. She watched with alluring fascination in the mirror as his hands moved over her flushed breasts, lingering. To feel his exquisitely knowing fingers on her skin and actually watch them move languorously over her at the same time in the mirror was one of the most beguiling, seductive things she'd ever experienced.

His mouth continued to make love to her shoulders and neck as his hands slid down her belly and over her hips. She whimpered and sagged back against his chest, lost in the sensations, the roar of her own blood pumping. He ground his erection against her.

She gasped at the carnal pleasure of it and the last of her resistance fell away. She didn't really want him to go when she'd been craving this very thing, especially loving him the way she did. Slowly, experimentally, she reached back and gripped his hips, hugging them tightly to her.

'Oh, God,' he murmured. 'Annie . . . tell me it's OK. Tell me you want this as badly as I do.'

In answer she undulated her hips, watching in the mirror as he grimaced in pleasure. He straightened and ripped his shirt off over his head and she caught the fresh scent of him. She realized then that his long hair was damp and clean, as if he'd just showered. For her. She gasped as his fingers grazed her nipples slowly.

'Tell me,' he said again softly, his dark eyes glazed and hot as they held her stare in the mirror.

She couldn't speak. His rough, strong fingers stilled and she nearly cried out with the loss. 'Please,' she whispered, leaning heavily on the sink for support, praying her legs wouldn't give out.

His hands lowered to her ribcage, her flat stomach, her hips, then to the tops of her thighs. Her belly quivered and she bit her lip to keep from begging. His fingers stroked her while she clutched desperately at the sink, blinking frantically to keep her eyes open, even as her vision started to blur and his face wavered. His hot, hard stare penetrated her while his strong fingers caressed her dewy centre, sending her to near-oblivion.

'Tell me you want me, Annie,' he said, his voice low and soft. 'Tell me to stay.' When she didn't answer, his fingers stopped and she whimpered again.

'Tell me,' he demanded, cajoled, and she could hear the shakiness in his voice.

He was as affected as she. It gave her strength. 'Stay,' she gasped. 'Please stay . . . just don't stop.'

His eyes softened even as his fingers started their delicious torment all over again, and in less than a minute she was rocking against him, the pleasure unendurable. 'Annie,' he whispered softly. But his next soft murmuring words drifted past her ears as she was hit with a rippling climax that left her gasping, trembling and shaken beyond belief.

'My God, Annie . . . you're something.' His disquieted eyes on hers in the mirror told her he meant it, told her also that he meant so much, much more.

She tried to turn, but he held her still, then with a rustle of his clothing moved close against her. Damp skin to damp skin slid together as she felt the hardness of him behind her. He groaned with pleasure, a deep, husky sound, and she closed her eyes, her body humming. When he thrust deep into her wet, silky heat, they both sighed.

With sure hands gripping her hips, he held himself deep inside her. 'I've dreamed of this every night and never did I remember it like this,' he whispered reverently.

Slowly he moved within her, stretching and filling her as no one ever had. She met his hard thrusts with her own, bracing her hands on the sink until he groaned and buried his face against her neck. When she turned her face to rub it against his, he groaned again, and when she blindly sought his lips he kissed her hotly, wetly, searchingly as he pounded faster and faster into her.

His fingers slid down her belly and stroked her until she couldn't contain her cries, caught in the grips of another seizing orgasm that stole her thoughts and reasoning. Then while she was still trembling, he leaned over her, wrapping both his long arms tight around her in a possessive embrace and came with a hot surge; filling her with joy, surrounding her with glory, freely offering her the only gift he had to give: himself.

'This didn't change anything,' Annie said, even as she snuggled closer to Noah's body. They were in her bed and the morning light was just beginning to streak across the sky.

He had been playing with her hair, but at her words he dropped the silky strand and sighed. 'I know.'

'I'm still leaving after my job is done.'

He said nothing, but pulled her even tighter against him and tried to still his sudden panic.

'Did you hear me?'

'Hard to miss it when you're yelling.'

'I'm not,' she said, lowering her voice anyway. 'I just wish you'd talk about it, that's all.'

'There's nothing to say.' And in childlike fashion he buried his face in her neck. The panic had spread into dread, icing his limbs. He would die when she left, he knew it.

He wished that he knew the secret to giving her his love, ensuring that he could make her happy. Never in his life had he successfully kept a woman happy. All he had done was annoy the hell out of his real mother, no matter how hard he'd tried. Rosemary had cared for him, supported him for a time, but never had he been able to make her love him. He hadn't even been able to keep his fiancée happy enough to stay with him.

How could he expect to keep this extraordinary, precious woman lying against him happy?

'I still love you, Noah,' she whispered, clutching him to her. 'That will never change.'

The words that should have struck terror in his heart worked like a balm, warming him. It left him with far more to think about than her roaming, questing hands.

They made love in the dawn's light; blazing, splendid, majestic love that was so perfect, so tender it brought an inexplicable wetness to his eyes and an ache to his chest he couldn't explain.

He didn't have to. Annie smiled a sad, knowing smile and softly rubbed her forehead against his, her eyes filled with her own tears that fell and mixed with his.

When Annie went to the big house for breakfast a short while later, she was stunned to discover that Noah had left town. He'd left her bed not an hour before and he had . . . vanished.

'He's gone?' she repeated to Rosemary, a hard ball of hurt and begrudging anger forming in her stomach where her hunger had been only a minute before. 'Gone where?'

Rosemary looked uncomfortable and turned away, making a show of getting a cup of coffee. She searched for sugar, then milk. Slowly she stirred the cup, her eyes averted. 'I'm not sure, dear. He just left. He said he'd be gone for a few days at least. He spoke to Ed and the counsellors to make sure everything was handled while he was gone. I thought he had told you too.'

'No.' She frowned down at her plate, heaped high with food. She had thought she was starving, brought on by a night of the most passionate, mind-blowing lovemaking of her life. 'Has he ever just left like this before?'

Rosemary fiddled with her coffee. 'I wouldn't know about what he's been up to lately,' she said bitterly. 'I don't even know what I myself have been up to lately.' At Annie's look, she sighed. 'But to answer your question, no, he doesn't usually just take off.'

Annie didn't understand.

Ed and two of the kids came into the kitchen for more plates and Rosemary waited diplomatically until the kitchen was once again empty. From the hallway they could hear the noisy sounds of kids laughing and talking, dishes clinking and silverware clanking. Morning was always a happy time around the Taylor House, especially a weekend morning. There would be no chores, no requirements. Just fun, free time.

'Noah didn't look too well when he left,' Rosemary confided gently, wearing a mother's worried expression. 'He didn't want to talk about it. How about you?'

'There isn't much to tell.'

'Hmmm.' Rosemary's eyes narrowed thoughtfully. 'I don't believe you, of course, but he'll be back.' And in an unusual move of friendship she awkwardly patted Annie's hand. 'Have patience. He'll be all right.'

At that moment, it wasn't Noah Annie was worried about. She had the uneasy feeling that if one of them was going to have long-lasting scars from this summer, it wouldn't be Noah Taylor. She sighed and brought a forkful of eggs to her mouth, forcing herself to eat. Her heavy heart thumped dully even as she told herself the harsh truth. Noah had never made her any promises. He'd never been anything but completely honest and forthcoming with her.

The sad truth was, he simply didn't owe her any explanations for his whereabouts. For whatever reason he had chosen to take off, it was his own business and she would do well to remember that.

And as for last night, well, she had no one but herself to blame for that. Even so, she couldn't bring herself to regret it. It would be hard to regret the most sensual, erotic night of her life.

For three days Annie was on edge. She didn't sleep, she couldn't eat, and for the first time in her entire life her camera failed her. No shot satisfied her, no scenery inspired her, and for the life of her she couldn't get the right lighting. Even her writing rang false, so she finally gave up trying to work. Rosemary was again ill, but with Ed back in charge she had little to do.

Without work, without Noah and without sleep she was a complete wreck.

Gerry found her sitting on the cliffs one afternoon, staring morosely out to sea.

He sat down next to her and for a long minute, neither of them said a word. Seagulls fly high above, glinting sharply against the brilliant sky. The ocean was choppy, thanks to the light wind, and both watched in silence as the birds glided effortlessly, playing in the draught.

'He didn't mean to hurt you,' he said finally. 'He couldn't help it, you know.'

It was hard to remember just how young Gerry was. He was looking at her with eyes that were far too old for a thirteen-year-old. 'I know. He would never hurt anyone on purpose.' Which didn't make it any easier.

'No, I mean that he had to go, but he's coming back.'

His face was earnest and . . . urgent. There was only one reason for that. 'You know,' she breathed. 'You know where he is. Don't you?'

Gerry shifted nervously. 'No, not exactly. But I know that he didn't go away to be away from you.'

His eyes beseeched her not to ask him more, but she wasn't that noble. 'What do you know, Gerry?'

'I can't,' he whispered. 'Please don't ask me. I promised him and . . . I can't let him down.'

Annie reached for a hand that was nervously clenching and unclenching sand and she relented immediately. 'It's all right, Gerry. I know how much Noah means to you. I wouldn't ask you to break your word.'

'I just wanted you to know, that's all. I think he'd be sad to see you this way.'

She didn't realize how much emotion she'd been showing. She certainly had never meant to let her pain show. Now she winced with regret. These kids had enough worries without having to divide their loyalties among the few people they cared about and trusted. 'How did you get so smart for a kid?'

He took her question seriously. 'I don't know,' he said. 'But I'm not a kid. Not any more.'

'No,' she agreed quietly, studying him. 'You're not.'

There was a wisdom about him that defied his years. Although not big, he was a formidable presence among the others. Few would mess with him, even the ones years older.

'I just wanted you to know that Noah didn't, like . . . ditch you or anything.'

'Well,' she said with an overly bright smile to hide the stab of pain, 'that's a relief.'

Gerry smiled back tentatively. He looked as though he had just dumped a large burden and Annie didn't have the heart to let him know he was sadly mistaken. Noah might not have meant to cause her pain, but one basic fact remained.

He hadn't cared enough to let her know where he was.

'So everything is all right now, right?' Gerry asked, rechecking.

'You bet. I'm fine,' she said, lying. She'd never be fine again. 'I'm just thinking about my work.'

'Martin's worried.'

'I'm sorry. I'll talk to him, OK?' She smiled and it must have been a good one because he looked even more relieved.

'Good. He's just a kid, you know.'

She nodded seriously. 'I know.' The concern that Gerry showed Martin was touching and it made her heart ache all over again. She hated knowing that she'd caused them stress, especially since Martin hadn't been sleeping well. Two nights in a row Ed had found him sleeping on the floor of Ed's room when he'd awakened in the morning.

She knew how Martin felt.

On the third day of Noah's absence, Annie was cleaning the bottom floor of the Taylor House. Rosemary was in bed, and, though Annie had tried to sit with her, the older woman had rudely refused the company, shouting that she didn't want a strange woman staring at her. Annie, trying not to take it personally, had tried desperately to find something else to do.

Ed had locked her out of the kitchen in order to bake, saying he didn't want her to jinx his work. Funny, she thought, but it didn't help her mood. She could have gone to the beach, where most of the kids were, enjoying the summer afternoon. But she didn't think she could summon the proper fun attitude.

So instead, she cleaned. She was no better at that than she was at cooking or laundry, but she had to do something – or die from thinking too much.

She was alone and struggling with Noah's disappearance. For days she'd been wondering what had made him run. Was it her? And if it was, then hadn't all her anger and hurt been for nothing because it meant that he cared – too much? That he was frightened? A half-smile tugged at her mouth. Noah frightened was not a picture that came easily to mind. He was fearless.

She'd have to be kind when he came back. No matter how much she wanted to wring his neck.

But what if his disappearance had nothing at all to do with her? Maybe it was just his computer work and he just hadn't seen fit to let her know. OK, she told her nervous stomach, that was just a worst case scenario. There was really no reason to panic until she knew for sure.

She pushed the vacuum past Noah's office door – the sacred tomb, she thought. Casually she looked over her shoulder, but she was alone. She tested the handle, surprised when it opened up to her hand. Pushing the vacuum in, she shrugged with resignation. She wouldn't stop now. Making a show of vacuuming around the piles of papers and books on the floor, Annie craned her neck to see what was on his desk.

When her elbow brushed against a pile, some papers fell. 'Oh, look at that,' she murmured to herself as she bent down to retrieve them. 'What a disaster it is in here.' And, using that ruse, she let her eyes quickly scan every paper in sight.

Nowhere was there a clue as to where Noah was hiding or what he was doing. Under the desk, the vacuum cleaner banged into a box. She bent and pulled it out, ignoring the fluttering in her stomach at the thought of how they'd made wild love in that very spot.

As she pulled the box out of her way, it gaped open

and she gasped in surprise. It was one of her own boxes, from her own house. In fact it was a box she recognized well – she had packed it herself.

What was Noah doing with her things?

She pushed the vacuum cleaner out of her way and squatted down to glance at the writing on the side. In her own scrawl was written 'LIVING ROOM – VACATION VIDEO TAPES'.

She sat back on her haunches, her hands on her hips. What the hell had Noah taken this box for? Yanking it open, she sorted through the cassettes, looking for any clue as to what Noah wanted.

There was nothing but vacation tape after vacation tape. Mammoth Mountain 1980. Vancouver, Canada 1981. San Francisco 1982. She smiled at that one nostalgically – she loved that city. New England 1983. Washington DC 1984. Her smiled vanished abruptly. That had been their last vacation as a family, because it was the following year that her mother and Jesse had been murdered.

'Find anything interesting?' a bored voice drawled behind her. She nearly jumped out of her skin.

CHAPTER 13

At his voice, Annie leapt to her feet, her eyes shining with embarrassment and anger. 'Well, Noah Taylor,' she said smoothly enough. 'How nice to see you.'

She shoved her hands in her shorts pockets and stared at him with a defiance that would have amused him if he weren't so surprised to find her snooping through his office.

'Did you find what you were looking for?' he asked again, his voice softer. God, she looked good. He had missed her – more than he had thought possible.

'As a matter of fact, I did.' Meeting his eyes with a grey fury that he wasn't expecting, she stepped around a box. It was then that he realized exactly what she had found. 'I found something very interesting indeed.'

His eyes flicked to the open box and his jaw clenched tight. 'You've been prying again, Laverty.'

'You bet I have,' she agreed tightly, and he was surprised to see her fighting tears. 'My parents always agreed that my curiosity was my worst fault. They were sure it was going to be the death of me some day.'

'It may yet,' he said in a strangely tender voice, taking a step towards her. 'Annie – '

'Back off, Bones,' she said evenly, backing away. 'I want to know why you have my stuff here. Why did you take my family's vacation tapes?'

'Aren't you glad to see me?' he taunted softly, desperately wanting to hear that she was, that she had missed him as hopelessly as he had missed her. 'Aren't you in the least bit curious to know where I've been the past few days?'

'No,' she said flatly, trying to yank her arm back as he snagged it in a tight grasp. 'Let go of me.'

'I can't,' he said, pulling her hard against him, drinking in her beautiful scent, her blazing eyes, her long willowy form. 'I'm too damned happy to see you.' He lowered his face to hers, stunned anew to see the tears still shimmering on her glorious lashes. 'What's this, Laverty? Are you that relieved to see me?'

'No!' She shoved hard at his chest, her eyes filled with panic. With reluctance, he let her go.

'What's the matter?' he asked her slim back as she turned from him. His chest tightened. 'Has something else happened?'

A disparaging sound escaped her and she shrugged. 'Nothing's happened. Everything is just as perfect as you left it. Now tell me why you have my things before I smack you.'

He smiled at her petulant tone. So she was just

miffed because he had left without a word, just as Gerry had told him she would be. He would have called; he'd wanted to call. But what the hell would he have said? As much as he had hated it, he knew he had to wait to speak to her in person. His smile faded when his eyes lit on the open box, and he wished she had been less thorough in her meddling. 'You're mad because I left, but – '

'I couldn't care less that you left,' she said, whirling to face him, her hair falling about her face in a curtain of gold. 'What I want to know is why you have my things. These are tapes that mean a lot to me, Noah. They're – '

When she stopped suddenly and covered her mouth with a shaking hand, his heart cracked. He desperately wanted to tell her why he had left, what he had found and what they had to do. And that while he was gone he had had another, more stunning revelation.

'Never mind,' she said quickly, heading for the door. 'I've got to go.'

'I'll tell you about the tapes,' he said gently, reaching for her. 'But there's something else – '

She pushed his hands away and hopped over some papers.

'Wait,' he called, cursing in frustration as he tripped over piles of papers and boxes. 'I want to tell you something.' She slipped out the door without another word, shutting it softly behind her.

'Shit,' he said softly, shoving his fingers through his

hair in frustration. He looked up at the closed door. 'I love you.' He kicked the closest box, then winced.

The door opened slowly and he swivelled back in relief, then sagged in defeat. It was Martin, looking small and uncertain.

'Noah?'

'Hey, Martin,' he said with what he hoped was a genuine smile. 'Come on in, bud. How've you been?'

Martin smiled back, his eyes showing his obvious pleasure at seeing Noah. 'You're back.'

'Yes, that I am.' He started moving boxes and files to clear a path from desk to door. 'Don't know how this office got so out of control.'

'Annie was trying to clean it for you.'

Christ, he hated that worried, nervous, wary look in Martin's eyes. And knowing he'd put it there this time was like a knife through his gut. 'Martin, everything is OK.'

'No,' he said slowly, shaking his head. 'It's not. I like you, Noah. I like you a lot.'

'I like you too, Martin,' he smiled gently. 'A whole lot.'

Martin's little hands fisted on his hips 'But I like Annie too.'

'Well, that makes two of us.'

'You left without telling her where you were going?'

'She told you that?'

'No,' he admitted, looking away. 'I could just tell. She faked like it didn't matter, but we knew it did.'

'I had a good reason, Martin,' he said gently, having no intention of sharing it. It was simply too complicated – and dangerous. 'But I am going to straighten it out.'

'You made her cry.'

'I . . . I – ' He stopped, feeling ridiculously chastened. By a kid. A kid who used to think the sun rose and sat on his shoulders but who was now looking at him with anger and reproach. 'I never meant to make her cry.'

'So why did you?'

Noah looked at Martin who was staring at him, waiting for an answer to a question that was so difficult he couldn't begin to explain. Because he was a jerk, he wanted to say. Because he was mentally challenged when it came to matters of the heart. Because he had never met anyone like her, and that alone scared the living daylights out of him.

He had made her cry. He'd made the only person he had ever *really* loved – could ever love – cry when all he wanted to do was make her happy.

'I'll fix it, Martin,' he promised the boy and himself. 'I will.'

'I hope so,' Martin said seriously. 'Because she's learning to cook and I think she's doing it for you, not us.'

Noah bit back his smile. 'Really?'

'Yup. Last night Ed taught her how to make spaghetti and the sauce was . . . pretty good.'

His smile escaped him then. 'Well, then . . . we can't have her upset, can we?'

'No,' Martin agreed solemnly. 'Tonight she's going to try cookies and I really want to see that. So do the others.'

'I bet.' Noah glanced down at the box of videos on the floor and was forcefully reminded that his problems – and Annie's – were far from over.

In some ways, he thought grimly, they were just beginning. 'Martin, I'll straighten things out, but could you do me a favour?'

'OK.'

'Since you're going to be hanging out with Annie today, could you let me know if she goes to her house?'

Martin looked reluctant. 'Like spy on her?'

Exactly. 'No, not spy. I . . . like her as much as you do, Martin. And I want to make sure she's OK.'

Martin's eyes widened. 'Is there someone trying to hurt her, really? Gerry told me he thought so, but I didn't believe him.'

He sighed. Gerry was too damn smart for his own good. 'I'm not sure,' he told the boy honestly. 'But I don't want anything to happen to her.'

'Me either.'

'So you'll tell me?'

'I promise. But what are you going to do?'

'I have something I have to do here before I straighten everything out with Annie.'

'Are you leaving again?' Martin asked, disappointment reigning over his features.

'No,' he promised softly. 'I'm not leaving. I won't leave again. OK?'

Martin smiled too. 'OK. You'll be here, then.'

'Yes,' Noah said, booting up his computer. 'I'll be right here.' And with any luck the whole mess would be cleared up within the hour, he thought as he started printing one of a list of files he would need.

He had hoped to have Annie by his side as he did this, but that too would have to wait. He had put the truth off long enough and he could no longer ensure anyone's safety. Real regret and loss shifted through him as he worked. He missed her.

And if she hadn't been so stubborn she would be here right now, he thought. She was hurt because he'd left without a word, but what she didn't realize was that he'd had to. He'd just explain that. She was a rational woman; she'd understand.

The night after the carnival, after he'd gone to Annie's cottage and they'd made love in her apartment, he had realized one short, terrifying thing.

He had lost his heart to her. Holding her in his arms as the dark night faded into dawn, he'd looked down into her peaceful, sleeping face and had known the truth. He loved her.

Scared sleepless by the thought, he'd got restless and gone to the beach to walk, but even that hadn't calmed him. So he'd gone to his computer to work on the city's programming and, in doing so, stumbled across a shocking truth. Something that had made him think that, if he looked a little harder, he just might find an answer to the questions that had been plaguing them about the fires.

And, less than a few minutes later, he was afraid he'd found it.

Even as he'd stared at the screen, wanting to deny it, he knew he couldn't.

So without a word, terrified by the unbelievable facts, he had left town to gain the proof he would need.

He had got it. Together with what he was printing, he was about to put away the most vicious, shocking arsonist this county had ever seen.

And devastate the woman he loved.

He was gathering everything he needed when Martin came running, out of breath, back into his office.

'Noah,' he gasped. 'She's gone.'

'What? Who's gone?' He thought of Rosemary and how easily it would be for her to wander off and get lost.

'Annie. She ditched me. She just got into a taxi.'

He looked helplessly at Martin, a sinking feeling growing deep within him. 'It's all right, Martin,' he said calmly. 'Everything is going to be fine.' He shoved the things he needed into a box and strode towards the door. 'I'll be back in a little bit.'

'You going after her?' Martin asked anxiously. 'Before something happens to her?'

'Yeah,' he said, hoping it wouldn't be too late. 'And then I'm never going to let her out of my sight again.'

Martin looked at him thoughtfully. 'Annie doesn't like to be told what to do.'

'I wouldn't dream of telling her what to do, as long as she agrees to do it with me.' He quickened his movements, cringing when he thought of how she must be feeling, thinking that he didn't love her.

He rushed from the house, dropped the box into his car and thrust it into gear, praying that he wouldn't be too late.

Annie chewed on her nails and tapped her feet impatiently for the entire short ride to Ross's downtown office.

Noah was back. And damn it, she'd nearly melted just from the sight of him. If she stayed in his office one second longer she would have been crying out her loneliness in his arms, making him feel even more guilty for what he couldn't give her.

She would be early, but Ross would understand. They were meeting for dinner, their weekly ritual since she'd been back. She was worried about Ross, noticing that he seemed weak and tired, much more than a man of only fifty should be.

Maybe he was sick. Maybe he was deathly ill and couldn't find a way to tell her. If something happened to him she'd be entirely alone. Granted, she'd been alone for ten years, but that was by choice – and she'd always known how to reach Ross. If Ross was gone, she'd be the only Laverty left. She'd be nobody's daughter.

In Ross's office his receptionist seemed surprised to see her. 'He wasn't in today,' she said, checking over his schedule. 'As far as I know, he's at the house working. Could you have just missed him?'

'Probably,' she conceded, though knew it was unlikely.

She was nearly an hour early. Maybe he had intended on meeting her here later, at the right time. Well, she'd surprise him and go to the house.

Anything to stay away from the Taylor House and its irresistible owner for a little while longer.

At the police commissioner's office Noah, the chief of police and the fire chief watched the Laverty vacation video in silence. When Noah switched it off, they all stared at him in horrified disbelief. One by one they looked down at the printed file in their hands.

'The voice that narrated that vacation tape is the same voice on the tape that was destroyed in the fire at my cottage,' he told them with certainty.

'It's Ross's voice,' the fire chief said, agreeing. 'But do you have any idea what you're saying? What you're accusing him off?'

Of course he did. He'd been sick as hell over it for days. 'Eighty per cent of the unsolved arson crimes of this county were committed when Ross Laverty was off duty,' Noah continued evenly. 'Starting twenty years ago when he first joined the force.' He pointed to the papers they were each holding. 'And the remaining twenty per cent of unsolved fires are small, petty fires that amounted to little or no damage.'

'Oh, my God,' the chief of police whispered, staring at the proof in his hands, a look of pure horror on his face.

'And Ross Laverty isn't his real name,' Noah said quietly. 'He was Bud Hinson before that. He lived in Texas – where he was a firefighter.'

'Was?'

Noah looked at the chief with apology. He knew how seriously the man took his job, how seriously he took the job of every firefighter beneath him. And everything Noah said went against the basic oath of a firefighter. They saved lives, not took them. 'He was sacked for setting a fire in an open field and watching it burn. Three kids who had been playing hide-and-seek there died.'

'Jesus,' someone whispered.

'He was Jack Halston before that, in South Carolina. There he was a ranger – let go for his inability to stop the local kids from setting fires in the woods.'

'But,' the fire chief said hoarsely, 'it wasn't kids setting the fires at all, was it?'

'No,' Noah said, feeling sick. 'It wasn't. But the kids were blamed. Even when an entire campground burned to the ground and thirty people were torched to death, including nine children.'

The chief of police looked as if he wanted to throw up. He and Ross had been close friends for nearly twenty years. 'But Ross isn't old enough to have had at least three other lives before this one. He's been here forever.'

And that was the crux of it. Everyone knew Ross, everyone liked him. Which made it that much more difficult to believe. 'He's sixty-one,' Noah told him gently. 'Not fifty. He lied about that too. And he's had two complete families before Mrs Laverty, Jesse and Annie. And each perished in mysterious fires.'

Everyone in the room thought about the unsolved mystery of Mrs Laverty and Jesse's death, and no one was left in doubt as to what had happened.

Annie let herself in the back door of her house and called to Ross.

The house was eerily silent and she shivered, suddenly frightened.

Then she laughed at herself. This was her childhood home, the place of happy memories. There was no reason to be afraid here.

'Ross?'

She stepped from the kitchen into the living room, seeing his tools scattered about. Then she saw his light jacket and smiled. He was here.

She took the stairs quickly, firmly squelching down

346

her uneasiness. Noah would kill her for coming here alone, she thought, then made a face. What did she care what Noah thought? He had coaxed his way into her heart, then into her bed, and then he'd deserted her the night after the carnival without a second thought as to how she would feel. It was still embarrassing to think about how easily she had given in to him and his damned sexy eyes, husky voice and knowing hands.

Oh, he needed her all right, but it wasn't exactly in the way she had wished for. She wanted him to need her mind, her spirit, her soul, not just her body. And until that was the case she had promised herself that she'd steer clear of him, for her own sanity's sake.

Strong thoughts, but the sorry truth was, she couldn't stay away.

She still loved him.

'Ross?' she called again, from the top of the stairs, smiling when she remembered how she'd smashed the mirror in self-defence against the fog and her own fear. Noah had tried gallantly not to laugh at her that night, but it really had been impossibly funny.

What was Noah doing with the Laverty vacation videos? The thought nagged at her as she roamed the hallway, cursing the fading light and the lack of electricity.

All Noah's own tapes had been destroyed in his cottage fire, along with the one tape he got of the arsonist talking.

She stopped abruptly as her heart tripped. Her

nightmares and skittishness had obsessed Noah into finding the arsonist and proving that all the fires were connected. And while her heart warmed at how much that showed he cared, it also told her what she didn't want to know.

The Laverty vacation tapes were connected somehow. There was only one Laverty left besides herself who could possibly be involved.

'Ross?' she called again, a shiver running down her spine at the silence that answered her.

A sound from above startled her until she realized that Ross must be in the attic. At the bottom of the narrow stairway, she hesitated. 'Ross?'

Slowly she climbed the stairs, wishing she'd brought a flashlight and shaking her head at her own nerves. How ridiculous to be scared in the house she'd grown up in. It made no sense.

Until she got to the top of the stairs.

From the city office Noah called the Taylor House. When he learned there was still no sign of Annie, he shook his head. 'I'm worried,' he told the other men in the office. 'What if she's with him?'

'He doesn't know we know,' the fire chief said.

Noah thought of how close to Annie the arsonist had been this entire time and he shuddered. If he lost her now . . . no. He wouldn't think about it, because it absolutely wouldn't happen. He'd see to it. 'We have to find her.'

'She'll be as safe as she's been all this time. For now.'

His gut twisted. 'No,' Noah said, with a sureness he couldn't explain. 'She's in trouble. *I can feel it*.' He looked at the chief of police, who stared at him for a long minute.

The man nodded. 'I've solved more cases than I want to admit on hunch alone. If you feel trouble, there's trouble.'

The statement didn't reassure Noah in the least. 'We've got to find them. She's not as safe as we think. He managed to find out about the video without us knowing; he could realize we're on to him. But once you get him, you've got to be able to keep him. Do you have enough to make an arrest?'

'We've got enough to lock him away for the rest of his life,' he answered. 'Which is a hell of a lot fewer years than I thought it would be.' He glanced down at the damning evidence Noah had spent the past three days searching for. 'Shit. I just can't believe it. All those years.' He rubbed his face. 'All those years. I thought we were on the same side. I thought we were friends.'

Noah didn't want to think about what he felt. Or how Annie was going to feel. It already hurt, knowing how much pain this was going to cause her.

'All those unnecessary deaths,' the fire chief said angrily. 'All those times I put my team in life-threatening, dangerous positions for fires that didn't have to happen. All that damaged property. It's god-damn sick is what it is. Sick.'

'Let's go,' said the chief of police. 'We'll start with the Laverty house. He's probably there and hopefully unsuspecting.'

Noah was not a religious man, but, as they drove, he prayed to every God he could think of that Annie was safe.

The light that shone on Annie's face went out, but she was momentarily blinded. A rough hand snatched her arm and dragged her into the attic, slamming the door behind her.

'Annie,' Ross said angrily in a hoarse voice. 'God-damn you. What the hell are you doing here?'

She still could see nothing, but her blood was roaring through her veins, her heart pounding so loudly she was sure he could hear it. 'You scared me to death, Ross. Why didn't you answer me when I called you?'

He said nothing.

She could smell her own fear. 'Turn the light back on.'

'I can't,' he said in rough apology. 'Annie.' He groaned. 'Why did you come here? You were supposed to meet me at my office, *not here*.'

'What's the difference?' she asked, relaxing a little. She took a deep breath to slow down her racing heart and strained to see him. 'What are you doing up here, anyway?'

More silence. Then he said harshly, 'Leave now, Annie. Just go and forget you came here.'

'What are you talking about?'

'Please,' he said in a tortured voice. 'Just go.'

Her heart started pounding again. 'Ross, you're scaring me. What's going on?'

Again, no answer.

She groped for him, but he had moved. And suddenly, in a room she'd been comfortable in since she was a baby, she was terrified. She couldn't even remember which way to turn to find the staircase. 'Ross? Turn the light back on. I can't see.'

'Go, Annie. If you hurry, you can save yourself.'

She whipped her head towards his voice. It came from the far left. A sudden flare of fire from the corner made her scream and she jumped back.

'Ross!' She crouched with her hands in front of her face to hide from the brilliant light. In two seconds there was a large, hot fire.

'Hurry, Annie,' he urged in a thick voice, staring at the flames. 'Go down the stairs. Save yourself. Please,' he yelled when she didn't move.

Annie forced herself to look into the fire. Eyes streaming, she saw him. He was hunched over a large bonfire, feeding it from a stack of kindling and wood at his feet.

God, oh, God, she thought. He's trying to kill himself. She couldn't let him do it. Without thinking, she ran towards him, straight at the very thing that terrified her most. Fire.

'Ross,' she cried, pulling hard on his sleeve and cringing away from the already powerful blaze. 'What are you doing?'

He was staring in fixed fascination at the flames. 'I can't help myself, Annie. God, it's beautiful, isn't it?' He roughly grabbed her, turning her to face the fire. 'Isn't it?' he asked again, his voice rising.

'No,' she sobbed, trying to turn away from the intense heat and ear-splitting crackling from the wood. 'No!'

'Yes!' he hissed, still holding her close enough to the hot flames that she could feel the hair on her arms singe painfully. 'Your mother didn't see it; nobody ever sees it but me.'

She blinked in growing horror as she struggled to focus on his tormented face. Sweat poured down her face from the heat of the flames and she jumped every time a new piece of wood was noisily digested by the fire. 'Oh, no,' she moaned, suddenly seeing clearly. Her mother and brother in the burning car. Her own house burning. Noah's cottage. 'It was you. It was all you. *You started the fires.* All of them.'

He was breathing heavily and his grasp on her loosened, but it didn't matter. She was riveted in place by the growing realization that the man before her was a perfect stranger. He was panting from pleasure, she saw with disgust. He couldn't keep his eyes off the flames. And yet he appeared completely unaffected by the incredible, growing heat that felt as if it was melting her skin.

'You killed my mother and brother,' she cried. When he didn't answer, she grabbed his collar and yanked him close, forcing him to look into her eyes. But the glassy eyes that stared back at her were vague and troubled.

'Yes,' he hissed again. 'I did. Your mother discovered the truth and confronted me, threatened to turn me in. I'd already rigged the car, just for fun. I never meant anyone to get in it. But she got scared and tried to run for help. I tried to stop her, but things went bad. It was an accident, Annie. I never meant – That's why I stole the earring.' He pulled it out of his pocket and stared at it, his eyes full of sorrow, madness. 'I just wanted a part of her too, just like you. I never meant for her to be . . . gone. Now she's gone. They're all gone. I can't help myself,' he whispered. 'I live to watch the flames. They got in the way, damn it; it wasn't my fault. People just kept getting in the way.'

'Oh, God,' she moaned, letting go of him as her world started to spin.

He grabbed her back and shook her. 'Even you, Annie. You wouldn't stay out of the way. It was me that night that set fire to this house – but I didn't know you were in it. You never came back; how would I know? I swear I didn't know you were here. Never would I have hurt you on purpose. Do you believe me?'

She stared at him in horror, the heat so intense she couldn't breathe.

He shook her, hard. 'Believe me!' he shouted. 'I want you to say it!'

'Ross,' she cried, trying to push him away. 'You're hurting me.'

'I dropped the camcorder when I heard you scream, Annie. That night I heard your scream and I . . . oh, God, I almost killed you. I lost it, I lost the camcorder then.'

'No.' She shook her head in denial, staring wide-eyed at his wild face. This wasn't happening, this couldn't be happening. Every exposed nerve screamed from the painful, intense heat and smoke.

Ross gentled his hold. 'That's why Noah's cottage had to go. I had to destroy the tape, and what a way to destroy it, huh? That fire was beautiful. God, what a fire that was – a quick, hot one.' His breath whistled out in remembered appreciation. His mouth twisted in a ghost of a smile. His eyes gleamed with insanity. She didn't recognize him.

Tremors racked her hot body as shock started to take over, and spots filled her eyes from lack of oxygen. She fought against passing out with every-thing she had, knowing once she did it would be over for her. 'Why the Taylor House?' she managed. 'Why, Ross? You could have killed those children.'

'No,' he said quickly. 'I was careful, I promise. I never would have let you get hurt.'

'Why?' she whispered, her throat screaming with pain. 'Why did you do it?'

For a minute his eyes cleared and he was the Ross she'd always known. 'You were getting too close, Annie. As much as I wanted you to, I knew I couldn't let you decide to stay. I had to scare you away.' His face twisted and he shook her hard again. 'Why didn't you leave, Annie? Why didn't you go? I don't want you to die.'

She couldn't stand the heat, couldn't stand the flames licking at her bare legs. They had to get out now or it was going to be too late. Already the fire had spread through half of the attic and was greedily devouring everything in its path. Smoke made it nearly impossible to see.

Ross was holding her in a tight grip that belied his years. Now that he wasn't looking at the flames, his eyes remained sane. *You have to believe me, Annie. I'm not a murderer. I wanted you to go to my office tonight so I could be sure you would be safe. Run. Now. While you can.'

'What about you?' she asked in growing panic, unable to think about what would happen to him if he stayed.

'Go,' he screamed, pushing her. 'Before it's too late.'

But it was already too late. Suddenly the narrow

beaming that served as the attic flooring gave away beneath the rippling blaze and the centre of the fire fell to the floor below.

Annie screamed again as the remaining flames leapt around them to grab on to the wall beams, climbing to the roof. Surrounded entirely by hot, scorching fire, Annie dropped to the floor, screaming Ross's name. Because of the smoke, she could no longer see him. No, not like this, it can't end like this, she thought wildly. Sobs stuck in her throat as she thought of Noah, then her mother and Jesse.

Huddling in a ball, she watched the very ground around her give way, dropping to the flames that roared through the second floor, then to the first floor, over twenty feet below.

CHAPTER 14

Five miles from the house, they heard the call come over the radio and the chief flipped on his own lights and siren. A mile away Noah knew they were too late. He could already see the smoke, rising dark against the deepening dusk sky. From the street, his heart stopped. Two engines had arrived ahead of them and were already working on the highest flames, but the whole Laverty house was engulfed.

And he knew, as certain as he knew his own name, that Annie and Ross were in that house.

Halfway to the door, two firefighters stopped him. 'You can't go in there,' one shouted. 'Get back.'

'There are two people in there,' he argued, trying to push around them, but they were strong and used to holding terrified, anguished people back from danger. 'Let me go.'

'No way, man,' one said, hauling him back. 'We have two guys on the roof and when the blaze is down some, we'll go in.'

He was left alone while they struggled to contain the

357

fire from leaping to the neighbouring houses. He put a hand to his heart as if he could actually ease the dull ache and the heavy pounding there, but nothing could. Annie was in there, he just knew it. And if something happened to her he would never, ever forgive himself.

She was in there, maybe dying and she still didn't know how he felt about her. If she died now, she'd never know because he had been too stupid and selfish to tell her. It couldn't end this way, it just couldn't. It wouldn't be fair. He blinked furiously, trying to see through the hot blaze, the thick smoke, the burning ash, but couldn't. The ache spread like a vicious disease throughout his body. Annie didn't know he loved her, had no idea how her very existence made his life worth living, how without her he would die.

A shout from above caught his attention and he strained his eyes, trying to see through the haze of smoke and ash. He could see the firefighters on the roof, but the flames were so hot and so big that he couldn't imagine how they were going to stay safe.

Though the night was cool, Noah was surrounded by thick smoke that made breathing next to impossible, and a heat that made movement difficult. Moving closer and closer without realizing it, his eyes searched desperately for any signs that the firefighters had found Annie.

When the roof collapsed suddenly and the two firefighters were swallowed up, disappearing into the blaze, a collective cry went up from the street.

Noah's heart, already dying, squeezed tighter in agony and concern for the men. Without thinking, he took running steps closer until a pure wall of heat stopped him short. He threw his hands up to cover his face from the hot sparks and ash as he sank to his knees with a desperate cry, unable to watch as the fire overtook the entire house.

And he knew, without being told, that there was no way anyone could survive the intense fire.

Annie groaned and went still. It was dark, but gradually her eyes adjusted. She was in her back garden and she knew if she thought about it long enough she would remember how she'd got there. But she didn't want to. She was on her back with soft, wet grass beneath her. Slowly, painfully, she rolled over and pushed herself to her feet to stare in shock at her house.

Or what used to be her house. Now, it was a sheer wall of fire.

And suddenly, she became aware of the noise; the crackling wood, the hoarse, distant shouts of men, a siren. Vaguely she remembered that she had been in that fire, but a clog of fear and panic came with that thought so she shoved it easily aside.

She didn't want to remember how she had got out.

The night was dark, and the smoke covered any light the moon and stars might have given off – which was probably why no one noticed her dark and huddled form standing off to the side of the back door, all alone.

Concerned in a distant sort of way, she walked carefully around to the front of the house, maintaining a safe distance from the heat of the blaze. Her thoughts were jangled and loose.

Stopping on one side, she blinked in confusion. Organized chaos was everywhere. Three police cars, two fire engines and two ambulances were parked haphazardly in the street. Water flowed down the driveway, hoses ran criss-crossed across the yard. Neighbours drifted in the street, in an eerie *dejà vu* of the previous fire. Officers, firefighters and paramedics rushed back and forth attending to their jobs, shouting orders and receiving news.

They were looking for her. Glancing back at the roaring blaze and flinching from the fiery heat, she started to remember. Whimpering, she turned away and closed her eyes until her thoughts again scattered and she could go on.

Unsure and wobbly, Annie stepped forward, but stopped abruptly at the sight not ten feet from her.

Noah was on his knees before the house, head bent and chest heaving. And something inside her cracked at the sight of the man she loved beyond reason. She knew from his pose of anguish that he thought she had perished in the fire. Her vision was starting to fade and the pain she'd been holding at bay was creeping up on her, but she tried to ignore it for a little while longer.

Dropping to her knees in front of him, she touched his parched and red cheeks, lifting his head with shaking hands to stare into smoke-drenched eyes lined with singed brows.

'Noah,' she tried to say, but all that came out was a croak.

CHAPTER 15

'Oh, God, Annie,' Noah moaned, yanking her against him and wrapping his arms around her as if he planned to never let go. 'I thought I'd lost you.'

The rest of his words died on his tongue as the lithe figure in his arms went limp.

'Jesus, no,' he whispered, even as he rose to his feet and ran with Annie towards the ambulance. Oh, God, he thought, don't let it be too late. Please, oh, please, let her live.

Yet even as they gave her oxygen, laid her out on a stretcher and prepared to care for her burns and wounds, Noah's heart sank. The paramedics wore tight, grim faces and Annie remained so very still and pale.

He insisted on riding in the ambulance and they agreed in the end only because it was easier and faster to do so, but he couldn't touch her because of the special burn suit they had her in.

So it was with bleak and dismal eyes that he kept a

vigil over her, wishing he could hold her hand. Wishing a lot of things.

Noah paced the hospital waiting room, alone with his grim and despairing thoughts. The fire chief had just left.

Both the firefighters that had been on the roof when it collapsed had been released with minor cuts and burns. Luck had indeed been with them.

Ross's luck must have run out. He didn't survive. The only mystery left: how had Annie survived?

Only Annie could tell them. But she was still unconscious, unable to tell them anything – especially what had happened in those last minutes between her and Ross. His gut tightened with fear, but he forced himself to relax. He simply had to believe she was going to be all right.

It was the what-ifs that were killing him. What if he had chased Annie when she'd escaped from his office and made her listen to his declaration of love? The fact that he hadn't was proof what a coward he was. What if he had trusted Annie with his heart sooner? She never would have been running from him in the first place if she had known how he felt about her. What if he had got to the Laverty house sooner than he had – would he have been able to get her out unhurt?

He desperately needed to believe she was going to be all right.

A tall, thin man in hospital scrubs came through the

double doors. 'You're waiting for Annie Laverty?'

'Yes, I'm Noah Taylor. Her . . . her – '

'Friend?' The man smiled gently. 'I know who you are. I'm Dr Mallow.'

'Annie?' Noah asked, his voice hoarse, his nerves leaping. 'Is she conscious?'

'No. Not yet.' The doctor took a deep breath. 'Her injuries are extensive, Noah, but she's going to survive.'

Noah's eyes closed and he drew a ragged breath past lungs that didn't want to function. 'Tell me.'

'Smoke inhalation – that's the dangerous part. But she got oxygen in time. She's got burns down the right side of her neck, her shoulder and right arm. Those are going to give her considerable pain and trouble, but I don't think skin grafts are going to be necessary.'

Noah held his body so tight it hurt. How was he going to handle watching Annie deal with pain? It should have been him, damn it. Not her.

The doctor touched his shoulder, and Noah looked at him. 'There's more.'

'Yes.' Dr Mallow's smile was grim. 'Believe it or not, she's a lucky young woman. Very lucky. She seems to have taken quite a fall. The fire chief said she might have fallen down at least one floor, possibly two. She's got a good concussion, a broken right collarbone, two cracked ribs and a sprained ankle.'

'Oh, God.' Noah rubbed his temples. What the hell had happened inside that house? And how many injuries did she have that no one could see? Like her heart?

A nurse waved frantically at the doctor. Dr Mallow squeezed Noah's shoulder. 'I'll be back when she wakes up, Noah. I've got to go.'

Noah sank into the nearest chair and let his head fall into his hands. She was in bad shape. Wait – how bad was the concussion? And what degree were her burns? He *had* to know.

He leaped to his feet and practically ran to the double doors, only to be stopped by a nurse.

'I have another question for the doctor,' he said urgently.

'I'm sorry,' she said calmly, blocking his way. 'He's busy now.'

'I just talked to him.' Noah tried to step around her. 'It's about Annie Laverty.'

The nurse's stern expression softened, but she held firm. She obviously was a pro at dealing with distraught family members. 'Maybe I can help you.'

'I want to see her.'

'Definitely not yet. She's still unconscious and in the burn ward.'

Sweat pooled at the base of his spine. 'How bad are the burns?' Hadn't he read somewhere that a burn was the worst kind of pain one could experience? He wanted to cry.

'I'm sorry,' the nurse said again, still calmly. 'I can't comment on that.'

Noah wanted to wring the information out of her. 'How about the concussion? How severe is it?' Was she in a coma?

The damn nurse looked at him sympathetically. 'Why don't you sit down? I'll tell the doctor you want to see him again. He'll be out as soon as he can.'

'That woman in there,' he said in a low voice, 'means everything to me. Do you understand? She's lying in there unconscious and alone, and all I want to do is see her. I've got to tell her – ' Oh, he was definitely losing it, telling a perfect stranger things he could hardly admit to himself. But pride had no place in that emergency room, none at all. 'I've got to tell her I love her and that she's going to marry me.'

'I see,' the nurse said kindly. 'This is very difficult for you, I know.'

'You can't know.'

'I do, but that's another story. I'll just go get the doctor and see what he says. We have a policy against visiting in the burn unit unless you're immediate family.'

OK, he was going to have to hurt this woman. Didn't he just tell her that he was going to be Annie's husband? 'Look – ' he started harshly.

'Noah.'

He turned to see Rosemary standing behind him, her eyes sane – thank God – and wide with worry. 'What's going on?' she asked.

The nurse escaped, wisely.

366

'I don't know anything,' he said, his shoulders sagging as he turned away from the doors. 'Not a damn thing.'

Her face reflecting her sorrow and sympathy, she came close and stared up at him. Then she sighed. 'Oh, Noah, I'm so very sorry.'

Unable to handle it, he turned away. But she grabbed his arm and turned with him.

'Are you all right?' she asked, trying to see his expression.

'I'm fine,' he said curtly, turning away again. 'It's Annie that I'm worried about.'

She stepped in front of him and gripped his arms with surprising strength until he was forced to look at her. 'I'm sorry about Annie, Noah. But I'm sorry for *much*, much more than that.'

'What do you have to be sorry for, Rosemary?' he asked wearily, his mind and spirit concentrating on Annie.

'A lot, actually.' Her eyes lit on him and her expression was soft and maternal, and yes, damn it, loving. He could feel his eyes ache suddenly and he shut them abruptly, knowing he was about to fall apart.

'I know you don't want to talk about this, but I want you to hear it, Noah.'

'Rosemary – '

'Noah, please,' she said, her eyes desperate. 'I – I'm not well and you know it. I may never get another chance, so please, hear me.'

He took a deep breath. 'Hear what?'

She looked at him, her heart in her eyes. Then she pulled him to a chair, forced him to sit and sat next to him. Gently she took his hand, and he saw how frail it looked. He squeezed it softly.

'I'm sorry, Noah. Sorry for many things. I'm sorry I wasn't more to you while you were growing up,' she said quietly. 'I'm sorry I never gave you the love and affection you so deserved. I'm sorry I wasn't . . . kinder, more like a mother to you.' She stopped and shrugged helplessly. 'It's just that back then I couldn't – '

As her voice broke, he started. Other than when she was sick with Alzheimer's, he'd never heard any emotion other than anger make that voice crack, so he didn't at first recognize the sorrow and regret for what it was. 'Don't, Rosemary,' he told her, holding on to his own emotions by a single thread. 'I know you gave me all you had . . . and that's what matters.'

'No,' she said, vehemently shaking her head. 'It's not. Don't you see, Noah? It's not enough. You needed more and I failed you.'

Just as he had failed Annie. His smile was sombre, bitter-sweet. 'Well,' he said with perfect understanding, 'you're here now.'

'So I am,' she whispered, her eyes full of gladness and relief. 'So you can forgive me?'

'After all you've given me, you shouldn't even ask. There's nothing to forgive.'

'I want you to be happy, Noah. I never taught you to be happy.'

He stood and stared at the nurses' station where bodies in blue scrubs bustled about in the insanely busy emergency ward. 'My happiness depends on what happens in there.'

Rosemary stood too and tentatively stepped closer. Then, after hesitating, she wrapped her arms around his waist and hugged him tight. 'It will be all right, Noah. It has to be. You deserve it.'

The compassion was too much for him and he felt himself losing it. He returned the hug for a brief moment, and then gently he pulled away, pacing the length of the waiting room while Rosemary watched, her eyes shining with tears.

Eight days later, Annie was released from the hospital. Grumpy, groggy, weak and aching, she was deposited into Noah's care by a starry-eyed, pathetically lovesick nurse who couldn't keep her eyes off Noah.

It was disgusting. And the sickening way that he soaked up the attention made her curse all men in general as hopeless beasts.

'You make sure she gets lots of rest,' the nurse was saying as together they wheeled Annie towards the exit. 'She needs to stay in bed.'

'I'll make sure she does,' Noah answered in a dutiful tone.

'I'll bet,' the nurse said with a sly glance and a giggle.

To Annie's endless repulsion, Noah laughed softly. The sexy sound made her grate her teeth.

'And lots of tender loving care,' the nurse went on in a tiny little voice that Annie was sure she meant to be seductive – not annoying as hell.

'I can handle that,' Noah assured her.

'Ooh, I'm sure you do that real well.'

Thank God the exit was looming up in front of them or Annie was sure she was going to throw up.

'And don't forget, she'll need help changing the bandages on her shoulder and arm. The rest have been removed.'

That was it. 'I'm right here,' Annie said through her teeth. 'Stop talking about me as if I were asleep. And I'll change my own damn bandages.'

The nurse pouted prettily. 'Now, honey, don't fret. Most people in your situation have trouble adjusting at first. Remember to call that number Dr Mallow gave you if you have any troubles, all right?'

Noah gave the nurse a sharp look and glanced uneasily at Annie. 'Now, Annie – '

'I don't need a shrink,' she said in a rising voice, knowing she was impossibly cranky and mean, but completely unable to stop herself. 'And what do you mean, people in my situation?'

'Well,' the nurse hedged as she stopped in front of the exit. 'Ninety per cent of burn victims who have

370

faced a life-threatening fire, as you did, need help to cope when they get out of the hospital. Dr Mallow explained all this to Noah and Mrs Taylor and everyone's prepared to help you. OK, sweetie? Ready to go?'

Now that they were facing the door that led to the real world she hadn't seen in over a week, a deep welling fear bubbled up from within. And panic that she hadn't even known she was harbouring overwhelmed her. She couldn't do it, she thought, gripping the chair with white knuckles.

The nurse nudged the chair towards the door and Annie nearly screamed. 'No,' she cried as she slammed her eyes shut.

She didn't realize she was shaking until Noah crouched before her wheelchair, gently prised her hands from the arm of the chair and covered them with his. 'Annie,' he said in a firm but tender voice. 'Look at me.'

She bit her lip and did as he asked, desperately fighting back the welling tears. He didn't laugh at her, he didn't mock her fears. He simply looked at her, his brown eyes filled with understanding.

'It's going to be all right,' he said softly, his eyes locked on hers. 'I promise you. Can you try to believe that?'

'No,' she whispered, horrified to feel the tears drip down her face. She didn't want to be crying in front of him, didn't want to appear so weak, but she felt so damn tired. And scared. And alone. 'No,' she repeated on a sob. 'I don't want to go. Don't make me.'

'Oh, Annie,' he said, his eyes reflecting his own anguish and sorrow at her pain. 'Please, baby, don't cry. The worst is over, really it is. It can only get better from here. And I'll be with you, I swear. I'll never leave you again.'

Oh, how she wanted to believe that.

'It's OK to be afraid, anyone would be,' Noah said, his eyes never leaving hers. His rough, but warm hands held hers. 'But I'll be with you and together we'll manage.'

How wonderful it would be to give in to that deep, caring voice. How easy it would be to drown herself in his arms. But even in her pathetic state, she remembered. She remembered that he held a part of himself back from her – the most important part. She remembered that he collected people about him who needed and depended on him. And she couldn't let herself be one of those people just in order to get his love.

She glanced outside again and all her brave inner words melted as the fear grew again.

'Come on, honey,' the clinging, irritating voice of the nurse droned, snapping her out of her blinding terror. 'You can do it.'

Damn right, she thought as she sniffed, then pulled her hands from Noah's. What was she thinking about anyway, giving in to the self-pity like a little kid? She was stronger than that.

'I'm ready,' she said quietly, and though Noah's small smile of admiration and encouragement gave her a quick boost, she had to be realistic.

Her house was gone, a burnt-out shell with nothing of what was inside left. She had no memoirs, no pictures, nothing but what was in her head. Her stepfather had nearly killed her, then saved her – for she knew without a doubt, despite the fact that the details were fuzzy, that it was he who had got her out of the house during the fire. But the man she had known all her life as a father had turned out to be a serial arsonist, a murderer and a wanted man in at least three other states.

And the worst thing of all, she thought as Noah gingerly helped her into his car, fawning and fussing over her as if she were an invalid – she had no future with the only man she could ever love.

Every day that passed was absolute torture for Noah. Annie insisted on staying alone in the small cottage. She refused to let him stay with her, though he knew she was having trouble sleeping because of the deep purple rings beneath her lovely eyes. And she refused to sleep in the big house where everyone would have loved to help care for her. Every time he tried to bring it up with her she threatened to go back east to her own apartment. The thought of her leaving struck sheer terror in Noah's heart, so he learned to keep his mouth shut.

It wasn't easy.

The hardest part was watching her struggle with the pain of the burns and the lingering nightmare of the fire itself.

Her first afternoon out of the hospital he settled her in her bed, his heart pounding with all that he wanted to tell her. But one look at her tight face and tense body told him that it wasn't exactly the right time. Still, he might have ventured it anyway – except for one thing.

Vividly he recalled their conversation about his tendency to attract only people who needed him. And though she hated knowing it, she did need him now. To announce his newly discovered love for her might ease his mind, but all it would do was reinforce the fact that she thought he could only love someone who needed him.

Which was ironic, since the desperate truth was, *he* needed *her*. More than he had ever needed anyone or anything in his life.

So he forced himself to wait until she was feeling less helpless. Until she was on her feet again.

Several days later he found Annie on her couch, surrounded by so many flowers he almost couldn't find her. Everyone had sent flowers – the kids, Rosemary, the fire chief, the chief of police, her editor – and it was ridiculous, but he was irritated. He couldn't even have a conversation with her without being interrupted by another delivery or someone coming to visit her.

And he so badly wanted to have a long talk with her about how he felt. He wanted to erase the weary fatigue etched on her face that tore at him so. He wanted to hold her until the haunted glaze in her eyes vanished.

'What can I get for you?' he asked, watching as she listed to one side. He rushed forward to plump a pillow behind her and she shoved at him.

'Don't,' she said weakly, leaning back with her eyes closed. 'Stop fussing over me as if I'm helpless. I'm not. I can take care of myself.'

'I can't help it,' he admitted, the tightly coiled anger deep within him overflowing at the injustice of what had happened to her. And he still didn't know everything, since she had refused to discuss the fire with him or anyone else. He knew she was holding back and that alone was enough to make him want to pound a wall in. He wished Ross back to life so he could slam his fist into the man's face or do some other mindless, savage, stupid physical damage that Annie would have scoffed at and called a sick male thing.

'Well, go away, then,' Annie griped. 'You're giving me a headache.'

'It's because you haven't eaten,' he reminded her, ignoring her mood. He headed towards the small kitchen that he himself had stocked. 'I'm going to fix you lunch.'

'You don't have to do that,' she said quietly.

'I know.'

He stood in the tiny kitchen putting a lunch together that he hoped would give her some energy, some life back. Which was ridiculous, he thought. He was acting like a nervous mother. Time was what she needed. Even so, he loaded a tray with warmed home-made chicken soup, toast, cut oranges and Seven-up. All the stuff that Rosemary had always shoved on him when he'd been sick – though the only one that ever felt better afterwards was Rosemary. The irony of it didn't escape him.

Carrying it back into the living room, he stopped short. Annie was fast asleep, tucked into the quilt he'd settled over her. Even in sleep her face was tight with pain and worry. He took the tray back to the kitchen and settled himself in the chair across from her to watch her sleep, zealously guarding her quiet, prepared to snarl at the first person to knock on the door or ring the phone.

Summer would be over soon, he thought, as he watched the light, cool breeze make the curtains dance over the open windows. Annie loved the summer; she always had. What would happen when the summer and her writing assignment were over? Would she leave? How could she even consider it?

He would figure out a way to convince her to stay. He had to.

When she eventually stirred two hours later, he straightened, having come to several conclusions.

She rubbed her broken collarbone and looked

embarrassed yet relieved to see him still there. 'I'm sorry. I guess I was tired.'

'With good reason, I'm sure,' he said. He knew she wasn't sleeping at night, but the stubborn, proud woman would never admit that she was frightened or that – heaven forbid – she wanted him to stay with her.

'Why are you still here?'

He sighed. 'You're a pain in the ass, you know that?' He came closer, then before she could protest he scooped her up in his arms and carried her out of the door.

'What are you doing?' she demanded breathlessly.

He didn't bother to answer. For one thing, she weighed a ton with the splint on her shoulder and arm and the heavy woollen blanket wrapped around her. And for another, what she didn't know would make her wonder. And he wanted her to wonder.

'Noah!' she clutched at him with her one good arm. 'Put me down.'

He kissed her forehead. 'Shut up, Laverty.' He carried her past the Taylor House and around the back. He walked past the tennis court to the cliffs and stood for a minute at the edge, watching the ocean and breathing heavily. She squirmed. 'Does this hurt your shoulder?' he asked worriedly, feeling sick at the thought of causing her more pain.

'No,' she admitted, resting her head on his shoulder. 'I've wanted to see the sea. I feel like it's been so long.'

He smiled a little at the pleased look on her face, ridiculously happy at her relaxed expression. 'You should have asked.' Carefully he lowered them both to the ground where they sat side by side, their feet swinging over the edge of the grassy cliff.

He took a deep breath. One decision he had made was to be completely honest with her, no matter what. 'Annie, you're killing me.'

That surprised her into looking at him. 'I'm killing you?' she repeated.

'I see you in pain and I want to smash something. I see you struggling with the images and nightmares from God knows which fire and I want to shout in frustration because you won't talk to me. I see you fighting emotions that I can only guess at and yes, it's killing me. I want to help you,' he said quietly as turned towards her. The soft breeze blew over them as he took her hands, eyeing her tired features, the crooked bandages she had obviously changed herself and her sudden wary expression. 'Please, Annie. Talk to me.'

For a long moment she simply stared at his hands holding hers. 'I'm sorry,' she said finally, softly. 'I've been . . . feeling sorry for myself. And taking it out on you.' She looked up at him with limpid grey eyes. 'I suppose it's too much to hope that you'll do the gentlemanly thing here and assure me I've been the model patient with the sunniest disposition you've ever seen?'

'I never claimed to be a gentleman,' he reminded her with a small smile. 'Besides, I've already told you what a pain in the ass you are, so the point's moot.'

'So it is.'

At the small flicker of laughter in her eyes, he gave her a look of mock wariness. 'What?'

'You're not a patient man, Noah Taylor. You put up with me a lot longer than I would have thought possible. Why?'

Because I love you. 'Because I've gotten used to having you around,' he said evenly. 'So tell me, Laverty.' He nudged her hands gently. 'Tell me what's on your mind or I'll sic the dreaded shrink on you.'

She laughed then, and the sound was sweet indeed. 'Oh, not that,' she said. 'Anything but that.'

'I mean it.'

A sigh threaded through her lips. 'Oh, Noah. I'm afraid.'

Her soft, short admission tore through him. 'Because of Ross?'

'No. He's gone. He can't hurt or frighten anyone again.' She looked at him. 'He saved me, you know.'

'No, I don't,' he said. 'Why don't you tell me?'

'I was mad at you for taking those vacation tapes.'

'Annie, I – '

'Quiet, Noah. This is my story. I've long since forgiven you for not telling me. How do you tell someone you suspect their father of arson in the first degree? Besides, as I stupidly stormed out of the Taylor House, it began to come to me. You had to have a good reason for having those tapes and the only reason I could think of wasn't so comforting. You must have realized you recognized the voice on that tape that was destroyed and you knew Ross narrated all our vacation tapes. So I went looking for Ross. Not a smart move on my part.'

He made a sound of distress, but she ignored him. 'I found him trying to commit suicide in the attic. I think he couldn't stand his obsession with fire any longer. Maybe he knew you were on to him, I don't know. When he saw me . . . he flipped. The fire had already started and he knew I couldn't get out. So he wrapped me in his arms and protected me the best he could, but we fell down the second flight of stairs. Hard. When I woke up, he was gone and I was alone in the back yard. I think he must have gone back into the fire. On purpose.'

'Jesus.' Noah sent a silent thanks that, in the end, the man had loved his daughter more than fire. 'OK. So you're not afraid of Ross.'

'No.'

He waited and when she didn't speak he nudged her. 'Tell me the rest.'

'I'm afraid that I won't ever feel better. I hate this.' She gestured to her bandages.

He took her fingers and brought them to his lips, watching her grey eyes darken at the touch of his mouth. 'Annie, you will feel better – I can promise you that.' He gently kissed her fingers. 'The worst is over.'

'But I feel so weak. And . . .' She stopped and pulled her hand from his, closing her eyes.

'And needy?' he finished softly, taking her hand back, wishing she wouldn't withdraw from him. Heart aching, he tugged her hand and turned her face towards his, waiting until her eyes opened. 'It's OK to need once in a while, Annie. You can't always be strong.'

'Well, that coming from you – the King of Need – doesn't comfort me much, thanks anyway.'

Anger felt good. 'Damn it, stop it. So I've helped a few people . . . so what? What, you've never helped anyone before?' He glared at her.

'Not like you.'

'Fine.' He stood. 'Wallow in self-pity. Drown in pathetic neediness.' He reached for her, intending to carry her back to the cottage, but she flinched back. He cursed and straightened, taking a few steps from her. 'But remember this. It's a lonely and selfish person who does those things alone, who won't allow anyone to get close to her, not even the people who love her – '

'What?' she asked hoarsely, sitting up straight. Her eyes were wide. 'What did you just say?'

Shit. Had it really just slipped out? And now, when she was feeling her all-time low? Great going, Taylor. 'Nothing. I didn't say anything.'

'Yes, you did.' She eyed him with narrow, enlightened eyes while he squirmed. 'Come back here.'

'No.'

'Please, Noah.' When he didn't move, she sighed. 'I wasn't making fun of you for helping people – you misunderstood. I'm in awe of that, Noah. I think you're the most compassionate, sensitive man I've ever met. I admire how you've taken the incredibly rough childhood you had and used it to understand and help others in the same predicament. The kids here all have a chance of a normal life because of you and that makes me feel . . . humble. And I want to be a part of that. I love those kids, Noah, and I want to help them too.'

She brought a hand to her chest. 'And though my burns hurt like hell, that wasn't the pain I was talking about. It's the pain in my heart from loving you so completely and – ' her voice broke and he stepped towards her, crouching down before her ' – I can't stand it,' she whispered, her misty eyes holding his. 'I know you love me, Noah. I just want so badly for you to know it too.'

Very carefully he pulled her into his arms and settled her on his lap, his body pulsing with the overwhelming love in him for this woman. The woman who loved him back no matter who he had been and what he had done.

'But I do know it, Annie,' he told her, his own voice gruff with emotion. 'I've known it for some time now. When I thought that you were gone . . . my life meant nothing. I know you think I need people to need me, and that may have been true – before you. But the truth is, *I need you.* I need your strength, I need the joy you bring me, I need to have you near me. I need you as I've never needed anyone in my life.'

Her eyes filled with joy, tenderness and so much love that they overflowed. And for the first time in weeks, the ache in his heart eased and his stomach unclenched. 'My life still means nothing unless you stay with me. You have to say you will, Annie Laverty, because otherwise the kids will string me up. They love you so. They want you to stay too.'

'Stay?'

'Yeah.' He kissed her wet eyes, her cheeks, her nose, her skin soft and salty from the ocean air. Then he kissed her lips. After a minute, he lifted his head. 'Stay,' he said again. 'And marry me.'

Those luscious lips of hers turned upwards into a surprised smile. 'You want me to marry you?'

'You're beginning to sound like a parrot,' he admonished gently, his heart pounding in anticipation of her answer. His arms tightened around her. 'What do you say?'

'You haven't told me that you love me,' she answered breathlessly.

'Haven't I? How clumsy of me – I did it backwards.' His lips lowered again to hers. When they were both dizzy from the delicious kiss, he stared in her eyes. 'I love you, Annie. I'll love you forever.'

'What took you so long?'

He looked at the sea. 'I had some strange notion that I couldn't care for you this way because we'd grown up together. I was worried about Jesse and what he would have thought. But mostly, I was scared.'

'Jesse would have loved this,' she said softly. 'But I'm glad you're not afraid any more.'

He kissed her softly and felt his heart grow that much stronger. 'I love you so much, Annie.'

'Well, then – ' she smiled brightly ' – there's only one question left.'

'Your job?'

'Naw.' She shrugged. 'Sue doesn't care where my home base is.'

'So what, then?'

She shifted to gaze at him solemnly and he prepared to promise her the world, the moon, the universe if he had to.

'Will you promise to do all the laundry?'

His shout of laughter echoed across the green. 'The kids have long since forgiven you for changing the colour of their uniforms from white to pink, but I promise. Hell, I'll even do the cooking.' He kissed her again. 'So, what do you say? Do you love me enough to marry me?'

'Oh, yes,' she breathed. 'I love you with all my heart. And there's nothing that I want more than to be Annie Taylor.'

'Good,' he said, lowering his lips again.

'Except,' she whispered against his mouth, 'maybe this.' And she whispered exactly what she wanted him to do to her and what she intended to do in return.

His body responded eagerly and he hummed his agreement, his love for her vibrating through his veins. And for the first time in his life his head was filled with exhilarating, glorious contentment; so much so that his throat constricted with the wonder of it.

'What?' she whispered, as always completely in tune to his quick change of mood. 'Sorry you've given me your name and part of your life already?'

He smiled, drawing her closer. 'No, Laverty. You *are* my life. You're everything I could ever need.'

EPILOGUE

Annie stood on the cliffs, looking out at the ocean. The setting sun seemed to set the choppy blue sea on fire. The turmoil on the sea matched the one in her heart. Fire.

Her eyes closed for an instant.

When she opened them again, the brief flash of pain was gone. After all, two winters had come and gone since that last fiery blaze where she'd almost lost her life. Her nightmares had stopped.

And she'd married Noah.

She smiled down at the brilliant diamond sparkling on her finger. Noah loved her. That fact would never cease to amaze her and was her greatest source of joy.

Married life with him had been anything but predictable, but they were happy. More than happy.

Yep, life was good, and it had just got better. But that didn't stop the twinge of nerves. She still had to tell Noah, and though she thought he'd be thrilled she still felt nervous. With a secret smile she headed down the steps to the sand, pausing halfway when a slight dizziness overcame her.

Her foot had no more hit the sand than she was whirled about and squeezed tight in a warm bear hug.

'Annie,' Noah breathed. 'I missed you.'

'You've only been gone ten minutes,' she said, laughing. She hugged him back. 'But I'm glad you're here. I have something I want to tell you.' She looked around her at the beautiful cliffs, the wide stretch of beach. 'And I wanted it to be here.'

'You have something to tell me?'

She smiled. 'Yeah.'

He stared at her in dismay. 'Oh, no. You've been doing laundry again?'

'No, you wretched, nasty man. That's *your* job.' She hesitated as her world tilted and she lifted a hand to her head.

'Annie?' Noah's worried voice penetrated her fog. 'Baby, what's the matter?'

It passed quickly. 'Nothing.' She smiled brightly, ready with her news.

He scowled deeply, supporting her. 'Your ribs bothering you again?'

Even now, two years later, the ribs she'd cracked that long ago horrifying night still gave her an occasional twinge. 'No. I wanted to tell you – '

'Your head?'

'No. Noah – '

'Annie, Christ. *Just tell me.*'

She laughed again, feeling so light-hearted and happy. 'I'm trying to. Sit down.'

'Why?' he demanded. 'You dizzy? Come on, we're calling the doctor.'

'I've already been.'

He went very still. 'What?'

She pulled him down to the sand. This stubborn, irritating man was *not* going to ruin this moment. Nerves leapt into her throat as she gently brought his large, warm hand to rest on her stomach. 'I – '

'Oh, God.' Noah looked down at their joined hands covering her middle. He yanked her on to his lap and tilted her head back to look into her eyes. 'You're . . . *pregnant*.'

His heart lay in those wonderful, expressive brown eyes and she relaxed. 'Yes, I'm pregnant.'

He stared at her, his mouth falling open. Then he dropped his gaze and softly, carefully caressed her stomach with a tender touch and an awed look on his features that brought tears to her eyes. 'Annie,' he murmured. 'Oh, Annie. A baby.'

She laughed, nervously. 'Two.'

His gaze shot to hers. '*Two?*'

She swallowed, and the tears she'd been holding back fell. Through a watery smile, she nodded. 'The doctor thinks it might be two babies, Noah. They can tell earlier now. Is that . . . OK?'

'Oh, yeah,' he whispered, his gaze never leaving hers. 'But I want them to be girls. I want them to look like you.'

She shook her head. 'I want one of each. Rosemary and Jesse.'

He smiled. His own eyes filled and he nodded solemnly. 'God, I love you, Annie. And my babies.' His hands touched her possessively. 'I know I'm difficult sometimes. But you always understand, you always forgive. I want you to know, you're my strength, my hope, my life. I never really understood family before, but I do now and you're all I need. It's your love for me that makes me strong.'

She kissed him, tasting their tears and a love so strong it could never be broken. She stroked his face.

'When you look at me like that,' he said quietly, 'I feel so loved.'

'You are loved.'

He smiled that beautiful, sexy smile. 'I'm going to remember you said that.' He stood and scooped her in his arms.

'Where are we going?' she asked breathlessly.

'Back. I can't wait to tell the boys.'

'You don't have to carry me.'

He held her close and stopped for a long, tender kiss. 'Yes, I do. I'm not ever going to let you go, Annie Taylor. You're mine now and forever.'

THE EXCITING NEW NAME
IN WOMEN'S FICTION!

PLEASE HELP ME TO HELP YOU!

Dear *Scarlet* Reader,

As Editor of *Scarlet* Books I want to make sure that the
books I offer you every month are up to the high standards
Scarlet readers expect. And to do that I need to know a
little more about you and your reading likes and dislikes. So
please spare a few minutes to fill in the short questionnaire
on the following pages and send it to me. I'll send *you* a
surprise gift as a thank you!*

Looking forward to hearing from you,

Sally Cooper

Editor-in-Chief, *Scarlet*

*Offer applies only in the UK, only one offer per household.

QUESTIONNAIRE

Please tick the appropriate boxes to indicate your answers

1 Where did you get this Scarlet title?
Bought in supermarket ☐
Bought at my local bookstore ☐ Bought at chain bookstore ☐
Bought at book exchange or used bookstore ☐
Borrowed from a friend ☐
Other (please indicate) _____

2 Did you enjoy reading it?
A lot ☐   A little ☐   Not at all ☐

3 What did you particularly like about this book?
Believable characters ☐   Easy to read ☐
Good value for money ☐   Enjoyable locations ☐
Interesting story ☐   Modern setting ☐
Other _____

4 What did you particularly dislike about this book?
_____

5 Would you buy another Scarlet book?
Yes ☐   No ☐

6 What other kinds of book do you enjoy reading?
Horror ☐   Puzzle books ☐   Historical fiction ☐
General fiction ☐   Crime/Detective ☐   Cookery ☐
Other (please indicate) _____

7 Which magazines do you enjoy reading?
   1. _____
   2. _____
   3. _____

And now a little about you –
8 How old are you?
   Under 25 ☐   25–34 ☐   35–44 ☐
   45–54 ☐   55–64 ☐   over 65 ☐

cont.

9 What is your marital status?
   Single ☐   Married/living with partner ☐
   Widowed ☐   Separated/divorced ☐

10 What is your current occupation?
   Employed full-time ☐   Employed part-time ☐
   Student ☐   Housewife full-time ☐
   Unemployed ☐   Retired ☐

11 Do you have children? If so, how many and how old are they?
   _____
   _____

12 What is your annual household income?
   under US $15,000 or £10,000 ☐
   US $15–25,000 or £10–20,000 ☐
   US $25–35,000 or £20–30,000 ☐
   US $35–50,000 or £30–40,000 ☐
   US $50,000 or over £40,000 ☐

Miss/Mrs/Ms _____
Address _____
_____
_____

Thank you for completing this questionnaire. Now tear it out – put
it in an envelope and send it before 31 May, 1997, to:

Sally Cooper, Editor-in-Chief

USA/Can. address	UK address/No stamp required
SCARLET c/o London Bridge	SCARLET
85 River Rock Drive	FREEPOST LON 3335
Suite 202	LONDON W8 4BR
Buffalo	Please use block capitals for
NY 14207	address
USA	

SUFIR/10/96

Scarlet titles coming next month:

THE JEWELLED WEB Maxine Barry
Reece Dexter only has to snap his fingers and women come running! Flame is the exception. She doesn't want Reece to give her his body – she wants him to give her a job!

SECRETS Angela Arney
Louise, Robert, Michael and Veronique all have something to hide. Only Daniel is innocent, though he is the one who binds them all together. It is Louise and Robert who must find the strength to break those invisible ties. Yet their freedom *and* their love carry a dangerous price . . .

THIS TIME FOREVER Vickie Moore
Jocelyn is puzzled: 'Who does Trevan think he is? He seems to know everything about me, yet I'm sure we've never met before . . . well, not in this lifetime. I can't believe he wishes me harm – but someone does! Can I afford to trust Trevan?'

THE SINS OF SARAH Anne Styles
But Sarah doesn't think she's committing any sins – all she's guilty of is wanting the man she loves to be happy. Nick wants to make Sarah happy too – but there's a problem! He already has a wife and Diana won't give him up at any cost. Throw in Nick's best friend Charles, who wants Sarah for himself and the scene is set for a red hot battle of the sexes!